I0699282

# Empire of Stars and Opals

*— ◆ —*

### Book One in the Serral Brook series

## Thora Wolf

Fall of Rome Books

# Contents

**1**

— • —

C hapter One

The planet's surface was mostly green. Where the wind was high, pale ellipses flecked white. Tall trees so dark as to be almost black reflected stands of those with crimson bark and copper leaves. The wavering shadow passing over the water looked small in comparison, as insignificant as their people, the remnants of a civilization that impressed only itself. A deep-gray cross shaped shadow evidenced that Imseth intelligence remained, or at least that their clever ways, their scavenging for parts and their will to fit them together was still intact. Below, the head-tossing herds of hooved beasts didn't know or care who flew overhead, the engines no more than a whisper, the gleam of silver appearing and then passing as silver always did. Bombs flared orange, shook the ground, then ceased for long enough that the young ones experienced them for the first time, again and again, inoculating, until the animals no longer felt fear at the trembling ground.

**2**

— · —

C hapter Two

When Serral woke under the iron gray ellipse of dawn sky though the aperture, her wrists were chafed raw, and the ground where her feel had rested was grooved where she'd kicked in her sleep. Foremost in her mind was cold, and thirst, and the resolve to remain apart from the people who had betrayed her, who had treated her like their enemy when all she wanted was to show how much she could do to help. An old man shambled across the field toward her, his ruined legs slowing his progress. Serral rubbed her face on her shoulders and put on a stoic expression. Whit's white beard tickled her forehead as he cut her ropes.

He stood back, crossing his arms, and growled. "Spook, your brother is not worth this."

Serral stood up and shaking, hugged his thin frame. He endured her affection without protest, standing passively until she stopped. Then he wiped his hands over his torso as if ridding himself of germs. She didn't mind. She knew Whit's ways. They walked together across the field. Lights were coming on in the milking barns high on the flanks of the pasture levels, and breakfast pots banged in the kitchens. He moved slowly, but mercifully, they met no one.

When they were safely out of the oculus and on the dirt path to the airfield, Serral felt her voice steady enough to answer. "I get why they didn't reprimand him, Whit. Brume is going to get recruited any day now. If he had this serious an infraction on his record, then his prospective assignment would be downgraded. But my getting a reprimand for insubordination is still bad, isn't it?"

"Yup, it is. That's what you need to learn. You're going to get recruited too, Spook. One day."

Serral had always liked her nickname. The old man had given it when she was little and she'd refused to enter the Yskeon. Serral couldn't remember why, but Brume said that she had fainted under the light beam, which was a terrible sin or a terrible insult to the Ysken, she couldn't remember. Most of the colonists thought calling her Spooky was derogatory, but Serral was glad she'd lived up to it and had given them a proper fright.

"It's two years before I'm eligible," she gave Whit a weak smile. "And you'll help me get my record fixed before then."

He spit, his light brown eyes bloodshot. "I'll try. No guarantees."

They reached the pump outside the hangar by Whit's workshop. The Bolt was covered again, but a tiny patch of silver winked in the rising sun through a tear in the canvas. Whit moved the pump handle, and water flowed into the basin.

"It's okay, old man. I can do it," Serral said. But she was grateful when he handed her the cup, and slumping to the stone plinth, she drank deeply, letting the cool water flow down her throat and onto her coverall where it drowned out the marks from her tears.

## 3

Chapter Three

Serral woke with a jolt when the can of green lubricant fell from her hand and spilled onto the floor. She rushed to clean it up, cursing herself for her clumsiness. The hard concrete had seen countless spills over the years, but quib lubricant had to be shipped in from Ingeni Station, and no one could predict when.

Whit was almost finished reconditioning an Arrow that had been shot down during a raid the year before. The machine looked great, its silver cross-wing bearing only a faint scar. It was fully functional now, hardened for space and ready for battle. Had he been allowed, he would have stocked it with surplus rockets and bullets. Then no one would be able to tell that the fighter plane had been in pieces at the bottom of a pond.

Serral smiled with pride. She'd heard Whit say it many times. The only reason he could return as many Arrows to the Military as he did was because he had her help. And Brume's. Where was her brother? She hadn't seen him since her sentencing. She wiped up the last of the mess and tossed her rag into a bin.

"Go on now, get some sleep," Whit called out from under a wing.

She went into the contriving office and called back to him, "I'm not tired. When you're ready to power that thing up and start the checks, just call me."

Brume was sitting at Whit's desk in the cluttered space, reading something on the liquid screen. "You're not allowed to work or play with others today, you know that," Brume said softly. "You might as well grab a nap."

He didn't turn his soft face toward her. He was eighteen, but still looked like an adolescent.

"Just because I'm entitled to time off doesn't mean I need it. They didn't break me," she said, suppressing a yawn. "Does the old man know you're snooping into," she peered over her brother's shoulder, "air traffic logs?"

"He doesn't care." Brume snapped the portal off. "I'm trying to see if any Transport 'Tainers have submitted a manifest."

"The military lets us know when they're coming?"

Brume scowled, a lock of auburn hair falling over his deeply-circled, jasper eyes. "Whit said rumor is the Recruiters are coming soon."

"And he has a line into what the military does?" Serral asked.

Brume shrugged. "Whit's got friends up there. You know that."

"Come on. They don't have any reason to tip him off." She wiped her hands with a rag, cleared equipment off a bench, and sat. "Does your extra paranoia have anything to do with yesterday?"

"It's not unrelated. Insubordination, what a crock." Brume scowled. "I would have taken my share of the blame, you know."

She picked up a small component, part of a ventilation system, though like all the universal components it had other uses. Serral wished she could research which, but that information was censored.

"Of course you would." Serral didn't add—*but you didn't.*

Brume turned his head. The back was ratty and still dusty from their adventure. Serral said nothing. They both knew that his recruitment meant their separation; Serral couldn't imagine life without Brume. When the subject of his move into space and the larger Imset diaspora came up, she always moved on to other topics. But she didn't remember him ever acting this worried. They didn't know exactly when, but they knew the recruiters would come soon. He was of age, as were most of the rest of his class. They both knew their time together was nearly up.

"Listen, Spook. You've got two years to convince the staff to change your insubordination charge to mischief."

"I know." Serral placed the component back on a pile. "Whit already promised to help me with Inoa."

"Whit has no pull with that witch, or you wouldn't have gotten such a serious charge. Think more creatively. Think of something else."

Serral fingered the component on the pile. It was pretty, colorless resin with veins of copper, like roots. "I'll ask Miss Pune. She likes me. You know what she said about my drawings."

"That they were brilliant, I know. I know." He clenched his teeth. "Liking your work isn't the same as being willing to risk her reputation for you."

"But the Bolt," she said. "That cave. It was worth it, wasn't it?"

His pupils were dilated in their red-brown irises. "No, Spook, you idiot. You're in big trouble."

"Don't be so dramatic."

"I shouldn't have let you. I just never thought you'd get in so much trouble."

"You thought they'd care more about the Azanta than about our adventure," she shrugged.

"I did. I guess Inoa thinks she is the only one who can dispense it, because it's sacred. Nonsense, of course. But she threw a fit. That's why they charged you with such a harsh sentence." Brume made fists, his breathing choked, his skin paling from its normal soft bronze. "Do you not get it? The cave showed us what we're not supposed to know."

"What? No, it didn't."

"Yes, it did. It showed that the legends are true. All the players in this war, the Harbs, the ones they serve, the Overlords or whatever you want to call them, and us. We are all related. We all came from the same source. We're the same people."

"Yuck. Don't say that. It's treason."

"It's the truth."

"So?"

"They're going to send us to die fighting our own relatives. And they don't want us to know. So they're going to make an example of you."

"Brume, you've upset yourself too much. Come on, before the worst sets in." She grabbed his arm. "You don't want to lose it in here with the breakables."

He scrunched his eyes closed and let out a soft moan, his voice rising to a high whine. "Insubordination is almost a death sentence. I'm so stupid. So stupid."

"Yeah, yeah. Come on," Serral said with forced cheer. "While I'm still alive. Breathe. One foot in front of the other. That's it."

She led him outside into the fresh air of the bone yard and maneuvered his quaking form behind the hangar. Junk, components, parts of planes and bits of equipment stood stacked in neat rows which stretched out in a large spiral shape in what Whit called an Imset Inventory. He'd taught them how to arrange pieces of broken machinery in specific order of size and function, so when they needed something, they had a system to find it. Whit said all real contrivers did this, because it confounded the enemy. Brume's coveralls were wet with sweat.

"Stop here," he said tearfully. They had a longstanding deal that he would keep himself together until she could get physically clear. Only then was Brume free to indulge his inner chaos.

"Further. We worked hard organizing this section."

Though Brume was taller and heavier than she was, Serral managed to get him twenty meters further from the hangar before his rage erupted. He grunted, then grabbed the nearest piece of metal, threw it to the side and reached for a pipe. He was halfway through wrecking a strut component when Serral quietly disappeared back into the office. He wouldn't want her to get caught in the crossfire of his aggression, she knew from long experience. But, nonetheless, she had scars on her hands, on her forearms, and on her forehead from the times she'd been too small, too slow, to get away. He never remembered hitting her. He'd cry for hours if she admitted the wounds ached or stung. She'd learned to keep her pain to herself.

The one time he'd willingly inflicted it was when she had coerced him into tattooing a celestial compass, the *heavenly hexagon*, on her back. They both loved the design. They'd had the drawing tacked up in their room so long, it seemed like a part of them, a reminder of the many hours spent dreaming about traversing one of the portworms to some unknown pocket of space where they could be free of the Authority and enemy raids and live and contrive in peace. He'd done a nice job with the tattoo, and it was the part of her she loved most.

Serral threw a red-brown braid over her shoulder and sat at Whit's desk, wondering what her brother had really been looking for on the liquid portal. Her gut twinged, a slurry of anxiety beginning to churn. Was she really going to be sent straight out into combat, because of her Bolt? The stupid Authority. Serral's eyes burned with fatigue, but she wanted to understand how she was in so much trouble. Whit had practically given her permission to fly the Bolt. Hadn't he? He'd known they were building it; they'd been working on it for months.

Yet, he'd stood silently by when Headmaster Bragg had read out the charges, saying nothing in her defense. Whit hated to speak in public, she knew. He was afraid of his own shadow. Maybe he had wanted to speak, but couldn't bring himself to say anything out loud. And, she supposed, as her Admin, he couldn't risk being reprimanded himself. Serral wasn't mad. She didn't want the old man to risk being sent back to the cities. He'd die there; he'd said so many times.

Only Miss Pune had raised her hand to speak on Serral's behalf, and Inoa had refused to call on her.

The sight of the Thantons in the cave with their blue eyes flashed into her mind, their benign gaze, so friendly, so unlike the look on Headmaster Brag's face when he'd said the words *night cinching*. Who should feel ashamed, Serral thought, she or the people who had no trust that someone they had been training for years who had stayed calm with them during dozens of raids, who had always brought in her agricultural quota or more, who had proven herself time and again to be a team player, ready to serve? Her head swam with fatigue and something else, maybe sorrow, maybe rage. Serral returned to the hangar.

"Have you eaten?" Whit growled, with a look that would have seemed fierce to anyone else. His white beard was stained red from Azanta.

It looked so ridiculous, Serral burst out laughing. "Why? Did you bake?"

"Go to the Caf. They still have to feed you. I've got him." Whit jerked his head in the direction Brune still tossing around furiously in the bone yard. "Go on."

Something wasn't right. Even after Serral let the kids on food shift sneak her a bake pocket and a bottle of fruit mead, exhaustion hung on her, and her stomach shrunk into a tight tangle.

The warren where Serral slept was silent at midday, everyone at work or in class. She pulled her covers over her head, wondering if Brume was still destroying things in the yard. His fits had a pattern long established; he'd destroy stuff, ranting and raving about injustice and corruption, then finally erupt in contorted tears. If it weren't for Whit volunteering to supervise them, Serral didn't know what would have happened to her brother. The old man said both he and Brume had bad things in their past that no one else could see. He insisted that Brume needed a lot of bravery to fight the horned, evil, imaginary Dantons that tried to drag him to their horrible depths. But she knew he worried about what would happen to her brother once he joined the Air Guard.

Serral scratched an insect bite, wondering which had set her brother off this time, terrifying specters of the past, or fears about the future. Soon, she couldn't feel anything but tingling dread. A darkness opened inside her, filling the space that had comforted her all night, a vacuum of unease. Something was happening, something not normal. Abandoning all hope of rest, Serral went out the tunnel, and looked up at the sky.

She gasped so hard, she choked.

**4**

C hapter Four

Above Chlore

If not for his elongated skull, Hallenander might have passed for his mother's kin. But the Imset were on the verge of extinction, and whoever his mother was, no doubt she was long dead and wouldn't feel the pain of the loss. He hoped to see the last of the wild Imset. His father had never shared his former concubine's name, but she had been full Imset. Perhaps she had come from an oculus colony like that they were soon to raid.

Hallenander felt marginally comfortable strapped into the observation chair. He sat passively while Helpers busied themselves with the business of flight craft, and he pretended not to note their every movement, every pull of lever and movement of long fingers across a console of instruments, for fear they would report his interest to his father. Hallenander was meant to be an Overlord, cold to his servants, indifferent to their activities. The best he could do was ignore the slender gray people as much as possible as they scurried to their tasks. As a child, he had asked why, if the Imset were such infamous outlaws, no one simply ended their misery.

"Oh no, your Sevenni Highness," his four palace servants had replied. "The Law dictates exile, not execution!"

"But doesn't forcing them to live in space, with no hope of a future home, amount to the same thing?"

He didn't remember what or if they had answered.

A Halo trekked silently across the sky, making a line toward the Imset Guardian ship hovering just above the atmosphere, spewing fighter planes into the pale membrane of exosphere. As they descended, Hallenander watched it recede against the black space, and strange stars, seeming to grow further from the green disc of Planet 30258. He shifted his gaze toward the armored pilots of his own ship, toward the four Xaff warriors who looked to him like ordinary long-limbed, bulbous-headed, black-eyed gray Harbingers dressed in armored space suits. Their air of intense malevolence centered around their small, slit mouths.

Hallenander sighed. He could do nothing about what was to come. The Xaff answered only to his father. Planet 30258 floated ahead. Even from this distance a rimeter above, the orb swirled white with cloud and glowed with life. He remembered his own planet, Evincio, as merely decorative in comparison.

"When we get closer, you could let me operate the controls for a minute," he tried. "Technically it would be legal, when we are near to the ground."

None of his four non-Xaff helpers replied. He had not expected them to. The ship shifted, and he felt a hint of planetary gravity taking hold. Hallenander watched the Imset ship grow in size as his own ship approached. It looked more threatening than in film strips and far more beautiful. Hallenander tried different places to put his hands, settling them at last under his thighs. He watched the Halo leap into action, pursuing two silver slivers, two cross-shaped Arrow fighter planes. Single pilot configuration, Hal noted, operated by actual Imset pilots, he knew, with all their predictable maneuvers. The Halo followed the fighters through the planet's atmosphere, gaining on them quickly and leading their enemy away from the goal.

Imset courage was legendary. But this was breathtakingly easy. The Halo plunged through the exosphere into blue sky, with a slight pop. The machine whispered changed direction, still chasing. Hal held his breath, under fire from the Arrows. His own ship's rockets streaked off into the air. Now the enemy planes flew away from the surface, trying to gain altitude and the safety of weightlessness. Even safe in the cockpit of the attacking Halo, Hal felt queasy.

The planet's surface was a wall pressing up against them, oceans and continents turning as they flew. The Xaff fired their guns and the Halo bucked. The Xaff stopped abruptly. The two Arrows exploded, twin flames moving past the window and disappearing against white cloud. The dogfight had lasted less than five minutes. Hallenander ran his hands over his helmet restlessly, lightheaded, and forced himself to breathe.

"Do not be sad," his four civilian helpers called out in unison, "the Imset savages are Ousians now, basking in glory."

He nodded, collecting himself. "If you say so. But I don't see why you had to kill them."

The Xaff pilots lifted their heads in unison but said nothing.

"It is their honor to die in such a way," the helpers chimed. Their bare gray head domes puffed and roiled with pleasure.

"You sound jealous."

They fixed eight shiny black eyes on him. "Funny jokes, your Seven-ni Highness. How could anyone be jealous of the Imset?"

Hallenander's skin flushed. He would never get used to the insults directed at his mother's people. "Are their lives really that terrible?"

The helpers looked out the window. For some reason, the pilots were taking them back into space rather than toward the surface.

"They are outlaws, sire. No such life matters until they are free of their Imset bodies."

"So you say."

"So say the Thantons," they replied.

Hallenander shook his long-skulled head in its helmet casing. "Yes, of course. The Thantons."

The Helpers hummed happily. Their heads rippled, each small wave of gray skin rising and falling in perfect unison, like sections of the same ocean. Hallenander sighed. His Helpers loved to talk about the goddess Ysk and her winged Thanton servants with their beautiful afterlife. He gave belief in Ysk the same amount of credence as he did the 88 Volterran gods. He was thinking about his lack of faith and didn't notice their Halo coming close to the space station until its silver casing was already disappearing from view. They descended again, this time quickly.

"Why did we touch the Imset station?"

"For the surprise, sire," his servants replied.

"What do you mean, for the surprise?"

They laughed, their gray head domes rolling, but did not answer. A forested continent lay below them rutted with pristine lakes and carved with tumbling streams. The Xaff pilots' gray hands moved gracefully across their control panels. He continued to note their movements. He would check them against his own instruments later. It annoyed him again that he couldn't be flying across this land alone, in one of his own ships. But at least he had been allowed aboard. The beauty below made the frustration worth it.

Hallenander wondered how many lush, lively planets existed in the universe. He hummed an old tune, and his Helpers chimed in, their slit mouths opening in song for his benefit.

"The Imset, the Imset, they crack their own bones.

The Imset, the Imset, they hurl only stones.

The Imset, the Imset, Ysk knows they have sinned.

The Imset, the Imset, they howl to the wind."

A long valley came into view, its grasses a thousand shades of brown and yellow and pale green. A herd of antlered animals looked up, shaggy and robust with health. They were close enough to pick off with a hunting rifle; males, females, and small juveniles with only sprouts for horns. And now Hallenander pondered the downside of his coming. He didn't want to watch death rain from above. The Imset did not deserve the slaughter the Helpers believed was their due. His uncle and the Eight Lords who supervised him had been right—Hallenander had been naïve about the war, about the universe and its brutal order.

But it was too late. Because ahead in the distance, a black lozenge shape appeared on the surface, half hidden by vines, its grounds rutted red with evidence of past bombardment. The oculus colony, a rare and precious pocket of Imset life in a world that wanted them dead. Hallenander imagined the faces of the children and their teachers and wondered if they knew their death was imminent.

The pilots made a sound in unison, a kind of deep grunting that sent cold, acid fear through Hallenander's blood.

The oculus was straight outside the window. And he could not look away.

# 5

Chapter Five

Sunlight angled down into the central field and assaulted Serral's eyes. Was it brighter than usual today, or were her eyes as off-kilter as her nauseated body? She lurched toward the water pump. Several younger children stared, unsure if they should greet or shun her.

"Still off limits," she said. But her mouth felt pinched, and she stopped.

Yellow sparks streaked across the clouds and left thin trails of smoke. A dogfight? She had heard about them, the battles that took place during raids, when their Imset Air Guard fighter planes rocketed out of the battle station to harass the much larger, attacking Harb halos. Her brows knit. Why was she seeing this? If the Air Guard was engaged in combat, the aperture should be closed. For a long moment, Serral wondered if she was in her dream. Her stomach churned, and she realized with a jolt that the sick feeling was not just a thing happening at the same time sparks flew across the sky. This was no dream. Everyone was going about their business, unaware. They didn't see it. She was the only one who understood a raid was in progress, that it was happening sooner than the expected date, and the oculus was about to be blown off the face of Chlore.

*No. No. No.*

The nearest alarm pole was halfway to the north tunnel. Serral stumbled toward it, fear racing up her body like a stain.

"What are you doing, Serral Brook?" Inoa shouted from across the yard, using the voice she reserved for dramatic sermons.

"Combat!" Serral pointed upward, her voice tumbling out too fast. "Sparks. Smoke. It's the Air Guard. Look!"

Inoa's robes billowed behind her, and she leveled her eyes at Serral, coming closer. "I realize you had a bad night."

Serral narrowly escaped Inoa's grasp. "That's not what this is."

"You're hallucinating."

"Can't you see them?"

Pure white clouds tinged with the gray of their own shadows billowed in a sky of serene, deep blue. Her stomach felt like she'd swallowed a handful of river rocks and the frogs who lived underneath.

"Come with me," Inoa barked.

Serral had no desire to argue. She pulled herself to standing, and with Inoa's hand gripping her elbow, let the woman guide her to the Yskeon. Inside the tower, the cool, shaded air surrounding the light beam was a relief. Water trickled in the pool which looked green and inviting in the center of the room. She wanted to sit and rest on one of the pews, but Inoa yanked her wrist.

"Ouch!" Serral took her arm back.

"Stop being a baby. You wanted to warn us of what is to come?" Inoa hissed. "Go on. Impress me."

"I never said that."

Inoa's eyes glittered dangerously. "I'm waiting. So are all the Thantons and Dantons in the Amperia."

Serral pictured the Thantons on the walls of the cave. "What?"

"I need to know now. Right now. Which side are you on, Serral Brook?"

A dam broke inside Serral, an electric sensation like something sick trying to escape. "What is your problem, Inoa? I've done nothing to deserve this."

"You have. You know you have. And I want to understand why. Who are you, child?"

There was a faint sound of trickling, and a delicious breeze off the surface of the pool. Serral's stomach was hard and cold, and her head was beginning to feel like it would float away. She wanted to stay there by the sacred water. And think.

"What do you want me to do?" Her voice sounded like someone old and tired.

"You saw nonexistent dogfighting, a moment ago?" Inoa pointed to the light beam. "What do you see, now?"

"You want me to read the light beam?" Serral blinked in disbelief. "I've never been trained in divination."

"And yet, you have visions. What else do you do, in secret?" Inoa crossed her arms. "For whom do you speak? Darkness or light?"

"I don't know what you're talking about."

"Foolish child. Now. Time is growing short." Inoa's black eyes flashed.

Serral forced herself to pay attention, though part of her screamed to leave, to go warn the others. Maybe she could get this over quickly. "Okay."

"What do you see?" Inoa growled. "What do you feel?"

Serral looked deep into the thick band of light that poured from the circular opening in the building's high dome. It was true that sometimes she had visions, heard what wasn't said, felt what was about to happen. But Brume had drilled secrecy so deeply into her that she barely wanted to admit her gift even to herself. The round pool below shone green and white and reflected clouds from the distant sky above the aperture. Her stomach lurched again. "The sky."

"Don't pretend you have no gift, girl. We both know you do."

The Yskeon faded around Serral, and with it, Inoa's voice. She stood in solid light. Reflections of clouds and sky and unspoken things moved in her peripheral vision and swam with dust motes, a glittering storm. The tiny specks shone brightly, like milky metal, but they were so small the effect was like buoyant opaline smoke, insubstantial, yet suggesting shapes of solid matter she could see, if the somethings would just hold still. What were the ellipses, then curved teardrops, then spiky fractals trying to show her? They had a meaning, she felt it. They had a message. It was almost clear.

*What are you trying to show me?*

A presence of electricity opened before her, then with fathomless power, it slackened like the graceful sparkling arms of a spiral galaxy, and she fell into it. She was lost, awash with the living light. All around her, diaphanous blue roiled and flowed, but Serral couldn't focus to see it clearly. A huge and terrifying presence hovered; it wanted her attention. That was all she knew. She felt intense frustration. What was the dimension she couldn't reach? It was so close, just beyond the unseen and powerful, a vibration like engines, voices of people she could not discern. The Ancient's carvings seemed to whisper to her. Something about getting out of the Yskeon, back to the yard. To the alarm pole. Groaning, annoyed, Serral closed her eyes and tried again. Yearning closed over her, and with it, she was back in the cool dark.

Yskeon. Inoa stared at her, slack mouthed.

And then the knowledge came, calmly, sharply, like hearing a song she knew but had forgotten she knew. "Inoa," Serral said. "Inoa of the Ovadathy. Please understand. There's going to be a... it is a raid." She spoke as if someone was speaking through her. "We have to raise the alarm."

"How do you know my full name?" Rage formed on the older woman's face, and then was replaced by realization. "Did they speak to you?"

But Serral was out the door, out into the square and across the field to the alarm pole. Above her, the air was electric, shrieking silently, and whatever was inside her stomach was answering, without words, urging her to hurry. She struggled for air, heaving open the heavy casing, exposing the red lever.

"You owe me an explanation!" Inoa shouted, but her voice sounded under water.

Serral pulled the lever to break the glass case, splintering it with her hands, cuts stinging up and down her fingers, welling with blood. For a long, chaotic moment, she waited. Then the sound began, the claxons, the whooping bells, and the deep rumble of the aperture starting its contraction. She leaned panting on the pole, the light above her growing dimmer.

Then she realized with a leap of agonized sorrow that it was too late. A grotesque shadow passed over the oculus' upper rings, moving smoothly across the oculus field, its alien bulk coming straight toward her. Serral's heart pounded a dark rhythm, and she understood something both horrible and inevitable. Her enemies had been in her trying to open the membrane to her mind. They had invited themselves in, and she had half allowed it, along with whatever else had been in the light beam, in the swirl behind her eyes. She hadn't understood what part friend, what part foe, and what part was indifferent universe that only observed. She should have listened to Inoa, to whatever the Thanton in the cave had been trying to say, to anything but this nothingness she'd mistaken for safety. Her enemies had found her. She had failed to guard herself against them. And now, her people were going to die.

From what sounded like a great distance, Serral heard a cacophony of alarms, and now screams, which was something new. The Imset never made noise when the enemy was near. The dark wheel of shadow crawled closer, its edges rippling over the weedy ground, until it stopped in front of her. Its enormous engine purred, deep and overwhelmingly powerful. She waited. Moments passed. The aperture had stopped moving. The facility contrivers knew better than to trap the aliens inside the aperture doors. When she couldn't bear the painful swirl in her gut any longer, Serral looked up. The Halo hovered ten meters off the ground. Colored lights pulsed silently while an array of guns emerged, all of them trained on Serral.

*This is good.* She thought. *I can draw fire while the others get to their hiding places underground.*

Serral stood straight, amazed how calm her body had become. The worst had happened. A raid had caught the colony unawares. The pain that had connected her to that danger was gone. She was ready for what came next. Whatever pain, or bleeding out, or darkness arrived, she was ready. If she were captured, at least some of her people could barricade themselves in their warrens, in safety. Her brain might be sucked out and turned to jelly, her eggs might be culled for experimentation. The Harbs were vicious to their prey. Serral's only regret was not saying goodbye to Brume. The rest of the colony had already discarded her, which, she decided, was for the best. Maybe Ysk, Goddess of the Imset Diaspora, existed, after all.

Serral laughed darkly. The wheel-shaped space craft moved a quarter rotation, and a large window appeared above, almost close enough to touch, surrounded by gun muzzles. Behind the glass, four Harb pilots in orange flight suits fixed on her from behind black helmets.

Behind the pilots, four helmetless Harbs, sat in a semi-circle. She sensed their chaotic joy.

*Why did they feel so excited, so happy? Did they hate the Imset, hate me, that much?*

In the center of the nightmare vision above her, sat someone else; a tall, larger, helmeted presence. Not Imset, though the face was far more similar to her own than any slit-mouthed Harb's. This person had thick lips, pronounced bones, and large eyes with whites and irises. *An Overlord?* Whit had always said Overlords were mythic, that they didn't exist, that their rumored large stature and distorted brain pan cones were the result of Imset trauma-addled memory. But there the person sat, staring at her ferociously like she was the one with rocket launchers. She wasn't impressed.

Serral felt sure he was male. His handsome, haughty face and elongated helmet meant he was a mastermind of Imset destruction and her mortal enemy. And yet, she felt calm. Time was passing. Her people didn't need long to lock down their warrens. Serral felt gratitude for that small blessing. And then, that small blessing grew, and she was filled with giddy, fizzing wonder. This Halo was not going to shoot today, so long as she stayed still, kept her composure, and endured their scrutiny. She did not know how she knew this. But she was sure of it, as sure as she had ever been, of anything.

She met her hunter's gaze. *Go ahead. Enjoy your savagery.*

The man in the long helmet started. His eyes reminded Serral of something, but she couldn't say what. His face was beautiful, made more so in comparison with the ugly gray Harbs lined up in front of him. Then his expression changed. The people in the ship looked at one another and at her. Chaos bubbled. They bantered in disagreement. The man's lips moved, and the others shifted in their chairs. Then they all stared directly at her. It was all she could do to remain rooted, unmoving, listening to the silence left behind as the alarms quieted. Somewhere The Authorities were shutting down power. Fear of fire, no doubt, after the bombs.

*You won't kill an enemy who doesn't fight back. Will you?*

Guns clicked and reversed back into the ship's lining. There was a pause. The only sound was the whirring of the Halo's engines. Then, from the creaky, old, half-open aperture, a drop of water fell onto her face. The Halo lifted, turned on its side, and shot away. Ripples of wind wake blew around her. The ship became tiny and disappeared in the span of a breath. Serral sat heavily on the ground, and then slipped to her belly, something invisible ripping out of her and into the sky. The ground felt soothingly cold on her cheek, her eyes sliding closed as her muscles slackened.

She saw nothing more.

**6**

C hapter Six

Serral woke in the Contriving office. Whit, Miss Pune, and Headmaster Braggs whispering in the background lulled her into feeling warm and safe. She heard the relief in their tones, their talk of plans and schemes. These were her people. They were still here. They sounded serious, which amused Serral. Not much mattered, she figured, now that they were safe from the raid. But then she heard them recounting the losses of the Air Guard. So she had been right; she had seen a dogfight. Or worse. She disappeared back into warmth and darkness.

In the cool of dawn, Whit, as usual, snored in his chair. If Serral squinted and listened only to the early morning birdsong, inhaled distant cookfires and the smell of the fields wafting in from the west, she could pretend everything was as it always had been. Everyone safe, the animals being milked, and her work cleaning and arranging spare parts for reassembly about to begin. Perhaps they'd send out salvage missions for the ships shot down in the recent battle. She straightened Whit's desk and emptied his refuse cannister. She cleared cups from last night's meeting and did it all silently so as not to disturb him. Then her eyes caught the liquid screen, and she froze. She knew that things had changed, that there would be consequences for whatever had taken place and her part in it. But she understood in that moment that things would never be the same. On the screen was a manifest for a Planet Protection Ship to be staffed by several officers and a Recruitment Team. She went cold. A recruitment team. Expected imminently.

Serral sat back on the cot, rubbing her eyes. A recruitment team meant that the of-agers would be shipped out. Never to return. Brume, Rafe, Lymm, their whole class. A Planet Protection Ship meant the Harbs had blown their Air Guard base ship out of the sky. She had met fighters when they visited on Myrth Day or came to pay respects to dead comrades. They were heroes. And now Chlore's constant protectors were likely all dead.

She ran through the tunnels to the Caf. Rafe and Brume were already there, nursing hot drinks, their faces serious.

She dropped beside her brother. "Your paranoia was correct, as usual. Or you knew?"

He shook his head, blinking slowly. "Listen. That's not the half of it."

Serral snorted a laugh. "I'm too tired for jokes, stupid."

"I'll catch you two later. Be careful, okay? Walls have ears." Rafe smiled sadly, picked up his tray, and left.

Serral downed half a food nutrition pocket and a cup of bark tea. Her brother's doughy face had never been so morose.

"Cheer up, for frick's sake. You're finally getting off this rock."

"There are some things you need to know." Brume spoke with uncharacteristic gentleness.

"What things? Am I in trouble for yesterday? They blame me for a Harb raid, now?"

"Not here. Rafe is right. We need privacy." His eyes darted around the Caf. "What I'm about to tell you is going to hurt."

**7**

—  ·  —

C hapter Seven

Evincio

Hallenander picked up and put down objects in his tower, unable to settle. He'd been directionless since his tutor had left him. Geddon had disappeared the day Hallenander had come of age, knowing they were both in danger. Hallenander was the master, but Geddon was the true leader of the two, with an air of command no amount of memory tampering could reduce. And he missed the Imset man, missed his way of listening with complete stillness and then, with only a few questioning words, delivering a sharp rhetorical blow that challenged the prince's thinking. Without Geddon's help, Hallenander struggled to understand the raid. He was not angry at the older man, not exactly. He understood the man's urge to run into the jungle and hide, his hope that in a world where he was hunted, he might find protection in the wild. But Hallenander knew Geddon to be thorough and exacting. He had respect for the man. And yet.

He had more on his mind. They had not killed the girl. Why? His Helpers had squealed at the sight of her, calling her *Thanton*, became hysterical in the light of her sullen glare. To his eye, she looked like no more than a shabby peasant. But he had been impressed by the way she challenged them, the way she looked death in the eye without flinching.

*The Imset, the Imset.*

The thought of their kind made him miss Geddon even more. To be abandoned by someone who ought to have been honored to serve should have infuriated him, but instead, it reminded him how precarious his position remained, how slender the tightrope he was carefully scaling, step by step. He could count on nothing. Trust no one. He opened his window to the night. A few village lanterns sparkled palely above the dark bay, the distant Reykos towers glimmering under a rising moon.

If Geddon were still living in the village, still climbing the steps to tutor Hallenander each day, no doubt the old man would ask probing questions about the raid, about the decision to not bomb the settlement, to not enforce the law. He might ask if this Thanton girl had a special look to her dark braids and slender frame that reminded the Helpers of an artwork. But no. The Helpers, the Harbingers, had no affinity for art or music. Their hivemind didn't lend itself to such things. None of the great works in the Palace had been created by their hands. They could imitate. That was all. Hallenander felt impatience rising in him, the quality Geddon had most counseled him to master. The Helpers had made him weak, the old man had said, and the Volettu of Eight were not his friends. They were there to carry out their duty to his father, the Opal-eyed Emperor. Nothing more.

"No one here, no one surrounding you, is ensuring your success," Geddon had said that first day. Brave for an Imset. "Your life is a performance for political ends."

Jarring, yes, but when the shock wore off, Hallenander felt clear. Felt like he could use the weight of his own power instead of succumbing to its crush. Geddon's habitual, brutal honesty made Hallenander love him. Trust him. The man was remarkable given that his mind had been wiped by Xaff doctors with their diabolical instruments.

Before Geddon, when he was a lonely child, Hallenander had floated on a cloud of deception and comfort, believing that the eight stern Companions he lived with were a kind of family. The men accepted his cheerful rebelliousness with stoic indifference, neither rewarding nor punishing him for it. Their seeming cynicism was chilling, especially in comparison to how desperate the Helpers were to please him, to carry out his ever more elaborate whim. But Geddon showed him that all aspects of this position as potential Heir were illusory. Geddon was gone. And without him, Hallenander would have to navigate his future with only his father to guide him.

Hallenander closed the window and opened one of a dozen ornate wood-and-metal chests that had been delivered to his chambers while he was in space. Coming-of-age gifts, glittering stones, metal of varying hues, from the people of the Worlds, his father had said. Hallenander knew that compared to the wealth of the Volterrans, these baubles held little value. Their point was ceremonial, an acknowledgement of his family's importance and power and maybe as hints of acquiescence to their ruler's scheme to put a half-blood on the throne, his solution to the lack of babies in the Empire proper, the shame of all Volterra. Hallenander rubbed the top of his head absently. He'd removed the circlet the moment he was alone and the hair tousling through his hand comforted him. Understanding the customs of people he had never met without Geddon's help drained him.

He picked up a pair of beautiful, ornate curved knives from one of the tribes on Gettyca, the planet he ought to be presiding over, his birthright, his supposed home. A gift from his father, they were black metal and amber in a chased silver hilt. Ancient, priceless, and rare, they seemed to him a sincere gesture, a reminder of the days when

Volterran nobles fought their own battles instead of letting the Xaff do their dirty work. His official coming-of-age had happened during a wan daylight ceremony attended by his uncle and the men of the Volettu of Eight. Their simplicity and obscurity was an insult. But he had to observe tradition, even alone in a party pavilion surrounded by Tyr concubines rather than an audience of his future subjects. He saw why Taurellio seemed agitated. Time was running out. Their experiment was soon to face its real test.

The coming-of-age ceremony had nearly not happened at all. The Eight lords appeared ambivalent about planning it, leaving most details to the Helpers, which was almost perverse in its dereliction of duty. But in the weeks before his birthday, his father had been insistent.

"I am Emperor Taurellio," he bellowed from the other end of the liquid device. "I demand that the Eloxiture in the Capital rule on this case immediately. They can deny you a real coming-of-age celebration, but they cannot turn back the clock, those Dantons."

"Perhaps they believe I'm too old to become integrated into normal society now." "Nonsense." His father laid a hand on his bare collarbone. "There is no longer any such thing as normal society. Only to admit such is considered blasphemy, apparently. We will deny reality until we are all dwindled to nothing."

Father was often full of energy and opinions, his teeth flashing and hands moving as he regaled his son with gossip and stories, sometimes for so long that Hallenander struggled to stay awake. But now the Emperor of the Eight Volterran Worlds appeared tired, his dark skin heavily creased. He spoke from his Gettycan Estate, and Hallenander found his lack of ornament or jewelry alarming. He was accustomed to full robes, collars, earrings, and a crown upon his father's head, always against the magnificent backdrop of the Great Palace, not the rural

Gettycan Estate. But until the government hastened their decision about Hallenander's legality, the capital would have to live kingless. Used to Taurellio's constant presence at court, his sycophants and rivals would be left idle, bored, their calendars filled with activities of no real import. Without their Emperor, Volterran society had no purpose.

"And they do miss me, I am sure. There are only sad little balls, now, and regional governors squabbling over their taxes."

"Which the Eloxiture uses as an excuse to stay off the subject of my claim."

"True. And now, my boy, to your adventures," Taurellio said, with an uncharacteristic willingness to change the subject.

Hallenander spoke about his fencing exploits, his masted ships, and other neutral topics, until his father abruptly claimed fatigue and the liquid darkened. Hallenander tapped the stand where the liquid device rested, hoping Father would return, but when he didn't, he read through journals from Volterra instead. He knew how perilous his father's efforts to install him as Prince were, how civilization itself rested on his success. The Emptiness was progressing. Fewer Volterran babies were brought to term, and those that were most often couldn't catch their breath and died. Burial cities grew bright with silk mourning kites. Schools were shuttered.

But despite their tears by day and manic parties by night, Volterran people did not want change, did not want to accept Hallenander's legitimacy. They saw no reason to allow a Hybrid prince. Such an act would signal the end of their civilization, their superiority, their noble right of overlordship and all its privileges. Their gods-given mastery over the Harbingers would be threatened. But the succession laws were unclear. Certainly, old traditions of blind adherence were as fervently practiced as ever. His father's people clung to their tribal dress and attendant rites as a drowning person clings to a float. Even before Geddon, Hallenander hadn't believed that he, a Hybrid prince, would ever dirty the polished stone halls of the Eloxiture with his half-Imset feet.

With his questions, Geddon had been quick to elucidate what the journals did not explain. What exactly did Alliance Law in the tomes negotiated between Volterra and the Harbingers have to say about a person of Hallenander's breeding? "If the Lords declare you a non-citizen," he said, his brow furrowing under his white mop of hair, expectation in his ambergris eyes, "do you think they'd let you continue to exist?"

"Surely the Harbingers would refuse an order to kill me."

Geddon made a hard face. "Do you believe they would make an exception of one Rakki, one Hybrid kid, when they've spent a century wiping out others with Imset blood?"

"Eighty-eight gods," Hallenander sighed. Geddon was right, but Hallenander felt sick admitting it. He had spent so much of his life in the company of those who equated silence with nobility that the exchange of honesty he had with his tutor always made him alternately nauseated and exhilarated. The man taught the possibility of freedom, of flight and adventure and honor, even in his fallen state.

It had been after this conversation that Hallenander had asked to study law. At first, he found nothing useful, but when his arguments with the men his father brought around became astute and accurate, he began to hold himself with more pride. He decorated himself as a member of his only official tribe, the Imset. He dressed as a man of the old planet and spoke as someone who could not easily be influenced by one of the Eight Lords on Evincio, who spent every official meeting and every informal dinner pressing him, looking for weakness. Hallenander had become strong, impassive, and quick to point out any small regulation or precedent that favored his argument. He enjoyed how much it irritated his uncle. The rare glimpse of fluster, a tiny edge of rage in the man's long face, buoyed Hallenander's spirits for days. Mimellio, his father's younger brother, could never quite disguise his contempt for Hallenander. He knew it irritated the emperor. But feelings were of little importance when dealing with the all-powerful Taurellio. He was a wise man, but not a patient one. Hallenander knew having such an ally was all that kept him alive, his potential for the same amount of supremacy hanging on the man's favor. So long as his birthright was still in question.

White stars silently exploded and faded in the sky far above the plateau, fireworks and the sound of laughter echoed outside the window. Hallenander put the journal down and watched the show as he had since he was a small boy, never knowing what in particular the Imset slave girls were celebrating nor why they seemed to be so happy about it. He committed himself to finding out.

**8**

— • —

C hapter Eight

Serral and Brume didn't talk until they had reached the top of their favorite evergreen. From the configuration of its gnarled branches they watched a murmuration of white birds strobe out and back to the east, their bodies flashing in the pale overcast sky like tiny lights. The formation's odd rhythm seemed foreboding. One of the birds peeled off from the group, but the others chased and surrounded it until they'd forced it back into their flying, moving mass. And then the flock dove under the canopy and left no trace.

Serral and Brume had found this tree years before, when the need for privacy and respite from Chlore's endless tasks pushed them out into the forest's elevated world. There, they could imagine that nothing existed but themselves, the sky, and the forest stretching out like blue-gray water. Serral settled into a crook and breathed in the smell of sap and needles.

"So. Spooky." Brume watched the birds disappear. He sounded strained. "Serral. Sister." He sagged onto an intersection of branches. His rusty hair spilled out like something alive. "I…"

"Did Whit tell you?" Serral interrupted. His hesitancy was a sign of nerves, and she was better off ignoring it.

"Tell me what?" His eyes were the one area where their coloring differed. Hers were yellow with green at the center, orange at the outside edge. His were red brown, the color of dirt.

"They're sending a new Planet Protector. During the raid, the Harbs must have destroyed the old one," she said.

He shrugged. "Probably why the Air Guard failed to warn us."

"Damn Harbs." She curled her lip in disgust. "They didn't even come here to destroy the oculus. They could have accomplished their mission without hurting anyone or breaking the law. They have no mandate to bomb a ship in orbit."

"Wait," he said, voice oddly flat. "You know the Harb's mandate?"

"What? Not totally, no. Obviously not. I learned the basics in history class." She picked at a knot in the tree's gray bark.

Brume looked at the horizon, his voice deadened. "Yeah, the whole thing is weird."

"What's wrong with you?" She leaned her forehead on a branch. "Just because you're getting recruited, you don't care about the colony anymore?"

He winced. "I'm trying to...tell you something important. Not about this stupid little colony."

"Sorry. I didn't mean that, it's just that some of us are stuck here."

"Okay, stop talking," he yelled, then visibly controlled himself. "We might not have much time. And I don't even know how to start explaining this."

"Look, I know what you're going to say." Rage jumped in her gut. "You and Rafe and the rest of your class are all about to graduate. The Authorities blamed only me for the Bolt excursion, because if they'd punished you, it would mean a straight ticket to the front and a real quick trip to hell. You're welcome."

"Okay." Brume's eyes squeezed. "Sure. The teachers were protecting us. Especially Rafe. Rumor is he's going to be sent to Amperia, but you know how reliable rumors are."

"What is your problem then?" Serral tucked a needle between her teeth, a bitter taste settling on her tongue. "You know other rumors? About you? About me?"

"Not really." He sighed, his face collapsing. "Nothing I believe."

"Are you crying?"

"No, of course not," he snapped. "This is hard. I've been keeping this secret so long that it feels wrong to let it out."

"Oh, for Ysk's sake, Bru." She slipped into a mocking voice. "*It feels wrong to let my real feelings out! Wait, is that breakable? Yay! Here's what I think of your glass, your paper, your resin! Say goodbye to your toys and portals! Whee! What else is there to smash?*"

"Ha ha. You want to hear it, then? Okay," he said, his voice barely audible. "When you were born on Quenetai, something very bad happened."

She sighed, disappointed. "You were two."

"Two and a half," he nodded.

Serral could think of several memories Brume could relay that came from earlier than anyone ought to be able to remember. It was part of his burden, his faultless memory. He was unable to forget anything, even when he wanted to.

"Okay. Tell me."

He took a deep breath. "Mommy and I were on the plain above the oculus. It was one of those stupid vertical ones, you know?"

"Suicide Oculi. Obsolete now." She spit the needle out and it fell into the branches below, out of sight.

"We were outside, even though the sirens were sounding. I don't know why. Maybe because Mommy was pregnant. And then, she lay down, and then, I didn't really see how, but she was crying and holding a baby."

"Me." Serral imagined the plane, the noise of the klaxons blaring, the chaos of a raid. It must have been terrifying. She didn't know she had been born during a raid. She didn't know Brume had been there. Why had he kept this to himself? She leaned closer.

"Yes, you. And Mommy was crying. But then she smiled. She was so pretty. She had blood on her, and she was lying down. Beautiful, really." Brume's voice was full of unshed tears. "And the air was full of lights," he whispered.

Serral saw it then, the configuration of halos, their incomprehensible colors, their smoke and glare. She felt punched. Something swooped inside her, a hard bat of fear, and something else powerful, but not wholly unfamiliar. Shame. "No."

Brume didn't hear. His eyes were on the sky. His fists were clenched, his voice shaking. "Full of lights, and the Grays came and took you."

"No, this didn't happen. Don't say this happened." The bat was swooping, careening wildly, looking for escape.

He swallowed, glancing at her with a look she had never seen before. As if he had only just noticed her, his sister. His voice was clear and low. "The Grays came and took you, and then Mommy made me swear I'd never tell. She said to just say we fell asleep with you on the ground."

He wiped his eyes on his arm.

"I don't want to hear any more." Serral put her braids behind her shoulders, checking to make sure her boots were laced for the climb down out of the tree. She felt the pull of gravity, of the long fall below them.

"And then Mommy, when the grown-ups came, she was..."

"Dead," Serral said. "Our mother was dead. And I was," the bat was in her throat, "where?"

"With me," he said cheerfully. "I was a good boy. I was holding you when they found us. I wouldn't let them touch you or take you. I screamed when they tried. Because I promised Mommy. And. Because. I saw you. With them. I saw you with them, Serral. And they took you into their ship, and I knew," he trailed off, rubbing something invisible off his face.

Serral leaned far over the tree branch and vomited. Then she stood on her branch, unsteady. Her hands felt far away, her arms like hoses in a broken Arrow, useless. Shredded.

She spoke in a flat, loud voice. "This is the meanest prank you've ever pulled."

"I'm so sorry," he said. "I've always been so sorry."

"I'm leaving now. I've got work."

"No. You don't."

Her scalp tingled with anger. "What's that supposed to mean?"

He sighed, pushing his hair behind his ears. His cheeks were spotted red, like a clown. "Whit was supposed to tell you. You've been relieved of all duties."

"I have?" Serral felt the branch under her feet sway. "Why?"

"We all have. All of us who are...who are being recruited."

Brume put his hands over his face and sobbed. Serral stared. She was used to seeing him in fits of rage. But this was different. He was crying like the baby he once was, who hadn't been allowed to cry over his mother. She had bled out in front of his eyes and then left him with a secret so overwhelming it might destroy him. If what he said was true.

But Serral realized with a prickle of pain, Brume never lied. She knew that as well as she knew her own name. He had carried the secret for fourteen years rather than expose why she always felt so strange, why she had been an outcast in her own right. She was the sister of a strange and volatile boy who needed her to keep him from destroying himself.

He had let the secret out. He had unearthed her identity, all that she had clung to, every moment she had thought she was the ordinary one, the one with something valuable to the Cause. But instead, she was unreliable and dangerous like Brume. Now they were both liabilities. With this confession, he'd tossed her into a new category, the one Inoa had branded her with: *outlaw*.

It made her furious.

"Thanks for the ridiculous story and the absurd rumors. I hope when you go up there, they assign you to write fairy tales for the civician children. No doubt they're feeble enough to believe your garbage."

"Spooky. You need to know this stuff. It explains so much."

She sighed, a cold fury enfolding her, and with it, a tender clarity. "Well now I do. Hope you feel better. That's always been what matters most. Isn't it"

She knew she was being cruel. He didn't answer.

In the bone yard, no one had cleaned up the evidence of Brume's tantrum. Serral started to put the pieces back in their long, curved rows: the small rods, bigger plates, the large components with their complex configurations. It was work she loved and soon was sweating from the effort. The components seemed to want to slip from her grasp. When one of the rods did finally, her left foot coming out from under her in a painful lurch. She slumped to the ground, and her eyes swam with tears. The forest was encased in shadow, the trees looking oddly like clouds in the midday light, like banks of vapor rather than solid objects. Only their creaking in the wind gave them away as real.

The cave carvings appeared in her mind, glittering with a silent message, the same message that had pulled Serral to them, had compelled her to fly the Aero. Whether she admitted it to him or not, Brume's words felt true, like the need to build a plane and to fly it to that pool with its particular prehistoric cave and its specific, moody message. Serral didn't understand, or even want to. She hid her face in her arms.

Inoa had been right. No night cinching or recruitment would interrupt the thread that was pulling Serral. She was that thing Inoa sensed her to be; a traitor, born to a traitor. Which explained why the authorities had always been suspicious, but also willing to watch and wait. They wanted to see if she'd show them something they could use to get rid of her, something disloyal. Or lead them to clues they could use for the war, if they really suspected her of being a spy. But she had only shown them that she was willing to bend the rules. Maybe that alone sealed her fate as a bad seed. Someone to send out as meat for the Harbs, to be shot down and forgotten. Like so many others.

# 9

Chapter Nine

Serral passed the next eight days organizing and tidying the Contriving hangar, the bone yard, and Whit's office.

"You should spend as much time as you can having fun, girl," the old man admonished, the tick on the left side of his face acting up. "Think you'll ever swim in a real lake again, once they get their hooks into you?"

His beard was red all day now.

"I don't want to leave you this mess. No one's going to look after you when I'm gone."

He watched her work. "Join us at the crescent fires tonight. Wouldn't kill you to be around your friends. Your brother will be there."

"What friends?" Serral asked softly. "You're probably the only one who notices when I'm absent."

"He's beside himself, you know. He's that worried."

She kept moving her hands, moving piles.

"You're loved, you stubborn kid. Believe me, friends are a rare resource. You never know where in the universe you might find someone you can trust." He stomped off, slamming the door.

But Serral wouldn't cross back through the tunnel to join the new class of recruits, for graduation or the celebratory crescent fire, to receive honorifics, diplomas and heartfelt words of love from the colony. They were all of age, had finished their schooling, and were ready for whatever assignment the authority deemed them fit. But what certificates had Serral earned? Not a one. No awards, not even the memory of a kiss stolen while huddled in the dark during a raid drill. Maybe it was just as well.

Lying in the hangar at night like another fuselage waiting for repair, Serral listened to the old Imset folk songs through the window. Her heart twisted with loneliness. Whit was wrong. She had no right to participate in the ceremony, to present herself as a helpful citizen, to show her face to those she had thought were her people. In these final days, she would remain with the half-built machines and her new understanding of her birth, excusing herself whenever someone from the oculus came to visit Whit.

On the fifth day Whit tracked her into the bone yard and said gruffly, "You've got a visitor. I am asking you, as a friend, to give her a listen."

Miss Pune stood next to the old man. She smiled. "A word, Serral. Please." Miss Pune's aquamarine eyes were set off by tiny gold-rimmed glasses and seemed uncharacteristically grave.

Serral nodded, and followed the woman through late-spring fields, hiding her face when kids greeted them from the crop rows and animal pens.

Miss Pune returned their hellos.

"People believe you hate them, you know," she said.

"They shunned me, Miss Pune." Serral stepped over a row of thorny bushes, keeping to herself that Miss Pune's had been one of the backs turned. Not that the teachers had any choice, but still.

"You were punished for misbehavior. It wasn't personal. But this refusal to say goodbye to us goes too far."

"I see. So, when the colony decides to punish me, it's fine. But if I decide to agree with you all, say I'm a menace and a bad seed, suddenly you want me around."

"Ouch."

"I don't mean you, Miss Pune. Or Whit. But everyone else just stood by and let Inoa make an example of me. Do they really think I'm going to smile and agree, shunning and cinching mean nothing? My Bolt sentenced to be sunk in the sea, just no big deal?"

Serral was crying.

"Come on. Let's talk somewhere we can't be overheard." Miss Pune pointed to their destination, a line of white-skinned trees marking a creek that wound through the fields in looping folds. Serral understood the area to be sodden and unstable, only good for fishing or hunting frogs. But she didn't question Miss Pune, who had been kind to her, especially as a drafting instructor, encouraging Serral's designs and contrivances, no matter how complicated. Serral followed the woman, and together they picked their way over small, grassy islands toward the trees.

"I doubt you can fathom the Ysken's full mandate. None of us can understand what has happened in the cities since...suffice it to say, the more volatile the war grows, the more extreme civician politics becomes in answer. Chlore is an example every side uses to try and prove its' point. And Inoa finds herself having to answer for the whole colonial program. It's more than a recruit is meant to know of, Serral. But the cities are divided, and the war is far from universally supported." Miss Pune shook her head, swishing the skirt of her dress to one side as she hopped onto a bank. "Inoa does not represent those of us who have known you since you were small. Many believe themselves to be your friends. Some deeply admire you for your contriving skills. That is why when you did something as extraordinary as build your own plane and flew that miraculous thing all over tarnation, the authority had to make an example of you. Because miracles are the Ysken's domain. Do you see?"

Serral hopped behind Miss Pune onto the loamy ground, and realized, as she landed, that after a few days, she might never feel a planet under her feet again, might not feel the cool splash of water on her ankles. Whit was right, she should be outside now. She should be burying herself in the jasper-red soil of Chlore, her home, rooting herself in it, like a tree.

"Miss Pune, respectfully. Flight is not a miracle."

"But empowering yourself is. Claiming freedom, refusing to be told that the only way out of the colony is when and how the Authority dictates. Cobbling together an aircraft without permits and taking flight without authorization can't be allowed. And I think you knew that. Certainly, your brother knew."

Serral wondered how old Miss Pune was. Her hands were gnarled from a lifetime of work, but her legs below her knee-length hem were smooth and strong.

The pair had reached a large meadow. Streamlets crisscrossed it in shining lines and reflected the white trees. Newly visible, a thin trail cut though the grass.

"Well. I hope she's happy," Serral said. "She's trying to get me sent straight to the front, so problem solved I guess."

They followed the trail and soon approached a small grassy notch between trees. To Serral's surprise, the place was outfitted with a crude pavilion, softened with old parachute fabric and ancient starship passenger bunks. It had the look of a secret sanctuary or a cabin in the woods on Old Imseth. Every bit of the structure looked as if it had come from the bone yard, including a heating unit and several stripped consoles repurposed as shelves. Serral smiled to herself. She'd heard rumors for years that Whit and Miss Pune sneaked off somewhere together.

"Your future is not yet decided." Miss Pune motioned to a chair. "That's what I brought you here to discuss."

Serral accepted a cup of warm spice broth from her teacher's flask. Sun speckled the fabric walls cleverly concealed under saplings and, she assumed, invisible from above. It was easy to imagine Whit spending the worst of his flashback moments here, a place so alive and green.

Miss Pune straightened her dress over her knees. "You have refused to acknowledge the admonishments of the authorities. That was not a good strategy."

Serral closed her eyes. She hadn't thought enough about positioning herself for the future. "I guess I thought Inoa had already won."

"Since when do you give up so easily?"

Serral faced Miss Pune. "You're right. I guess I don't know why I've let the whole cinching and shunning thing get to me."

But she did. Brume's confession had flooded her with so much shame, she had forgotten that others didn't know her secret, but still saw her as a member of their community. That wasn't the whole reason why Serral felt defeated. Her dreams haunted her. The glittering blue of a Thanton's eyes, the feeling she was supposed to be in the air, that her destiny was above and not in a station but outside, in the sky. They left her with the feeling that she couldn't control her fate so much as let it unfold, because forces bigger than she, bigger than Chlore, bigger than the Authority, were at work. She winced at the absurd idea, shaking it out of her head.

"What should I do?"

"Whit and I have convinced Headmaster to update your records as best he can, showing clearly that while you have not yet reached certification, your ability to fix machines is outstanding. Extraordinary, really. A number of contrivances we use in the fields and in food gathering are owed to your inventiveness. The Warren Falla murals, the reconditioned cleansing area, all the work you did to improve the fish reef. Your plow makes every planting smoother. These have all improved not just nutrition, but well-being in our community, Serral. These are empirical facts. We have made sure your file contains all the ways you personally have contributed to the survival of this colony. You are needed for the future of all Imset, not only here but all over the diaspora. Alive. Not doomed to die as a regular soldier, fodder for the Harbs."

"My plow? The fish reef? You think the Military cares about those things?" Serral's neck flushed with embarrassment and anticipation. No one had ever talked to her this way before. Her tears fell, and she made no effort to wipe them.

"The Military wants to win the war, regardless of what the cities want. As they say, *there is no way...*"

"*But the planetary way.* I know." Serral shrugged. She had never thought deeply about the meaning of the slogan. It had always been empty words, like *Imseth Forever,* something nebulous but comforting, wishing eternal life for the dead husk of their former planet.

"You have contributed a great deal to this community. You deserve the same fairness of review as any other recruit. I am not alone in believing that."

"And other people are not alone in thinking I should slink off and die."

Miss Pune gripped Serral's wrist, her hand stronger than it appeared, her voice low and strong but gentle. "Child, there is much you don't know. Listen to me now."

Serral nodded, her eyes blurring. She was feeling overwhelmed. But the pavilion was comforting, and she had no place to go but the hangar which was full of bitter memories.

"I can't tell you everything, you know that. You wouldn't want harm to come to Chlore."

"Of course not." Chlore was hers, would always be hers, no matter what kind of monster she was, deep down. She would protect her home with her life.

"As you know, an Air Guard tour is ten years. If you survive those years, you may return to a planet or live a decent life in one of the floating space cities. Such things are still possible for someone with extraordinary focus and ability. Child, all things are still possible for you."

Serral couldn't think of a reply. Survival still sounded nearly impossible, but she didn't argue. Miss Pune's hand felt warm on her arm, and the wind blew the grass across the marshy field, so it swayed in the sun like dancers to a crazy tune.

"Whatever you have to do, survive your tour. You are a capable, imaginative person, Serral. You see possibilities that others do not. Please find it inside yourself to get through your stint in the Military. Do you understand?"

"Thank you for trying to help me. Maybe if they're smart, they'll listen to you." Serral turned her hand upward, so Miss Pune's fingers rested on her palm. "Even if the worst happens, and they send me right to the front, I promise to try."

"This war is devolving. We don't know what is going to happen. And you will have difficulty pretending to be an obedient soldier."

Serral laughed. "What about Brume? He's worse than I am."

"True, but we are speaking of you now. Mine the memory of your accomplishments for strength. If you get the chance to stand out, take it. Become someone they don't want to risk losing. Know that you are special and use that knowledge to stay alive."

"This is the opposite of what you people have been telling me all my life."

"It is. You are not a scrap rat anymore, Serral. You are now a soldier of the Imset. And like all Imset, you must do anything to survive. Anything. Understand?"

Serral felt a slight pulse of energy, and a faint pop in the air. Spacecraft had entered the atmosphere. The recruiters. Fear shot through her body. So soon. Far too soon. She put her head on Miss Pune's shoulder. Her scent was comforting, bark and soap.

Miss Pune pushed Serral's face up to meet her gaze. "Choose right now. Do you want to survive? Because if you don't, I promise you, you won't."

The marsh grass suddenly lay flat, then sprung straight.

"I want to survive. I do."

"You will see ways out that others do not." Miss Pune stroked Serral's cheek, her blue eyes blurring. "Let no one tell you what is real, and what is unreal. Trust only yourself."

Whit's husky voice carried from outside the clearing. "They're here. Better get in formation, Spook. Quickly now."

She sprinted toward the airfield. Other children were running in from the fields and disappearing into the tunnel. Just like a raid, getting to places. Only this time the formation felt far more ominous. Her last time running to places. She tried to take in a few final glimpses of Chlore. Once recruited, no one who grew up there was ever seen there again.

A shadow moved over the courtyard, the craft dwarfing the oculus. The whole colony seemed to tremble. People stood in their assigned rows, teachers, admins, and the class of recruits. Serral took her place at the end of the line. She had never stood with this group before. There was no designated place for her. No one looked at her. They all gazed up at the recruitment ship.

A massive silver Transport 'Tainer lowered its legs to the ground. Serral recognized it as a Jiniper 7 Catamaran with its two gargantuan hulls and seven long jets. Its Imset seal was tarnished and old, and the pockmarked jets looked like they had been through far too many debris fields, but the ship's sheer size commanded respect. Excitement surged in Serral's chest. She would fly again, soon. She was going into space, and there was hope she'd live long enough to return to Chlore one day. Maybe she would find a way to travel to all the destinations on her back tattoo, to traverse each of the six port worms, see everything the universe could show her. *All things were still possible.*

The ship's doors opened.

Four bots emerged. Together, acting as one, they unfurled a large fabric tent until it stood flapping in the wind, clean as nothing in the oculus ever was, bright as clouds. Each surface bore a sharp Imset star, giving the structure a faintly royal flair. The bots disappeared inside the tent, and two humans strode down the ship's ramp.

They were the oddest-looking people Serral had ever seen, though familiar enough from educational strippies. By the looks of their hairstyles and flimsy clothing, they were Civicians, space dwellers. One was a man, soft and fleshy, the other a woman, angular and regal. They shimmered with tiny stars that Serral realized were jewels in their earlobes and around their necks. The sight unnerved her. She had never expected to see anything so precious or rare, so far removed from the work of saving Imset civilization. The pair moved slowly toward the tent, speaking quietly to one another. Serral noticed the headmaster wringing his hands. Inoa stood as still as a heron. Strangers patrolled the line of authority figures, occasionally addressing one or another directly. Serral didn't hear what was said, only that the adults she knew seemed suddenly small and plain, their white heads bent in deference.

Then all the of-agers moved to stand in line, were handed small totes, and made final turns to wave goodbye. Clearly, they had been briefed on what to expect. Serral had not. She moved to the back of the line, behind a kid named Cecil who ignored her. Inoa continued staring, but then, To Serral's amazement, she made a hand gesture, from her heart toward Serral.

Serral laughed in confusion. Inoa's hand dropped to her side.

"Serral Brook?" said the man who had come from the ship. "Don't keep us waiting, Col. We've been processing stinky scrap rats for weeks. Even our bots are petitioning for reassignment."

Inside the tent, cold lights shone down on a shining metal table. The recruiters sat peering into a single liquid portal, its light reflecting in their eyes. Serral stood, checking to see if her one photograph of Brume was still in its place on the inner pocket of her tunic where she kept it wrapped securely in resin. It was the only possession she cared about, other than the Bolt, which was lost to her.

"Miss Brook," the tall, regal woman said. "You are an odd one."

Serral stood in front of the two of them, feeling like an offering at a buffet table.

"You two are Military?" Serral asked, instantly regretting how dubious she sounded. "You know about contriving?"

The man's eyes were small in his flabby, colorless face. Only his voice sounded muscular, almost musical. "We are contracted to the Military.

And by their jurisdiction, we are charged with evaluating each of you strapping young illiterates for fitness to serve."

Serral didn't reply.

The woman, her white hair pulled back tightly, said. "Are you a prize? Or a punishment?"

"Uhm." Serral tried to think of something to say. "I have some skills as a contriver. Ma'am."

The woman gestured toward the liquid screen. "Oh we see how your supervisor and his girlfriend have kluged all this nonsense together about how useful you are, blah blah blah."

The man smiled cheerlessly. "Sorry hon, but there's no trick that hasn't been pulled on us before, and better."

"Trick?" Serral swallowed. In the corners of the tent, the bots sprung to life as if from a hidden signal. They swiveled, preparing to dismantle the tent. Serral remembered Miss Pume words. "No. I really did all that stuff. Did they tell you about..." She paused. "The Bolt?"

The woman replied, "Authorities will say anything to keep their kids alive in space. I understand. They love you, though they can't admit it. If your authorities and teachers here fail to follow proper boundary protocols, they'll be yanked right off these cushy assignments and sent back to some slum on Amperia or to a barge in the cluster to work as domestics. Some people love planets. We get it."

"No, I really did." Serral felt her throat drying.

The bots grabbed each of the four metal support poles. Time was running out. Miss Pune had said there was a chance Serral would be seen as an asset. But clearly, Miss Pune had been naive. Serral had been correct to feel cynical. But standing in front of these nasty people, she regretted being right.

The man closed the liquid portal with a snap and stood to join his comrade. "Basic training for you. Just like most of your friends. It'll be fun."

"Basic Training?" Serral asked, her voice rising. "You've already decided?"

"Nothing to decide." The woman shrugged. "You're sixteen?"

"Yes Ma'am."

The man picked at his teeth with a pale finger, reconsidering. "If you're kicked off the plantation, you go straight into Basic."

"It's rules, sweetheart," the woman smiled faintly. "You'll have to get used them."

"Can you tell me where my brother...?"

"We're done." The woman waved. The tent suddenly rose, lifted by bots, and folded closed. "Go."

The first thing she noticed on the ship was the smell of space, its mixture of chemical and physical odor. The next was the presence of other recruits. Strange, mysterious kids of all shapes and sizes who watched her with curiosity when she entered the ship. Serral too was intrigued by them.

Then the door shut, and the 'Tainer lurched. And the lot of them rose quickly into space.

## 10

C hapter Ten

The Portainer was overloud, extra bright, and contained too many people. Everywhere were other kids in bizarre versions of standard, gray Colonial coveralls. Most were deep in conversation. The ones with shiny black horns attached to their clothing were bragging to the ones with ink for sleeves. A group of fur-draped kids blinked through tinted goggles, patting the back of one who seemed to be overcome by the light. A couple of others sat on their heels, rocking and humming. One group wore frightening face paint. Were they trying to smile? Serral drew her lips up in greeting, then scurried past their smell of wood smoke and animal fat. The conversation noise was deafening, voices she didn't know, accents she couldn't place. And everywhere, nervous tension.

In the Caf, Serral found Rafe, Lymm, Brume and another boy from their class, Tuane. The food counter was crowded with kids, all cheerful and excited. Unlimited food. Who wouldn't be happy about that?

Tuane narrowed his eyes at her. "You two even get recruited together. How'd you manage that?"

"Inoa."

"I looked at Whit's liquid," Brume broke into the conversation. His brown eyes were scared, though he was trying not to let it show. "We are lucky to have left the planet when we did."

Serral whispered. "The Planet Protector didn't come?"

Brume shook his head.

"Dantons in Hell," Rafe cursed. "Chlore needs protecting."

The ship lurched. Was that normal? No one else seemed to notice. Serral hoped it was just the exit from Chlore's atmosphere that rocked the ship, or maybe a pulse. She had watched the education strippies on space navigation model over and over, played with the sim until it broke, and she'd had to build her own. But the actual experience of space travel was new. She didn't know how to gauge the shaking the 'Tainer was doing, the loud sounds that emanated from its shell.

"Let's find a porthole," she said.

Serral, Brume, Rafe and Tuane scrambled out of the Caf and ran to the starboard side of the hull. They flung open doors, finding kitchens, bunk rooms half occupied by kids, and an abandoned utility closet. Finally, they discovered a huge vertical pod tube with a small opening next to an emergency air lock. The gap had weak gravity, so they vaulted to the window. The view was of a narrow slice of stars.

The 'Tainer lurched again. Alarms sounded. Serral didn't care about alarms, she was used to them, but a sudden smell of smoke frightened her. It could be coming from anywhere. The ventilation system piped throughout the ship, she was sure. She forced herself to breathe evenly. The air wasn't poison. Yet.

"There, six o'clock," Rafe said in his best trying-to-stay-calm voice. A Halo.

Their heads touching, the three watched through the window as three other silver wheels joined the first. Then, in formation, the four ships flashed patterns in yellow and red, while coming closer to the 'Tainer.

"Why aren't we fighting back?" Brume whispered.

A massive vibration shook them, and then it stopped abruptly. A streak of shiny silver whooshed by the window. It separated and dispersed itself into a batch of missiles that was moving steadily out towards the Halos. There was a series of small explosions, bombs fizzling without oxygen to feed them. The Halos shrank to the size of Serral's palm.

"They'll pursue." Serral tried to anticipate what the alien pilots might be planning. She felt tremendous anxiety and tried to reassure both herself and her friends. "But it's okay. We'll pulse."

The stars outside the window grew fuzzy, then disappeared. All alarms abruptly ceased, and their glide grew smooth.

"How do you know these things?" Tuane asked, eyes wide.

Rafe smiled, making her grow hot with embarrassment.

"Why do you think we call her Spooky?" he said.

Brume looked sideways at his friend. Rafe took the cue and stopped talking. When they got back to the commons, no one seemed to have noticed the violence that had played out beyond the porthole. They seemed inoculated to emergencies and sirens, and mayhem. And maybe this kind of thing was to be routine for the next ten years of space travel.

Serral stopped a proud-looking girl decorated with numerous earrings and a series of metal plates that joined in a flexible mask over her face. "Is that smell and all the munitions going off normal?"

The girl laughed. She said her words with an odd lilt. "Smoke happens every time we pick up new recruits. Firing weapons? At least once a day. I'm amazed this craft is still flying. We have no one guarding us, you know. Not a single Arrow. How do they expect to win the war? Honestly."

The girl smiled at Rafe. "Hello," she said. "I'm Thandra. I come from the first colony to be recruited, so I know just about everyone."

Rafe smiled back. "We must seem boring to you."

"Oh no. You are the strangest we have yet met. Chlorans, you with your easy lives."

"Our what?" Tuane said.

Serral was amused by Brume, who couldn't seem to speak at all.

"It's a pleasure to meet you," Serral said, glad to make a friend.

Thandra invited them to sit with her in a corner of the large lounge. She pointed to kids across the room with a long, metallic fingernail. "Those are the Huvians." She gestured towards a group of goggle wearers. "Those there? They lived in caves. All this sensory stimulation is hard on them."

There were kids with decorative horn scales she called Nisstopians. "Ask them about their *charismatic leader*," she said.

Thandra was beautiful. In the cracks of her face plates, Serral could see her olive skin and the cleft in her chin.

"And the muscular ones?" Rafe pointed out kids who had sliced open the sleeves on their coveralls to make room for their bulging biceps.

Thandra sighed. "The Mon. There are only four of them, sad to say. Life was difficult in their colony. They lost their oculus and have been on the run for years. They say the planet Mon is filled with ferocious animals which they used for food when they could but also succumbed to. Eat or be eaten."

The group sat in silence, contemplating, before Thandra spoke again. "How often was Chlore raided? Rumor is only twice a year." Thandra's voice had an edge of disbelief.

Rafe and Brume exchanged a look. Rafe said, "Is that not normal?"

She rolled her hazel eyes playfully. "Oh, come on, don't play with me. We just met."

No one responded.

Thandra blinked. "Are you kidding? Once, Mons was raided every day for sixty days. And the Nisstopians? They all have hearing loss from bombs. Our colony, Petris, had so much damage we could only use a third of the structure. Sometimes we had five raids in a week. We never went a month without one."

Brume's dark eyes met Serral's. "It sounds like Chlore was harder to reach than other planets."

"No." Thandra said. "The reason you got recruited last is that you are closest to Hevoxin. Easy to reach from anywhere. Chlore gives the most recruits, and they don't want to pay to feed you any longer than necessary. Or so I have heard." Her eyes grew comically wide, teasing. The group went silent again.

"So the rumors are true?" Brume finally spoke, voice flat. "The colonies are almost all extinguished? From what you say, we are a vanishing breed."

Thandra smiled. "I'm just another recruit, darling. But if you look around, do you see the only hope of a proud people? Or a ragtag bunch of freaks, barely able to keep it together?"

Serral scanned the room. One of the Huvians was whimpering, pressing his goggles onto his face while his friends encircled him with their bodies.

Brume changed the subject. "You said Chlore is close to Hevoxin?"

Serral smiled wider thinking of the other side of the universe. She might not live long, but her dream of traversing one of the port worms was about to come true. "We're going to traverse Hevoxin? The wall? Or the nebula?"

Apparently not everyone obsessed over the Heavenly Hexagon of cross-universe travel as much as Serral and Brume.

"How should I know?" Thandra groomed one thick eyebrow with her metal-covered fingernail. "I wasn't even aware there were two port worms in Hevoxin. I thought there was one."

"Oh no," Serral blurted. "One leads to a totally different part of the universe than the other. It's a mystery why the Ancients..."

She felt Rafe's hand on her arm and fell silent.

"Please excuse us. We're geeks." Rafe said. "There's not much to do on Chlore."

"No, I imagine not."

Brume's face froze, angry at being categorized, Serral was sure. She was relieved when Rafe changed the subject back to rumors, which Thandra tore into hungrily. She explained that on a normal recruitment cruise, there were presentations and programs to keep the children busy. But this trip had only a skeleton crew who made little effort to prepare their charges for what would come next.

"The crew runs if we try to ask a question," Thandra said. "We've been on board for two weeks, and so far, all we've seen are the same boring strippies about the beautiful Lost Planet Imseth."

They laughed. Serral could have recited the narration of those strippies by heart. The rivers and valleys, the large modern cities and rolling expansive oceans all owned by the Imset people. They had been on the verge of solving ecological collapse, when the brutal aliens invaded, augering themselves into people to the point of death and insisting that Imseth belonged to a giant, previously unknown political system that had rules no Imset had ever agreed to, let alone been aware of. And so, the bombing began and couldn't be stopped, until the planet was lost. In the darkness, heroes emerged. They stole tech from the invaders and created the space cities that gave egress to the deserving few who would start civilization over again, one day. Serral thought of the strippies as she did the slogan *Imseth Forever* on the wall of the Caf, or the four-point silver star; a simple reminder of who they had been, when they had been something. The only evidence she'd seen of their once-great civilization was the Air Guard. And this ship, which looked sleek enough despite its feral, dirty cargo.

"Thank Ysk we have new people to talk to," Thandra said, turning her attention away. "I keep trying to piece together what the world is really like."

The four friends left Thandra while she was teasing a passing Huvian boy who was trying to pry his goggles off and seemed to like the attention. He laughed and tried to pull her hands away, his eyes pressed shut. "They said they would give me drops to fix it."

Serral and the three boys moved through a series of common rooms, all populated by groups of strange kids. Serral couldn't believe the variety of ways their fellow scrap rats had been molded by their planets. The only thing special about those from Chlore were their long, matted braids and the impressively thick patching on their coveralls. The others were distinctive in their oddness. It wasn't only their costumes and physical forms, but also a rawness in their personalities. She sensed a low hum of suspicion, of anger, and a kind of jumpiness, that reminded her of Whit. These people had been traumatized, and while they were still young, their hope felt somehow wrecked.

Serral found the manic flirting and giddy friend-making overly dramatic. She followed the boys from room to room, looking for a couple of free benches. Some of their new mates had integrated into new groups and were lost in conversation. Some people sat slumped, fabric hiding their heads, trying to sleep or block out the hubbub. But most seemed to be enjoying the party.

Eventually, Tuane spotted an empty alcove and the four settled on the floor. For the next couple of hours, they traded theories about why the Air Guard hadn't protected them on the way off Chlore.

"Maybe they did," Tuane said. "There were explosions."

"I think this ship fired off one round." Brume looked at his thumb, then bit a cuticle.

"Miss Pune told me the war is getting worse," Serral said. "She said to pay close attention because nothing is the same as it was, and no one can prepare us."

Tuane tossed a black braid. "How would she know?"

Brume stared at Tuane until he fell silent.

"That Halo cluster was trying to kill us," Serral said softly. "That wasn't just harassment."

"I'm sorry." Tuane made a gesture of peace. "But how do you pretend to know these things?"

Serral picked at the patches on her coverall, watching the tiny old silver star wink. "Logic. Fire needs fuel. That's always been the reason why we don't fight in space. You expend a lot of ordinances that can only fizzle without the air of an atmosphere. Or if you get close enough to an enemy ship to attach a viable explosive, you put your own ship at risk. Rarely worth it. Right?"

They nodded at her recap of what they had learned in early grades.

"Obviously," Brume said.

"But the Harbs fired anyway. Because there wasn't much risk in it. Our crew aren't fighting back." She whispered. "Something has changed."

"It's a worthy theory, Spook," Tuane said.

"Not enough data to be sure." Brume shook his head. "But it is possible."

"As always, they don't tell us anything. So, whatever we make up in our own heads is as valid as anything else, I suppose." Tuane looked around the room. "Now is your chance to learn if anyone outside of our own little world thinks so too.

"I am attempting to understand," Serral replied. "Try it sometime."

But he was distracted by five odd-looking kids. If they weren't so young, Serral might have mistaken them for crew members, with their cropped hair and stiff black coveralls, their bright Imset insignias glimmering silver over their hearts.

"Sharp," Tuane said admiringly. "So, when do they turn us into soldiers?"

The chemical shower stung.

Afterward, Serral sat on an exam table while a white-haired, young-looking tech examined Serral's limbs. "That is the ugliest, most homemade heavenly hex tat I've ever seen."

"Is it common to ink the hex?" Serral hated feeling so innocent.

The tech smiled. "There are no original ideas, Hon. But just so you know, the 'Thors aren't crazy about the map."

"The 'Thors?"

"Oh for Ysk's sake. The Authority."

"Oh." Serral craned her neck, but she couldn't see her back, or the map Brume had tatooed.

"Look." The tech pushed a robe up over Serral's shoulders. "I've razed a hundred face tats and sealed two hundred ear holes today. If you promise to be discreet about that scrawl, I'll let you keep it."

"Thanks," Serral said. "You seem to be short staffed right now. That must be hard."

The tech smirked. "What are you angling after, Col?"

"Just a question." Serral ignored the flush crawling up her skin. "Did anything unusual happen today?"

"You mean, did they shoot at us? Yeah. But it was nothing."

Serral's neck pinched as the Medic injected her with a tracker. "Ouch."

"It'll stop stinging in a minute. Okay, lie down. Time for the main event."

"Lie down?"

"It'll only take a second." The tech prodded Serral's body with gloved fingers. Serral tried to lie still, but she felt a strong urge to fight the woman off and run.

"No oves, kid?"

"Oves?" It took Serral a second to register the question. The tech was asking about her ovaries. "I don't have any?"

"Nope."

The pressure immediately ceased, and the tech snapped off her gloves. "You never bled, huh?"

Serral grimaced, thinking of what Brume had told her. She'd been with Harbs, for who knew how long. Of course they'd harvested her. They'd have wiped her memory too if she'd had one as a newborn. Her face grew hot.

"I'm only sixteen."

The tech nodded. "Yeah. That's not unusual for a Col. Stress messes with hormones. But anyway, you're the lucky one. Nothing for me to excise." She winked. "I'd keep it to myself, though. The other girls are going to feel rough tonight."

"Only the girls?"

"The boys have nothing the Harbs want, other than their lives. Girl bodies, different story. But don't worry. You'll never come face to face with any Harbs. And if you do, it won't be for long."

"Okay." Serral felt frozen. She noticed that the tech was tall and pallid, obviously a space lifer and someone who knew all kinds of things about Imset life that no Planetary kid could. Ten questions coalesced in her mind, all competing to be asked.

"Go on, get dressed and get out. I got a ton more of you stinky Cols today, and then we're all done for this year." The tech handed her a pair of folded black coveralls, underthings, and a sleep set. Serral inhaled the first new clothing she had ever owned. It smelled like chemicals.

In the next room Serral sat in a bot chair while its mechanical arms cut off her braids. Seeing the long, auburn coils lying dead on the floor filled her with a strange sensation of rebirth. She laughed softly to herself, as a vacuum sucked them away.

Her friends looked bizarre in their new black outfits and stubbled heads. Tuane slept on the other side of Rafe, Lymm and other friends scattered around randomly wherever they could find a place. When the lights faded to darkness, Serral expected to lie awake, worrying about another attack or trying to manage her newfound excitement. But she didn't even have the will to change into her new sleep set before exhaustion took hold.

She floated in velvety blackness, warm and relaxed as a blue light threaded across the sky in dots and beams that throbbed in mysterious swoops and bends, disobeying the rules that light was meant to follow, sometimes refracting into a rainbow, other times shimmering like water. It beckoned her, signaling something vitally important. If only she could fly closer to find out what. But the scene was loud. Huge creatures flew around, blackening her view. Misgiving overwhelmed her. And then she was awake, feeling cheated.

Because, in reality, something was deeply, terrifyingly wrong.

**11**

— • —

C hapter Eleven

Serral's ears ached from the morning cacophony aboard the ship. The common room lit up, darkened, lit up, darkened. Kids rubbed sleep from their eyes and roused friends. Serral stood, trying to keep her feet in the swooping surges of gravity. Brume rose next to her. Rafe shook Tuane to wake him. Kids shouted to one another about *instructions* and *crew*. The ship lurched, and they floated up, clinging to one another and grabbing pointlessly at their blankets. Grav came back on abruptly and they all fell back down onto the floor, hard. Shrieks erupted, fear and pain. Serral landed awkwardly but managed to stay upright. The four of them grabbed hands to steady themselves.

"You all okay?" Rafe asked.

Brume grabbed at his side where it had collided with the floor, his breathing ragged.

Serral pointed to the passageway. "The porthole. Now."

"Where's Lymm?" Brume mouthed.

In their new clothes and shorn hair under harsh green light, it was hard to tell anyone apart. The four of them slipped through clusters of recruits, trying to shout over the din. Screams erupted as Grav blinked off again, then back on, sending them tumbling to the floor all over again.

Serral and Brume pulled themselves out into the passageway. Serral grabbed Brume's hand, and Tuane took hers. Kids around them were doing the same.

"We need to get back to the window." Serral motioned. Her insides felt gelatinous. She passed an elevator, its doors opening and closing erratically like a spluttering mouth. Mercifully, the alarms quieted the further they moved from the common areas and toward the central cavity.

"What is the point of this?" Tuane said.

"We want to see if we're under attack or having mechanical failure." Brume said, shambling along.

"Attack?" Tuane said. "Might as well start praying."

"The ship got away once before," Serral said. "The Med tech told me it was a normal thing."

"This doesn't feel normal," Rafe said.

"There," Brume said through gritted teeth, another vibration rocking the ship. "Seemed closer before."

They reached the pod tube. The door was ajar, wedged halfway open, an angry ping emanating from its emergency locks.

"What if we can't get back out?" Tuane said. "What if we get in trouble?"

Brume gasped, short of breath. "Wake up. This is war, you idiot."

"Do whatever you want," Serral said. "I'm going in to look."

"Look, I'm sorry you got cinched." Rafe grabbed the handle and looked straight at her. "But that flight was the greatest experience of my life. And I'd follow you into hell."

The mud in Serral's gut instantly calmed, and she grinned. Beyond the door, the hatch to the pod was jammed, though Serral couldn't tell if it was because of a power outage, or if the opening had shifted during a vibration.

"One, two, three," Rafe said. "Push."

Their limbs quivered with effort. Grav failed again, but they were through. Behind them the ship was silent and dark.

"Hold on to each other," Rafe said. "If you lose your grip now, you'll be in trouble."

The cavity smelled like smoke and ozone. Serral didn't look at the long, empty bay. The space was ominous, caverning out into blackness where instead of red flashes of emergency lights, there should have been an ambient glow, exit signs, something that signaled a functioning ship. The window was barely visible, just a faint reflection of glass and a glimmer of stars in deep black beyond. They pulled themselves to it, and Serral went rigid. Outside, off to one side, almost out of view, floated a massive Harb cluster ship tucked inside four circular battleships, colored lights on all five crafts blinking into the darkness of space. They were Halos, just like the one she'd seen on Chlore. One of them was detaching, unhinging like a glittering bracelet. Tekkus swarmed, the small ships emerging as soon as their host ship was free of the core. A vacant space was left where one Halo had flown free, out of view. The 'Tainer shuddered again.

"Not normal," Brume said. "No return fire."

"We're just sitting here waiting to die," Serral said quietly.

Tuane made a strange sound in his throat. "Where is the damn crew?"

As Serral's eyes adjusted to the dark, blinking rows of red lights beckoned her attention to four launch tubes. Three were empty. One contained an object, invisible but for reflected patches of red-silver where the lights flashed, like a piece of equipment sputtering as it sinks into deep water.

"They abandoned ship," Serral said.

Brume swore. "We are nothing but meat to them. Nothing but a bunch of..."

Rafe put a hand on Brume's shoulder. "Shut it. Now."

The ship creaked sickeningly.

"There is one escape pod," Serral said, surprised at how steady her voice sounded. She felt detached from her body, no longer nauseated but coldly calm. "And we are going to take it."

"We have to get the others," Tuane said in a high voice. "There must be more pods. Enough for all of us."

Vibrations shimmied through the hull, followed by deep metallic pinging, and a loud hiss.

"No time." Brume's eyes, wild, surveyed the sky outside.

"Come on. The others will find their own." Rafe hustled Tuane toward the tube. "Like you said. A 'Tainer this big must have plenty."

Tuane took one look behind him, then followed as the four friends dragged themselves in the empty gravity across the cavity and toward the pod. They pulled the emergency safety latch and the pod's doors opened to accept them. It was compact, with six seats and four large portholes showing dancing light in the large core cavity outside a transparent launch tube. They scrambled to strap themselves to seats. The doors sealed, and the craft buzzed like a living thing. The oxygen inside was rich, and clean, and Serral gulped it against the realization that her head felt light, floaty. She had been breathing too much carbon dioxide. They all had. She panicked. Life support aboard the main ship had failed, she now understood. The reason the ship had grown silent behind them was that in the overfilled common areas the other recruits had passed out from lack of oxygen. Her head filled with tears so hard and angry they couldn't be shed. Outside, in the vast bay behind them, orange-and-blue monster tongues of flame erupted.

Rafe was calming Tuane. "We'll wait things out. If the 'Tainer doesn't go into distress, we've overreacted. If it does, we'll be..."

The Ecto escape pod shifted and its windows went dark. Serral felt a swooping sensation as they shot through the tube, away from the recruitment ship and its passengers, the crew who had seemingly failed to do anything to protect them. Grav disappeared, and with it, the tugging sensation in Serral's chest. The Catamaran appeared outside, then grew smaller, cracks becoming visible in the space between pontoons. The Harb battleship, a second Halo, hovered at a distance, fully detached now.

"...jettisoned automatically." Rafe trailed off.

They rocketed away from the broken ship, cracks in its hull gaping like knife wounds, gas and debris flowing out, dots of horror. Serral wanted to close her eyes, but they were locked open. She did not want to accept what she was seeing. One pontoon disintegrated. The other broke into flame-fringed parts. Tekkus fighter ships swarmed back toward their base ship. Serral felt herself at a great distance from the inside of the pod, from her situation. Everything had happened so fast, she couldn't be sure she wasn't dreaming or still in the cave of the ancients, watching the destruction of a whole generation of recruits in some kind of hallucinatory strippy. This couldn't be real.

A mechanical voice came over the pod's speakers. "*Welcome passengers and thank you for strapping into this unattended ECUnit. We are now in deep space, and you may move about the cabin freely. Nutrition and personal care facilities are located at the stern. Please observe all posted regulations, make yourselves comfortable, and enjoy your flight.*"

They sat quietly, looking dazed. Brume had his eyes closed, his breath staccato.

"Are you okay?" Serral said, unbolting and moving closer to him.

He grimaced. "Wind knocked out of me. Bruised a rib, I think."

"We have to keep an eye on it," Rafe said. "If you start to have real trouble breathing..."

"I'm fine," Brume said. "I'm lucky to be alive."

Serral touched a hand to his side, and he cringed. "Anything else hurting?" she said.

"Leave me alone." He opened his eyes to glare at her and then shut them again.

That was a good sign, acting like himself. Serral moved to the other side of the cabin and tried to catch her own breath, which felt uneven and strange though her head felt less dizzy. Her brother's eyes had been like dry stones flashing hard at her. She hadn't looked directly into them since their time in the tree when she had left him after his terrible confession. She wondered if she'd ever see them soft again. Life had changed. Her own eyes tingled, pinpricks of strain and something else, something too powerful to consider.

"I'll see if there's any water." Tuane strode to the back.

Rafe approached her, his voice low. "For the love of Ysk, Spooky. When did you realize they'd abandoned us?"

She counted Tuane's steps behind her, twenty, and mentally measured the area of the pod. She cursed inwardly, understanding how many more kids they could have folded inside. Had there been time. Had any of them been alive. Which she doubted. Outside, the cluster ship reintegrated its Halos. The fifth gently aligned itself while the fourth merged with the whole. From the little pod's distance, the cluster was as pretty and shiny as a silver top in a picture book, something a toddler would spin on its axis for fun.

"I didn't realize anything. I didn't even imagine it. I just wanted to go see if there was a full-blown attack or just another skirmish." She wiped her eyes on her sleeve. "The Authority must not have been expecting such firepower so close to a port worm. Isn't it against the rules of war?"

Rafe ignored him. "What were you expecting, Serral?"

"I don't know. I wanted to see what was happening," she said. Her scalp tingled.

He continued, his voice oddly soft. "Will they come after us now? Do you know?"

Serral paused. Her gut felt queasy and sour, not jumping with fright. "I think they'll leave us alone."

"What makes you think that?" Tuane returned with water. She wasn't used to him without his braids or the old vest he used to wear covered in pockets. In his new black coveralls, feet in socks, he looked as vulnerable as a child wandering away from the crescent fire on a summer night, oblivious to predators watching from the dark.

Brume swiveled in his chair, listing to one side, but alert. "I admit, I'm also curious why you think they won't attack us. They just got done destroying an entire Jiniper Seven. Like it was nothing. What makes us worthy of survival?"

She sighed. A tiny spark of energy flitted around her head, looking for purchase, and a memory appeared in her mind: an Air Guard Vice Marsiant sitting comfortably in Whit's office. She had been ten or so. The man had been impressive to look at in his sharp black uniform gleaming with silver stars, his close-cropped white hair and fighter pilot's lithe build. He was visiting after a Myrth Day fire, and the three sat by lamplight, Whit and the man chewing on Azanta leaves and contentedly telling stories of past glory.

Serral had only recently started working for Whit, and Brume hadn't yet begun. He must have been out with friends, up all night for the holiday fires and celebrations. Serral smiled, thinking how even then she would far rather spend a free night in the presence of a war hero than singing and dancing. She listened to the men chat for hours. Whit told her to go play or find a place to sleep, but after she served them tea and cakes, he'd let her stay. She'd be the one to pull blankets over Whit in the wee hours while he slept with a rare smile on his weathered face. She must have asked questions, because the uniformed man, whose name she didn't remember, told her that the enemy was like a hive of bees, and not to be afraid of them. He said, "If you can get one of them to do something, they'll all follow along. No minds of their own, you see. It's maddening, but also, we can use it against them." Then he held a finger to his red-stained lips and made a shushing motion, as if she should keep his words secret.

"I don't know for sure why they won't attack, obviously," she answered Brume, "but, we're unarmed, I guess, and I don't think they kill the defenseless."

Rafe stared. "How do you figure?"

Brume coughed. "That's just a legend."

"Of course," Serral said. A picture came into her mind, of standing in the central field with the Halo hovering above her. She felt the low vibration of its propulsion systems. She sensed its big, black, gleaming eyes on her, the strange sense of elation they shared. The mysterious, gesticulating Overlord. "The other day when they raided, they could easily have killed me. I counted ten guns, at least. I am pretty sure, if I'd tried to fight back, they'd have shot me dead. The only thing I did to defend myself was not give them a reason to attack."

"Highly speculative," Brume said dismissively.

Tuane rolled his eyes. "You don't know what else was going on. They probably got called away to help take out Chlore's Air Guards and figured you were just one squirt, not worth wasting a bullet on."

"I'm sure the authorities covered this part up, so you might not have heard," she said. "But the aperture was wide open. It would have taken no time to bomb us all. Leave nothing but a smoking crater. I half expected them to. I'm still kind of shocked they didn't."

She said nothing about the Overlord. But the moment remained in her memory like a diorama in a traveling museum; frozen, vivid, and baffling. Her body felt rubbery, her mind overloaded with images. She was beyond being afraid, except the creeping worry that too much was happening too fast, and she was getting lost.

"Those legends are garbage." Tuane turned his head away. "Anyway, even if it's true, whatever the "Tainer pilots did to defend us was weak at best."

"We shot at them. During the skirmish, before we pulsed. The Med Tech said so," Serral said.

"But when you were on planet, what options did you have?" Rafe smiled at her with sad eyes. "Up against them by yourself in the middle of the oculus. How could you have fought back even if you wanted to?"

"I don't know," she said. "But there's always some way to fight back."

"Stop talking," Brume said in the robotic voice. "The Authority forbids speculation about enemy motives. Remember?" He gestured around the interior, as if pointing out invisible listeners.

Serral answered, overloud. "I have no idea what the gray Dantons are thinking, and I don't want to know."

"There's no weapons on this ship, right?" Tuane said.

"Of course not." Brume closed his eyes, breathing slowly. "And if there were, we still wouldn't engage. If they wanted us dead, we would be."

Serral and Rafe exchanged a look. Brume's lips moved, prayer-like. But Serral knew he wasn't praying. He was silently reciting things he'd read, epic poems or directions for the resin printer, anything at all. He was talking himself down from a fit of rage, and he wouldn't return to them until he felt calm. Outside the window, battle debris glimmered in the distant darkness, though whether from fires or reflections of distant stars, she couldn't tell. The Harb ship was nowhere to be seen.

"They're gone," Serral said. Her voice sounded hollow.

Tuane pressed his hands into his face, tears leaking between his fingers. "I don't know how you're all so calm. Just about every friend I have just died."

"We're as upset as you are." Rafe patted his back. "At least they didn't suffer."

"Of course they suffered," Brume said darkly. "But you're right. It was quick."

Serral wished she felt close enough to Brume to ask why he had returned from his frazzled state so quickly. Space seemed to agree with him, despite its terrors.

Tuane straightened. "What is wrong with you?"

"Same as you, I'm upset," Brume said. He sounded the same as always, toneless and awkward.

"Hey," Rafe said. "We're safe for now. Let's focus on that, okay?"

A hard cloud of pain was forming behind Serral's eyes. She swiveled her head, trying to let go of the muscular clamp seizing her shoulders. Fingers touched her neck gently, dislodging a bit of the tension. Rafe, with a light smile, grimly plopped down near her. She smiled back, flushing a bit, his touch comforting. A new sensation.

"Thank you," she said. "I'm sorry about Lymm, and everyone else."

Even without his shiny hair, Rafe was beautiful. His strength and grace seemed odd without it, like an animal in a cage far from its natural habitat.

"She'd be glad that at least a few from our class escaped. And, let's face it, none of us expected to survive our tour, much less grow old."

Brume glared at him. "I did and I do. And those civician cowards can't stop me."

"Let's assess our situation," Serral said, taking charge before Brume fully lost his composure. "Status report?"

"Sitting ducks in a tiny can in the middle of deep space?" Tuane ran his hands over his head as if he'd just noticed his missing braids.

"Yup," Rafe said. "In a ship that seems to have everything we need to survive for now."

"Good. Let's review options." Serral tried again, louder.

Rafe laughed darkly. "We have options?"

"Always," Brume said darkly. "Though you probably don't like some of them."

"Focus." Serral stood up and moved to examine one of the consoles. "Is this pod controlling our trajectory, or is it momentum? Are we in fact unarmed? How much fuel do we have? We need some specs or a manual or something."

"Ship? What can you tell us about yourself?" Tuane called out. "Ecto? Pod? ECUnit?"

No answer. They all tried summoning the mech's voice again, but they found no wake word to rouse her.

"Will the Authorities abandon us, too?" Tuane said. "I mean, we just got our asses handed to us in battle. Won't they be worried about contact? How will we explain this to them? In a way that seems loyal?

"They can't execute every Imset who's ever lost against the Harbs," Brume said. "They'd have to commit mass suicide."

"Brume!" Rafe said darkly. "Some sensitivity."

"No doubt this pod has some way of self-destructing, if it comes to that. But let's think a bit more positively," Serral said. "Look for a portal, or a liquid display, or anything useful."

"Didn't he just say we were fine?" Tuane said.

Brume started humming ominously.

Serral spoke over him. "Think about if we were in the oculus and our warren collapsed. We would need to let the others know how to find us and dig us out."

"You're right." Tuane's eyes opened wider as he warmed to the task. "Okay. So I reckon we're about thirty hours out from Chlore."

"Right," Rafe said. "Headed for Hevoxin, if what the tech said is true."

Brume stopped humming. "Wall or Nebula?"

"I'm not sure it matters," Serral said. "Either way, there's a shipping lane. That might be our best shot for getting noticed. I'm sure this pod has a beacon. If we could find our way to one of the worms, we could use it to get noticed and scooped up by scavengers."

Rafe looked at her with an expression she couldn't read, possibly admiration, but maybe pity at her naïve hope. She shrugged. It was clear to Serral that the pod was meant to be operated by trained staff. There were three important-looking consoles in the bow with complicated surrounding equipment. Somewhere there had to be hidden data; charts, access links, something useful, invisible to the enemy but accessible to them.

"I found something," Tuane said, moving his hands over a toggle. At first, nothing happened but a blare of static and scrambled images they all knew from propaganda strippies, music and scenes from the lost planet that would be familiar to any Imset. "Must be broken."

"No," Serral said gently. "Keep going."

"What's the point?"

But as Tuane said it, the garbled media faded to the Imset insignia, and then a holo-board sprang up, displaying a beautifully detailed version of the Heavenly Hexagon. A mechanical voice, deep and old-fashioned sounding, said *"Travelers, you are here. Follow violet protocols. Best of luck, and Imseth Forever.*" In the center of the board, a small red spark throbbed, marked by a tiny letter E, almost invisible in the cottony field of stars.

"Us," Rafe said.

"What's that?" Tuane expanded the chart, again and again, until their red flicker was surrounded by a sparse scattering of stars. Closer in, the two Hevoxin Portworms loomed, vast and mysterious, their walls glowing sockets of unfathomable depth. Another tiny blip pulsed, this one orange, next to a minute letter T.

"We seem to be heading toward it," Rafe said.

Tuane squinted. "T. For what? Are there any planets that start with T?"

Brume scowled. "Ninety nine percent of green planets are Harb controlled. We'd best hope it's not."

"What do you think violet protocols are?" Rafe asked.

Serral rotated back and forth in her chair, gazing at the console in front of her. It was nearly smooth, made to be difficult for the enemy to use. She doubted there would be any more information available. "I don't think the Authority would load anything in here as sensitive as the location of a named planet. This is a civilian craft, remember, from a non-military ship."

"What else could it be?" Tuane asked. "What other kinds of places exist? I understand they can't teach us that, but sometimes all the secrecy seems self-defeating."

"It's bad timing, for sure," Rafe said. "Clearly we are in a situation no one anticipated."

"Or if they did, they didn't care enough to prepare us." Brume leaned his head on his arms.

"There's no lack of caring in this." Serral ran her hand across the glossy component in front of her. "Just an assumption that passengers would be willing to stay passive, which obviously, was the old war. Not the one we're fighting."

"If it were a planet with a colony, they might be looking for us," Rafe speculated.

Brume looked doubtful. "Chlore was the last colony on the list, at least according to Thandra."

"It might be a science facility," Rafe said.

"It's not a planet," Serral said.

"Why not?" Rafe's amber eyes questioned.

"See this configuration?" Serral pointed to a star field. "This is Chlore's sol. See there? The twins, the horns, the golden crown?"

"Oh yeah," Tuane said. "You're right."

She spun the chart. "Here's the movement of the 'Tainer. We only pulsed a short distance." She traced a zig-zag line with her finger. "This is that nebula we saw, from the porthole."

"They all look alike," Tuane said. "How do you know it's that one?"

"Not important." Serral didn't want to take the time to explain. It had to do with the quality of stars and how they looked like an arch that jogged her memory, gave her a familiar feeling. "We changed direction here, and then pulsed to this point."

"Hardly worth it," Brume said. "A lame attempt to look like we were leaving the system."

"Yeah, it didn't fool the authority," Serral said. "They knew we'd be headed to the worms."

Brume pointed to a place on the interactive map near their red avatar. "And this is where the 'Tainer disappeared."

"What if T is for *Terminus*?" Serral said.

"A Terminus?" Tuane asked. "Like the ones in a strippy?"

Serral shrugged. "Some of the things they show us must be real."

Even the name Terminus was old fashioned, a throwback to the early days of interstellar travel. It called up images of people moving around the universe for reasons other than just the war, a time when the Imset were still colonizing, still exploring. A more optimistic era, Serral guessed, when they truly believed they'd have their own planet again someday.

"What a thing," Brume said. "First a Jiniper Seven, then an Ecto, and now a Terminus? If it weren't for the mass extermination, this journey would be really fun."

The others looked at him, and after a moment, shared a moment of reluctant laughter.

"We were probably supposed to arrive there sometime tomorrow," Rafe said, looking over at Brume.

"So, maybe some people were going to be left at the Terminus to connect with another ship, or ships. The Jiniper couldn't escape until those people were dropped. So, after the skirmish at Chlore, we pulsed here," Serral moved her finger to a point on the map. "And the Harbs were waiting. It must have been obvious where we were headed since we were so close to both portworms. For a reason we don't yet know, the Harbs attacked. The recruitment ship's crew must have anticipated a possible confrontation, which explains why so few adults were aboard. The ones who were, waited until the Harbs appeared, and jettisoned. And, I assume, are now headed to the Terminus too?"

"So, you don't think they even tried to rescue us?" Rafe asked softly.

"Of course they didn't." Brume sounded surprisingly resigned. "You saw that ship, the third-rate people on board treating us like disposable objects. They probably sold their Ectos long ago and pocketed the money."

"They sold ships meant to rescue colonial recruits in case of trouble? Things must be desperate. Or else Civicians are simply evil," Tuane said.

"Evil, or just greedy," Serral said.

No one spoke for a while. Stars shone outside the windows.

"The surviving crew won't be expecting us." Tuane grimaced.

"Nope," Brume said. "They won't be happy to see us, either."

"Come on," Rafe countered. "Put yourselves in their shoes. The attack happened so fast." His voice softened. "We didn't bring anyone with us, either."

The others stared at him.

His face clouded. "I'm just saying, we're not better than they are. In fact, they were brave to go on a recruiting mission at all under these circumstances, if Serral is right, and the rules of the war are changing."

No one argued. He was obviously wrong.

"Okay so they left us to die." Tuane's face shifted as he processed the truth. "I guess that means we have to get to the Terminus before they do. Though they might throw us out an airlock once they get there."

Serral pictured an airlock, sealing in the lifegiving oxygen and heat any living being needed to survive. Being sucked into space was a terrible death. No spacecraft, regardless how large and established, even the vast floating Imset cities of the Diaspora, could guarantee invulnerability to it. Their teachers cited their hatred of Space as a reason to seek planetary assignments, gravity and oxygen and the safety of a planet, illegal as the Harbs deemed such life to be for the Imset. Ancient rules broken by generations past on a ruined former planet, disregarded by them, professional rule breakers with strong bones and the skills to start again. Upstarts and rebels. Not devious, bejeweled criminals who abandoned kids in the cold vacuum of space.

She smiled. "I have an insurance policy in mind."

Her hands continued to explore every part of the ship, slowly, gently, relentlessly.

**12**

C hapter Twelve

Tuning in different channels on the portal from where the star chart projected, they found reports of Harb activity near the Vexpo Void, a safe distane away. They found some maintenance reminders, but nothing else useful.

"Does it look like attacks have spiked?" Tuane asked.

"These are general warnings," Brume said. "Nothing sensitive."

Serral scrolled. The liquid had protocols for hailing vessels and entering stasis, which she skimmed. Nothing about colors, violet or otherwise. Stasis, the long-term slowing of metabolism to just where cells were alive, but inert, seemed like a death sentence. An even darker worry prickled in the back of her mind, deep and thrumming, and she pushed it away. She sensed a fate even worse than going to sleep and never waking up. It was a feeling of such intense vulnerability that she couldn't let it in for more than a moment. She looked around the small vessel.

"I need to understand what this little ship has in store for us. Is she controlled by us? Or by someone else?"

"The crew are not going to murder us, Spooky," Rafe said. "They don't want us talking about what happened, but let's not get confused about who has power in this situation. They promised a crop of recruits. We can still get them paid for delivery. Think about it. Money is what motivates people like that.

"Of course they wouldn't waste our little lives," Brume said overloud, sarcastic. "We're their best and brightest hope for the future."

"Would you give it a rest?" Tuane said, squeezing his eyes tight. "We've all been through it. We all know the situation is dire."

"No more talk," Serral said. "Unless it has something to do with Ecto propulsion systems."

The boys settled down to gnaw on ration bars and to grab some sleep. Tuane hummed himself an old lullaby, and the other two sang along, softly, like they were back home, content on the planet Chlore.

Serral followed a link to writings pertaining to Terminuses. There were diagrams for a standard size, and variants for larger or smaller stations. But no instructions. The plans laid out docking as if it were so simple the ship herself could do it. Then a status bar popped up, with coordinates and a timeline.

"Hey!" Serral shouted. "Look! We are definitely headed to the Terminus. It has us arriving in three days."

"Okay," Rafe said. "Something to work with."

"There's no way of knowing when the other ships jettisoned," Tuane said. "It could have been hours before we left."

"Not to be negative," Brume said, "but I think you're pointing out that the crew could arrive and leave without us, since they don't know we're out here, and even if they did know, they might leave anyway."

"Stop. For Ysk's sake. All we can do is try to beat them there and trust that they won't commit outright murder when they see us. Which they won't. I think I can guarantee that they won't, but you have to stop talking me out of trying."

Brume looked out at the stars, expressionless.

"Take a break." Rafe motioned for Serral to move away from the console. "I'll check the antennae for transmissions. Get some rest."

Serral nodded. "Stored transmissions could be from a hundred years ago."

"They might be from Old Imseth, wouldn't that be interesting? We could hear our ancestors screaming to be rescued," Brume said.

"Honestly, from the bottom of my heart," Rafe said, "give the attitude a rest."

Serral used the small restroom, then, instead of rejoining the others, she started poking around the surrounding components. The main panel, abutting the propulsion cavity, was heavily insulated. It looked like heat cladding for entry into planetary atmospheres. But there was a chance it was covering life support systems. She hesitated. If she broke a heat shield, the pod would be ruined for landfall. But they'd already established they were going to a space station and not a planet, and her curiosity overcame her. She broke the covering and breathed freely when she saw what lay underneath: a cone-shaped casing marked with bars and codes. The propulsion system. She pried the covers off the remaining two consoles. One held the controls for the burner, and the other held a nav computer, the one that had set them on their course in the first place.

"Good little pod."

It took her six hours to find a way to control the burner. And by that time the boys were awake and watching her work.

"Why wouldn't they give the pilot controls?" Rafe asked.

"I think because of the beacon," Serral said, peering into the cavity.

"What do you mean?" Tuane asked. "Of course there's a homing beacon. How else are you going to be rescued?"

'Harbs, dummy," Brume said. "You start piloting to a city, or the convoy, and they can follow you straight there. Why do you think they have the First Imperative?"

"I know all that, stupid. I'm just asking why it's okay to head towards a Terminus?"

"Not much of a target. Only a handful of people on a Terminus, I'd bet." Serral held her hand out for a needle wrench, which Brume wordlessly supplied. "And whatever happened to the peace agreement? The cities are supposed to be off limits to Harb attack, so long as we don't try to permanently settle on a planet."

"Maybe they think Chlore is permanent. It's been around for a while."

"They don't think that. Otherwise, they would have bombed while I was standing there below them, the best target ever."

Rafe laughed. "Spooky knows how the enemy thinks."

Serral lowered her face to hide the heat rising on it, the shame creeping up, threatening to overcome her. She forced herself to focus, though the machine was beginning to blur in front her. How long since she'd slept? Was it back on the floor of the Jiniper? It felt like years. When they had secured the casings again, Serral strapped herself to the seat and entered the codes Brume read out.

"Okay, that's as fast as we can manage." She wiped sweat from her brow with her shoulder. "We still need to figure out how dock."

They all stared.

"Dock?" Tuane said. "You sped up the ship without thinking about docking?"

Serral saw again in her mind's eye, orange and blue flames ejecting from the core of 'Tainer, the horror ballooning out in bright gas. "We decided together to do this."

"Together?" Tuane's face contorted with anger. "You must be kidding me."

Brume hissed: "How about some gratitude, Tuane? Did you fail to notice Serral saved your life, you whiner?"

"Shhhh," Serral hissed. "Stop."

Rafe got between Tuane and Brume. "Enough."

"I'm a whiner? That's really something coming from you, Brume the Gloom. You want to hear what people said about you on Chlore?" Tuane's voice grew cold. "*You're* the monster people fear. *You're* the one who hurts people. And your sister, she is just plain weird."

Hatred gleamed from Brume's dark eyes. "Don't you dare."

"Tuane is right," Seraal said, weariness flattening her words, hoping to diffuse the moment. "We're a bunch of freaks from a broken-down backwater the Authorities obviously decided to abandon. No one is going to protect us or save us. We have to save ourselves, and that means all of us."

"But docking, though?" Tuane gave her a raw look. "I'm sorry. But we trusted you and now it turns out you don't know what you're doing."

Rafe put his hands up in a conciliatory gesture. "Think Tuane. We have to get there before the crew, or we risk them doing to us what they did to the rest of our recruitment class. Do you think they're going to send search parties? Or, maybe you'd rather go into stasis, and sleep until someone finds us? Have you not heard the rumors about what goes on in the war? You want the Harbs to wake you up and eat your brain?"

Tuane sagged in his chair, defeated. "What happens if we overshoot?"

Serral sighed. "I don't know. Believe, I guess. Trust that Imset tech still works, even if its people have lost their way."

Brume cleared his throat, a fit roiling there, and pressed his palms on his eyes.

Rafe sat next to Serral. "Rest now. We're all feeling the lack of sleep, suffering the delayed effects of trauma."

"Enough with all the leadership, Rafe," Tuane said through clenched teeth, "No one's going to give you good marks on your behavior now. You're not in Med training."

Serral felt the blood drain from her face, surprised she still had the energy to be shocked. "Med training?

Rafe rolled his amber eyes dismissively, but she saw his relief at admitting it. "I don't know. The recruiters said I was going to Cam.. .Cam..."

"University," Brume called out. "On Campion."

"The City of Learning, Rafe?" She forced a smile, her eyes blurring. She wasn't sure if her emotion was jealousy or simply the fear of being separated from him. They had never been alone together, but always with Lymm and Brume. Yet he felt like the most important person in the world now. And he was going to where she would never be allowed to follow. University. A regular profession that the whole Imset race needed. Her shame at being unfit for a normal life flared. But it wasn't his fault she was tainted. He didn't even know she was. If he did, his blue eyes wouldn't be fixed on her with such softness. "That's great. You'll make a quality Medic."

No one spoke for a while. Serral ignored Rafe's silent plea to meet his gaze. She busied herself sealing up the console, and then hurried to a part of floor near the bow where she pulled a blanket over her tired body. She didn't remember ever feeling so exhausted, like she was walking through quicksilver, her arms and legs dragging behind her while she tried to escape a murmuring presence striating out in gleaming waves of blue, gold, and white. Shapes dissipated like the rings on a pond, all around her, over and over, rippling and bending in a way that made no sense. What was causing the disturbance? And when it sank into the silver, where did it go?

When Serral woke, a space station spun gracefully outside of the window, silver and black, its hull and arc spinning in in precise opposition, Imset sigils as fresh as the day they were applied. The boys couldn't hide their relief.

"Look at that. Have you ever seen anything so beautiful?" Rafe said softly, handing her a hydration cannister.

"Wow." She gaped. She'd been in contact with tech, both Imset and Harb, all her life. But this space station made battle arrows and Harb tekkus look like crude toys. It must be at least a century old and had the attention to detail her predecessors had loved; observation decks, extra spokes, an extravagant number of windows. The cities' symbols were painted alongside the four-point star, just like in a strippy. This was a more sophisticated world than any she'd known, full of wonders. The station spun and she counted eight docking bays, all unoccupied, their arms and hoses neatly folded. She sighed. They were either the first ship from the battle, or else the last, to arrive.

All at once, Serral realized the pod was going too fast. The station was growing nearer but the little craft was on a trajectory to hit and bounce off it. What could she do? She silently cursed the boys for not waking her sooner. There was no time to think. Her heart fluttered.

The pod lost power. Serral felt the cutoff of Grav in her bones, in her sinews, an ache she had never known and didn't understand. G forces? A sudden feeling of unpleasant floating followed, and a silence so deep she thought she might drown. There were no planets for thousands of rimeters, no green or oxygen rich places, no forest or fields. The sensation of not belonging was a form of pain. And yet, she had always dreamed of this, of being weightless, far from everything she had known, the future unwritten and full of possibility. But she hadn't imagined the depthless soundlessness, the obliterating nothingness outside the ship's thin skin.

She felt a new heaviness and then a mechanical force lifted them, then rotated, clicked and groaned. The pod erupted in cheers and gesticulation, though she was unable to make a sound or catch her breath. Through the window, she saw long arms of station apparatus surround the pod. Forward motion stopped abruptly, and her stomach fell back into place. She heard sobbing, though she didn't know from whom or if they all let the same helpless relief followed immediately by the cold, rigid anticipation of whatever would happen next.

**13**

—  ·  —

C hapter Thirteen

Fresh, green-smelling air welcomed them aboard. A mech voice began a speech, getting as far as *"This Terminus is designed with safety in mind, but that doesn't mean a space traveler can't expect some..."* before devolving into gibberish, and then silence. While clearly old, corroded in places, shabby in others, the Terminus seemed clean and in decent repair. The place cheered Serral. It reminded her that the Imset were capable folk who could design lovely tech. The four friends wandered. They came upon several large common rooms which looked to serve a multitude of functions. A towering atrium grew plants, green and purple and bright with flowers. A strongly worded sign warned *DO NOT CONSUME THE FLORA.* Serral peeked under massive leaves revealing pink fungi, minuscule neon-green frogs and iridescent beetles. None fled in fear. Everywhere moss had overgrown the plant beds. It crawled over floors and up walls like a rebellious carpet. Water dripped. She closed her eyes, breathing in the familiar comfort of growth, of life.

A loud, orange, yellow, and blue color scheme signaled to Serral that the Terminus hadn't been intended for Military use. She knew very little about civician Imset life or about the time before the convoy, when Imset people traveled freely. But she imagined her ancestors feeling comfortable in a place like this, a place a million miles from the filth of Chlore or the chaos of what she had seen from the window of the pod. Lights blinked on an off while she walked through the outer reaches of the station. The Terminus sensed her and created a comfortable environment in which to explore. If she had to spend extended time there, she didn't mind. She could be happy in the grand, arching green space for a long time. Large windows looked out over the stars and the distant Hevoxin Nebula. Its garish cloud was bright enough to power the array of solar panels sitting like epaulets on each of the station's arms. Serral smiled broadly. It felt strange on her face, and she realized the last time she had turned her lips up in that way was in the cave, a handful of days, a million years ago.

The four friends met up in a Caf big enough for a hundred. Tensions had eased among them, and they helped one another figure out the food printers and the beverage spouts.

"I feel as if I've gone back in time," Rafe said. "Or into the future, I guess, depending on how you look at it."

"I know," Serral said, biting into a pale biscuit more delicious than any she'd tasted. "It's hard to tell how old this place is, or what it was intended for."

Brume breathed in contentedly. "I love this place. I hope rescue never comes."

Serral tipped her head to one side. A thought crept in and with it a measure of panic. "Where did the recruiters say you were going? Before the attack? Where were you to be stationed?"

Brume looked at the ceiling, avoiding her eyes. "What makes you ask that?"

Serral felt something heavy settle into her already-cluttered collection of worries. "Were you planning to tell me? Or were you just going to slink off?"

He shrugged. "I didn't know what the orders meant. Only that they said Ingeni."

Serral's throat closed, and her face burned hot. *Ingeni.* The center of contriving, of planning and building, nothing but machines and builders in the whole, seemingly limitless station. Her brother was going to the city of her dreams. While she went to Basic. She forced herself to breathe.

Brume was talking about not being able to get by without her. The others laughed. She smiled feebly, playing along, but she could see by the tight look on Brume's face that he understood how gutted she felt. How being left behind while he went on to the place they both wanted to be, the place they knew to be their best possible hope. That he had been given the future she wanted, the future she had laid out for him a million times in minute detail. She wondered if her many descriptions of Ingeni's imagined wonders had helped him create that future for himself too. And while it hurt her to think of him getting what she had wanted for herself, there was some comfort in it. If it came down to a choice, of course it was better for him to be sent to Ingeni. He wouldn't last a day in Basic. She knew that. But the place inside her where relief had taken hold when they landed on the station, turned bitter. She congratulated Brume woodenly, and he still refused to look at her. She knew he was thinking about what he had told her, how she was unfit for the cities or any place else a traitor wasn't allowed to go. How she was tainted. And once again, shame welled up inside her, and with it, anger. She put down her food, her appetite gone. The others moved on to other subjects. No one mentioned Ingeni again. No one had to.

After they cleaned the meal, they settled down in a common room to read the station's collection of pamphlets, trashy books, and much-creased pieces of Imset propaganda. Serral found a dated-looking messaging portal. She composed a distress call with the details she could remember from their experience on the 'Tainer, then hit send. When that was done, the Terminus felt too spacious and colorful, a hint of what the cities must be like, a taunting reminder of where she would never be welcome, where she would never go.

"Guys, I'm just going to the pod for a while."

Rafe and Tuane watched her go. Brume didn't look up from his book.

The interior of their Ecto pod felt cramped now. She opened the hologram of the larger universe. It was beautiful. She enlarged a quadrant here and there and admired the many structures of known space she had access to, milky nebulae, various irregular galaxies, suns with their planetary arrays and scatterings of moons. But the worms didn't open for her, their dark centers mysteriously opaque. She touched her familiar sun, wondering if she'd ever visit Chlore or fly in a Bolt again. A voice inside her told her to stop being a baby, to focus on the impending arrival of the 'Tainer crew, and come up with a plan beyond sending a signal out to the Authority. Who knew if they were listening, or if they cared about what had happened to a doomed shipment of colonial recruits, or if they even had the resources to investigate such a thing. She thought about the arrogance of the recruiters, how dismissive they had been, and doubted it. When she closed her eyes, there was nothing on the other side but a dark storm of worry, of something coming from a great distance, something formless and powerful, searching for her, calling her name.

She woke with a start. The pod was silent and peaceful, Chlore showing in the holo before her like a beautiful green ball. Her breathing was shallow and fast, like she'd been running hard, away from something bent on tearing her apart.

"Get a grip," she said to herself. And then she shut down the holo and left the pod.

She figured the boys were still lying around the lounge, relaxing, though she knew them well enough to understand they weren't truly calm. They'd learned how to deny stress, how to give the outward appearance of cheerfulness. It was what colonials were famous for, after all, their ability to deny the Harbs any excuse to drop their bombs. Emotions only served as bait. Serral walked slowly across the expanse of the station's shining floor.

"Look at all this garbage!" Brume called out. "It's hilarious."

He handed her a thick pamphlet titled "Death Before Augering," which featured cartoon-like drawings of Harbs and Halos. The Harbs' heads were exaggerated, their eyes overlarge and their expressions un-realistically fierce. The Halo ships looked like hoops. The Overlords were only mentioned in passing, as a "deep alien mystery" that no Imset would ever solve. Readers were admonished to "protect your knowledge" by "utilizing items of last resort" rather than be captured. Its tattered back cover said, "Stray thoughts kill tots," and "Sacrifice for the Cause, as the Cause has sacrificed for you."

"So funny. Right?" Brume said, his mouth upturned, his red brown eyes flat.

"Sure, funny," she choked.

Something was breaking loose in her gut. She barely made it to the hygiene area before her meal came back up, followed by tears. She curled into a ball on the cold floor, horror washing over her, Brume's testimonial about her birth came racing back through the fog of recent days. Images of a mother bleeding out, of a baby, of her in Harb arms, of a small boy watching it all. She wheezed, unable to catch her breath, her body flashing with panic. Maybe it wasn't true. Maybe he built the memory on a story, or a strippy, or something someone said. Yet, Serral remembered, the Medic had said she had no eggs to be culled. And she also knew, as well as she knew to read Brume's face to anticipate a meltdown, that her brother was both fully sane, and completely sure that what he had told her was real. It became clear to her in that moment, that he had always loved her despite it all.

"Spooky! Quit staring at yourself in the mirror. Come play," Tuane called through the door.

"One minute." She dried her eyes and then rummaged through the hygiene area's first aid kit until she found a syringe of Zanoth, an Azanta-based med. There was a chance it would hurt her, but she doubted the rescue med would be left in the kits without a warning symbol if it were dangerous. She injected herself in the stomach, the needle prick a welcome reminder that her body still existed under the layers of panic, and immediately the drug flowed through her, finally relaxing her breathing. Her face looked blotchy and blue-shadowed, but that might be as much from space as anything else. In moments, Serral felt real again, a bit thirsty, but normal enough. She drank cool water from the spigot through her hands, letting it splash on her face and onto the black jumpsuit that still felt stiff and strange and new.

She rejoined the boys. Puzzles and games and cards were spread everywhere. Brume watched her make herself a cup of tea and sit down. She forced a smile, and he looked away.

"We'll know if you two cheat," Rafe smiled, dealing cards. He'd shaved off his stubble and looked almost like himself.

Serral flushed. "Before we start the game, can anyone think of anything more we can do? To prepare for the arrival of the crew and recruiters? Assuming that is who took the other Ectos."

"No. Everything here is good." Tuane dealt the cards. "You said we landed in time."

Serral sighed. "It's all a guess, Tuane."

"Listen," he said. "Your guesses have been amazing."

Serral spoke without thinking. "What do we do if Harbs show up?"

They looked at her with disbelief.

"Quit worrying," Brume said. "If we get attacked, we die. We won't even feel it coming."

Looking from her cards to the vaulted garden, it was hard to imagine anything bad happening here. The Terminus had obviously seen many years of service, but it showed no signs of trauma. Either Harbs didn't know about it, or they didn't care. With the help of the injection, Serral banished worry from her mind. She played a long, satisfying game of pixeter with the boys until the lights in the station dimmed for the night. They converted four lounge chairs into tented beds and settled in. The station hummed contentedly and the four reminisced about their lost friends, and what had happened. They lay on their cots in silence, stunned by the reality that fourteen children they'd grown up with were gone. Then Rafe gently steered the conversation to lighter gossip, and they talked late into the night. Serral learned how she and her brother were known around the colony. People thought Brume was crazy. No one wanted to cross him, for fear of retribution. He was considered irrational and frighteningly vindictive.

"Vindictive?" she asked, laughing. "Brume?"

"Ah, little sister is the last to know," Tuane teased.

Brume laughed maniacally. "But no one bothered you, did they Sister?"

Serral had no answer to that. She'd always had the sense that kids were intimidated to speak to her or to get close, but she'd believed that being a sibling meant you already had a best friend, so she hadn't cared too much. She was grateful for her dose of meds, or she'd have had to contend with all this news instead of letting it wash over her. She yawned.

"And you, Spooky," Tuane said into the darkness. "You were considered really odd."

"So odd," she said, "that I had to be cinched."

"Everyone knew that cinching was just for show," Tuane said.

Rafe turned over in his tented bed, a muffled sound. "You never heard because you hid yourself away, but our whole class voted you an honorary member. For sheer guts alone."

"What?" Pleasure flushed halfheartedly up her body. "An honorary member?"

"Whit loved you. Miss Pune bragged about you all the time. You were loved, Serral. No one wanted to shun you."

She smiled despite her numbness and fatigue.

"If you hadn't pissed off Inoa, you'd have gotten a slap on the wrist," Rafe said.

"You want to know the weirdest thing?" No one answered, so Serral said to herself, "What's odd is, I don't even know what I did to make Inoa hate me so much."

"Shhhhh," Brume said. "Time for sleep."

She didn't, though. Sleep wouldn't come. Tired as she was, she climbed out of her cot and returned to the pod.

When Rafe arrived at the hatch carrying a bottle of ale and a plate of food, Serral felt no surprise.

"You must be hungry." He sat next to her on the floor and pulled a space blanket over them both.

"You're really going to Campion?" she asked, surprised at the pain that reared up inside her.

"Are any of us going anywhere?" He handed her a glass of something milky with a frothy surface.

She drank, glad for the drink's fizz and its distraction from the swirl inside her. It was her first taste of ale. She'd always been too young. "Is it true," she asked, "that once a person goes to the cities, they never leave?"

He grimaced, the clench of his jaw reflected in faint starlight. "I don't know. I don't want to be overly optimistic."

She laughed. He always had a way of putting things in perspective. What good was getting off the Terminus if it only meant a lifetime in space? And yet, that was what both he and Brume had in store.

He drank a swig of ale. "You know what they say about the cities, what it's like for colonials there."

She didn't know what was real and what was rumor, because the strippies always insisted planetary citizens were just as important as those who lived in space, but in reality, everyone knew that Civicians looked at people who grew up on a planet as hopelessly backward, without status, money, or connections. But she hadn't been allowed to know much of anything real about Imset life, other than what they would need to start a new colony, once the war ended. Even questioning the Imset diaspora was forbidden, not that anyone would. Showing disrespect for the flight from the dead planet was too un-patriotic for the colonists. *Their peoples' brightest hope, the only way forward.* The propaganda she'd heard all her life spun in her head, an array of images, she knew, designed to stir emotion. But none of them resembled the Terminus, or the snotty recruiters, or even the visibly bored Medic who'd performed her health intake. The truth was, Serral knew practically nothing of the people she was slated to fight for. Her ignorance had been designed. Was it really to protect her from Harb augering? She reached for the ale, not wanting to think about it anymore.

"They'll love you, Rafe," Serral said. Then she laughed again. "Sorry. I seem to have lost my mind."

"Nope. You're sane as rain. I'm the one who's slowly waking up to reality." His hands found hers. "So, listen. If I have to go, I want to remember you. All of you. Not just because we've been thrown together. I don't want you to think I'm a creep. I've been thinking about this for a long, long time."

His face came close, and she smelled his peaty scent. His lips were surprising, first because they felt rougher than she had expected, and then because they took her someplace far away, where time had no meaning. All that existed was his body on hers, his hands, his torso, his short, soft hair. She was lost, surfacing only with brief realizations that her experience was more vivid than she could have imagined. She felt eclipsed, enveloped in his shadow, disappeared in warmth and dank and a kind of joyful stillness. Finally, he pulled away, and they sat in thick silence. Serral was filled with bittersweet joy.

They sat watching the stars, her hand in his.

"I'll kill all the Harbs I can. Once I get to the war. I'll do it for you, Rafe. Even if our people never get to live on a planet again. At least I know you and Brume will be safe, in the cities, living a terrible life, of course. But alive." She was crying.

He lifted her chin. "Listen. I probably shouldn't say this. But I've always had a feeling about you. Not just that."

His face took on an embarrassed expression.

"What feeling?"

"That you're different. Meant for something greater than this. Does that sound weird? If it weren't for what you've shown us in the past bunch of hours, I wouldn't mention it. But the more I see you doing things like taking us on a joy ride and just randomly finding a cave of the ancients, and then somehow anticipating two raids in a row, one on Chlore and now the attack on the 'Portainer. I just can't help feeling like you are not a normal girl."

She laughed. "I bet you say that to all the girls."

He put his hand on the side of her face. "Don't underestimate yourself. You are alive for some reason. I'm not religious. But even I can't deny you are in the middle of too many weird situations for it to be a coincidence,"

Brume's voice in the tree telling Serral she had been in contact with the Harbs the moment after being born flashed through her mind. Had he told Rafe? No. Not a chance. "They're sending me right into combat. If I'm special, you and I both know I won't be for long. I'm glad you and my brother are both going to be safe in the cities. Promise you'll remember me."

"No one who knows you will ever forget you, dummy. That's why Miss Pune was trying to get you to the crescent fires. People wanted to celebrate you. You just wouldn't let us."

He held her hands in his. His hands felt warm, calming to her fluttering heart. The thought of being cared for by him, by her community, annoyed her.

"It's too late to be sentimental. We're Scrap Rats. We can't afford that."

He kissed the top of her hand. "I never learned how to properly stow my emotions. I always blamed myself for the raids. I thought if I could only follow protocols and feel nothing, Chlore would be safe. I didn't get that they told us that just to shut us up."

They sat so close she felt him breathing. "Will you try to look after Brume?"

"I will try. But he'll be okay." Rafe took her hands in his, his face shadowed. "He's getting better. Have you noticed?"

"He is," she agreed. He hadn't broken down, she realized, since they'd left Chlore.

"Maybe he always had the capacity to handle things. Maybe it was being on planet. Who knows? But one person you can count on to take care of himself is Brume."

"Kiss me again," Rafe whispered.

And she disappeared.

The day passed quickly in the station. They put everything back in place, then tidied the surprising amount of dirt they'd created. No one had much appetite for dinner. Rafe read aloud from a ridiculous novel set on Old Imseth, a mystery story so circuitous they couldn't tell if it was fantasy, or if the lost planet had just been absurd.

Just before nightfall, two Ectos arrived, disgorging five Military crew members and passengers: Pilot Crigsen of the Air Marsiant, a medic who was a civivian Mate and Captain, two Recruiters, and two colonial girls. One of them was Thandra whose eyes were unfocused, expressionless, and blank. The Recruiters brought her and the other girl by the arms and led them away towards the center chambers of the station.

"Don't fret children," the white-haired Captain said to Serral and the boys, striding into the station and sniffing approvingly. "We have arrived."

"Glad you made it," Brume said, over loud. Rafe's grabbed his elbow and Serral made a face to shush him.

"Yes, you must have been very frightened," the Captain said. His name tag read *Thrish*. "Tell me, how did you manage to escape?" Thrish's eyes flashed, his thick neck bulged with veins.

"Pretty random," Rafe said. "There happened to be an empty ECUnit near us."

"Ah, dumb luck." Thrish feigned concern. "Well, not to worry. I'll need to speak to each of you about the attack, of course, to be sure you're clear about what happened. It must have been very traumatic for you. How sad, to be the only ones who escaped. What an incredible thing."

None of the four Chlorans returned his large, false smile.

**14**

C hapter Fourteen

Over the next two days, Serral was interrogated five separate times by four different people. Each time she denied knowing anything about how the 'Tainer was destroyed except that the Harbs attacked and she fled, which was true.

"What will you say, when the Authority asks?" Captain Thrish peered over his glasses and smiled his insincere smile. Pilot Crigsen sat at one of the Caf tables nearby and took notes. The four friends were scattered around the large room, each, like her, explaining for what felt like the thousandth time.

"We woke up," she said. "We ran to the porthole to see what was happening."

"How did you know where that porthole was?"

Serral shrugged. "We had snooped. We wanted to see out the window; it was our first space flight. You know, rude colonials."

The Pilot Crigsen, Beatty, sniggered. "That you are."

Thrish's smile dropped. "You just randomly found the circulation tube, and the Ecto?"

"I guess. All we had to do was open a few hatches. They weren't locked, and no one told us we couldn't. Anyway, we weren't looking for anything in particular. We were scared, and we went to look out the porthole. The ship began to disintegrate, we saw the pod and jumped in. No thought went into it."

"You were much luckier than the rest of the children."

Serral studied her hands on the table. She knew better than to admit the surge of anger that flowed into them. "We were. Sir."

Thrish rapped his knuckles. "And where did you think the adults were while you were exploring the ship?"

Serral swallowed. "There was no time to wonder about that, Sir."

"And you helped yourselves to the last, and only, remaining Ecto."

"As you know, we colonials are taught to hide in tubes."

His eyes flashed, then he relaxed. "True. I was a scrap rat once. I remember cringing in the burrows, trying not to think thoughts that the enemy might exploit."

"Exactly, sir." Serral watched his face, wondering if he meant to sound sarcastic.

"So you were looking for a tube to hide in."

"Like I said. It all happened so fast."

"Exactly." He leaned in toward her. "There was no time. The attack came on very, very suddenly."

Serral locked eyes with him. "I...yes."

He sat back, nodding to Beatty. "And that is how you're going to explain it, when the Ninitan picks us up."

She nodded, mind racing, facial expression flat. What was the Ninitan?

His eyes bored into her. "We were attacked in the middle of space. Which isn't normal. Understand? No one knows how to respond to such a thing."

"Of course not," Serral said. "Everyone knows the enemy never attacks in space."

On the second night, Serral spotted Thandra and the other girl, Selmina, drinking tea in a common area. She hurried over to them.

Selmina had glossy skin and shining green eyes. Like Thandra, even without ornaments or hair, she was incandescent. Her accent was deep and musical. "My new friend," she said. "Believe me when I say that we went to sleep on the transport Portainer and woke up on the escape pod just before boarding this station."

"No memory of the attack?" Serral whispered.

"None at all."

Thandra spoke under the sound of tea pouring. "You know, the officers are extremely worried about what happens when the Ninitan shows up."

"What is the Ninitan?"

"They didn't tell us," Selmina said quietly.

Thandra shrugged. "A ship containing people who matter, if their paranoia is any indication."

"Friend Serral," Selmina spoke quickly and quietly. "Why did we evacuate the transport Portainer?"

Thandra whispered: "Everyone died, right?"

"I think the less you know, the safer you'll be," Serral said.

"Tell me," Thandra said, her expression serious.

Serral dawned a false smile to cover, and then hastily explained what she knew. While she spoke, four of the white hairs encircled them.

"Children, what are you whispering about?" the Medic asked. "I remember you. The girl who didn't need to be culled." She sat down with them, her face a mask of disapproval. Serral left quickly, wondering if she'd see Thandra or Selmina again.

Another night passed. She and the boys slept in a common room. By now, it had become obvious that the white hairs had a separate area onboard the station that the friends didn't have access to. Serral assumed Thandra and Selmina had bunks in the restricted area, too, because they disappeared at lights out. They seemed to be on the side of the adults, whether they wanted to be or not.

On the fourth day, the Ninitan came into view. They all stared through the station's large windows, speechless. Serral didn't know what to think about the hulking, insect-like contraption. It looked like a child had constructed it by gluing together a dozen broken battle ships. There were patched up scars, wounds repaired without any effort at symmetry, and not a swipe of fresh paint. If Serral hadn't known that the ship was Imset, she would have been frightened of it. She knew its arrival meant rescue, but she felt concerned by the hulk's aggressive disregard of grace. It reminded her of the oculus.

Which in turn reminded her that her ten-year tour was now about to begin.

"Ugly Nina," Thrish said, smiling. "Right on time."

"You know this thing?" Brume asked.

"Of course," Thrish said. "Every Pilot remembers the ship on which they learned to fly."

"Yeah? How many hours you have to fly to make Wing Commander?" Tuane asked.

"Loose lips, my friend," Thrish gave Tuane an assessing glance. "Anyway, I only made it as high as Crigsen Pilot. But I miss the thrill every damn day."

Serral hated Thrish in that moment. She had never heard anyone talk about the war as thrilling.

The Ninitan opened a huge mouth, and its windows went dark. Serral could see the innards of the ship. Its contraptions closed around the Terminus completely.

They were enveloped and aboard.

Serral couldn't take in all the details, but her impression was one of Military might and precision. Everyone wore black, everyone had white hair, and no one looked at her twice. She saw at least a hundred such people, Harb killers all. Her concern left, and she wanted to shriek with excitement.

"This way," a Whitehair said.

The four friends followed him down a confusing array of corridors and through common rooms. They passed clusters of uniformed people doing incomprehensible things. The Ninitan was as patched-together inside as it was out; a mismatch of sleek white, industrial raw and battered metal. Her size and complexity thrilled Serral. But that wasn't all. There was an intensity in the walls, a tension. Serral believed she could spend a year exploring the old ship and still not decipher all her mysteries.

Their escort left them at a desk occupied by a bald, scarred, old Whitehair whose name plate read *Master Syrtient*. Only one rise rank above Crigsen, Serral wondered how many tours the woman had seen. The Master Syrtient typed their names into a portal, and then gestured for them to wait in a large lecture hall. Serral's heart sank at the empty seats. Rafe held her hand under the desk, and they watched a strippy called, "What the Authority Wants You to Know." They were to listen carefully to any and all instructions, learn what various klaxons and alarm beeps signified, and above all to never use an air lock unsupervised. The threat of space was ever present on the station.

Two new Whitehairs came into the hall. They called out for Rafe and Brume. "Come to the exit, if you please."

"If we please?" Brume asked. "What's happening? Where are you taking us?"

The men didn't answer. An elevator door opened. The soldiers gestured for Rafe and Brume to enter.

"Wait a minute," Tuane called out. "Wait."

Rafe looked back at Serral, confused. Brume had a smirk on his face. The doors snapped shut.

She and Tuane stood in the sudden silence, speechless. A young Whitehair came through a side door. Serral couldn't move, because if she moved, she would make it real. Her brother, and Rafe, gone. She was unlikely to see either one of them again. Pain closed around her chest. She had known the parting was coming, and yet, she was unprepared for it. She felt dull and stupid.

"Hello!" the Whitehair said. "You're late."

Tuane accepted two crinkly packages from the man. Serral forced her wooden legs to move, her eyes to focus on the floor in front of her. She and Tuane shuffled down hallways and up an elevator. They were stunned. Tuane looked young and inept. Serral felt a strange pulling and floating sensation. She told herself she'd get used to it, that it must be normal, that a ship so large must have inconsistent grav. The lighting went to half-power. But not as an emergency signal, because the ship ran silent. No vibrations, no explosions, no reason for her breathlessness. "Are we in a worm?" she asked the Whitehair

"Yes, Col," the man replied. "We're in a port worm."

Tuane sighed audibly. Serral wished she could see out a window.

"Which?" she pressed. "Hevoxin Wall, or Nebula?"

"Yours is not to question why."

Minutes passed. Finally, there was a lurch, lights came back up, and the three continued down the maze of corridors.

Their escort left them in a bunk room with instructions to change and report for training. There was evidence of other trainees about, but Serral couldn't tell how many. She removed coveralls from the crinkly packet. They were embroidered with a silver Air Guard In-

signia and black and white identity patch. Serral touched them rever-
ently, knowing Whit would chastise her for her admiration.

"My name, it's next to a four-point star," Serral said.

"Crigsen Serral Brook. You're Military now."

"Air Guard," Serral whispered. "We're Air Guards. Do you feel
different?"

He shook his dark-stubbled head. "Maybe I will, though. Once I see
combat and my hair turns white."

"You mean, when we kill Harbs."

Serral's body surged with clean, hot rage. She pushed the memory
of Brume's smirk, of Rafe's lips on hers, out of her mind. Colonials
don't have the luxury of a lover or a brother, of hoping for children or
a future outside of war. She knew that. All her training was right under
the surface, the promise she had made to Miss Pune to stay alive, the
warnings and instructions Whit had gently instilled in her. Even Inoa's
unexpected gesture of love clicked into place in Serral's mind, the way
the old woman had seemed to send her off on a mission of importance.
So what if Civicians were selfish and corrupt, like the recruiters and the
Catamaran crew? They couldn't take away her memories of the boys
she loved. No space dweller could remove her hope for a planet, and
end to the war, a future. She was glad she hadn't been sent to Ingeni,
or Campion, or wherever else they sent recruits who weren't fit to fly
combat missions. She was glad to have survived the last weeks. Serral
Brook was a proud, scrappy Colonial, born and raised for this. Even if
she held a secret shame, the only other person who knew was gone for
good. She rubbed the stubble on her shorn head. It would be white
soon enough. She was ready.

"I can't wait."

**15**

—·—

C hapter Fifteen

"Dantons in hell, only two of you?" A boy with red stubble and freckles called out as Serral and Tuane entered the sparsely populated lecture hall. "Heard there was a terrible accident. Know anything about that?"

Serral counted seven other recruits, and all looked as uncomfortable as she felt. She and Tuane exchanged glances. What should they say? What should they keep to themselves? Who could they trust?

"What have you heard?" Serral asked.

"Well, we were supposed to get a full recruitment class. And instead, there are less than ten of you."

"Oh yeah?" Tuane played dumb.

"Rumor is," a tall girl with a scar on her neck spoke out. "The rest are orbiting the moons of Xozaa."

Serral didn't know the expression, but its meaning was clear enough. A metaphor for *no longer with us*. "Sounds cold."

Stubble-face looked frustrated. "You know how rumors are. Idle gossip."

Serral nodded. She wasn't sure why she didn't give the boy the information he wanted. Old-fashioned mistrust of strangers, she supposed, made all the stronger by their journey. For good measure, she added, "I'm sure our superiors would tell us if they thought we ought to know."

He looked at her squarely, blue eyes evaluating. "You're right. Why should you trust me? I'm a scrap rat, same as you. I get it. Name's Mazith."

"And I am Omiviah," said the girl with the scar.

The group introduced themselves around. Names flew by before Serral could memorize them. Her new peer group. She hoped she'd be accepted by them more than she had been growing up on Chlore.

"Oh m'Ysk. He's here," Omiviah said, awestruck. "Master Syrtient Nothrim."

Everyone rose abruptly and stood at attention.

An ancient-looking, kind-faced Whitehair entered the room and introduced himself as Corliss Nothrim. He wasted no time. "Children, you have a date with destiny," he said. "You will complete your training in record time." His face crinkled into a sincere, sad smile. "The Imset cannot afford for you to arrive late."

Training consisted of early morning fitness, lectures until lunch, SIM in the afternoon, and strippies every evening. Serral had no trouble keeping up with classwork. During her years working for Whit, she had read extensively on physics, contriving, and navigation. Worried she would annoy the other students, she did not raise her hand to answer questions, but Nothrim soon realized that if he couldn't get a response out of the others, Serral could supply the correct answer. She helped Tuane. Before long, her classmates did their outside schoolwork wherever she was, so she could help them when they got stuck. She didn't mind. Most of the other classmates came from a colony called Gyuzith. It was made up of seven oculi in the middle of a shallow sea. The Harbs didn't raid there often, because, Mazith said, "We were already doomed. No way the colony could last there, long term. If our pumps stopped working, we'd flood. If we forgot to close the apertures, we'd flood. Sometimes we'd wake up in a hard rain and the furniture was floating. We'd spend a week drying it out again. I guess the Grays figured one of these days we'd all drown. Problem solved."

Tuane and Serral exchanged glances and the others laughed.

"How often did they raid, though?" Serral asked.

"Every couple of weeks, according to people I've talked to," a boy named Kameth said. "Not often. You?"

"Tell us the name of your colony again," another girl next to him said.

Tuane answered, explaining Chlore's wetlands and forests, its farms and fish reefs, but dodged the question of how often raids came. Serral felt ashamed that her colony hadn't known the kind of hardship others had. She had to push away the dark cloud of guilt. The class was learning how to kill Harbs. She would focus on that.

"We loved our raids." Omiviah said. "The bombs killed enough fish to keep us fed for months."

Serral enjoyed the sound of their laughter. The Gyuzith recruits were easygoing and hardy, and their humor was all as black as the fish joke. Tuane spent most all his time with them, especially a wiry girl named Lanshoo.

By unspoken agreement, no one mentioned the subject of combat. Nothrim insisted the class learn to fly first, learn to stay safe while operating a craft capable of decimating any one of their colonies with an accidental push of a button. He told them, cryptically, that once they killed their first Harb, they'd never learn another useful thing.

Serral often lay awake at night, while the others slept, and thought about those words. She wished she had her brother to talk to, to explain to him the unspoken enticement the instructor dangled, to discuss the threshold that a first combat represented. But instead, she would wander the Ninitan in her mind, and wonder if he and Rafe had arrived at their cities safely, or if they were still in transit, or had been separated, or if they'd encountered any attacks along the way. She felt herself in the center of the war, where important decisions were made, and wasn't optimistic. Nothrim had implied what Serral already sensed; the war was coming to a head. She wished she could sit under the stars and contemplate her place in the order things, take time to think about where she was in the universe. But nighttime in Basic was meant for sleep, and sleep only. At lights out, their windows were sealed, darkness fell, and no one wandered. Serral's body ached with fatigue, but foreboding kept her mind in a constant state of alertness. She was left trying to calm herself, hoping the sick anxiety in her gut would unsnarl. Most nights, she could relax enough for a few hours of unconsciousness, and then jack herself up in the morning on energy drinks from the Caf to make up the deficit.

Weeks passed. Her uniform hung slack; her face lost its healthy, planetary glow. The stale air and tasteless food of the space station did not nourish her. She was sleeping less and less, averaging an hour or two, and was sometimes so tired that Nothrim's lectures sounded far away and the air around him seemed to sparkle with a chemical shimmer. She tried to look out the windows during class breaks, tried to escape to the observation decks. But the stars were all nonsense, constellations so strange and overly bright they looked unreal. Serral wondered if the Ninitan was pulling a trick, showing a projection instead of real space. But that seemed far-fetched. How could a person harm the Cause by looking out the windows at the stars? There was much she didn't understand.

She loved the Ninitan for its scrappy character. But Serral suspected that if she stayed on board much longer, she'd grow too weak to leave. In desperation, she went to the Med bay. A crabby white-haired Medic gave her a shot and told her to come back the next day for another. But unlike the Zanoth she'd had on the 'Tainer, these meds left her groggy and made it hard to follow Nothrim's lectures. She wouldn't go back for more.

Eventually she and the others heard rumors of a recruitment 'Tainer that had been attacked traveling an old and well-traveled route. Carrying enough escape pods was too impractical for modern times. Such craft were scarce. The transport company wasn't held liable for the cost of training the recruits. No one knew why the Harbs bombed the ship, but the consensus was that Harbs were insane murderers no one could fathom, and it was dangerous to try.

"The cost of training? Is that what they're calling our lives these days?" Tuane said.

Unlike Serral, who had shrunk since they boarded, Tuane looked taller and bigger since they'd arrived on the Ninitan. His arms and shoulders were round with muscles, and he carried himself with a new swagger. He had made new friends which added to his confidence. On Chlore, Tuane hadn't spoken much to Serral, and now he returned to that habit, treating her like an acquaintance instead of a lifelong mate. She didn't mind. At least he enjoyed space life.

One day, she and the rest of the recruits were in the bunk room before class housekeeping and lounging in a rare moment of unstructured togetherness. Usually, their days were busy with training and classes, strippies and recently, lectures from officers about combat strategy and tech.

Lanshoo rolled her eyes. "You don't think the Authority regards us as full Imset, do you?"

"We're just scrap to them," Omiviah said. "And we always will be."

"They should love us." Kameth threw a ball in the air, catching it and tossing it. "It's not costly to build their disposable army. The colonies produce all the soldiers they need."

"Except for Air Guards," Serral said. "Air Guards cost a lot to train, right?"

She had never seen money, but she knew about it. On Chlore, they had no need for it, and if the adults owned any they kept it in banks in the cities. Once, she'd heard Whit complain that money was a scam designed to distribute property to the Authority when people inevitably died in space or on planet.

"Has anyone offered any of you a salary for your service?" Kameth asked idly.

A girl named Soo hung upside down from a bunk. "They don't want to make commitments. If they can't properly evacuate a transport ship, you think they've got the capability to organize payment for our service?"

"*Survive the tour and be a hero to the Cause,*" her large friend Bridla intoned, repeating a phrase included in many strippies. "*You can't help anyone in an Ecto.*"

"I wonder where heroes go after their tours," Tuane said. "The ones I've met don't want to be locked up in a city, that's for sure."

"Might as well get through the ten years before you worry about it."

Serral didn't join the group when they left to watch the evening strippy. Earlier they had watched the educational content, so what remained was morale-boosting, patriotic fare espousing the glories of city life; patriotic assembly atriums on Amperia, life-giving vertical farms of Sperr, a diverting gaming palace in Asundi, a group of earnest students listening to a lecture on Campion, and then a long section of the sinister magnificence that was Mollith who protected it all. *Each*

*City unique and special. Each keeping the Imset comfortable until they win the war and claim their new planet.*

Serral didn't want to hear any more. The strippies seemed as fake as Thrush's smile when he'd told her to keep her mouth shut about the 'Tainer. She missed Brume and Rafe. The one thing that diverted her from her sad heart and sick stomach was the SIM.

At first, her facsimile combat missions went by much like everyone else's. She'd strap in, complete her checks, then head into whatever combination of Tekkus and Halos the machine threw at her. This SIM made the ones on Chlore look like toys. It felt real inside, complete with sound and special effects. At first, the foot and hand pedals confused her, and she often fired her weapons when she meant to feint or the other way around. But her time preparing to fly the Bolt paid off, because after only six or seven days, she was able to shoot or avoid getting shot more often than not. She began noticing patterns in how the simulated enemy approached combat. They tended to attack in even-numbered groups in an overwhelming chase toward a single ship, leaving themselves with unguarded flanks. The way to win those fights was to do the opposite of what they expected, to go at them hard, make simple evasive rotations or flips, actions that seemed obvious. Soon Serral was killing the entire wolf pack by causing them to accidentally kill one another. In those moments, she found her mind reaching out to see what was next, to see who was out there. But no one was. And then the next wave of attacks would come, and she'd try new configurations and patterns of defense. She loved the game. It made her forget her body and how wretched it felt. Anger and cunning blocked her feelings of weakness. Time had no meaning inside the SIM. She knew her turn was over when the lights went up revealing the internal workings of the machine.

When she stepped out, the others who had been watching looked at her with annoyance and envy. Tuane made her explain her decisions over and over, until she finally asked him to stop. By the end of a month, she had to take her turn in the SIM last so that the others wouldn't miss meals. And then came the day when during the morning lecture, a broad, bald, half-mech officer stood at Nothrim's side.

The old teacher grinned and said, "Class, you are in the presence of a legend. Air Vice Marsiant Duglak has seen more action in this war than any soldier alive. He personifies sacrifice for the cause. I'm confident you will give him his due respect."

The class applauded dutifully. It sounded small, only ten of them clapping, so some made their colony growling sound to show reverence.

"I'm Duglak, just Duglak," the man growled, holding up his mech arm to silence them. "It's time to give your nursemaid, old man Nothrim, a round of applause. He believes in your potential, which is more than the rest of us can say." He clapped his real and metal hands together theatrically.

The students lined up and shook Nothrim's hand.

"Watch out for Duglak," the old man said softly to Serral when she passed him in line. "He's uncomfortable with your SIM stats. They're better than his."

She tried to catch his eye to see if he was joking, but Nothrim had moved on to the next recruit in line. She thought his face looked more pinched than usual, and he leaned toward the door, like a man in a hurry to be gone.

Then, without further ceremony, Nothrim saluted them and strode out of the classroom. The trainees took their seats and focused on Duglak, who paced, his machine parts shining in the lights of the lecture hall.

"We're in a time crunch, children," Duglak began loudly. "You need to be soldiers and not whiners. I know that won't be easy for some of you."

Serral saw her classmates weren't responding to this insult any better than she was. It sounded generic, like a speech he'd given many times before. Tuane flinched with annoyance.

"You have no right to take an attitude," Duglak edged away from the dais. "You haven't done anything yet."

They sat up, feigning respect.

"With one notable exception, not one of you shows any particular feel for flight," he said, continuing to stride back and forth across the front of the hall. "If you plan to live out your tour, you had best get on that, and I mean now, children. Now. Serral Brook, stay behind. The rest of you, go SIM like you mean it. There's a fight-to-the-finish brewing. Tomorrow, we start in real planes."

A collective gasp went up. Duglak's half-mech face twitched.

"You thought being in the Military was going to be fun and games? No crop raising here, Cols. No lazy afternoons catching fish. You're soldiers now! Better start taking your training seriously, or your tour will be over right quick."

The rest of the class filed out, silent, and Serral could see by their straight backs that they were nervous.

"Miss Brook."

"Yessir," she said, buoyed by curiosity.

He didn't look at her. "Come with me."

She followed Duglak down the endless hallways she'd grown used to on the Ninitan. Whitehairs saluted him as they passed. Ignored her.

"In here, Princess," Duglak muttered, seating himself at a desk. He regarded her, standing at attention. "Sit," he said.

Serral sat opposite him.

"I apologize," he continued. "I thought you'd be," he coughed, "more robust. Most of your life spent on planet, you know, your performance thus far. I can see now you're a mere whisp of a thing.

"Don't worry about it, sir." Both fear and annoyance overpowered her nervous stomach; "I've been called a lot worse."

He half-smiled. "I bet."

The office was sparse and over-warm, decorated with shiny award plaques bristling with insignia and photographs of an all-flesh Duglak standing with various people. He typed into a portal, clucking at what he saw there.

"I guess you're a bit of a light finger," he said. "Requisitioning an Ecto, flying a Bolt without permission."

"It was my Bolt. I built it," she said, "and I couldn't exactly submit an official request for the escape pod. All the adults had already evacuated. Our ship was under attack."

His eyes flashed. She saw in his bionic face that he was amused.

"I see," he said.

"I'm not supposed to recount that, of course."

"I have the report of your actions as well as, let me see here, Captain Thrish's efforts to suppress said report. I'm sure it won't surprise you that he offers a totally different series of events than you. In fact, he goes as far as to suggest that you and your friends might have caused the destruction of his ship by your haste in abandoning it. And, it is true that you arrived at your pickup hours before the rest of the crew. So, someone is lying."

"Thrish tried to threaten me. It didn't work. He and the crew were gone by the time we poor, spoiled recruits even knew we were being bombed. I'm just lucky he was sure he'd gotten away with it, or he'd have left me to rot in deep space like he did the rest of my classmates."

Duglak looked at her for a long while. Her face felt sweaty, and she pinched the skin on the palm of her hand to make herself stop talking.

"Brook. I'm not stupid enough to believe the cover story of a contractor who'd take a recruiting run in today's war. Thrish must have been desperate. His sponsors are only paid for the children they deliver. He turned you over to us because he wanted the money, pure and simple. His report is an attempt to wiggle out of liability, and," he gestured at his portal, "it says here he did. I only mention it to point out that everything you touch seems to wind up exploding."

Serral thought about Thandra and the other girl on the Terminus. Where had Thrish delivered them? She took in Duglak's words and vowed to return to them later, when she had time to sift through their meaning.

"Don't cry, little girl. You were correct to report what happened. You were correct to abandon ship. But this meeting is not to praise your instincts or to chastise you for the brazen theft of Military surplus you refer to as *your Bolt*."

"I'm not crying, sir," Serral interrupted. He glared at her, and she fell silent.

"The point is, not everyone would act under those circumstances. Most would end up floating in the starry fields or buried on some squat under Harb shrapnel." He watched her for a long moment. "Are you going to argue with me, Brook? Because nothing belongs to you, including your life. You know that. That is the price Colonials pay for being planetary."

She shrugged. The flow of information Duglak provided was so unlike anything she'd heard that she wanted only to keep him talking. "I understand, sir," she said. "Mine is not to question why, etc."

"Good. As for the Bolt you stole, your supervisor isn't authorized to have a machine like that himself, much less loan it out to children."

She said nothing.

He smiled. "But I knew Whit way back, when we were both intact. He was a true man of the cause, before he lost his nerve."

Serral jumped at the mention of Whit's name. Duglak held up his mech hand.

"Don't get sore, I'm not judging him. He did his part and more. Hell, he's still doing it. I know he's lying for you. I can only assume that he has good reasons."

Serral felt heat emanating from the old man and then realized that it came from his chair. He needed to keep himself warm. His mech parts she figured, needed it for circulation. She felt sorry for him.

"Whit believed in my skills as a contriver, sir. I'm an Air Guard Crigsen now, and I don't think that's what he wanted for me."

"And what do you want?" His one brown eye bored into her.

She met his gaze, and her blood lust rose, pushing out the chronic, sick feeling, clear and sharp and powerful. The thing within her that wanted to murder Harbs was like a tendril of a plant that needed only a shaft of light to grow mighty.

"I want to chase them down and kill them all. Every last gray, squishy one of them. Sir."

He nodded. "Good. That was the correct answer. So let's talk." He leaned back in his chair. "Your SIM stats are," he tapped his mech fingers against his flesh hand, "unusual."

"Thank you, sir."

"I'm not sure that's a compliment."

"Sir?"

"This independent streak of yours worries me."

"I follow orders, sir."

"That is a bald-faced lie, Miss Brook. Unless you want me to believe someone *told you* to put your colony in danger by flying all over the planet or that someone *told you* to escape while the rest of your friends burned to death."

"You're right." There was no hiding from this old soldier. "I acted of my own volition, taking a flight on a home-built plane filled with three passengers who were not disciplined at all for our insubordination. And you're also right that no one told me what to do when our crew abandoned ship without us. I had one chance to jettison to safety, and again, I brought along friends. Those things I did on my own. I provided needed medical herbs to my colony, and I saved three lives. My only regret is that there wasn't time to save more kids. I wasn't enough of a maverick to do that."

"Oh gee, no one told you it's dangerous to be Imset." Duglak's expression remained mild. "What are you doing here, Brook? Really. Truly?"

"Sir?" She made a sound of frustration. "I was recruited."

He leaned forward and watched her again. "I think I understand who you are."

"Oh?" Sweat prickled her short hair, but she didn't move.

"It's obvious if I read between the lines." He reengaged the portal.

Serral wanted to inch away, but her chair was bolted down.

"You pulled a raid alarm," he read. "And then proceeded to what, meet the enemy? Face to face, in the yard? Did you offer them tea, Crigsen?"

"I would have, but for the cannons they had pointing in my face."

"Duglak," a woman entered, tall with kinky white hair and a fierce look in her eyes, "are you interrogating Crigsen Brook without me?"

"Air Marsiant Slook," Duglak made a half-hearted salute. "Brook is my student now. I don't expect I need your permission to speak to my mentees, do I?"

"Power grabber." Looking Serral up and down with a cheerful expression, Slook ignored his question and sat in the remaining chair. "What did I miss?"

"We were going over a near-miss on planet Chlore."

"Oooh, straight to the good part." Slook leaned toward Serral. "Please continue."

Serral told her version of the raid, of seeing the Halo up close, leaving out her sighting of the Overlord. She had never felt so important recounting a story. When she thought about her full truth, about the birth story she kept to herself, her stomach tightened into painful knots. But if Duglak knew anything about her origin and her possible contact, he wasn't saying. Slook listened carefully, her face still. Serral trusted the woman.

When Serral finished speaking, Slook sat back and smiled. "What is the relationship between your knowledge of the raid, and your escape from the 'Tainer attack?"

"What?" Serral looked between them. "I don't understand."

There was a long silence. Serral felt sweat trickle down one side of her face. Slook and Duglak waited in silence for her to speak.

"How could those two things be related? One was a raid on planet. Another was an attack in space. It couldn't have been the same Harbs, could it?"

"You tell us," Slook said. "Do you think it was the same Harbs?"

"Honestly, how could I know?"

"Don't faint, Crigsen." Duglak stretched out his leg and rested it on a stool next to his chair. "The Marsiant is just trying to check out a theory."

Slook flinched, shooting Duglak a look. "We'll talk again, Brook," she said. "You're dismissed."

Serral looked to Duglak. He nodded. "Go on."

That night Serral tossed and turned, delirious. When she woke, the other recruits had moved to another part of the bunk hall. At breakfast, they grumbled about how loudly she had talked in her sleep. The rest of the day was an effort to stay awake while Duglak and a couple of contrivers taught them how to suit up.

The next day, the contrivers lectured them on safety. A sad strippy explained how emergencies in space quickly became deadly. If you failed to seal your coils, you would die. If you failed to properly secure the air lock, you would die. If you did anything other than follow the protocols with total accuracy... *We will die*, they chanted.

After three days of suit and air lock drills came Ecto training. Serral learned that she had ejected the Ecto from the 'Tainer without preparing the tube, a ship-endangering move. Her face grew stiff when she learned how whole stations had been set on fire by fool moves like hers. She and Tuane shared a look.

Later, though he rarely made the effort anymore, he caught up with her and said, "I saw the rockets hit it, Spook. There were tons of explosions. It was the Harbs."

Her cheeks felt frozen.

"We have to focus on the future, Spook. We need to survive our tour. Okay?"

"Yeah."

"I'm serious. Look at you. You look like a damn ghost. You don't eat. You yell about Thantons in your sleep."

"I'm sorry." Serral tried to remember dreaming of Thantons, but what came to her mind was the cave, the rock wall carved with spaceships, stars, and the large, winged people with their arms raised in blessing. Or for something else? She felt the mineral air of the place in her lungs, and the ominous gaze of the glittering figure's blue eye. She shook it off.

He touched her arm. "We're all on edge, Serral. But think about Brume. And Rafe. Don't you want to see them again?"

She nodded. It was what she wanted most.

Three days later, Serral and Tuane shared an Arrow for their first practice de-dock. They never left the protective seal of the Ninitan's harbor mesh, but the exercise proved tricky anyway. They were a meter away from the air lock, and the Arrow refused to move closer.

"Tuane, are you sure we released the aft pressure hose?" she commed.

"I'll go back and make sure." He released his harness.

"No, don't. I'll com in. They'll send someone to fix it."

"What? That'll lower our grade. I'll just double check." And he was out of his seat, moving away from the place he'd been instructed to remain. Moments later, Serral saw the aft hatch open and Tuane step out of it, his helmet shining in the Ninitan's lights. He stopped, frozen. She commed him. Once, twice.

Something was wrong. A terrible feeling of panic and dread came over her. She commed to the contrivers: "Mayday, mayday, my flight partner has left the ship and will not reply to coms. Please advise."

In moments, the Arrow began moving the last meter into dock. The cockpit portal showed a crew grabbing Tuane's limp body and dragging it into a nearby airlock. Serral hurried out of the Arrow and back inside to wait for a contriver to remove her suit.

Kameth took her hand in his and led her away from the airlock. He was crying. "Why would he do it?"

Her stomach imploded. She was enveloped by fear and a creeping understanding that she could not, would not accept.

Duglak pulled Serral away and told Kameth to get back to barracks. "Sorry, kid," he said to Serral. "It's the nature of war. We do dangerous things for a living."

At the debrief, she sat in invisible cotton clouds, numb with shock and sorrow listening to Duglak explain the unexplainable. Tuane had gone out into space without sealing his helmet. The vacuum and cold had blinded him, and then he'd simply frozen. It had taken seconds. She put her head in her hands, her will the only thing keeping her from dry heaving.

"This one is not on Brook," Duglak said. "Tuane had obviously rushed through pre-flight protocols and left the craft to fix his screw up, because he wanted to cover his error. He was a bright young man, but he made a rookie mistake."

When the meeting was over, Serral wandered until she found an unoccupied conference room. She sat under the table, and cried until she had no tears left. Then she curled up, head pounding, midsection exploding with darkness, and fell asleep. She dreamed of Thantons, flowing and ebbing silver, blue and black, like water, like mist, untouchable and cold. When she woke up, her grief had turned to rage and had hardened, transformed into a scar, into a fragment of the invisible encaustic surrounding Whit, and Duglak, and every other Whitehair. She couldn't possibly kill enough Harbs to avenge the invisible thing they'd stolen and would keep stealing until no Imset were left to hold onto it, and it dissipated into the vacuum of space.

Serral moved numbly through the rest of her training; advanced flight craft, warcraft, and advanced navigation. She earned top marks in her class.

Duglak ribbed her about her high marks. "Best out of seven. Pretty impressive."

"Sure, the Harbs will check my stats before they kill me."

Duglak blinked. "Who knows. Maybe you'll be the one to single-handedly win the war."

"Someone has to."

Their graduation ceremony was short and grave. A hundred officers and crew lined the sides of the training theater, applauding as each of the recruits were made Pilot Crigsen. A camera flashed, and they were handed a new uniform with more badges. Serral did not smile.

There was a party that night in the Caf. They had ale and a planetary style cake. Duglak told stories about great and mighty maneuvers he'd seen pilots perform in his long career, trying to inspire them. Serral picked at her slice of cake, but it tasted like resin foam. The ale was worse. When Slook came to sit with her, even an offer of cider didn't tempt her.

"You're a wreck," Slook said, her white curls cascading down the sides of her long face and disappearing haphazardly into her silver-emblazoned uniform. "Nervous about combat?"

Serral shook her head. "No. I'm looking forward to Harbicide."

"Right." Slook sipped her drink. "Hey, now that you're no longer Duglak's creature, I have a situation I'd like your help with."

"A situation?"

"An opportunity." She stood up, put down her drink, and then scanned the room. "Come with me."

Serral followed Slook deep into the Ninitan, passing from the training sector through offices and private quarters, past well-staffed strategy rooms, and on and on. As soon as they entered a sleek, new section of the ship, she started to feel seriously ill. Her midsection was on fire and burning with a foulness that threatened to crawl up her throat.

"Air Marsiant," Serral said, her hand on a wall, "something's not right here. I think I should go back."

Slook's smile dimmed. Her hand was warm on Serral's shoulder as she pushed. "Come on. It's only a bit further."

Serral's feet shuffled unwillingly, her body wanting to refuse. "Where are we going?"

"Straighten up, Soldier." Slook pulled her along. She touched the patch of decorations and insignias on her chest, revealing a small camera lens. "You're being recorded."

Serral forced herself to stand tall. "Yes sir."

They came to a series of cage-like rooms, each numbered, doors open and empty. They stopped in front of a closed door within hardened walls. A plaque read *T-111*.

"The brig?" Serral whispered.

"Don't worry. I'm not incarcerating you." Slook let go of her hand and turned. Her warm eyes looked amused. "Why do you think you're here, Crigsen Brook?"

"Because you brought me." That sounded aggressive. "I mean, because you had an opportunity, Sir."

"Stop talking like an imbecile. I know you're bright. Try harder."

"May I speak freely?" More than anything, Serral wanted to turn and run away. She struggled for air, her eyes filling with tiny black dots. Her body was betraying her.

"Of course. With me, honesty is a requirement."

"What is happening in there? What is happening to me?"

"Sit." Slook's face grew serious. "Stop fighting it."

They perched on a bench against a cool metal wall. The brig was silent, but Serral sensed other people, people who called out to her wordlessly. She struggled to stay conscious, blinking away the dark haze engulfing her vision. She spoke haltingly. "What are my orders, Sir?"

"Orders. Oh, you willful Colonials. I was once like you. I believed in the clarity of instructions, of being told what to do. You see how well that's working out for the Imset." Slook crossed her legs and leaned back. "We are on uncharted ground here, my dear. I do need your help.

But it would spoil things if I said too much. I want to hear directly from you. Do you understand?"

"No. I don't." Serral rubbed her eyes. "I'm sorry."

Slook pushed her white curls off her face. "Tell me your impressions."

Serral grimaced, short of breath. "My impression is, with respect, I don't want to be here."

"No?" Slook smiled. "We all do what we can to help the Cause. I'm just asking for you to use your imagination about what that might mean." She snapped her fingers in a show of impatience. "Observations. Now."

Serral's eyes traveled down the clean, white hallway. "That is the only occupied cell in this unit."

Slook clapped her hand, "Yes!" she laughed. "Very good. You couldn't possibly have known that."

Serral forced words out of her throat. "This place smells like something is very wrong."

"Hmmm. That depends on your perspective, I suppose. The situation is complex. Please continue."

"What is this *situation*?"

Slook shrugged, her white hair coils bounciing down her back. "I can't tell you that. I'm not sure others would find it as objectionable as you do. But your reaction makes me think you are uniquely qualified to help me deal with it."

"I think you've got me confused with someone else."

"Oh, no. I've been tracking you for years, Brook." Slook looked serene. "You were born at the exact moment Quenetai Sci Col was destroyed."

Brume's story. Serral looked for an escape.

Slook put her hand on Serral's shoulder again. "Of course, you don't remember. But had you and your brother been inside, you would have died. Everyone died that day. Everyone except you two, defenseless kiddos. Now, how did that happen, do you think?"

Serral leaned over her knees, her shame a pit too frightening to look into. "How should I know?"

Slook ignored her question. "Then sixteen years later, when your Air Guard was disengaged, from out of nowhere you pulled the raid alarm just as a halo came to call. And, as if that weren't unlikely enough, the enemy chose not to kill you. I'm sure I needn't tell you, a story like this is never heard in the world of the Imset."

"I wouldn't know, sir." Serral blinked, her vision still swarming with black. What drug had she been given? "I was only recently given security clearance."

"Any theories?"

"Theories?" Serral gasped. "I have no idea why anything has happened. I was a newborn on Quenetai. I have no memories of it. And on Chlore, I saw a dogfight in the sky and knew that couldn't be good. So, I pulled the alarm, just as we were trained to do." Her voice felt tight and raw, but she was relieved something logical came from it. "That is the Ysk's honest truth, Air Marsiant."

Slook showed no reaction, but continued, gazing into Serral's eyes. "And now, despite your recruitment 'Tainer being destroyed, and with it almost all of your recruiting class, you wind up here. Again, the lone survivor but for the children you brought with you. I'd say you are either very lucky or mighty special, Pilot Crigsen."

"Lucky." The bench felt cool under Serral's hands. She wanted to press her forehead against it. "I don't feel well, Sir. I think if it's all the same to you, I would prefer to talk more later."

"Nonsense." Slook stood. "Stand up. I want to introduce you to someone."

A black tunnel solidified around Serral's peripheral vision. "Sir."

"That's an order," Slook said. "Stand up."

"Sir." She tried to stand, but her body wouldn't respond.

Slook regarded her with a predatory gleam. "Serral Brook. If you intend to survive this war, I suggest you start showing some loyalty to the Cause. Now. Or I'll have to put another very murky report into your already questionable record. And that," she crossed her arms, "would be the end of your luck, I'm afraid."

"Yes, sir." Serral shut her eyes, begging her legs to lift her off the bench. A vibration shimmered in her head, something like what she'd felt during the raid on Chlore except this felt dark and desperate. Serral counted her breaths, one to ten. Ten to one.

"Get inside that cell, now."

Slook gripped Serral's wrist so hard it hurt and yanked her to her feet.

Serral stumbled, then righted herself. "Yes, sir," she said. Fear was joined by a pallid note of curiosity. If she could survive whatever ordeal Slook had in store, maybe she could learn something.

"I will be waiting." Slook unlocked the door to cell T-111.

Serral walked inside, and the door closed behind her. She looked around the cell, and then turned and pounded on the door, unable to form words or keep the screams from rising through her like the blare of hoarse, pointless klaxons.

## 16

Chapter Sixteen

*Ours is the making*
*Of a million alluvial orbs*
*Circling a thousand loving suns*
*Under one sacred visage,*
*Divine Ysk*
*And her spectral company of Thantons.*
*We offer our greatest treasure, Sacrifice*
*Willingly, joyfully*
*Lowly slaves that we be.*
*Humbly we wait*
*For the winged ones to bestow*
*Love everlasting, on our grateful ousia.*
*Our time will come,*
*In the fullness of Ysk's plan.*
*We Harbingers of death, of life*
*Beloved of Ysk*
*Tenders of her desire*
*We give thanks for the heavy duty*
*Of caring for each living thing*
*She has placed upon us.*

*Each creature,*
*Every blade of grass*
*And vast living sphere.*
*Our efforts are immeasurable,*
*Our tribute is universal.*
*The world echoes with the sounds of all Ysk's creatures.*
*Oh orchestra of love!*
*Oh universe of joy!*
*And promise of life, free and unfettered, whole and perfect,*
*As we have crafted it.*
*Praise be to Ysk,*
*Our lord.*
*Praise be to the Thantons*
*Who carry out her will.*
*Amen*

**17**

— · —

Chapter Seventeen

Serral slumped to the floor of Cell T-111. The place smelled of blood and waste and despair. She was not alone. Before her stood three Harbs, their long, naked gray bodies and bulbous heads bruised and bloody. She stared, her chest jumping, her stomach flattening to lead while she and the prisoners studied one another. More than dread or anger, Serral felt surprise. She was standing face to face with live, albeit injured, Harbs. It was unreal, and yet, her nose told her, it was real.

The aliens she'd seen on Chlore had seemed large, but these gray-skinned people were just under two meters tall, their massive skulls at her eye level. They were so slender she could have fit her two hands around any of their narrow waists, though their shoulders widened to the same girth as her own. Their arms were pitifully weak looking, their slender necks overtasked with holding up their huge heads. Were their ballooning head domes hollow? They looked as if pierced, they would pop. Only their eyes, though swollen and crusted with scabs, looked formidable, black and shiny as beetles, blinking slowly as they stared. Their small mouths made straight lines below the slit lumps of their noses. Except for their different bruises and the black blood caked on various parts of their bodies, Serral wouldn't have been able to tell them apart.

*Harbs.* Why did she not feel fear? Her body had regulated somewhat and settled. Serral watched the three gray creatures, and they watched her. Their expressions didn't change, and no one moved. But the feeling in the room slowly shifted from stark suffering to something more hopeful. Her heart rate slowed and hardened. She understood. She was in control. The people before her, she understood, were happy to see her. But they wanted something from her. Something they needed, something they yearned for.

Minutes passed. Serral felt a thread pulling at her breath, something subtle yet persistent; an idea, a thought, but not her own. The air popped without sound, without vibration.

Serral realized in the core of her being what the aliens wanted. It was simple, so simple. The trio of Harbs standing like nightmare statues before her wanted more than anything for her to kill them. They were eager for it. They would be devastated if she didn't. They held their hands palms up, and bowed in submission, in invitation. Their gray head domes fluttered, their skin moved over the actions of something muscular and brain-like beneath. It was both grotesque and fascinating.

"You're in pain," Serral said softly. "And they don't know how to get any more information out of you."

They raised their eyes to hers. She felt they understood.

"They are testing me to see if I am loyal enough to kill you."

They stood motionless.

"You're waiting. Is that right? For me to put you out of your misery?"

Their head domes rippled faster. Shiny wall-mounted cameras looked down from a corner. Serral was sure Slook was watching. Was she pleased? Or was she still parsing meaning out of Serral's birth story, looking for ways to use it against her?

"Which one of you is first?"

None moved.

"You don't speak Imset, do you?"

Their heads grew still. The two on either end took the hand of the one in the middle. Serral sensed that they were ready. And so was she.

"Here goes. This one is for my mom." Serral took the distance between her and the Harbs in two strides. Their smell of filth made her gag, but her hands found clammy gray flesh. The first Harb neck snapped like a twig.

The others didn't move. They looked at their dead comrade, then turned back to Serral.

"This one is for my dad."

Snap.

"And this one is for my friends on the 'Tainer."

By the time Slook had rushed into the cell, yelling something about "misunderstanding," the slender gray bodies had collapsed on the floor, eyes closed, heads rounded and small. They looked like gray-skinned dolls.

Slook's voice writhed around Serral like an angry snake, yelling about stupidity and rashness. But Serral was impervious. A mysterious and wonderful revolution was happening inside her. The sick feeling was gone. She felt sure, and clean, and confident. A surge of wellbeing pulsed into her fingers, her toes, her ears and her hair. It was followed by a shock of electric, giddy joy. Serral turned from the heap of Harbs and walked out of the cell. At ten paces, she felt a hand on her arm and realized Slook was still yelling at her.

"Where do you think you're going? I haven't dismissed you."

"What are you so upset about?" Serral breathed deeply, her body floating on a cloud of vitality. "They're dead."

Slook's face contorted. "I know that, you stupid Col. Just like every other Harb we see. The unusual thing was nabbing a live one, and we had three. Now they're dead. Which I will be blamed for. But worse, there were tests planned, experiments I'll never get to try. And we need those tests, that information. Badly. I'm not even allowed to say how badly. So, I hope you're happy."

Serral smiled. She felt a hundred rimeters distant from her superior officer's rantings.

"Why are you smiling? This isn't funny."

Serral shrugged. "Air Marsiant. I'm not that gullible."

"Oh, you think you're so smart?" Slook said. "You failed the test."

"No, sir. You failed." Serral rubbed her hands on her coveralls, trying to clean the Harb remains from them. "You sent a soldier into a room with a bunch of enemies, right after talking about how she was a borderline traitor."

Slook's eyes widened. "That's not what I said. I said you had escaped from the Harbs three times, and no one else has ever done that. You're a mystery, is all. This was an opportunity, and you blew it."

"You said to open myself up to my feelings. Which I did. I hate Harbs! I've seen what they can do. You've seen it too. How could you not be the one to break their necks on sight?"

"That's not all there is to war. The Imset have to face reality, Pilot Crigsen. We need a new way to fight. We need to think of the larger picture."

The lovely feeling vibrating through Serral waned slightly, replaced by a soft calm. "New way to fight? What new way to fight?"

Slook looked around, then hissed. "Not here."

Slook led Serral out of the brig, down myriad hallways, to a combination office and quarters section. The place was blank and anonymous, the opposite of Duglak's lived-in room. The lights dimmed, and Serral realized the late hour.

"I have to get back to my barracks."

Slook sat heavily and poured them each a glass of amber liquid. "Sit down. You've got the Thrill. You won't sleep for hours."

"The Thrill?"

Slook nodded and knocked back her drink. "The sweet nectar of killing Harbs. It's addictive. So be careful."

Serral declined her glass, so Slook downed it too. The warm, powerful surge through Serral's body was intoxicating enough. She'd heard of how good killing felt, but nothing could have prepared her for the fullness of contentment than ran through her body. She thought of Whit, and his need for Azanta. There was so much she didn't understand. But she was learning.

"So. The prisoners are dead, and we can't bring them back. What can you tell me? Anything you noticed? Felt? Saw?"

She had noticed things. How should she express her observations in words? "Those Harbs weren't soldiers. They were ordinary servants, and they wanted to die."

Slook leaned forward. "How do you know?"

Serral thought in silence for a moment. "Piecing together reports, we think there is a separate class of hardcore Harbinger soldiers. And then there are ones like those, meek and nonthreatening, the worker bees, if you will. We took them off a transport, after a fierce battle."

"We're attacking in deep space, now?"

Slook shrugged. "They started breaking the rules. So, we did, too. It was a golden opportunity for us."

"One you won't get again any time soon."

"Correct. Regular Harbingers will no doubt have more soldiers accompanying them, in future."

"I don't think they fear death much." Serral ran a hand through her short hair. "Those three were waiting patiently for me to put them out of their misery."

Slook sat back and stared. After a pause she said, "We don't understand how their hierarchies work. Or even how many different types there are."

Serral thought about the Halo, how some of the gray people had seemed ready to kill her, others had emanated friendliness, and the tall one hadn't been a Harb at all. "At least three. I saw at least three when they came to my oculus."

"Where you weren't augered?"

Serral stretched her feet out in front of her. They seemed a long way away. Thrill sizzled pleasantly through her body. "I saw them visually. And the ones I killed, they didn't reach into my mind."

"Then how did you know they wanted you to murder them?" Slook fingered her glass. Her anger seemed to have been replaced by curiosity.

"Intuition." Serral made her face blank, though she felt dishonest. "And maybe wishful thinking."

A smile flitted across Slook's face. "We only recently began to risk interrogating them. I mean, how do you start? And how do you protect yourself from being augered? I've searched for years for someone who can speak their language. Which is probably a waste of time, but you can understand why it would be useful."

"So." Serral turned a new idea over in her mind, examining it with fascination, aware that under different circumstances she'd be furious. "You were willing to sacrifice me, on the off chance that I could communicate with them? You thought maybe I'd survive being augered?"

Slook's brows furrowed. "Those Harbs were weak, away from their ship. And like you said, they wanted to die."

"Help me understand. I'm just a rude little colonial and have been trained to avoid contact on pain of death." Serral sniffed her now empty glass. It smelled of old, brown grass from some planet she'd never seen, a lovely aroma, deep and pungent and sad. "What about the way you nudged me toward treason?"

'Don't be such a baby," Slook glowered. "I would have covered for you. But anyway, you don't need that now. You lived up to all their expectations. After this, no one will look askance at your patriotism. Whereas I'm back to the drawing board."

"You've taken Harb prisoners before."

"A few times over the years," Slook shrugged, "But it's not easy. They usually commit suicide. Or kill one another."

"Does the Military know you're...?"

"What? Interested in alternative methods?" Slook scoffed. "Obviously. Don't romanticize the Military or the Authority, for that matter. They're as desperate as anyone else, these days. Why do you think they recruited me out of teaching on Campion?"

Serral didn't flinch at the sound of the university city. Rafe was becoming a distant memory flavored lightly with nostalgia. Her new love was the Thrill. "So, you're not a soldier?"

"I am. Have been since the war went bad. We all have to pitch in, Brook. I have a long record of distinguished service, believe it or not. Though, you're right, even I have to follow hunches as well as rules. And my hunch about you, I'll be honest, I'm disappointed." Slook pulled on a fuzzy white hair coil. "In your record, it's so clear. You anticipate their moves. You knew who was in that cell, even if you didn't have words to say so. You can almost feel them reaching out to you with their minds, can't you?"

Slook stood, and Serral took the hint. They moved toward the door. Serral felt the trap looming. "Not exactly. I can tell something bad is happening because my stomach ties in knots. But I have no idea what."

Slook's brown eyes softened. "That's at least something." She patted Serral's hand absently and then said, "I knew you had intuition about them. Yes. Intuition. That's what I'll put in the report."

The lights lowered another grade, signaling the day's end.

"I'm sorry to disappoint you, sir. But I'll be honest," Serral said.

"Oh?"

"You knew I'd fail this test. Otherwise, you'd have given me more of a clue. If you'd trusted me, you'd have told me what I was there for."

Slook crossed her arms. "It's a difficult thing, this war. Anything I tell you can get back to them, and as I'm sure you know, if one Harb gets hold of information, that means they all have it."

"I thought that was just a legend."

"Who knows, really?" Slook tipped her head back, curls trembling, and made a bitter sound. "Sad. I won't be able to take you back with me."

"Take me back?" Serral stood, surprised. "You were planning to take me to Mollith?"

"I hoped," Slook shrugged. "Listen. If you come across anything I could use, get word to me. Got it? I need straws to grasp, Pilot Crigsen."

The door closed on Serral's salute.

She made it back to her bunk right before the lights went completely black. The warm, excited feeling mellowed slowly and left her conflicted. Had she committed a terrible blunder? But parts of her refused to worry. A welcoming darkness descended inside her eyelids, and the vaulted heavens opened like a glimmering cavern, winking blue, full of promise.

Next morning, Bridla and Kameth made shocked faces in the hygiene area mirror. "Holy Dantons."

Serral started, not knowing the face staring back at her. Her hair was bright white.

"Snow top!" Kameth scoffed. "I thought we were friends!"

Serral had no words.

Prinsloo gaped, angry. "You've gone and murdered Harbs without us! No fair!"

Serral's muscles glowed, and she felt a smile grow on her face. "Oops."

They all laughed.

That afternoon, Serral received an order to appear at one of the cargo bays. She and a group of Whitehairs strapped into seats on a transport and left base, though no one told her where they were going, and she felt content not to ask. The Ninitan looked benign now, its spidery hull as much an admission of Imset weakness as strength, she thought. The war had gone bad, Slook had said. They endured the sick sensation of traveling through the port worm, everyone continuing their conversations as if they weren't being twisted and pulled into threads and knit back together. Serral rubbed her back against the seat, her tattoos itching suddenly, as if to remind her they were there.

When they came through the otherside, a medic joined them. "Injection for Pilot Crigsen Serral Brook."

"What for?" Serral asked, baring her arm.

The medic, young and of indeterminate gender, looked bored. "Powers-that-be think you could use a little extra boost."

The Med Bot pushed the dose in slowly. Whatever it was burned, and then filled Serral with fog. "Feels like sleep meds."

"That and a bunch of other goodies to get you strong. It'll take four days to reach the Tuval. You can catch up on your rest."

"The Tuval?"

The medic looked down at Serral, pity in their gray eyes. "You're headed to the front, Pilot Crigsen. Enjoy your peace and quiet while you can."

A disembodied fatigue washed out the last tendrils of Thrill. Her head slumped alarmingly to one side. "Hey..."

But she couldn't complete the sentence. The last thing she saw was the medic's arm reaching over to flatten out her chair.

**18**

C hapter Eighteen

Hallenander hesitated in the elevated passageway between his part of the palace and his uncle's. The sixteen ancestral busts were indifferent to his presence, their stony cheeks contemptuous below the high crests of their head domes. He could name each one, eleven men and five women who had ruled the Worlds. These were only the most famous of his father's forebears. The Chi'irea line stretched back two thousand years. When he was a child, he had liked to reach up and touch the cold, smooth faces of these sculptures, imagining their love for him, the monarchy's best hope.

Now he reached over and slapped Banthalat III, making his pedestal wobble. Four Harbinger servants rushed to straighten the statue before it fell.

"Honestly, Helpers. You can't save his life now."

They stared, head domes frozen.

His change in attitude toward the elders occurred when Hallenander first understood that Imset women lived in the Xalavria, that it was their laughter he heard at night. As a boy, he had liked to lie in bed with his windows open, imagining his mother up on the plateau. Then, one day he heard the thread of a deeper voice, his uncle's basso profundo unmistakable out there in the midst of silvery giggles, and all at once he understood what was happening. He'd seen Imset, both in the village and at a great distance on the clifftop. But they had been abstractions, part of the scenery, perhaps someone he spoke to in passing. Not someone he laughed with. Not someone he could be with intimately. He thought of his aunt, his cousins, the people who expected Uncle Mimellio to uphold the standards of their lofty race. He had closed his window and spent the rest of the evening trying to wash his embarrassment off in the shower.

The day that Hallenander realized the depths of palace hypocrisy marked the end of his trust in his eight wizened advisors. But he didn't tell them. Instead, he fulfilled their assignments, learned what they had to teach, met all their requirements. But he could no longer look at the men in their Kohl-rimmed eyes. To him, they were, and always would be, the keepers of slaves, exploiters of Imset women whose memories had been tampered with to make them more compliant. The insult of it, both to the distant Volterrans who fancied themselves moral people, and to his mother's misbegotten Imset people, weighed on him like a soaking-wet cloak. But with no way to erase their stain, the Eight would insist that Hallenander share in it. They were unable to accept that while they enjoyed Imset slave girls, Hallenander did not and would not, regardless of how embarrassed that made them feel. But oh, they were persistent. Thank the eighty-eight gods they had settled on procuring an Imset tutor for Hallenander instead, a man who instantly earned Hallenander's respect.

Hallenander made a gesture of entreaty to his ancestors, asking them to protect Geddon the beloved tutor, wherever he had gone.

Hallenander sighed with frustration and entered his uncle's great room. For reasons none but the Harbingers knew, the great homes on Evincio were styled more like those on the lost planet Imseth than planet Volterra. And, as always, Hallenander had the urge to flee, but instead, he sat in the accustomed chair, and his uncle, like always, kept him waiting. Once, bored, tired of waiting, Hallenander had stalked off, and his uncle had refused to grant him another audience for nearly a year. He studied the familiar room. It felt smaller and more ridiculous than usual with its carved medallions and swags, its repeated motif of a golden kite with a soaring tail, its sheaves of wheat, and colored jewels, and the Eight World planets, each depicted with a small sigil signifying their unique culture. His favorite, the Gattycan eye.

Uncle Mimellio spoke from the doorway. His low voice was reedy and well bred, that of a buyer continuously evaluating the same shabby wares. "The servants neglected to tell me you were here, Hal. I daresay you haven't waited overlong?"

Hallenander made a small bow. "Waiting for you keeps me young, uncle. I feel like a ten-year-old boy, awaiting my examinations."

The smile dropped from Mimellio's long, dark, bony face. He sat heavily, crossing his legs under his linen tunic. "Ah, but you are a man now and answers are murky. His Royal Highness expects your case to be given consideration in the Eloxiture before the quarter is out."

Hallenander could say nothing more until the precise nature of his uncle's summons was stated. Mimellio signaled for the servants to bring a tray. Hallenander sipped the tea, according to ritual, then they both dipped their cakes. His uncle praised the food as he always did, though the cakes were identical to all previous offerings. Hallenander made a show of agreeing with his uncle.

Finally, Mimellio cleared his throat, and addressed Hallenander with narrowed eyes. "We of the Eight, we request of you, that is to say, it would cheer us a great deal, it would help us feel that you are truly our prince, if we were to share with you our amusements and, how shall I say it, our entertainments."

Hallenander pondered his carved leather brogues. "You want me to take a Companion."

"Yes." Mimellio smiled again, his wide brows rising. "If all goes well, one day you will be required to woo women of your own society, that is to say, the noble women of Volterra."

More noble than Hallenander, it went without saying. "I see. So, fraternizing with a slave is good training, is that it? Use Imset girls for practice?"

"Hal. Your superior pose is tiresome." Mimellio rubbed his eyes. "This is for your own good. For the good of your future and in keeping with your father's wishes that you be socially nimble."

"Ah." Hallenander fingered his gold watch chain, crossing the legs of his Imset-style trousers. "You wish to help me overcome the handicap of my being half Imset by letting me loose on captive Imset slaves."

Mimiellio's face went rigid. "Do not let the women hear you speak so. It would hurt their... feelings. It would."

"And we wouldn't want to hurt the feelings of our captives. Or, perhaps, have them understand that they are captives? Eh?"

Mimellio held up his large hand. "Enough. Their memories have been altered, of course. It would do them no good to understand that if not for their extraordinary brilliance, our Helpers would have left them to their doom, shared by so many of their race. Life on the run in space, or as dirty planetary animals left to be hunted."

Hal gave his uncle a conciliatory smile. "It is not my wish to cause offense."

"A Companion may be treated as a guest, as you would any other beautiful and charming women. You must learn to converse amicably, to give your jewels away at the gaming tables, and yes, to flirt. Flattering girls, enjoying their attentions, keeping them appropriately infatuated are necessary skills. And I do not say this to be critical of a new-made man such as yourself, but your earnestness will hold no appeal to any practiced courtier. It will be seen as weakness, Hal, as the hallmark of a rude provincial. You must learn to float along on a cloud of amusement and let politics appear as an afterthought. If you do not, the nobility will turn on you, and no amount of book learning or sportsmanship will change their minds."

"Ah, well they have Eight worlds, and I only one. I concede I have much to learn." From long practice, Hallenander kept his face still and his voice even. "And if taking advantage of slaves does not amuse me, Uncle? What then?"

Mimellio put his long brown hands on his linen-clad knees and faced Hallenander with seriousness. "Hal, do you not see that their lives now are preferable to the filth and degradation of any ordinary Imset?"

Hallenander sighed. "I see that you are determined to tell me so."

"It is for your own good."

"Very well," Hal conceded quietly. "But I ask something in return."

Mimellio's held his hands out, indicating the whole world. "Is there anything that you do not possess?"

Hallenander did not mention the knowledge of his mother's identity, the legal rights in Volterra, or the access to all the great libraries in Gettyca. Instead, he said in a clear voice, "I want to learn to fly a spaceship. After I have been granted that, then I will take a Companion."

Mimellio looked perplexed. "Fly a spaceship? Of all the degrading occupations for a nobleman, or even for a member of the Sevenni Family of Chi'irea..."

"And one more condition, sir." Hal stood, signaling their meeting was about to end. "I will require the freedom to select the girl I find most pleasing without opinions or protestations of my elders. Do you agree?"

Mimellio's long head crest dipped down his back and he laughed. "Of course, my dear boy. Any Imset girl you like. But as for flying, I cannot authorize that."

"Then I will ask my father."

Mimellio rose and then bowed. "By all means, let my brother be the one to explain to you the risk the of the Worlds' press getting wind of a hobby so Imset-like."

"As you say. Let him lecture me on the role the Harbingers play in our lives and my moral obligation to depend upon them."

Mimellio rubbed his hands together. "If you don't care for the feelings of our Helpers, I know I cannot sway you. But still! The ladies of the Xalavria will be overcome with joy. They have been yearning to meet you."

Hallenander waited until he was outside of the great hall to let his eyes roll.

**19**

—·—

Chapter Nineteen

Serral stirred when an announcement pierced the blackness that held her down. Her mouth was crusted with old spit, and a stench rose from her body. She missed most of the mech's words, but gathered their meaning: passengers were to prepare for an arrival. She used the common hygiene area, then ate in the small Caf. For the first time since Chlore, her body felt simple hunger without a throb of anything painful to go along with it. She forced herself to slow down and enjoy the food; dark bread with a savory spread, cool sweet fruits she did not know the name of, and dark, bitter tea.

"How long before we get there?" she asked a white hair in a civilian coverall.

"To the front? A few more days."

The front. Serral thanked her and returned to the serving area for dessert. While she was letting sweet brown paste slowly dissolve onto her tongue, the mech voice announced a rendezvous with a Terminus. People moved on and off, but she stayed where she was, the woman's estimated time of arrival replaying in her mind. No definite location, no real time frame, no way for Serral to plan how to spend what might be the last hours of her life, if the adults back on Chlore were to be believed. Even now, when a ship was about to enter a war zone, the

Authority did not see fit to be honest with her. She thought about escalating a complaint, but decided against it. Her body was slowly recovering from its long sleep, and she was enjoying feeling rested. Her seat had a good view of the stars. There were old print magazines from the cities tucked in a small unit by the door full of articles about the five stations that held her people like fish in a can. The photos did not look bad, though, and the writings were of a positive slant. Serral found them amusing and spent the day reading about the diaspora's many brilliant solutions for planetless-ness. When she had read through most all of them, she wondered darkly why they were still fighting this war. Life in space was evidently great.

The next day they passed through a Portworm. Serral figured it was Obbney, but either no one on board knew, or the information was classified. Serral did not care any longer which point on the heavenly hex she was passing through. But she was sad to not have Brume along. She was beginning to get used to the stretching, weightlessness swim of the passage. She kept her eyes on the starry membrane of wall, hoping for a seam, a rip, some way to see to the other side. But all she saw was milky, glowing striations that dwarfed their transport and the handful of other ships crossing in the opposite direction, tiny flashes of silver in the white. Her heart squirmed at the sight of so much activity. Wherever they were, it was closer to civilization than she had been before. She waited to sense that Harbs were near, that they were trying to speak to her as their ships passed, distant chrome walnuts in the worm's vault, but she felt nothing. She did not want to think about killing the three Harbs, about what had happened before they had slumped limply to the floor, the way she had surged with life. Because, when she did think about it, her hands went numb, and she would have to roll the fear out of her shoulders until they came back to life.

On the third day, a Syrtient with a mech arm stopped by her chair, scanning the tracker the 'Tainer medic had injected into the back of her neck. She had forgotten about it. "Pilot Crigsen Serral Brook."

"Yes, sir." She tried to stand, but he gestured for her to stay put with his metal hand.

"You are now on active duty." He told her where to report on the Tuval. "Have a good tour."

She did not know what to say. He was on to the next passenger before she managed to mouth the words *thank you?*

Within an hour, a gray disc appeared on the horizon. Serral watched with growing excitement until it resolved into a large, impressive star ship. If the Ninitan was an ugly, patched-together hulk, the Tuval was a shining, silver egg. They embarked onto her arrivals deck, and Serral felt the pride of the ship. Squadrons' worth of Arrows entubed and ready, dozens of white-suited contrivers, the low hum of equipment being tested and perfected; this was a place of excellence, of Imset swagger beyond anything she had imagined. The Tuval seemed to say, *come get a piece of this.* She simultaneously ached to fly out in one of the battle Arrows and wished she could stay aboard forever.

Her new CO was a fish-eyed, wiry Master Syrtient named Jeslo. Her office was sleek, but it smelled as much like quib lubricant as Whit's had. Serral waited while Jelso, white hair sticking in all directions like a satellite, her cheeks marked with vertical seams, read her file.

"Sorry, kid. I'm not seeing it." Jelso's huge, pale green eyes darted from her liquid portal to Serral. "You're not ready for flight battle yet. Why'd they send you? Why'd they want to get rid of you so bad?"

Serral shrugged. "I don't know. Maybe once I'd killed those Harbs, they thought I was ready for more."

"You killed them with your bare hands. Which is a-okay by me, but not how we typically conduct Harbicide. To be in the Air Guard, you have to use rockets and bullets. Make sense?"

"Yes, sir."

"All right then," Jeslo typed onto a pad. "If you want to go straight into combat, I won't stop you. But, like I said, you're not ready."

"I'll do whatever you think I should, sir."

"Yes, you will. I'm going to have you run some drills. Put some meters on you so you won't get shot within the first five minutes."

"Thank you. I appreciate that."

"Never thank the Military. Never curse the Military. The only one who gives a shit about your life is Ysk. Talk to her." Jeslo scrolled through the liquid. "Brook. Here's my concern. You got a hex tat on your back, is that right?"

Serral's neck prickled, a warning. "Yes. On our planet, lots of kids had ink."

"Oh sure, and they're all of the worms and where to find them." Jeslo met her eyes, expectant.

"I don't understand, sir."

"Cols. Never as ignorant as we pretend, am I right?" She smiled mirthlessly. "Your record shows who you really are."

Serral swallowed. "The insubordination charge was disputed by several staff members."

Jeslo let out a high-pitched scoff. "Shut it. You've been insubordinate in many ways. It's an illness, you know, wanting to be special."

"Yes, sir." A prickle of cold spread slowly down her shoulders.

"You do know why the colonies exist? Why the Imset sacrifice so much, and the Air Guard fights so hard?"

Serral shrugged. "To grow soldiers. To keep a standing populace of planetaries for our new home planet?"

"Ha! No. It's to make meat for the Harbs. To keep them busy while the Cities finally conclude we'll never win the war. To try to wear the enemy down. There's an infinite supply of them, you know." Jeslo grimaced. "We can no longer afford to be picky."

Serral waited for her to say more.

Jeslo put her feet up. "We'll start you in the pocket, twelve hours a day, until you show us you're ready to fight. Dismissed."

Jeslo's harsh talk made Serral feel comfortably insignificant. She finally felt at ease everywhere she went on the Tuval. She knew what to do. No one looked at her twice.

At her first meal in the Caf, returning pilots sat in disheveled heaps drinking hydration cannisters and shaking with what Serral reckoned must be the Thrill. Two white hairs nearly came to blows, yelling about missteps out in space. Black-uniformed guards came from nowhere and pulled them apart. Their bodies immediately went slack, and they slumped silently in their seats. A few minutes later they shuffled out together.

She found a new bunk. Three roommates came in, ignored her, and hurled themselves into bed. They fell asleep immediately. It took Serral longer. She thought about what came next. Wondered what *the pocket* was. Twelve hours of flying a day, for who knew how long. She hoped she was up to it.

The next morning, a large, female Crigsen came to her bedside with a scanner, then she showed Serral to a locker. "Store your uniform in there and anything else you care about."

Serral had nothing but her uniform, the photo of Brume, and some spare underclothes, but she nodded.

"Have you written your letter?"

"My what?"

"It's standard. Come with me."

They walked down lacquered hallways that curved gradually with the shape of the ship until they arrived at a large equipment room hung with flight suits and apparatus. The big woman opened a portal and brought up Serral's file. Serral dictated a short letter to Brume, telling him to have a good life. She wrote another to Whit.

A Master Syrtient, Pollux, instructed her to suit up.

A young contriver named Zero checked her zippers and seals. He helped her choose a helmet. "This will configure to you. Don't lose it."

She nodded, her chest rabbiting. Zero told her to follow him, and soon they arrived at a dock full of hatches, entubed planes, and a large bank of windows protruding out into bright, white space. *Were they on a planet?*

"What is that?" Serral pointed at distant wrinkles that looked vaguely like the sea floor.

"The pocket, of course," Zero smiled conspiratorially. "You didn't think this station was all crammed with Imset, did you? It's as empty as a Myrth Day candy bowl after the fires go out."

Serral laughed remembering colonial life. An Arrow's star-shaped belly flashed past the window. She gaped. She'd never been so proud of her people.

Zero checked her harness. "Remember, if you fall asleep, you die."

Serral locked her helmet down, and Zero helped her into the smallest Arrow she had ever seen, one barely larger than herself. But the dashboard matched those of the fighter models and had weapons controls at her feet. She was training for combat, no doubt, and to stay awake. Two extremes of life for a fighter pilot. Flying in the pocket looked interesting enough, but her body called out for more Thrill.

Serral completed her checks and entered the flow of traffic. Other pilots commed to her, each relaying their distance and position. She promised to stay out of their way. Below her stretched curved walls studded with equipment like an inside-out sea urchin.

She quickly grew to love her sweetly nimble little Arrow. The first hundred orbits around the pocket went by, and then another hundred, like a carnival ride in a strippy, and then she stopped counting. The landscape below her resolved into familiar landmarks; the docking areas, a dozen or so dormant 'Tainers tethered to the wall, large picture windows, arrays of harsh lights, and several observation bubbles poking out like eyes from the field of interlocking components.

"What's your call sign, tiny?" The com made her jump.

She said the first thing that popped into her head. "*Spooky*, over."

"Nose up, Spooky. You're losing altitude."

Serral jerked to full attention and nosed back up, away from the surface. She checked her instruments. Sure enough, she'd slowly devolved into a wider rotation. Another hundred rotations and she would have started shearing off antennae.

"Thanks," she said, "and you are?"

"Sidewinder. If you see me dip, do the same, okay? Over."

Across the pocket, one of three other Arrows waggled his wings. Serral set alarms to sound every fifteen minutes, then drank hydration fluid. She had six hours left. Halfway through. The light in the pocket remained bright. The afternoon wore on, and two of the Arrows disappeared. She practiced aiming and arming, then commed to Sidewinder that she wanted to try some tighter circles.

"Good idea. Just don't go above fifteen hundred meters or you'll get caught in the storm."

"The storm?"

"Where the G starts to collapse on itself, nearer to the center. Windy. Hard to control these little planes."

"Copy that. You're an Ysksend, Sidewinder."

By the time her twelve hours were up, Serral felt like the pilots she'd seen in the Caf, exhausted and wobbly. She staggered to the common area. Her thirst wouldn't be slaked until four bottles were empty. Finally, as she was about to start on her food, a short, stubble-skulled guy about Brume's age came over and set down his tray.

"Spooky. Sidewinder." His name tag read Voomish. "Congratulations, you made it through your first day."

She motioned for him to sit. "Tell me, how do you stay so alert?"

"Some of it's practice. Some of it is a little treat you can get from the Medic if you ask nicely." His smile showed crooked teeth placed like one had gone missing and the rest had crowded into the gap. He was a scrap rat, one of her kind. Since coming aboard the Tuval, she had become aware of the rustic, planetary quality of scrap rat skin and of their brutally stocky, solid bones. Others she saw in passing were obvious Civicians, and while she knew she was tougher and physically superior, the condescension in their perfect demeanor and slow-blinking eyes made her angry.

"That's it?" Serral chewed her main course, a savory meat dish she couldn't identify.

"Okay, this is embarrassing," Voomish sighed. "I pretend I'm hunting Harbs."

"This is useful information."

They both laughed.

"You pretend you're in combat?"

"It makes the day go by much faster. I run whole long dog fights in my head. I've been flying in there for ten days now. I think my time is almost up."

She started in on a cup of yellow pudding covered in unidentifiable fruit. It was delicious. "Why do they have us flying in the pocket anyway?"

"Safety, I guess."

"Seems hazardous to me."

Voomish scratched his ear. "I guess the Military wants us to at least have a chance."

They chewed soberly.

"Have you fought much?" Serral said.

"No. But you have." Voomish studied her hair. "Is that why you're in pocket? Did it not go well?"

She calculated her answer, "I did kill Harbs, but not in combat exactly."

"What do you mean?" His eyes narrowed. "How'd you get that snow top without combat?"

She hesitated. "Hard to explain."

"Huh." Voomish looked away. "I didn't realize there was another way to do it."

Serral wanted to change the subject. "You've heard the war is complicated and getting worse all the time. Right?"

"Yes. Obviously. But what else are you up to? Any tactics I can steal?"

"I wish." Serral smiled. "Thanks for your help today. I really appreciate it."

That evening she couldn't sleep. Everything that had happened flashed through her mind, from the flight to the cave of the Ancients, her encounter with the Harbs on Chlore, Brume's secrets, then recruitment, escape from the attack, their time on the Terminus and her kisses with Rafe, killing the Harbs on the Ninitan, and her brief training in the pocket. A lifetime's worth of events compressed into a few weeks, maybe months, she didn't know. It felt like years. The boys must be in their respective cities by now, starting their new lives. Civicians. Destined to follow the politics of those who wanted to give up and let the Harbs drive them into permanent exile. She felt a new feeling of paranoia growing in her heart. There in the darkness, the soft hum of the Tuval comforted her. But every time she closed her eyes, she was back in the pocket, rotating around and around. Sometime after midnight, her three bunk mates clomped in and fell heavily into bed. She hadn't met them formally, didn't even know their names. Her bunk shook until the woman above her quietly blew her nose. Another woman's voice called out "It wasn't your fault. Go to sleep."

Then all was silent. Serral lay awake for hours.

The next morning, she tried to explain to Zero that she was too tired to fly safely. Her eyes felt raw.

His civician's slender fingers worked on her harness. "Sorry, kid. If we let every tired pilot sit out their sorties, we'd have no one left to fly."

"Do pilots ever get breaks?"

Zero tucked a strap away and smiled knowingly. "Once you start killing, you won't want breaks. Just get these training flight hours out of the way."

Then the delirium started.

## 20

— · —

C hapter Twenty

It started as an unreal feeling that crept around the edge of Serral's vision. To counteract it, she summoned her fantasies of combat, thinking back to the SIM, picturing the Halos she'd seen attacking the transport 'Tainer. She trained her unloaded weapons at random things, an antenna, a bulky component, or other landmarks she could pretend were oncoming Harbs. Voomish didn't return, and the other Arrows that she saw didn't hail her. They came and went in short stints. Most of the time, she was alone in the pocket. Her head felt too light, almost detached from her shoulders. Her ears buzzed. At the end of the day, she tried flying in the storm area, testing how the Arrow moved in the vortex. She had tried to ignore her sense that time was passing irregularly, that she felt simultaneously in the cockpit and out of her body. The weird tugging she'd felt near Harbs returned but was flavored with awe. An unnamable force hovered, wanting her attention.

That evening, exhausted, half out of her mind, she took Zero's advice and went to the Medotel. A tall, clean-scrubbed Medic named Olik gave her two bursts of foul-smelling nasal spray and told her to go straight to bed. "If you wander, no telling where you'll wake up."

Serral didn't hear her bunk mates come in.

She had no memory of waking the next morning, suiting up, doing checks or strapping in. Zero gave her helmet a gentle knock, which jolted her to attention. "Stay awake, little Col. You can do it."

Afterward, his face full of rage, Serral realized that Zero wasn't that much older than she was. "I told you to stay awake, you idiot. You almost crashed."

She mouthed how sorry she was, but he just pulled her from the cockpit and tended to the plane.

"You were lucky. No major damage. Thank Ysk."

Trying to recall what went wrong, every window had been a Halo, every antenna a Tekku. She returned to Olik who said she had blacked out during flight. He gave her more sleep spray. She didn't try to change his mind.

Her experience was similar to the gossamer membrane inside a worm, a sea of warmth and light. Serral had never felt so safe. Arms held her, an embrace full of meaning, espousing her worth. She wanted to stay.

When she'd woken up in the pocket, Zero's voice screaming in the com, the nose of her Arrow approaching the wall at full speed, Serral remembered only a handful of words. She righted the plane, but only after she'd snapped an antenna which bounced off her windshield with a thud. She'd followed Zed's admonitions calmly. Her mind kept repeating words: *destiny*, and *an enemy who is not an enemy*, and with a yearning that could not be ignored, pulling her toward *the surface*.

The surface of what?

That night, Jeslo came to see her in the Medotel. Disappointment in her tepid green eyes. "I have no choice," she said. "You understand. I'm sorry."

"I know. No more pocket."

Jeslo swallowed, her jaw clenching. "You wrote your letter? Ready for combat?"

Serral nodded.

"Report to Fithu. He'll look out for you as best he can. Good luck."

Serral closed her eyes, wanting the starry place.

Fithu was a handsome Air Vice Marsiant with an office adjoining a vast, busy contriving bay. The room held fifty or more tubes, with scores of Arrows to fill them. The soldiers working under his command bristled with energy and purpose. Serral felt a tiny pang. Once, she would have considered this place paradise.

Her new commanding officer looked back and forth between his liquid portal and Serral, a furrow between his brows growing deeper.

"My dreaded file," she said.

"I have no idea what to make of this collection of bizarre tales. I'm not even sure I believe half of them."

Serral couldn't contain a laugh. "Me neither."

"There's only one pertinent detail I care about, and this doesn't contain it." He gestured toward the portal dismissively. "The question is, what will you do in combat?"

Serral shrugged. "I will kill Harbs, Sir. I can't wait to kill me some Harbs."

He gave her a long look. "Don't take this wrong, Pilot. But we Imset have limited resources."

"I understand."

"Good." He typed into a pad.

"So, are you going to risk an Arrow on me?"

"Most people aren't that eager to go get shot at." Fithu said, questioning. "While we're on the topic of space flight, Jeslo said you have a tattoo of the celestial map on your back."

She touched her shoulder absently. "Something we did as kids. When being an Air Guard was our idea of the greatest thing in the universe."

"Ah. Back then. Before you grew up."

"I'm sixteen, sir. Still a kid. Still think those in the Air Guard are heroes."

"Don't bullshit me, Brook."

"No, sir."

Fithu blew out a breath. "There are limits to what you and I can discuss. You understand that?"

"Yes. In case I get augered."

"Before we go any further, I must ask. Are you suicidal?"

Serral laughed, then saw on his face that his question was serious. "No," she said.

"And are you planning to desert?"

"Of course not. I want to kill Harbs. Doesn't it say in there that I've killed before?"

"Yes, it does."

"So, you know that I am serious. And, it also tells you about the attack I survived on the way to Basic, right?"

Fithu nodded. "Yes. Quick thinking, you had."

"But I'm not sure it explains what happened. What I really saw."

A cloud passed over his eyes.

Serral nodded. "I know. Not to be discussed. But, sir, I think I survived for a reason. So I could do my part."

"All right." He typed. "Your contriver will be Ephany. She's from your home planet. Do everything she says at all times. She'll let you know when I've found you a squadron."

"Thank you, sir. Really. Thank you."

Ephany was 24, with a shock of bright silver hair eternally trying to cover her left eye. Her white coveralls stretched across her curvy form appeared attractively ladylike, but her tough, planetary stride brooked no nonsense. She and Serral greeted one another like old friends, with a warm Chloran hug and shoulder clap.

"I remember you! From when you were in Warren Falla with the little-ies. Oh my, how you've grown. Only, you're too young to be here. Where is that rascal brother of yours? Tell me everything."

The two planet mates enjoyed a long evening of stories and snacks in a back room. For hours, Serral updated Ephany on every person on Chlore. And Ephany told Serral all the gossip from her time, which took just as long. By the end of the night, they were laughing so hard they both slipped off their palates and onto the floor. Serral was tired, but the lights shone brightly.

"No dark hours in the contriving bay?" Serral asked?

"Naw, combat happens at all hours."

Serral looked around at the comfortable makeshift lounge. Tools and equipment. Hydration bottles and overstuffed pillows. "You sleep here?"

"No. Fithu lets us use this place, you know," Ephany winked. "For necessary purposes."

The next day, Ephany introduced Serral to everyone they came across, contrivers, support workers, mechs and soldiers. She showed her "the good bunk room" and "the decent food line." Serral's face ached from forced smiles. Ephany took her to a large picture window in a co-worker's quarters. A gorgeous azure planet hung in the view above them.

"Sapphire," Ephany said. "They'll waste everything we have left on that rock."

"Why?" Serral stared, mesmerized. "What besides its beauty is so special?"

Ephany pushed bangs off her eyes. "Rumor is, command wants that planet, and only that planet, and if they can't beat back the Harbs and take it, the war is... I shouldn't say any more," she grimaced apologetically. "We'd better get back. Pisclan squadron is due to land any minute."

"Pisclan squadron?"

"Yeah, traditionally our squads are all named after stuff on old Imseth. Pisclan, Eos, Liklantis, all those places."

"Kind of sick, don't you think?"

Ephany laughed. "Welcome to the Military, little girl."

Alarms wailed. The crew sprang into action. Air locks swung open one bay after another and revealed seven post-battle Arrows. All wore signs of violence, bullet holes or shattered glass, and one poured smoke from its starboard engine. Crews peeled pilots out of their planes and led them away. Several pilots had to be carried straight to the med center.

After the landing bays cleared out, the crews hooked each fighter plane to a tow bot, which dragged them, one by one, into the bowels of the service bay. Serral noticed the blood spatters on the floor and the concern on Ephany's face.

Serral grabbed a mop and started cleaning. Whit's words came to her again. *Whatever happens, survive your tour.*

**21**

—·—

C hapter Twenty-One

Serral's days slipped into a rhythm. When she'd learned her way around Arrow battle components, she began to assist Ephany in the post-battle repairs. Ephany did not allow silence admist their work. She filled Serral's ears with stories about her life, her lovers, soldiers and crew members, people who were no longer there. People she would probably never see again, because the Imset were a *doomed, tragic race.*

Serral said, "You never know, Ephie. Everything you think you can count on can just disappear, like magic."

"So true." Ephany looked at her for a moment, then kept working.

She dreamed of the starry place at night and each morning, hated to wake up. Nevertheless, after only two weeks, Ephany told Fithu that Serral had completed her training and was as skilled a contriver as she'd ever seen. Serral was assigned to a squadron.

"This is the Final Offensive," Fithu explained, apologetic, and offered her a new badge for her black uniform. "I'm not authorized to tell you that, but I did anyway."

Serral sat next to him in the storage bay while he poured them each a cup of cider he'd stockpiled from his planet.

"The thing is," he said, exposing a silver tooth, "the Civicians want to end the war. Command has convinced them that we can take this one planet." He waved weakly. "And of course, they won't say, 'why this one?' I'm guessing it's because it has an excellent airfield and a lot of cultivated land. Course, it also has a nest of Harbs as big as this station, but apparently, they believe we can defeat them."

"Do you think we can, sir?" Serral took a sip of cider. Pilots and contrivers passed by the open door. Some peered in, curious. But no one entered.

Fithu sighed. "I'd be lying if I said I agreed with every decision Command makes, Crigsen. But I do what I'm told."

Her squad leader was a broad, muscular Syrtient named Sly. He and five other pilots wore gray off-duty coveralls. They looked Serral up and down as she entered his office, crowded with their arrogant presence. She met their gazes. It felt important to be unimpressed.

Sly's voice was tangy and fluid, though where he was from Serral couldn't place. "This here is our new pinkie finger."

Serral saluted. She wasn't sure what a pinkie finger was, but figured it referred to the final flyer in a five-arrow formation.

"What's your call sign, Crigsen Pilot?"

"Spooky, sir."

He sneered. "Spooky, eh? You don't seem scary to me. No offense."

She smiled. "You don't know me, sir."

The others exchanged glances. She thought she heard a derisive sigh. But no one said anything.

"Spooky this is Manster, Vis, Mogil, Wastrel, and Liphal." He waved one of his beefy hands across the line of impassive faces.

A bunch of planetaries, Serral figured, none older than about twenty-two. They stared, challenging her. Pilots, she was coming to understand, had eyes like this, unfocused and roaming, one moment piercing her with glare, the next looking over her shoulder as if the enemy were about to appear there

Sly finished his introductions with a mock salute. "Welcome to Lukadio Squadron."

At the sound of the name, the pilots simultaneously made a loud, shuddering war grunt, both silly and terrifying.

Sly addressed the room. "They tell me Spooky here is a raw, green rookie. Apparently, she almost met some Thantons in the pocket. Scared her contriver half to death."

The squad murmured a sympathetic laugh.

"Obviously, she's young and short on hours. But as you can see by her snow top, she's a murderer."

Manster and Liphal gave her nods of approval.

"And she has two other things going for her that most fresh new Cols don't." Sly stood behind Serral and put a hand on her shoulder. "Spooky here was number one in SIM on the Ninitan."

Mogil shrugged. Liphal rolled her eyes.

"Oh no, you're not getting it. This young lady wasn't number one in her class."

Manster started to object.

Sly's voice got loud, "She's number one ever. In the history of the fleet."

Serral flushed with surprise. The others stared.

"She's built planes out of scrap with her bare hands and taken them for joy rides, am I right?"

Serral looked down at the table, suddenly sweating.

"And that's not all, folks. Spooky here is, can I say it?" His ebony eyes shined.

Serral put her hands over her eyes, wishing she could slip out and escape.

His voice fell an octave, "She's well known in the fleet for," he paused theatrically, "insubordination! She secured prohibited materials for her supervisor. She was reprimanded for disrespect to her Ysken."

The soldiers oohed teasingly.

"She stood up to a Halo all by herself with no weapons and her colony wide open for attack, and the Grays got so spooked they up and flew away without shooting a single rocket."

They ahhed respectfully.

"And then of course, the piece of resistance," he winked again. "Air Marsiant Slook put her in a room full of enemy POWs and she..."

"It wasn't a room full," she interrupted. "There were only three of 'em."

"...and she dispatched those old Grays, by herself with her bare hands."

"They were half dead already," Serral said quietly.

The room went silent.

"They needed killing," she said, still with a hushed voice. "I thought that's what they wanted me to do."

Sly laughed, repeating, "*They were half dead already.*"

Liphal mocked, "*I thought that's what they wanted me to do.*"

Suddenly everyone was laughing.

Manster leaned forward and shook her hand. "Welcome, pinkie finger. I'll be on your left side from here on in."

Everyone started talking at once, saying *she was all right, she was going to fit right in.*

Serral blinked. The talk of her record stirred up a familiar layer of shame. But that was not appropriate, not now. Never had she expected what she saw before her, a room full of swaggering fighter pilots applauding her defiant ways.

Slowly, a smile spread over her face.

Lukadio Squadron taught her their protocols, their formation patterns, their responses to various situations in battle. She tried to take it all in. She asked questions. But at night, she floated in membranes of stars. Music emanated from the edges of her mind, a flute song that reminded her of a Halo's rainbow lights. She woke feeling rested.

Sly said after five days, "I never seen a rookie so calm, Brook. You are a spooky one."

On her eleventh day with the squad, Serral woke to Liphal shaking her by the shoulder. "It's time to hunt, baby."

Ephany helped her into her plane, and Serral performed her checks. Her mind felt sharp, calm, and focused. She strapped on her helmet, double-clicked her harness, and tightened her flight gloves. This was it. She suppressed a grin. If Inoa could see her now.

The Arrow moved into the black tube ready for takeoff. Reflections of her ship's lights dotted the walls. And then, with a swoosh into space, she was shot out of the belly of the Tuval and found herself flanking the rest of her squad.

Almost immediately, she flew into near-total death and destruction, the Arrow soaring into a debris field filled with floating broken parts of ships and horror. It was all she could do to avoid hitting the larger objects, spinning and gunning through the chaos to stay astride of her team.

When they reached the far side of the destruction, the atmosphere turned silver with the shine of the Tekkus that swarmed like a flock of sharp-edged plates, Halos with their wheels aglow in colored lights and Arrows raging around like bees. Tears streamed down Serral's face. She fought back sobs as tracer bullets created an enveloping, bright spider web of threat. The quad had no choice but to scatter, leaving Serral to try and follow Sly's directions by herself.

Later, she tried to remember exactly when she'd stopped following his orders. The Lukadio squad was heading due north, close to the edge of the exosphere, and preparing for entry into the planned battle. She made it through the barrier to planetary space, the moment of burn not as bad as she'd expected. And then the familiar pull of gravity helped regain her wits. But by then, she'd been hit on the left flank of her Arrow and was losing pressurization. She commed. Sly barked that she was fine, to stay in formation. She ignored the cold that seeped onto her left foot and arm. Avoiding rockets and trying to keep up took her full attention.

But then the mutterings began, a moment when Serral realized she was hearing a private conversation. She wasn't frightened. Or surprised.

She kept in formation and attacked one of the Halos. The squadron hit it with two rockets and tried to avoid another squad that came in from the south. Serral was numb, and she'd lost her port guns. But she kept going. She used her starboard rocket launcher to land a blow, and when the Halo exploded, Serral was hit with a jolt of poisonous electricity that turned into the sound of screaming and then into a wave of deliciousness as the Thrill washed through her. The squad came over her headset, euphoric, full of congratulations.

"You're good luck, kid!" Manster commed.

"It was all of us," she said.

Hours later, Ephany helped Serral out of the Arrow, making disapproving clicking noises with her tongue.

Two steps out of the plane and Serral fell hard, tasting metal, emotions numb. It felt like she had been flying for days. Maybe she had. She had killed many more Harbs, then limped alongside the rest of her squad until the beautiful Tuval came into view. She had never felt so exhausted, yet filled with elation, the Thrill. It reminded her of the one time she had tried Azanta, only a hundred times more potent. Killing was a drug. She understood how easily she could become addicted.

Ephany wheeled her to the Med Bay on a well-worn gurney. No one looked twice at them as they passed out of the bay and into the belly of the ship. Pilots were always being transported from combat, it seemed. Serral closed her eyes, but the day's flight replayed in her mind, explosions, dogfights, the sight of the enemy in the distance. A Medic put her arm in a bot. The mechanism shot her with numbing meds, then started cleaning and stitching her wound.

"Rookie choices, pilot. The cold saved your life," the Medic said, his face greasy-looking, scrubs splattered with dark spots. His name tag read *Somi.*

"What does that mean?" she asked.

He tapped on his portal. "The bullet entered near an artery. The hole in your suit meant your blood froze, closing the wound. If you'd been flying lower, or taken longer to leave atmosphere, you'd have bled to death."

Serral looked back at the medic, stunned.

Somi snapped the portal closed. "Understand this, kid. You're a resource, not to be squandered. Next time you get shot, you come back in. If your SL doesn't have time to authorize it, just know that the Military would rather you break formation than die for no good reason. Got it?"

Serral pulled her arm out of the bot and took note of the puffy line running from shoulder to elbow. She stretched and wiggled her fingers. "When can I go back to work?"

"Be careful," he shook his head.

But Serral was already gone.

# 22

C hapter Twenty-Two

"Okay, good luck charm," Sly commed while they waited in their tubes. "This mission is for recon as much as hunting, got it? Stay focused."

The five flew in precise, geometric formation straight toward Sapphire's surface. Three things happened at once: the Arrows pierced the hot white lava between space and exosphere, Serral's hearing became scrambled, and rockets exploded like orange puffballs all around her plane. Voices yelled incomprehensibly in her ears, but at a distance, like screeching insects. She had no idea what they were saying, or who they were talking to, or where exactly they were.

Her Arrow whipped through atmosphere and flame. Serral maneuvered, searching for her squad, unsure of her next tactics. She checked for wounds; not shot. Silver ships spouted orange flames, obscuring her view. Were they Harb or Imset munitions? The shine of swarming Tekkus drew her attention, Halos with their wheels aglow, Arrows raging around like bees. Tiny explosions, little orange splatters of flame. Where was her squad? She gunned it. Everywhere were ships, explosions, and fire. An Arrow came screaming past, firing rockets. She narrowly avoided being hit.

Her com sounded like tearing metal, incomprehensible. Where was Sly? She couldn't hear anything but blood in her ears and the click of her chattering teeth. She noticed a familiar pressure and understood that it had been trickling through her head like an underground stream, unseen and rushing, since she'd broken atmosphere. Thoughts and feelings, not her own.

Familiar black dots gathered around the corners of her eyes. The battle stretched out over the blue planet; silver objects, orange flames, black smoke trails. She tried comming again. Either she had lost her hearing, or her com was out. In desperation, Serral closed her eyes and asked Ysk for guidance, but heard the voice of another reply.

*Thanton, your gentle murder is too great an honor.*

The words came through her mind like an electric shock. Serral heard her own scream.

*Oh, do not be afraid, divine soldier. We are coming to you to collect our sweet destiny.*

Behind her, four Tekkus appeared on the horizon.

She forced herself to stop screaming. She plunged down, away from the battle, leading the Tekku squadron to a high, complicated pile of cumulus to the north.

*A perfect place to be given immortal life, oh daughter of Ysk.*

"Stop it!" she screamed. "Get out of my head!"

A low buzzing was their only answer.

Serral slowed at the edge of the cloud bank. Maybe it would buy her time. White, all white, all around. The enveloping mist felt heightened, like the moment before a lightning strike. Serral felt the Harbs enter the clouds. She spun her Arrow to face them.

*Thank you, good lady. We will tell the souls of Amperia of your noble actions!*

"Shut it!" Serral shot four rockets. Flames lit the mist around her.

But something felt wrong. She throbbed with goodness and giddy joy. And also, overwhelming rage.

The clouds parted. Serral retched. In the eye of stillness floated a majestic Harb battleship, a silver permutahedron that Duglak had once called a Walnut. From it, voices bubbled in quiet cacophony. Serral told herself to breathe, commanding her body to cease its shaking. She willed herself to stop hearing the boil of souls across the clouds, and a membrane she didn't know she commanded rose up and flapped as taut as a sail in high wind.

Silence.

Breathing evenly again, Serral circled back around.

What should she do?

A tug came through her consciousness. She let the membrane slip slightly.

*What?*

The answer was overwhelming. The need. The desire. A ship full of Harbs, like the eight she had just killed, all asking for her favor. Begging her to bestow her deadly blessings upon them.

*No!*

Serral shut out the babble and sent her Arrow skyward. She had to do her job, had to find her squad, be the pinkie finger. Get away from this nightmare hallucination of jabbering Harbs. She streaked across the sky, straight toward the front, and tried her com again.

"Where in the seven hells of the Dantons have you been, Spooky?" Liphal sounded relieved. "We were sure you'd gone down."

"No, I'm good. I just lost my com for a while. Got four Tekkus, though."

"Nice." Liphal gave her coordinates.

Four more Tekkus appeared on the horizon, coming fast. Like they knew where she was.

"Spook, you got company," Manster commed. "We got ammo left. Sit tight."

Would the Harbs blast through the squad to get to her? Her gut told her they would. "No." Serral commed back, "Not enough time."

Four explosions. More Thrill. Serral joined Manster on his right, took her place in formation.

"We're heading back in, Pinkie Finger. Sly's orders."

"Roger that," she said. She didn't add that it wasn't safe for her to be aboard the Tuval. That it wasn't safe for her to be with other Imset. The Harbs knew where she was and wanted her to come kill them.

"Crisgen, you will follow orders." Sly's voice was gruff.

"Copy that, Squadron Leader. I'm right here," she answered. But as the Arrows entered their tubes, she realized that a part of her was still on the battlefield. And always would be.

Ephany helped Serral out of her Arrow again, and Serral realized that she'd been hit. Her ship had a shrapnel hole straight through the starboard side. Her left foot was white and covered in ice.

"Uh oh."

Ephany shook her head. "You're a thrillist, Ser. And it's going to get you killed."

Serral hobbled to a waiting gurney.

**23**

—·—

C hapter Twenty-Three

"Idiot kid," Somi scowled. "Next time you'll lose your toes."

Serral ignored the Medic. He'd been fussing with her for two hours while the Thrill slowly wore off and her frostbite healed. She wanted dinner and her bunk. But Fithu and Sly were waiting for her outside to debrief. She would have to forgo rest and try to ignore the painful tingling in her foot.

Somi unhooked the bots. "Like I told you before, when you get shot, come in. No one will think worse of you for it."

She nodded. "I told you, if I notice I will."

"Notice. Or you'll get bionic real quick."

"Thanks, Somi," she said and pulled on her booties. "You're a miracle worker."

"Wish we'd stop needing so damn many miracles."

Fithu and Sly were huddled over a liquid portal. Sly's biceps were prominent under rolled-up sleeves, his posture casual, but Fithu looked serious.

"Sit, Crigsen." Fithu motioned toward a tray of sandwiches on offer.

Serral gratefully tore into brown bread with cheese-like filling. She drank half a cup of hydration before realizing the two men were staring at her intently. "Sorry," she said.

Fithu rotated his portal so it could be seen by all three of them and cued up a strippy. "This is your Arrowcam, Brook," he said.

On the portal, the first moments the squad reached the front came into view. Manster on her left, large chunks of debris separating them. Then explosions lit the feed. Serral's audio came through. She tried to reach the squad. They responded, all of them, though she didn't appear to hear. The Arrow's rockets passed, and the camera shook in a way she didn't remember. It must have been when she was hit.

Fithu indicated a reading in the footer. "Your pressure is danger-ously low here. The air temp is outside normal limits."

"You got dinged by shrapnel. It happens," Sly broke in.

Fithu said in his rich, reassuring voice: "A more compliant pilot would have returned to ship at this point."

She nodded. "I just didn't notice. I was distracted."

"I'll bet," Sly said.

Fithu continued, "Here is where things get a bit baffling."

The strippy continued: Serral tried to com again, and again her squad replied, Manster even yelled at her to stop screwing around.

"You couldn't hear us, apparently," Sly said.

A root of worry sprouted in her chest. The rest of the strippy continued to show the flight as she remembered it. Her time in the clouds, her slow arc around the large silver Walnut.

Fithu stopped the feed.

"Can you explain any of this?" he said, his voice tinged with awe. "You'd just bumped into a battleship. And kept going. I'll tell you honestly, Brook. That doesn't happen. You should have been blown right out of the sky."

"Before you ever even saw the thing," Sly said.

"I was running scared. I guess I thought I'd hide in the clouds and try to get my com back. I didn't know where my squad was." She took a deep breath. "And that this big ship appeared."

Sly cleared his throat. "And you didn't die. Which is... very strange." Sly met her eyes, his expression hardening.

Fithu waved his hand to silence Sly. "But a Tekku squad came after you immediately."

She nodded. "Right. And I killed them."

"Yes, Pilot Crigsen. You killed them."

"Yup, you did." Sly rubbed his head.

The replay continued. It showed Serral's climb back to the front line. Her audio kicked back in and recorded the moment she volunteered to kill the second set of Tekkus. Time seemed compressed. Her words and the four explosions simultaneous, as if she'd commed her intentions as an afterthought.

"Wow," Serral whispered. "I don't remember it happening so fast."

"No?" Fithu stopped the strippy and typed onto a pad. "How do you remember it?"

"I guess more slowly. More naturally."

"Naturally? Are you kidding me?" Sly shouted. "There's nothing natural here. Eight rockets, eight ship-killer hits," he glared. "Who are you?"

Serral jerked. *They knew.* They knew that she had some mysterious visibility to the Harbs, that they tracked her wherever she went. No matter what she said now, she couldn't possibly explain away this evidence. Unless.

"Respectfully," she said. "Calm down." She summoned her memories of Brume, how he would handle interrogations after they'd overplayed the rules, after the many times he was accused of wrongdoing.

"I'm not sure what you want me to say, but it does sound like you're accusing me of something."

Fithu turned to Sly. "Not another word."

Sly glared at her.

She channeled her brother. "So, is it unusual to kill eight Tekkus on a sortie?"

Sly shook his head, muttering.

Fithu gave her a kind look. "Yes, Brook. It's never been done by a rookie, particularly without any misfires or wasted ordnance. Even our most seasoned pilots haven't had days like yours. At the very least, they'd need to come in and reload."

"I see," she said. "So, what does it all mean? My actions, that is."

Fithu sighed. "I have no idea."

Sly shivered theatrically. "It means you are Spooky. As hell."

"Told you I'd be honest," she said through a mouthful of food. "I was trying to kill Harbs."

Sly's mouth twitched.

Fithu typed. "Air Marsiant Slook will be here in less than a week to do her own investigation."

"Investigation?" A feeling of panic and shame rose in her chest. She would have to come up with a better response, or they would know she had a connection to the enemy. That she was, despite her killing, a traitor to the cause. A breaker of the First Imperative. She kept her face impassive, grateful for the energy the Thrill offered.

The two men looked startled.

"No wonder we're losing the war. We're not going to get very far if every time a pilot has a good day it warrants an investigation."

Sly laughed. Fithu pointed to Serral and then to the door. "Go."

She saluted crisply. But once she returned to the bay, she felt herself covered in cold sweat.

*They knew.*

Ephany, red-faced and wild-eyed, met Serral near the bay door. "You are amazing," she said.

Serral let the older girl put her arm around her shoulder. "Holy smokes. At least someone thinks so. They act like I did something wrong."

"I got some Chloran bark beer. It'll help with the Thrill ache."

Serral wanted to sleep, but she followed Ephany to the storage bay. "The Thrill ache?"

"How you feel when you come down."

"Ah." Serral took a seat on the cushioned pallet and picked up a metal cup. She'd been too stressed to notice that the Thrill was wearing off. Her foot tingled.

"Okay." Ephany settled in next to her. "I have a confession to make."

"This isn't really from Chlore?" Serral looked into her cup.

"It is. I am." The older girl wiped a tear from her eye. "But also, I'm a spy."

"A spy?" Serral smiled, still channeling her wicked brother. "Who for? Because I got news for you, Inoa can't cinch me now."

Ephany laugh-cried. "I thought you'd be mad. No. When you came on board," her voice dropped to a whisper, "Slook took me aside."

Serral forced another laugh, convincingly, she thought. "Ysk's army, that woman is obsessed with me."

"And she said she couldn't say why."

"But she had reason to believe that I was some kind of secret weapon, blah blah blah."

"She said I ought to keep an eye on you and then report back to her."

Serral toasted her friend with the metal cup. "And she brought you bark beer."

Ephany nodded. "So, there's some kind of connection between how you fly and her obsession?"

"Obsession? Maybe." Serral paused. "Okay, if I tell you something, can you keep it under your hat?"

"I just told you, I'm a spy."

"No, don't worry. This isn't anything the Military cares about. It's about Chlore."

"Oh. Okay, lay it on me."

Serral heard Whit's advice in her head, *survive your tour*. It swirled sourly. But she kept talking. "So, my brother and I flew a lot on Chlore. Much, much more than my record shows."

"Really?" Ephany said quietly. "Why did they cover it up?"

Serral hesitated again. "Because it would implicate the adult staff. They wanted me to be a killing machine. That's why they sent me off early. Or so Inoa said."

"The new Ysken?"

"Yes. She used some kind of magic on me. She was convinced that I was an anointed something-or-other. I don't know. Anyway, they knew I was building planes. They knew I was flying around the planet, practicing, shooting at rocks and stuff."

Ephany gasped. "She *marked* you?"

Serral shrugged. "Is that what it's called?"

"So, they trained you before you even came of age?"

"I still haven't come of age, silly."

"Oh, Spooky. This is so ugly."

"You think? I mean, they're as desperate as everyone else to get this war over."

"I doubt that." She shifted onto her elbow. "The cities are openly crafting the wording for our surrender."

Cold shimmered through Serral. Was it anger? Fear? She continued her deception and said, "I need to go out again tomorrow."

Ephany sat up. "Are you allowed?"

Serral smiled. "Oh yeah. Fithu specifically said."

"Okay then." Ephany smiled. "I'll make sure your Arrow is all ammo-ed up. But seriously, try not to draw so much attention to yourself."

"Of course," Serral replied. "I just want to do my job."

That night Serral dreamed of Thantons, a man and a woman. The woman held Serral like a baby and whispered familiar words to her: *destiny,* and *her enemy who was not her enemy.* Music vibrated, a heartbeat both as enormous and mysterious as the universe and as tiny and ordinary as human cells. The woman was named Zaphia. The man, stern and watching, was Woseth. Serral knew he was upset, but not with her. His sorrowful unease bothered her, a rip in the order of things. She understood that the world was not right, and that she was expected to help fix it.

She woke to Manster shaking her shoulder. "They're gunning for you."

Serral wiped her eyes, still half in dreams. "Don't worry. If anything out of the ordinary happens again during a battle, I'll just scurry home to the Tuval, okay?"

"You're a talented pilot, Serral. But if you step out of line again, they'll have to do an investigation. Which means you'll have to spend some time in the brig. No airtime, kid. No more Thrill. Can't imagine you'd like that much. And we'd have to replace you, which none of us want."

Serral considered the danger of being locked in the depths of the Tuval, unable to fight or evade the Harbs. What would the creeping, electric voices do then? How would they beg for their *sweet freedom*? If something happened to the Tuval, the war would be over. And they'd all be dead. Brume and Rafe would be stuck in the cities forever. And it would be her fault.

"Thanks, Manster. I appreciate the warning. But nothing's going to happen."

"Good." Manster's expression pinched tightly. "Who are you, really?"

"Nobody. Seriously. There's nothing special about me."

He shook his head. "Maybe you don't understand how bizarre yesterday was. But everyone else does."

"I thought this planet was important! And we were supposed to win it, and all that."

"Sure. But the strategy is simply to stay put and keep at it, wear the bastards down. No one pilot is going to do that all by themselves."

She gave him her brightest smile. "Got it. Thanks."

He seemed satisfied. "Watch out for yourself, Pinkie. There's something going on that none of us understand. And it can't be good."

The next day Serral was in her Arrow before the others were done with breakfast. No one spoke to her, but no one stopped her, either. She watched the lights of the bay through her helmet, thinking they had never looked so bright and perfect and Imettan. She didn't cry. She wanted to. She didn't know when she had ever felt so alone. But then she remembered. The night alone outside, when a Harb ship was advancing toward her, like a preordained destiny, too powerful to run from. Too scary to do more than stare down.  She finished her checks.

Ephany smiled. "This com will not fail you."

"Thanks." Serral triple checked her harness. The others were still getting ready. "You think you'll ever get back to Chlore?"

The older girl checked Serral's helmet seals and kept her eyes on her work. "Don't get sappy," she said.

The day was quiet with only a few skirmishes, two lonely Halos hustling off far below, seemingly uninterested. Manster commed, "Remember, if anyone sees that battleship, they're to call in the coordinates and scram out as fast as possible. No heroes."

Serral watched the Tuval fade into blue. The fighters settled into a classic Air Guard orbit, their five-Arrow formation in synch. They orbited once, twice, and saw only clouds, sky, and planet below.

Serral felt the attack before it came. The voices called to her, grabbed her attention. She tried hard to keep the door to her mind closed. Though she was expecting it, still tears came. A lump in her throat, Serral turned off her com, and left position, gunning her Arrow so fast it would be long moments before Manster could react.

The Tekku squadron was still low in the sky, the first four sets of saucers well ahead of the second. Then they emerged from high, white clouds in neat, flashing rows. Serral waited until she was almost on them to release her rockets. She repeated the process twice and then swung around the cloud bank. She knew where the battleship was hiding.

A green continent came into view. She descended below the cloud cover and noticed a notch set in a recess over a bay. In it, a tiny gray-white grid studded with whitish rectangles that sat below two glinting pieces of blue-green glass and a couple of paler lines that stretched out into the landscape. Settlement. The thing the battleship was protecting.

She headed toward it, four Tekkus tracking behind her. She pretended to fall toward the grid. They followed. Her squad dropped below the cloud cover but still far in the distance. She had to force the battleship up and clear of the clouds so the squadron would see it and turn around.

She released the fury of four bombs.

Someone whispered to her. She was getting close. Thrill surged inside her, sparkling bright, and was mixed with a mysterious compulsion to go toward the ground. She heard the whispers of Thantons. A powerful force was in motion and her job was to surrender to it. She let her Arrow spin wildly. She retched, pulling back into straight flight. She was over a jungle now, a snaking green river. There were white mountains in the distance. She was alone.

Serral rocketed back around toward the settlement. Two objects gleamed glassy below her on a green hill. Her window went white, then blue, then white, and then she saw it, moving horizontally over the bay.

Where were the squadrons of Tekkus that ought to come meet her? She let in the whispers about *sweet release*, and *the Ouserium*, and *duty*. Serral retched again. Her head was full of argument, of nonsensical babble. *Come to us, Thanton*, electric songs, hundreds of voices.

She swung her plane around again. Far away, shimmered a glimmer of wings. Arrows. Her squad. That wasn't right.

*It doesn't matter*, she thought. *All is as it should be.*

She saw her shadow flash on the surface of a cloud. So good, her ship, so light and fast. She had no regrets. She whispered a last goodbye to the sweetness of life. Memories of Chlore and her brother, of Rafe, of Whit and of her blue needle tree flashed through her mind.

The Arrow's wings screamed through the air, too fast, her instruments failing, their readings nonsense. The ship groaned ominously. Serral unloaded her ordinance, rat-a-tat-tat-tat-tat-tat-tat-tat-tat-tat-tat. Her tail buckled with the change in weight, and momentarily skidded sideways through the sky, spinning, losing control. Falling.

The Thrill filled her, too fast, making her empty stomach jump. She righted herself, the sea only meters below, the battleship slipping down toward it, wounded but alive. Voices screamed in her ear, afraid and thankful, a crowd cheering.

*Kill us, sweet Thanton. We have waited so long for you!*

And then a deep, electric gong surged against the chirping chorus, saying *It is not for you to choose to die. You do not have the right.*

The right? There was no time to understand. Serral pushed her Arrow to the limit, steering it in a loop so steep her eyelids ached and her lips trembled. The monstrous permutahedron was a silvery heart that must not keep beating. She had to kill it, had to make her final act wipe away her shame, making the world right again. She would answer the voices with her own scream of rage.

Serral dove the Arrow into the ship, into darkness and pain. A terrible sound of twisting metal fought a Thrill so high and tall, it threatened to engulf her. She began to drown in flames. But Serral flew on, into a sparkling, cool sea, where the flames went out, and her worries faded into the lapping of waves.

# 24

Chapter Twenty-Four

A man of fifty, lean and white-whiskered, wiped his hands on a rag. "Hallenander, don't make me regret contacting you. I appreciate the food, but this is dangerous."

"How close are the Wilter to finding you?" Hallenander placed a wicker hamper on a worktable in the large, immaculate hangar and ignored Geddon's words. "Do you need more weapons?"

"Any excess they will find and steal. Best keep them here."

"Will they not eventually raid this place?"

"The Wilter are genuinely convinced that this quadrant is haunted. Rest easy." He bit into a sandwich.

"If I were capable of resting easy, we would not be here."

"No, I suppose not," Geddon said. "This is delicious. How goes your negotiation?"

Hallenander explained his bargain with Uncle Mimellio. Flying lessons in return for the agreement to take a concubine.

"So, you finally gave in?"

"I agreed to choose a girl but on my own arbitrary whim. My choice cannot be questioned by the Volettu."

"Ah," Geddon said. "And how long do you think you will be allowed to pretend to be selecting such a friend?"

"Long enough to learn to fly. I will make sure of that."

"What does the Syxarit say?"

Hal chewed on a toothpick. "I will find out soon. We are to speak later today. But Master Geddon, if you are forced into hiding places, can you trust your former crew to protect you?"

"Of course." He ate another bite of his sandwich. "Go on now. Do not be late to speak to your father."

Hallenander left the hangar and drove his shining Bisbee through an elaborate, swirling mosaic of broken planes and pieces of components until he reached the end of the airfield, where he gunned his carriage onto the road back to the palace.

"You are the light to my day, my son," his Sevenni Highness Syxarit Taurellio Chi'irea of the Eight Volterran Worlds said, smiling.

"And you are the day," Hallenander replied into the liquid portal. The pale sun of Phrygia poured through linen curtains that blew open and closed, intermittently revealing the wheaten fields of his father's estate.

"Volterran men do not fly space craft," he said, the lines of his chiseled face deepening. "We do not drive Bisbees or plow the field."

"I'm not asking to plow the field or sweep the floor. Though I must say, Bisbee driving is not to be eschewed until you've tried it." He lowered his voice. "May I speak freely?"

"One moment," Taurellio said to Hallenander. And then, to someone beyond view he said, "Come here, child."

"I'm no child." An ugly, bright-eyed girl of twenty appeared in the portal. "Hello, cousin."

"Bellex!" Hallenander said. "Good. You are the only one I would feel comfortable hearing the paranoid rant I am about to go on."

"Hoorah. It's been at least a week since we heard one of those," she said, looking up at Taurellio. "May I?"

"Of course," the King said, "Far be it for me to waste time the two of you could use to gossip and scheme."

"There is no time left, apparently. As you are well aware, Hal, the Eloxiture and the Jalophians now insist it will take years to render their decision. Especially the Eloxiture, with their nobility and pride, cannot begin to imagine a world without their perfect blood," Bellex said. "Those shortsighted beasts."

Taurellio nodded. "Should they take long enough that a majority in favor of accepting Hallenander as Heir is lost, we will never be able to create legal standing. And you know how much our Helpers the Harbingers rely on the legality of everything."

Hallenander rubbed his head. "What will happen?"

He didn't mind the idea of staying on his lonely planet forever. But if he became illegal, the Harbingers would be forced to restore legal order. Unless he found a loophole. The easiest thing was to become Heir. But more than ever, he needed to be able to fly away if they did not. Where to, he still needed to research. But there were many green planets. And his kind were not specifically forbidden to live on them, like the poor misbegotten Imset.

"The older ones are dying off." Bellex smiled wickedly. "The helpers tend empty halls, and the birds fly free in the orchards. Sort of romantic."

"Now you are being morose," Taurellio said.

Hallenander rubbed his circlet absently. "I may outlive this government's legitimacy, and if that happens, I cannot swoop in after everyone is gone."

"Obviously I have considered this." Taurellio held up a hand. "Do not plague me with the consequences of my gambit. You know my only choices were to fail in my duty or to place my faith in you."

Bellex said, "Well and rightly done, uncle."

"Bellex," Hallenander said. "If this topic hurts you, we can speak of it later."

"Oh, don't be stupid. If I could bear children, you would not inherit the throne, I would not have you as a friend, and my life would be unbearable. Do not fret. It is not your fault I was made this way."

Taurellio kissed her head crest.

"I was made this way," Bellex continued. "But you are healthy and hale, oh my noble Minsyx, and when you arrive on the throne..."

"If I arrive," Hallenander said, "I shall endeavor not to fly spaceships or plow the fields. But if the government cannot bring itself to shift the throne to such an inferior specimen as myself..." He stopped before using the word Hybrid, or its equivalent, Rakki.

"This is known to me," Taurellio said peevishly. "And was even before you were conceived, Hallenander."

He decided not to hold back. "Yes, but back then you believed the legal ramifications of my making to be simple. Either your Rakki son would be accepted as full Heir, or he would not. And the thought of an Eloxiture so stubborn and unyielding..."

"Just say it—prejudiced and cynical," Bellex said.

"A government inclined to allow its members to die, because it did not have the majority of votes needed for a legal transfer of power..." Hal began.

"Enough." Taurellio waved absently. "You are afraid of the Harbingers and what will happen by their hand if we all disappear before you are given the keys to the Empire."

"Ought not I to be?" Hal said. "Here on Evincio the sky lights up with fighting, and the Imset struggle to gain a foothold while the Xaff continuously cut them down."

"I wish I could come see!" Bellex looked amused.

Hallenander said, "No one who sees it can remain ignorant of the real power our servants wield. To enforce the law. Whatever the law is deemed to be. If I am Heir, they continue to harass the Imset. If I am denied, what project will they move onto?"

Taurellio gazed wordlessly into Hallenander's eyes. Then he gave a tiny, nearly imperceptible nod.

"My mistake was to task you with study of the law." The older man stroked his braided beard, smiling to show he meant no harm. "Our servants put duty above all things. If it became their duty to place us side by side with the Imset, then they would do it."

"What?" Bellex acted bemused. "How could they?"

Taurellio cleared his throat. "There are decisions to be made in the halls of Alliance Rule which could render us traitors. But let us move before it comes to that. With the end of the Imset war, which is imminent, we find our servants with a surfeit of ways to prove their worth to Ysk, their god. Time to resolve our legal matters."

"We are vulnerable. I am glad you said it, father," Hal sighed.

"Us, at the mercy of the Harbingers? You? The greatest Syxarit who ever lived? You who have sacrificed all for the sake of his people?" The young woman caught herself. "I'm sorry, Hallenander. I didn't mean to be rude regarding your birth. Forgive me."

"Of course not," Hal said. "You are only saying what everyone knows, that the Volterrans would prefer a full blood ruler."

"But you make a valid point, Bellex," Taurellio said. "If a solution can be found to save us if the worst case happens, it might benefit us all."

Bellex gasped.

"Thank you, Father," Hal said. "I will tell the Volettu."

Taurellio looked amused. "Your uncle told me of your capitulation."

"What?" Bellex demanded. "Hal, what did you promise?"

"Nothing of lasting import," Hallenander said, breaking into a broad grin. "Now I must find a flight instructor."

"Not your tutor?" Bellex asked. "Was he not a great starship commander?

"Once, but no more. The Harbingers took that part of his memory. But I will find someone. I hear rumors of wild Imset in the jungle. They are shot down every day."

"In the meantime, put your entourage at ease," Taurellio said. "Make them think you are one of them."

"Of course."

"My boy, if the Volterran people could see your cleverness and cunning, they would be desperate to have you." Taurellio's eyes disappeared into smiling folds.

"Thank you," Hallenander said. "Cousin, I will tell your father of your sweetness and loyalty."

Bellex laughed. "Pah, he'll only ask why you are bothering to speak to me when you could be giving your report to your father."

"Tell my brother Mimellio that his child is well loved here. He is liable to ask for her back, and I cannot part with her," Taurellio said.

The portal went blank.

Idly, Hallenander commanded the liquid to show his favorite static camera, the one he sometimes watched for hours. It came online and showed the familiar large, vaulted room filled with long, carved benches that encircled a parquet marble floor. Volterran men and a limited number of women gathered in clusters of two or three, moving together in a five-minute choreography that ended with the entirety of the people seated, ready for the day's business.

A man named Grand Xupior Diall Padmillian rose to the dais. He was joined by a woman, Magistrate of Vincture Chyn Sesthia. Hallenander bit his thumbnail, he knew them both well. The branches of assembly, the Eloxiture and the House of Jalophians, were called to order. *Both branches*; such a meeting was assembled only in times of crisis.

The liquid went dark.

Hallenander tried to make it come back up, but his servants didn't come when called. They were behind the sudden failure of signal. They didn't want him to know what was being said about him in the halls of Volterra.

**25**

— · —

C hapter Twenty-Five

Hallenander headed out to check on the caulking of his yacht and told Uncle Mimellio as much. Mimellio replied, "Your father indulges you." He straightened the shoulder mantle over his white, gauze toga. "After you have satisfied yourself that your toy is in good order, you are expected at the Xalavria. Wear your best Imset finery, as you seem to enjoy looking like a savage dandy, as if your situation were not precarious enough. And don't be late. Tender feelings will be trampled if you appear indifferent. Do I make myself clear?"

Hallenander nearly laughed aloud at the irony of his uncle warning him about the *tender feelings* of caged slaves. He descended the palace ramparts and continued through steep white villas and green gardens until he arrived at the village with its white Yskeon and fountained square. Imset people bowed respectfully as he passed. He had long ago asked them not to make a fuss; he preferred to lose himself in the illusion of being an ordinary man in a regular settlement on Imseth.

The village gave an illusion of idyllic beauty and quiet with its hanging gardens and neat stone fences. Hallenander believed that the only people who could teach him to fly were members of the Wilter who would kill him and themselves rather than help him, who they would doubtless believe an enemy. The planetary girl he had seen in her oculus had looked at him as if she wanted to kill him with her bare hands. She wouldn't know the difference between him and one of his father's warriors. Doubtless the Wilter would hate him even more than she. But there had to be a way. He took out his key and was about to slip it into Geddon's old door, when he noticed a dramatic shift in air pressure. The sky darkened. Hal felt a crackle of electricity and looked to the sky for an answer.

Out over the sea, a majestic silver ship hovered too near the sea wall. A single Arrow circled impossibly fast, shooting rocket after rocket into the ship's side. He had never seen such a display of nimble flight, now fast, then slow, under and over, a pilot either crazy or supremely gifted or both. Imset villagers came out, staring open mouthed at the Arrow that screamed over their heads. They watched it circle back, shooting, its rockets disappearing into the ship's silver skin. Explosions and shock waves echoed through the valley.

The battleship lurched. The attacker raced into a high arcing loop and then returned with a peal of speed. Imset people moved up the hill, some running, others stunned stationary, unable to take their eyes off the fight. Hal wound through them to the strand.

The Arrow was moving fast, a bird hunting fish, intending to dive. Hallenander's heart jumped at the pilot's foolish bravery. Here it came again, this time in a nearly vertical angle, faster and faster.

*No, no.* He couldn't let it happen.

Voices gasped in horror as the silver cross plunged into the silver orb, its deafening roar abruptly silenced. The battleship rocked with explosions. It listed, orange flames shot out and pushed the Arrow away and into the water. Steam hissed, the water roiled in anger, and the Arrow disappeared. The large battleship shuddered, then fell onto the beach, rolled into the water and sent thick pillars of vapor skyward.

Xaff on war Bisbees streaked down from the palace.

The Arrow floated helplessly in the chop, flaming but intact in only a meter or two of water. Hallenander plunged into the bay and staggered over rocks to the silver plane. The water was hot on his legs. The escape latch seared his hand, but he managed to release it. The burned and blackened pilot, half submerged and unmoving, didn't respond to his command to eject. Hallenander felt for the lever and braced for release. The harness came free from the fuselage, and water poured in, swamping the craft, and carrying it under the waves. He held the pilot's light body under one arm and used the other to staunch flames on their flight suit. Hal shouldered the pilot and ran to where four Xaff patrols had gathered on the strand, guns pointed. He motioned for them to accept the broken pilot into a jump seat.

"Is he alive?" Hallenander shouted.

The Xaff gathered around, assessing, and then nodded. There was life left in the body. A *she*, not a *he*, though he didn't know how the Xaff were so sure.

"Have this pilot healed immediately. Tell the medics to use all their skill, do you understand me?"

They nodded again.

"And," he put his hand on the nearest soldier's arm, meeting its black eyes, "No memory manipulation. To disobey me in this would be a great breach of duty."

The four soldiers snapped a salute and with haste glided their land craft up toward the palace complex.

Hal stood dripping onto cobblestones, his hands hurting, his nose full of the smell of charred flesh. The villagers stood numbly on the strand. Planes no longer disrupted the silence. The four Arrows had evaporated from the horizon which now faded into grays behind the darkening islands. Nightfall was near. The only battle evidence was knots of muttering Imset, their eyes streaming with tears. They stared at him in passing, and he knew they were waking to a new reality of war and the existence of other Imset outside their curated village.

Hal hurried past, up the hill, taking the stairs by twos. He had just enough time to have his wounds ministered to before doing his uncle's bidding and getting himself to the Xalavria .

The Helpers in the Medotel immersed his hands and arms in the glittering gel they used to repair wounds. It was cool, immediately soothing the pain of his burns.

"Is the pilot being seen to properly?"

Their head domes roiled. "Your Sevenni Highness, she is receiving the best of care."

There were sounds of feet shuffling in another room down the hall, but as always, the Helpers spoke in their silent way, so the only other noise was of sucking and ripping.

"She? The pilot is female?"

He had forgotten that the Imset allowed women to fight. They were rumored to be fierce warriors, though like so much mythology about his peoples' cousins, the Imset, Hallenander didn't know what was true and what had been invented by the Harbingers. The image of the girl on his planetary visit came to his mind. Certainly, she had been brave, like this pilot. Fearless to the point of suicide.

"Please remain still, Sire,"So this pilot is a sacred warrior with nerves of steel."

He allowed himself a small smile. There could be no one alive more suited to teach him what he needed to learn.

If the pilot lived.As he mounted the steep road to the palace, possibility bloomed in his mind. Just when he needed both a flight instructor and an Imset Companion, one had quite literally landed at his feet. The skies were clear now. It was as if this miracle had never happened.

**26**

— • —

Chapter Twenty-Six

She plunged through darkness, disembodied. She flew into silver, a place starlit and exuding infinite love. The plunge repeated, over and over, falling and catching and holding her carefully, then breaking free and soaring, losing the sky, returning to the warmth and safety of the unnamable. A smell like the Thanton woman from her dream, like snow, like potato blossoms, like rain in a lily pad, washed over her. The woman hovered on the other side of a curtain moving invisibly in black wind. The sun was down. But it would return. Serral understood this. The woman, serene, beautiful, and awe inspiring, had a name. *Zaphia.*

Serral slid into the feeling of hands on her arms and feet on her legs and the coo of voices lulling her to sleep.

Rain pelted her with pebbles. She was churned in a vat of thorns. But the intensity eased, then slaked, and she became aware of her skin touching warmth. She felt the sweetness of a body, of clenching and unclenching. She heard a sucking noise, like feet moving through mud, and realized with bleary amusement she was causing it. She breathed but tasted nothing. She bade her eyes to open, but they refused. Then the voices became sharper saying words like *do not move, Thanton*, and *mistress you must rest.*

Her state was unfamiliar but did not frighten her. She dreamt of diving into nothing, into the curtain of silver with the woman on the other side, galaxies above her head, a crown of stars. Serral was a dolphin, and this was the ocean, black and warm, full of the voices. Serral understood that the people she heard were Harbs. Fear crept into her body, slowly, painfully, but with calm familiarity.

She let the darkness take her. Thantons flew, their iridescent wings carrying her safely, over land, windy oceans, clouds, and the glint of ships passed, and bombs exploded. Then she felt the warmth of arms around her, heard the beat of hearts and wings as one, life and flight one condition now, as effortless as breathing.

Serral saw the Universe as if from the heavenly fields of Astulia, from the highest height, with the perspective of ages; she saw the failed salvation of the winged spirits, their sorrow, their impossible attempts to reach pilots in Arrows or Halos, all people inside them similarly deaf to the comfort they offered. Songs, hauntingly beautiful, sung in vain. People thinking, people comming to one another, pilots and soldiers, servants and then children on land, running to an oculus, bombs exploding. A colony, not Chlore, just another colony enduring the war.

Serral saw children die, their souls rising like smoke into the arms of her friends, the Thantons, Zaphia and Woseth. Then the songs rose in chorus, the tears turned to stars, and she understood how tenderly the Thantons cared for the souls they were meant to watch over. She felt their tears on her face, and their anguish, their frustration.

And she asked the Thantons, quietly but with force, *where is Ysk, in all this? If you are here to make Ousians of these children, where is your Mistress?*

And suddenly, Serral was awake. She gasped a breath of fresh air. She opened her eyes to a white room, a bed, curtains blowing, and red blossoms in a vase. Her feet lay far below her head, under a white blanket. Her hands moved to uncover herself. Two feet, two hands, a torso, hips and belly, a body, complete. She looked at her fingers, her wrists, her fingernails. These were not hers, not covered in nicks and scars or a bullet wound, no frostbite ruination. No evidence of her life before.

She sat up, knowing before she looked what she would see; four Harbs in Medic scrubs, in blue paper masks, staring at her with shining black eyes, their head domes puffing with satisfaction. They bowed to her.

*Awake, awake, at last! And your body, is it to your standards, dear Thanton?*

Serral screamed, a harsh, guttural rasp, scraping her throat. *Where am I?* And then she realized with a combination of horror and familiarity that she had been riding her enemies' wave of common thought for days, weeks. Augering with the telepathic minds of the Harbingers all around her felt normal. Her heart sank. She put her head in her hands. What was worse, her resolute treason, augering with enemy minds, or being their captive? She screamed again, this time ending with a sob. She opened her eyes and gathered herself. The window was open. What was on the other side? She saw only blue sky. The four Harbs kept their attention on her, holding out their slender gray hands in a gesture meant to soothe.

She was dead. Dead. Why was she there, with a whole, painless body, surrounded by her enemies? A memory came to her, of hiding in places during all the many Harb raids on Chlore, how the kids were trained to slow their breathing. Put their big emotions away. Be warriors. Be calm. Be still. Wait for the sounding of all clear.

*Be comforted, dear one. You are safe here. You are under His protection and ours.*

She messaged them back, *Who is He and why am I under His protection? Where is this place? What will you do to me?*

She must have shouted into the river of voices, because the answer came as a cacophony of notions, most reassuring, others electric and dark, swirling together into a jarring stew. She shut them down and forced herself to breathe evenly until her mind cleared. The Harbs dropped their hands. She felt them gnawing at her mind, trying to get her to open up, to get her to listen.

She put one foot onto the cool, stone floor. Then the other. The four Harbs took a step toward her, and she ran for the window. Her feet tangled. Hard tiles met her cheek with a sharp pain, her lips under teeth instantly filled with blood.

Serral sunk over onto her back there on the floor, studying the underside of her bed and the high ceiling above. Her straight white hair fell around like spilled water. She shook off her daze and forced herself to focus and assess. She was a prisoner of her enemies. They had a plan that involved reanimating her body. They wanted her alive. She had failed to obey Imset law and end her life. She considered her remaining options.

The Harbs moved closer as if to lift her back into her bed, saying soothing words, insisting she needed rest.

*Shut up!* She augered. *Get out of my head!*

Silence. The only sound was wind in the curtains. Outside, the sky was blue. In the corner of the rectangle of window, a silver dot hovered past. A spaceship. The war was going on, out there. The Imset were trying to win this planet. Or were they? The people on Chlore were trying to raise a new crop of recruits. Or were they?

She had no idea how long she had been asleep. In stasis, in space, a person can remain inert for decades. If Air Marsiant Slook were here, what would she say? What if the war was over, and Serral was no longer part of a Cause? And her life now had no connection to the fate of all Imset?

Her Medic helpers moved to put their heads together. Their big gray brain bulbs roiled. They were talking. She knew. Her situation upset them. She didn't need to auger to see that. Why had they kept her alive? If they wanted to suck all her knowledge out of her, obviously the had had the time to do it.

Serral pulled herself up.

I'll get back in bed. Don't worry.

They turned, their heads smoothing to gray skin, their small mouths upturned in grins she suspected were for her benefit.

"Don't do that. It looks terrifying." She said aloud. Their mouths returned to small, flat lines. "You understand Imset."

*Yes, Mistress.*

The answer sounded in her head.

"Why?"

*So we may speak to you.*

*Why?*

*Because He wants you to live. Do you not want to live?*

She did want to. She felt as brilliantly alive as she ever had. The sky out the window beckoned to her with possibilities. She had a second chance. She was whole, and would be strong soon, and she could speak to the Harbs in their own language.

*Why didn't you mess with my memory?*

*Because you are protected.*

*Am I?*

She was protected. Whatever that meant. An idea began forming in her mind. Revenge, and violence, and something more difficult. Subterfuge. Intelligence gathering. Espionage.

But they had not wiped her memory. She was healthy and whole, albeit too weak to run yet, and a bit dazzled by dreams of flying with Thantons. Still, she had a chance no Imset had ever been given, at least none she knew of.

Miss Pune's face smiled at her, through time. Slook's curls shimmered from across the universe, her curiosity like a jolt of cool water. *I need you to find out what they're up to, soldier. I need you to survive.*

# 27

—·—

BOOK TWO

## 28

—·—

C hapter Twenty-Seven

Hallenander sat heavily at the opposite end of the long table. "I have here," he reached into his jacket pocket, producing a small folio of papers, "an agreement signed by you, witnessed by our friends the Harbingers." He waved the papers toward the other seven men of the Volettu seated along the sides of the table.

"A fallen pilot is not fit to be your Companion, Boy." Mimellio speared another buttered fish from a platter. "I would have told you as much before you put the servants to the trouble of saving her."

"I quote, 'Hallenander may take any healthy Imset girl as Companion that he finds pleasing,' end quote."

Laughter broke out around the table.

"He has you there," a wizened man in a blue tunic said, one jeweled finger pointing to the papers. "A contract is sacred. Though I am surprised you allowed our little paradise to be written about."

Mimellio waved him away. "Tuss, nothing from this world will remain except our jewels and perhaps this boy, here."

"I am no longer a boy," Hal said. He held up his chalice, and a Harb servant filled it with wine. "This I know because if I were, you would not pressure me to spend so much time with your artistic friends. You would not need me to guarantee never to let your wives know what you have been up to. Not to speak of your friends, who might think less of you for being with Imset women. or more realistically, might fly into rages of jealousy."

The men laughed again and pounded the table.

A canny-eyed man to Hal's left said, "Your Sevenni Highness, the magnificent building you've had the Helpers constructing over these many long months, all the nailing and pounding and consternation, you must surely have it occupied by a lady as elegant and refined as the tower itself. Do you not agree? A random pilot, who has no training and no finesse?"

Hallenander ate a pickled cumquat. "Who is to say the pilot is not elegant and refined, Lord Lollio? You have not met or tested her. She might be a princess in her world."

A man in a velvet coat with fur collar sighed. "She could be. The servants claim she is a veritable Thanton."

The men made dismissive noises.

"The Harbinger Helpers have no higher compliment than to name her a divinity, but as they are so devoted to her wellbeing," Lord Eltu said to Hallenander. "Why not avail yourself of their skill and make the girl, how should I say it, acceptable? Wipe her memory, so she can be at least demure and subdued?"

Hallenander shook his head. "My dear Lord Eltu, I prefer my Companion in her original state."

The men booed.

"For my own reasons. If, after I have satisfied my curiosity..."

The men laughed raucously.

"If I find that her wild and uncouth nature bores me...or I fail to subdue her myself. Which I look upon as an amusing challenge..."

Hands pounded wood, and the men whooped.

"...then I will consider having her memory wiped. But I do not want that now. And never did I agree to it." Hallenander shook the pages in his hand.

"Hallenander," Mimellio said, lowering his fork and leaning toward the table, his face growing red. "Do you mean to offend the other ladies with this insult? Your choice speaks louder than words. They will know you do not find them as appealing as a lowly Imset soldier."

The men fell silent.

Hallenander put the papers back in his jacket pocket. "Is it for the other ladies to decide who I choose to befriend? Are they our equals in this important decision?"

The men exchanged amused glances.

"Let us speak of what matters in this business. You need me to do what you have done and mingle with the Imset women. Thus, when we return to the Worlds, no one can stain your reputations without the risk of sullying my own, and thus that of my father." The room felt tense, but no one spoke. Hallenander pressed his point, "I am willing to do what I can to ameliorate shadows falling on the reputation of any man who returns to the Worlds knowing that his behavior here on Evincio might be viewed by those at home with less than proper perspective. This choice of Companion makes my task easier, because I desire the challenge of it. It is in all our interests for you to accept her. If the other women are offended, what is that to you lofty and superior beings? I am only a Rakki, only half Volterran, but even I see how absurd it is for you to fret about the passing feelings of Imset captives. Of all of us here, as one closer to them in genetics, one would think I am more occupied with their tender hierarchies. And I believe it is perfectly fine for me to choose any of their race I wish. It amazes me that you would care. Really. Is not the purpose of the Xalavria our diversion, our amusement, indeed, our pleasure?"

The looks between men became severe.

"Calm yourselves. I will certainly partake in all the same activities as you. I will be similarly compromised. And happily so." Hallenander held up a hand to retain command of the conversation. "After all, you have sacrificed nineteen—or is it twenty? —long years here on my behalf, rimeters removed from real Volterran women, not to speak of the arts and amusements of home. One would have to be cruel not to understand that gentle, refined Volterran citizens have a deep need for distraction...affection...proper stimulation. It's only natural. People at home might be shocked, but we are all in it together. Or we will be soon, if you agree to my choice."

The room erupted in discomfited harrumphs, but he spoke over them. "I am delighted to place my reputation alongside those who have served my father loyally, regardless of the sacrifice. I mean it. I ask only that you allow me to decide on the method. And the other girls, delightful as they may be, cannot be allowed to influence me. Be assured gentlemen, in the important matter here, I shall carry our common secret to my grave."

There was a pause while the men considered, some glaring, others stroking their beards and whispering to one another.

"Of course, you are right, Sire," Lord Tuss said. "A Volterran man such as you, or such as you will be no doubt soon, need not be troubled by the delicate feelings of lowly Imset. Yet, there are politics in the Xalavria, my boy, just as there are everywhere."

"I understand, old friend," Hal said, anger piquing his voice. "And I refer you to my father's greater wisdom. At placing me equally to a Volterran man in spite of my questionable citizenship. I am sure he understands how you might see me as less able to rule, as questioning my choice of Companion obviously does."

The men gasped.

"Oh now." Maurdoy, a keen-eyed man in gray silks, raised his hands. "Of course, Lord Tuss is not questioning your rights, Hallenander, not your ability to rule when that time comes, which no doubt it will. No one questions that. Of course not. We here in this body all believe you to be as noble and intelligent as any full-blooded Volterran."

There was an awkward silence.

Hallenander made his face serene. "But of course, my Lords. How could I doubt that, given your many years of sacrifice and devotion to my cause?"

The men looked relieved.

"Secure as I am in both my status as enlightened Volterran man and in the blessed full support of my father," Hal said, hoping to silence them for good, "know that the pilot is the Companion I choose to install in my folly of a building and enjoy as I will."

The men muttered.

"No need to be demeaning, speaking of your courtship as if it were already done, and the women we offer beneath you." Mimellio shook his head. "Imset that they be, the Xalavria women are not animals."

Hal's eyebrows shot up, but he said nothing.

Lord Eltu handed his plate to a Harbinger servant, who scurried off with it. "You are indeed Taur's son. But be advised: lovely, amusing, and skilled they may be," his eyes twinkled, "there is no thornier adversary than an Imset lady."

The men laughed.

Tuss said in his quavering voice, "If you do not believe him, ask the Xaff."

Those around the table grew sober.

Mimellio clucked his tongue with distaste. "As always boy, you are a trial to me."

"I am keeping my agreement, Uncle," Hal said. "I assure you, my Companion will cause no disturbance in your contentment."

Mimellio gestured for dismissal and moved on to his dessert.

Hallenander's mind was preoccupied with one thought as he moved through the palace to the Medotel. *Finally, the pilot was awake.* She could begin teaching him to fly. Hallenander stalked the carpeted corridors and stone staircases that lead to the lower palace and ran scenarios in his head: decisions those in the Capital might come to and verdicts the Law would render about each. If he was deemed permanently illegitimate, without hope of appeal, Hallenander had no doubt the Xaff would be forced to kill him. The image of the girl's fighter imploding the Xaff mothership played in his mind, the explosions, the smoke, the water seething with heat and the bodies of dead Harbingers. He didn't know where he could run to, if it came to running. But even if he ended up in the same way the pilot had, it was better than just waiting like the puppet his father's people thought him. Become Heir or fly into the unknown. Of the two alternatives, only one was under his control. Fly, take to the sky and never come back. Search the universe for some key to ending the Xaff's endless war, to the mysterious origins of the Alliance and its ruthless, cruel sense of justice. Refuse the hierarchy of races and rights. Bring the whole filthy enterprise to light.

If he survived. He would show them the true meaning of justice.

He took the stairs to the Medotel two at a time. But despite what his helpers had said, the girl remained inert in her bed. Her mouth was open, and hair covered her eyes.

"Why is she asleep again?"

"Sire, she sleeps most hours. It is part of her healing."

"Is it?" Hal walked closer. She looked the same as she had since emerging from the healing bath with new limbs, and skin, and hair.

The medics had regrown almost half of her body and had boasted of their miraculous efforts, as if it had been their idea to bring her back. Her long white hair cascaded around smooth skin, her smallish Imset features peaceful. Only her eyelids moved. The servants called her Thanton but had told him her name was *Serral*.

"I must speak with her. When will she wake again?"

Their black eyes blinked back at him as one, "When she has rested enough, sire. She is still very tired."

"No matter what happens, do not allow any Xaff near her. Agreed?"

Their head domes puffed with indignation. "Certainly not, sire! She is to be protected. All know this. All obey."

"Good," Hal smiled. "You are certain to be rewarded in the afterlife for your devotion and sacrifice."

Their bulbous gray heads puffed with pride, and they bowed again. But Hallenander was already down the hall, and out the door.

**29**

—  •  —

C hapter Twenty-Eight

Serral heard commotion in the hallway, and this time her legs held up as she crossed the room. She made it to the door in time to see a tall man with an Overlord's crested head disappearing down the hall.

She augered casually so as not to arouse too many responses. *Is that him?*

*Yes! The Minsyx, the prince, a noble Rakki who is your protector, Mistress.*

Hmmm. *Protector from what?*

Voices talked over one another with indignation and disapproval. *The Xaff, the men, anyone who would do you harm.*

She resisted the urge to laugh.

*Where are the men?*

*In the Palace.*

*Are there other Imset here?*

*In the Village, in the Xalavria.*

*What is the Xalavria?*

A burst of excitement: *your home, Mistress. Soon. If you pass the test.*

*What is it?*

*A place of Imset wonders where the women are beautiful, and the nights are full of artistry. But perhaps not for you, Thanton.*

Serral left the connection in her mind open, waiting. The energy around this "Xalavria" was respectful and a tad longsuffering, but the Harbs didn't see it as a prison. She smiled at the thought of meeting her own kind.

*And the Village? May I go there?*

*Oh no,* they burbled, *the Village is only for him, because he likes to see his mother's people out the window of his tower. It is not for you! You have not been wiped.*

*The other Imset, they have all been wiped?*

Serral climbed back into bed, tired, pulling the covers over her head, trying to shut off the resounding reply: *Yes. Of course. Imset are dangerous, surely, Serral knew that? Only when wiped can they be docile enough to keep as friends.*

*Friends. What kind of friends?*

*Sincere, loving and fun Companions that brighten up the boredom of Evincio.*

*Boredom? Is this a dreary planet?*

The sky looked blue. She smelled greenery, plants and the sea. The place felt lush. How could it be boring? But what did she know. She was a scrap rat. Her standards might not be very high.

*It is the most beautiful planet in the galaxy, Mistress. Fit for the royal entourage.*

*The royal entourage?*

*The Sevenni Family. His family.*

*He is a prince?* That hit her in the stomach. The Imset hadn't had royalty since they lost their planet. Being noble had not saved anyone. It seemed silly and archaic. But possibly, interesting.

Leaning back on her pillow, Serral thought about the rock carvings in the cave on Chlore, the impetus for the hallucinations that had comforted her in semi-conscious states. She felt the glittering blue-eye stone, watching her.

*How does the politics of Harbingers and Volterrans work?*

*The politics, Mistress?*

*Yes. Your people are capable of miracles. Why do you serve the Volterrans? Are their miracles better than yours?*

There was a titter of laughter on the thought river.

*Oh no, not the Volterrans. They depend on others for everything.*

*Others? You mean, the Harbingers? Or are there other races I don't know of?*

More laughter.

*We are all one race, Mistress. All related, a thousand, thousand generations ago.*

*What? No.*

Silence. She sensed they didn't like this subject. There was a color of pain, a tinge of regret. Discomfort. Shame.

*Where did the original people come from?*

*She saw a swirling cone of stars. There was a pulling sensation. She heard music being played on an instrument she couldn't name. A feeling of jubilation, of the presence of Zaphia and something bigger than what she could see. Time. A thousand, thousand generations.*

Then nothing.

# 30

She woke to the sight of silver ships outside her window, flashing in the setting sun. There was an airfield to the north, and she pieced together a map in her mind, sharing it with her helpers from time to time via augering to see if her image was correct. They supplied her with details, willingly, though sometimes she felt walls of secrecy, or ignorance. She couldn't tell. With the Helpers, ignorance passed for all versions of the word *no*. The Medotel where she was installed occupied a low series of buildings northwest of the palace complex which towered above a steep valley that fed into a deep-water bay. She had fleeting memories of her battle over the village, of the crop grid surrounding it and the bay below. But her recall of the actual crash was disjointed. Most of what she remembered was the overwhelming feeling that she had to stop the battleship. It would have followed her back to her squad and come after her on the Tuval. She was still sure of that.

*Two questions, Helpers.*

*Yes, Mistress?*

*One, what is the purpose of the lights on the Halos?*

*Oh, that is simple. They are intended to draw the attention of the silly Imset and draw them into a fight. The Xaff who pilot the Halos love fighting the Imset above all things. The Xaff are our most exalted martyrs.*

*Second question: What is my purpose here?*

There was a collective groan, as if the medics had been waiting uncomfortably to answer.

*You are here to kill us, Mistress.*

She sat bolt up. *Am I?* She sensed confusion, argument.

*If you so choose.*

*What? So, I can just kill anyone I want?*

Laughter, with an edge. *Funny jokes, Mistress! Of course, you may not kill the People, or him.*

*The People? The Imset?*

More laughter.

*Imset are not the People.*

*Then who?*

*The People are the vast ones. The People of the Worlds.*

Serral got a visual of tall, handsome men with the long hairless crests of Overlords.

*Oh, the People. I get it.*

*But it is your choice, Mistress. Thanton. Divine warrior who has come to us in the form of a lowly Imset soldier.*

Her skin itched. She stretched out a perfect, scarless arm.

*Why do you address me as Thanton?*

*Ah, you are still joking with us! But we will not be fooled. We are devout subjects, and it is our honor to bend to your will.*

*Seriously. Why? Isn't a Thanton an agent of the Ouserium?*

*Yes, yes, yes.*

The woman in her dream, Zaphia. Now, that was a Thanton. A winged, huge, translucent, powerful creature.

*I'm not.*

Serral broke off. Why not let them believe she was an agent of Ysk, or whatever they wanted? The image of Inoa making a sign of love at her as she was sent off by the Recruiters flashed through her mind. Rafe telling her she was meant for something important. Brume confessing that she had been in the hands of the Harbs when she was born. Who knew what kind of mark they had left on her? She could auger. Was that strange? Or did other Imset have the ability too, and were only prevented by the First Directive? Or was it evidence of some early intervention, something the Harbs had left on her when she was a baby?

So much she didn't understand. She needed more, much more. Hope blossomed in her chest. Regardless of whether she deserved it, this opportunity had come to her. She was not going to waste it.

*I see. Sure. I can kill Harbingers if you want. But I really prefer if you serve me, first. Show me your worth. You know?*

*Oh yes, we do know. We serve the People, but there is no challenge there for us. We have served them for a hundred generations. Allow us to serve you, Thanton.*

*Okay. Can I ask, why you are so anxious for death?*

She thought she knew the answer to this one, the ecstatic humming of the Xaff warriors as she hunted them in her Arrow. But it didn't make sense to her, how killers like them would twist fighting into some kind of sacred martyrdom. The thought made her feel a throb of nausea inside.

*We are not anxious at all! But we want to go to the place of souls and wait for our next life. Which we will make magnificent. Such is our mission. Our vow. Our purpose.*

*Your next life? What makes it better than this one?*

*Oh, we cannot say yet. You will see, Mistress. You will no doubt live and see what kinds of beings are worth becoming, the most noble and vibrant of people, neither cynical nor feral. People with lives worth living.*

*So, you don't want to die. You want to be reborn.*

*Yes! That is it. We desire a new life, a better life.*

*I get it. I will see what I can do.*

She bit her lips to keep them from seeing how the thought of killing them all amused her. Not that she hated them specifically. These Harbs had carried her like a helpless baby, fed her, healed her, talked to her for hours as she slowly came back to life. But they were still Harbs. If her purpose was still to kill them, she could live with that.

*Oh, thank you!*

Their head domes roiled with pleasure.

Serral intermittently thought and questioned. She asked for paper and graphite and began sketching. She drew a map of the planet, Evincio, with blank places the medics eagerly filled in. Below her, the bay and islands out to sea. No one lived on the islands. Her people lived in houses between the palace, and the water.

By late afternoon, Serral had the lay of the land, but for two mysteries. One, a place the Helpers shrouded in a mysterious electricity, the *Reykos*. On her map, they stood looking like two glassy knife hilts jutting from the opposite side of the valley on a spit of land overlooking the ocean. The other mystery was the *Xalavria*, where, when healed, she might go live with other Imset women. Though, her Helpers questioned why she would choose that fate when she could instead stay and *kill us, giving us the highest honor, a place in the Ouserium and... a next life of perfection.*

*I thought we agreed I needed some time to see how deserving you are.*

*Yes. We agreed with your divine wisdom. Of course.*

*Why are you so eager? It seems okay here. I've seen a lot worse. No one is bombarding you. The food is the best I've ever had. Are you unhappy?*

*Oh no, do not concern yourself with us. You have to rest and heal.*

*I want to know more.*

*You must rest.*

*Just a few more questions.*

She pressed on. The Helpers never refused to answer, but sometimes their words did not coalesce clearly in their collective mind. The concept of the Reykos was fuzzy, hard to hold onto, and the idea of a perfect life was wrapped up somewhere inside the fuzz.

The Xalavria was nebulous and confusing, but for a different reason. Serral's Helpers considered themselves superior to the Harb *staff up there.* Their disdain brought a smile to Serral's face, the idea that some Harbs were of higher status than others. They could not explain the hierarchy, and after a while she understood that it was because they didn't grasp it themselves. Harbinger life seemed to be divided into cells. Her helpers know their own business, and not that of the other teams around the place. They were almost as ignorant of the larger world as she had been when stuck on Chlore with the other scrap rats. SThey seemed interchangeable with their similar bulbous, gray heads, their shining black eyes and small faces, and their long, soft limbs and hands. Everyone is tribal, she thought.

*We hope you will remember our good service when you make your choice, Mistress.*

*Of course, I will!*

Yet she was surprised when her four medics came forward, removed their surgical masks, leaned toward her, and offered their heads.

*What are you doing?*

*We are waiting for you to kill us, of course! If you feel we have done our duty and deserve your favor.*

She sat back on her pillows. To no one, she whispered "This whole martyrdom thing is getting very annoying."

*Not today, friends. I'm feeling tired now.*

The thought river seethed with tension, like a sudden wave crashing over her.

*What is happening? I thought I was supposed to rest. I'm feeling very weak now. I want a nap.*

*Oh, no rest now, Mistress! The People are coming for you. You must decide to be a Thanton or a Companion!*

They scurried out of the room. A Thanton or a Companion. She rubbed her eyes. The air seemed charged with sudden anxiety. She was not a Thanton. Obviously, she thought, standing on her very real Imset feet, brushing her tangled, mortal hair out of her face. The alternative, Companion, the name given the Imset women in the Xalavria, seemed the only option, though when the Harbingers thought of it, their feelings were complicated and unsettled. The vibrations were dangerous.

Maybe the people in the Xalavria would enforce the First Directive the moment Serral walked in. But she doubted it. Weren't they all in enemy hands? Why was her treason any more serious than theirs? She wanted to see Imset people. She yearned to be with her own kind, even if the Harbs weren't crazy about them. But not yet. She needed more time to rest and gaze out the window, gather intelligence and information from the thought river. She had so many questions. And she felt tired. She wasn't ready to meet anyone. She hadn't thought that she, a lowly POW about to be sent to a camp with a fancy name, would. It must be connected to being a Companion. She was not ready for this. Of all the things Serral had been trained for, contriving, survival, planetary colonial establishment and management, worship of Ysk, interplanetary navigation, nothing seemed useful for this situation.

"Why can't I just rest and be peaceful for a while? I only just got out of the goo. You yourself said I needed more time."

*They're coming now*!

Serral cursed.

*Where are you going?*

They didn't answer.

Serral followed the medics into the hallway. She had never been past the door of her white room except to use its small hygiene annex. She knew well the view out the window of a barren courtyard below but had only glimpsed the rest of the Medotel through snippets of the thought river. She believed the Overlords would come from the north entrance, the same doorway the man had disappeared into when she had caught sight of him.

*You have decided to be a Companion? We are not sorry. We have done our duty for you, and one day Ysk will see us rewarded.*

*Yes, of course.* Serral tried to soothe their obvious hurt and anger, *Do not doubt your efforts are appreciated. By Ysk. And by me.*

They purred, content in her favor.

*You are indeed divine, to choose duty over glory.*

Duty? She thought privately about trying to meet other Imset, about learning what they did in their valley and if they had a resistance movement. *Yes! My duty is to be a Companion to the... To him.*

She got a visual of something golden and ornate, maybe a crown, she wasn't sure. She recalled the Overlord she had seen on Chlore during the raid, the way he had gestured to the Harbs like they worked for him. *Um, exactly what is he a prince of?*

*He is prince of this planet, Evincio, and one day perhaps, of all Volterra.*

Volterra? Her mind struggled with the unfamiliar word. Her medics gesticulated and bowed, their head domes ruffling more violently than she had seen before.

She encountered the unfamiliar vibrations of new and different Helpers. Twelve Harbs wearing ludicrously embellished dress uniforms arrived and flanked the door. They bowed deeply, then stood at attention. Serral restrained laughter.

*They shall be here soon, Mistress. Hasten to ready yourself. It is expected that you wear a costume, for the People love Imset exoticism.*

*Imset... what now?* Serral augered. No one answered. Exotic seemed the least likely word to describe her people.

One of the Harbs opened a door, revealing a multitude of bright colors and mirrors. It smelled like spring rain on flowers.

*Come inside, quickly.*

Racks and shelving surrounded her with fabrics in a rainbow of hues, wealth beyond her imagining. Gold and silver gleamed. Cases glittered with jewelry. It was like an ancient treasure cave in a story book. Was it even real? Serral stood on the threshold, stunned. Would she be punished for trespassing? Her new Helpers put their squidgy gray hands on her back and gently pushed her forward.

*Dress yourself!*

*In these things? What kind of costume are they expecting?*

*He has chosen for you to dress like those in the world of Imset entertainment.*

She thought of an old strippy with women in satin and men in dark suits. She recognized the period as Old Imseth, the period her schoolbooks had called The Skyscraper Times.

*Why must I pretend to be from another time?*

*Because all Companions must! So the People can remain amused and pretend to be visiting the Lost Planet! Hurry. They are coming. And they do not like to be disappointed.*

One of the helpers pulled something from a rack. A dress. The fabrics were actually garments, a whole roomful of costumes. She moved toward them, her nose filling with smells of fine silk and flowers. Perfume.

Serral pushed the bright garments one by one across racks. Each was a masterpiece. She worried her hands would dirty them.

*How do I decide what to wear?*

*This is clothing sewn for you at his order. His jewels, for your use. Choose a gown, please. As a Companion, you are meant to know what to do. He said you were ready.*

Serral flinched, said *thank you*, and closed her mind. She had never worn anything but coveralls, her flight suit, or her Medotel gown. The pressure to make herself presentable to alien strangers caught her off guard, and her stomach rebelled.

She stepped into the room and looked in its mirror. She hadn't seen herself since the Tuval, and other than her long, white hair hanging down over her shoulders and the now smooth skin of her once-scarred forearms and hands, she did not know what to expect, so that when she saw the entirety of herself, she gasped.

A different girl stood reflected in the mirror, a prouder and more beautiful version of herself. She was taller, her neck longer, and her face more symmetrical. The only feature that remained the same was her eyes.

She turned in front of the mirror, heart fluttering. No tattoo of the portworms. She held her fingers to the ship of her skull. No tracker. Serral felt for the first time since waking up how far she was from all she'd known. Someone knocked at the door, and a small voice called out in halting Imset, "The People are on the move."

"How long before they arrive?" It was a relief to speak out loud, to learn that the Harbingers could if they chose.

"Soon, Mistress. Please complete your preparations."

Each of the dozens of gowns was covered in fine embroidery or emblazoned with gems. A table held troves of sparkling jewels. There were shoes and bags and accessories whose purpose she did not know, all elegant, all singular. The designs were unmistakably Imset, straight out of an elegant strippy. One had no sleeves or even arm holes, the next had only one shoulder. Another was so complicated, she didn't know if it was a dress or a cape, or something else entirely. A lace piece made a noise as if her hands were tearing it. She threw them down in frustration. The floor was littered with shimmering piles of color.

"How are these supposed to work?" she said to herself.

From the other side of the door came the small voice again. "You are not yet prepared for presentation?"

"Almost," Serral said. Her eyes fell on a gray lace gown with a pale under layer, simple as a night dress. She tore off her Medotel gown and slipped the garment over her head. It fell to the floor, leaving her arms and shoulders bare.

"I am not naked!" she called out in triumph.

"Good," the voice said. "You must come out!"

Serral felt an electric shock in her core, a zap of Harb interference she recognized. She communicated in thought. *Why are Xaff here? I don't want to fight.*

*The warriors are guardians of the People.*

*I refuse to be with Xaff.*

*But Mistress, they want a good fight with you. We hope you send us to the Ouseria before that time, of course, but all have need of redemption.*

She was tempted to give them their wish and murder them then and there. If they wanted the peace and love of the afterlife, why not? But The People—whoever they were—might not like it. And the Xaff were scarier than the Harbs she had killed on the Ninitan. She would be late. She touched the jewels on the table, looking for a sharp needle or garrote to protect herself with. She could snap Harbinger necks. But only if they let her, like the ones on the Tuval. Not Xaff warriors, she suspected, who craved combat. And what of the People, who had all the power? Serral had a strong sense that they would not enjoy the spectacle of a silk-clad Companion strangling their guards to death.

*I told you, I am not a Thanton right now. I am a...* what was the word? *I am a Companion.*

The telepathic landscape popped like an uncorked bottle, the Xaff withdrew and Serral felt a palpable relief. She wasn't the only one who didn't like the warrior Harbs. That was interesting. Much to think about, if she could get on with becoming a Companion and all that it meant. It couldn't be worse than going into battle, but still her stomach knotted with worry and uncertainty. She could only survive this if she figured out the politics. She wished for more time to quiz the medics. But her time had run out. She had better get through this meeting, and then figure out how to get back to her people.

Chains and gems slipped from her fingers. No weapons there. They knew who she was. Her bare feet felt cold. Harbs again knocked on the door. She grabbed a handful of diamonds, which turned out to be a cascading collar of white metal and flashing pale stones that fell over her like raindrops. Opals. Lovely. She looked like a long silver stem with a sparkling cape draped over her shoulders. She pulled her hair out from under the necklace and let it fall behind her. Maybe she should hurl herself at the men, kill a few of them somehow and get herself killed. If she met with them like a normal person, had a conversation with those responsible for killing her family, bombarding her home, murdering all the kids on the recruitment ship, what did that make her? Could she force herself to get through this, stay alive, keep gathering information in hopes that she could get it to Slook, and help the Cause?

Collaborator. That was what it made her.

A part of her stilled. Her heart slowed. She had been cinched in the Oculus square, felt the scorn of her whole community. According to her brother, she had been a traitor since birth. Inoa had accused her of hiding something. Her superior officers had threatened her. She could live through this. The Harbingers found value in her. Didn't that mean something? Wouldn't it be worse to disregard Slook's instructions to listen and learn? Her arms fell to her sides. She smiled.

The feeling Serral had just before being shot from the Tuval settled into her chest. Resolve. Blood lust. Will.

If this was a fight, she would take it. She didn't need to auger to feel the vibration of the men's feet on the stairs, the rhythmic fall and rise of their large bodies in the Medotel's foyer. Serral slipped out of the clothing chamber and back into her room. The bed was made, the window closed. The only sign she had been there were pencils and a stack of papers.

*Friends, what do I do?*

*Stand and be correct. Speak when spoken to. They will tell you when to present yourself.*

*Friends, please do not mention to the men my ability to communicate with your language.*

A ripple of confusion crossed into her mind.

*I am still a Thanton if I choose to be. But the men do not need to know this. Because if they do, they will interfere with my duty. Do you understand?*

The thought river heaved with recognition.

*Of course, Mistress. They are heathens who do not believe in the Goddess and those that serve her. We will protect your divinity.*

*Thank you, friends. And, most importantly, do not let the Xaff wipe my mind.*

*No? But the others all have their memories altered.*

*The other Imset may have wiped minds, but they are not Thantons. Are they?*

The twelve Harb servants lowered their head domes, which puffed with agreement.

*He has already given you his protection. We obey you both in this matter.*

*He has? He doesn't want my memory wiped?*

Thunderous footfalls reached her door. Eight massive men entered in pairs and stood in two rows, still as statues. Each had a long, hairless head crest with elongated, elliptical skull domes ascending past their ears like skin-covered hats. Some had braided beards. Each one wore a different outlandish, heavily decorated outfit. Native costumes, Serral decided. They smelled fresh like a newly cut field. Perfume, it must be, or scents used in laundry. Each man wore his own style of jewels, lots of them, silver and gold and stones.

She shivered.

As one, the stone men's heads swiveled and they stared down at her, their almond-shaped, iris-ed eyes smeared in black kohl, thick mouths pursed like they were ready to order their servants to squash her like a bug.

She held her head higher.

The one nearest to her wore a white dress-like garment and sandals. He glared, his chiseled face daring her to spoil his perfect pleats. She bit back a smile, overcome by a yearning to throw mud on him. She reached for some of the hate that had always bubbled in infinite supply within her, but all she came up with was terror. She called to her usual warrior feelings. But the strangeness of the situation made it hard to focus.

More footfalls echoed down the hallway. All eight faces rotated. Serral forced herself not to flinch or show fear, but it took all her concentration. A ninth person entered the room. He was dressed in somber tones and strolled slowly between the others. This man was younger, smaller, and more graceful than the others. He turned his head toward her slightly, and Serral gasped in recognition. This man with his long, crowned head dome was the same man she had seen in the Halo that day on Chlore.

It was him.

And he was the one she was to work for?

Serral's skin tingled. She summoned her comforting memories of Zaphia. There was no coincidence. All the events of her life had meaning. And purpose. She was supposed to be meeting this alien, though Zaphia had neglected to tell her why. He looked directly at her, and then took her hand.

"Please be calm. I will explain everything when we are alone." His voice was low and accented. He sounded posh.

Serral made an awkward curtsy, mimicking an old strippy, but the eight men didn't notice. They spoke to one another in a language that sounded like breaking glass in a half-remembered dream. They were angered by the way the prince had greeted her, and White Dress's rage crept up his face like a rash.

But before he could speak, the man holding her hand said, "My name is Hallenander."

White Dress interrupted with a series of syllables that Serral took to be the rest of Hallenander's long, royal moniker.

She pointed to herself and croaked out, "I'm Serral."

"I know," he said.

Of course. The Harbs had told him everything about her.

"I apologize, but my advisors want to know your qualifications for becoming a Companion."

"What kind of qualifications do they expect?"

He said to the men, "She is an artist. Allow her to show you."

And to her he said, "Draw. My understanding is that you are skilled in this area."

"Draw?"

His eyes flashed intensely, but he spoke in measured tones, "Prove to them that you are an artist of great talent, a rare and exceptional person. Please."

"And if I don't?"

He handed her the drawing pad and box of graphite. "Then you will have no purpose, and they will allow the Harbingers to use you as they will."

Serral nodded. She drew Hallenander, then White Dress, then several others. She channeled Miss Pune, and the long afternoons they had spent sketching while Serral prepared to apply for advanced contriving. The mood in the room shifted, voices only cracking glass instead of shattering it. She sensed the moment when their babble turned into grudging respect.

Hallenander bent to where she sat on the bed. "Good. You may stop now."

And then the men turned, let Hallenander out first, and exited without a word or a backward glance, their long backs and arching head domes bobbing away down the hall.

Serral fell onto the bed and closed her eyes. When the Medotel was again silent, she augered for her Helpers. But none were near, only a crew of workers chugging happily to a cleaning job. She moved to the closet, removed her costume, and put on a fresh nightdress. When she re-entered her room, she found eight Harbs in drab clothes, waiting.

*Hello, Companion of Hallenander!*

*Why are you here? What is happening?*

*You are to go to your new home, of course! We will pack your things and deliver them to you later.*

*I see.*

They offered her a dark gray coat and a pair of satin slippers.

Serral found herself outdoors in the warm, late afternoon, breathing sea-fresh air. The last time she'd walked outdoors was on Chlore. How long ago had that been? She had no way of knowing. She took a few awkward steps. Her body was surprisingly strong considering that she had spent days in bed, and days before that lounging in the goo bath. She looked around this planet, the place the Imset had tried to conquer during the Final Offensive. They had failed. But she could understand why they wanted the place. A perfect planet. Beautiful as her own, though different in all its details. Evincio was warmer and had more varieties of green than she had ever imagined. A white stone castle rose like something from ancient Imseth, all towers and colored windows and wide verandas.

Liveried Harbingers helped Serral into a shining black-and-gold Bisbee. They drove down past Xaff castle guards who stared straight ahead. She kept her mind closed to them, and they didn't seem to notice her. She marveled at the landscape. Each element was incomparably more amazing than she'd expected: curlicued, topiary gardens, vine-covered cliffs rising above the palace. They hovered over parade grounds bordered with ramparts and a steep stone road that led to white buildings framed by emerald-green trees. She saw the flat market square and beyond it, docks lined with masted ships.

It was strange to see the harbor where she'd crashed look so peaceful. Boats rocked gently like no war had disturbed them, like no Harb battleship had ever rolled into their sea. To the south rose a tall bluff, capped with glittering, blue-green glass buildings, the *Reykos*, she realized. Serral was glad for the break from the decorative fakery, from all the imitation of her people's lost planet. The blue and green towers were truly alien, cold and gleaming. She could not see the airfield beyond the towers. It was hidden below the crest of the cliff.

The road turned abruptly, and they hovered up a plain road leading through steep walls of jungle. Monkeys and birds shrieked in the dusky shadows. The Bisbee climbed hairpin turns until a long, green plateau rising inland toward a distant mountain range revealed itself. A jungle continent, forested and pristine.

The carriage stopped.

*And now you go in, Mistress.*

*This is the Xalavria?*

*Yes.*

*And what happens here?*

Her drivers communicated a vision of fireworks exploding, frighteningly similar to battle but joyous, nonetheless.

*You are expected, Mistress. No doubt the others are angry with Helpers for our lateness!*

*It's not your fault.*

*Oh, but we are responsible, for we are the Harbingers! Our brethren inside will be suffering much harsh language, suffering for their duty. Such is the will of Ysk.*

*Right. Okay. Thank you for the ride.*

Serral jumped out, and the carriage glided away. She turned toward a tall gate that gleamed in the twilight, and her anger surged. The doors were constructed of pieces of old Arrows, numbers and markings left visible and melded together in a solid wall of dead planes. The message they sent was clear: we win, you lose.

Party noises emanated from the other side of the doors; laughter and music. What would happen if she ran into the dark jungle, hiding and running until she reached the mountains? She would miss out on the chance to get into the enemy's royal inner circle, which felt like her duty, though she knew it was against the First Imperative. But maybe she could find other downed pilots there and live with them like a regular colonial. Even as she pondered it, she knew it was impossible. The Xaff had too much killing for her to do. They would never let her go, even if this man did. And he seemed to have gone to a lot of trouble, or his servants had, to regrow her and make her all new. Why not?

She knew.

Xaff would find her. Just like they would have if she had stayed on the Tuval. They would always find her. They might not kill her immediately. They might agree she was a Thanton, and therefore she'd spend her days ritually killing them while they pretended to hunt her. She'd send them off to their next life with good marks, absorbing more and more Thrill until she was nothing but a shell for their death energy. And then, if she were lucky, they'd let her die.

Serral knocked on the silver gate.

## 31

C hapter Thirty

"You must be joking," came a voice speaking rapid Imset. "Mimellio told me she was plain, but this is too much. Ever hear of cosmetics, hon?"

Women laughed.

"Hello?" said Serral.

"Come in, come in," people said. Women, in clumps and groups, all watching Serral. Someone swung open the gates. Serral walked onto a seeming strippy location, a fake place made of artificial scenes, what her textbooks would call a *theme park* were it on old Imseth. The women parted and she moved between them toward a large, circular drive that stopped at a kind of depot with a painted sign that read, "Xalavria Station." She couldn't see beyond, because the road, sidewalk and platforms were crowded with Imset women.

"Hello," Serral said to them.

A small, red-haired lady in satin sleep clothes and high heeled shoes with round clumps of fur on the toes gave Serral a wide, theatrical smile. "Hi doll," she said.

It was the same voice she'd heard when she entered, that had called her plain.

"I'm Serral."

The crowd laughed so loudly that Serral almost put her hands over her ears. She'd become accustomed to the quiet of augering. This cacophony was overwhelming.

A girl with long, dark hair parted in the center and a floor-length dress approached.

"Don't talk to her," someone called out. "She's above you."

"Above me?"

Several people laughed. Serral estimated there were nearly a hundred women, many speaking to one another behind their hands, looking her up and down, and laughing. Humiliation crept up her back, but she stayed calm.

Serral looked into Callia's pretty face. "I am so glad to see you all."

"Do not sully her reputation," the redhead said. "I don't care how desperate you are."

"It's okay, The Imset are all desperate. Right?" Serral said. "Hi. I'm Serral"

"I'm Callia," the pretty girl said. She smiled and motioned for the others to be quiet.

"Nice to meet you, Callia."

"This is Riellen," Callia said, motioning toward the red-haired woman. She ran through further names; Cheloa, Alisse, Lady Midrey, Lady Irie. Serral stopped trying to keep them straight after twenty.

Callia moved in for a hug. When her lips came near Serral's ear, she whispered, "Riellen is the one to watch out for, she is out for your blood."

Serral smiled. The feeling of being shot into a dogfight remained in her core, the coiled snake of violence she would unleash if anyone tried to touch her. "Seriously?"

Callia stepped back. A handful of others came close and kissed the air near Serral's head, whispering welcome they seemed not to want the others to hear. They smelled of perfume. Serral found herself in a circle of women as the crowds drifted away into the Xalavria. "Child, best you understand how things work here," Riellen said, lighting a small brown tintorello. Serral tried not to stare. She had only seen tintorellos in strippies. TCallia took her by the elbow. "Ri, I'll get her a drink of water. She's already worn out."

"Worn out? More like dragged out. Look at her. What can he be thinking? Subjecting us to this insult."

"Excuse me," Serral's hands balled into fists. But she didn't feel like punching anyone. She felt like crying. How was it that meeting her own people felt so weird, and fake, and disappointing? Did they not know there was a war on? "Do you have any idea what your people would say if they saw you in this... facsimile of Imseth?" Serral struggled for words.

Riellen and the last remaining women turned away.

"Leave it," Callia said in a stern tone. "Our memories are wiped. We don't know shit. Neither do you. Understand?"

Serral nodded and turned to follow. "I'm sorry."

"Don't worry. You've been with them. Makes you forget yourself." Callia winked one dark eye.

"Right," Serral said.

Callia took her into a hygiene room tiled in pink and black. There were chrome sinks and stalls, and Serral recognized Harb handiwork everywhere: the neatly rolled towels, the fragrant flowers, the sparkling cleanliness of every surface. She wished to auger and ask for a quiet place to rest. She had finally found other Imset, but all she wanted to do was hide. She sagged with disappointment in herself.

"Drink," Callia offered her a paper cone.

Serral gulped the water gratefully. "I need to understand how it works here," she said. "The politics. The whole being above and below thing."

Callia spoke softly and quickly. "Don't talk, just listen. You're more protected than she wants you to believe. You are as high as her, and if Hallenander becomes Heir, higher. He has already chosen a persona for you. He has built you a fortress high on the hill, which is more than any of them would do for their girls."

"They said I need to play the part of Companion. But come on. Even in front of my own people?"

"You don't have to dress or speak for us. But remember, at all times, who your Master is. You represent him. The Imset stuff is irrelevant here. Your only protection is your relationship with Hal. Do you understand?"

Serral looked in the mirror. Her eyes looked huge. "Why are you helping me?"

"Later. They're waiting, and we give them no reason to find fault. No reason. Decorum is important."

"Okay." Serral understood the meaning behind Callia's words. Serral could not repeat the mistake she had made on Chlore. She would make sure this group did not discard her like nothing. She would ingratiate herself, even if it meant pretending to be a lady in a strippy instead of the scrap rat she was. "What do I do?"

"When we walk out of here, Riellen is going to try to stick you with a humiliating backstory, to show that even though you're with Hal, she's boss."

Serral straightened the long hair of her strange reflection. "A backstory?"

"The story of your character, the role you play here. Your period and genre."

"The helpers told me I am supposed to come from *Skyscraper Times*?"

Callia smiled. "He likes that era. He pulls his own costume from there, since he can't claim clan rights on any World. It's a power move. Very Hallenander."

"You sound like you know him well."

Callia put her hand on Serral's wrist. "Later. When Riellen tries to change your origin story, remind her that Hallenander himself wants you to work the specific strippy, *Deco Drama*."

"What do you mean, work that story?"

"You're acting as if you're a character from *Deco Drama*. The famous strippy about a bantering couple in the skyscraper times? Enemies to lovers, you know. Snappy chatter. Inuendo."

"I have never seen that strippy." In the mirror her face looked pallid, like she was about to pass out. She pinched her cheeks, thinking about flying in the pocket and Zero's voice screaming for her to wake up. "Doesn't matter. He has. It's how he dresses too. Surely you noticed he looks like an old Imset gangster? If they were young and handsome."

Should she admit that the only glimpse she had had of Hallenander was of a dark, graceful figure whispering to her to draw as if her life depended on it? He had worn fine clothes. But she had no education in the language of clothes. For her, a nice outfit consisted of clean coveralls. She was in over her head. It seemed important not to admit how far. She smoothed her hair in the mirror. "Deco Drama. Okay. Thanks."

Callia removed her hand from Serral's arm, "Since Hallenander has chosen you, you must be careful to stay away from girls of lower status. Does this make sense?"

Her mind cried out *no*, but Serral nodded.

"I'm not a Lady Companion, like you. I'm not even a Companion," Callia said.

"What are you?"

"They own all of us, don't fool yourself. But..." Callia's long eyelashes fluttered, her beautiful face looking frustrated. "I'm a friend of Hal's, informally, not romantically. That's why I'm helping you. Because he's a good man, in his way. Arrogant, angry. But not a monster, like the others. You can't be seen talking to me. But because I have no Master directly over me, I have no real status. I'm here for entertainment purposes and other things I can't mention right now."

There was a sound of laughter outside, and Riellen called out to them to hurry up.

"What is Hallenander? Besides someone important?"

"Oh. Man. You know nothing, do you? There is no time for this now. If you get through today we can talk again. Probably."

"Please. You have to help me understand what is happening, why we are at war with one another. I am... lost."

Callia leaned in close enough for Serral to smell her sweet perfume. "He's Rakki. A Hybrid. But he's the emperor's illegitimate son, and since they are having trouble producing any children over in Volterra, Hal is their best hope."

"Rakki?" Serral repeated. "Emperor?"

"Don't say the word, *Rakki*. Don't let on that you know anything at all about their situation. For us they are mighty Overlords. They think we know nothing. It is best to keep it that way. Understand?"

Her mind spun. A soldier in the heart of enemy territory. The consort of the future emperor. No memories of her education or time in the military rose to guide her. This was unknown territory in every possible way.

"In a minute, I'm going to have you go out ahead of me because, as I said, you have higher status. Riellen is counting on retaining her queen bee position here, as Companion to Hal's uncle, Mimellio. She might pull it off, since Hallenander is only a Rakki and not legal. If he becomes Heir, you will be the highest status Companion here. If they rule against him, you'll be nothing. Understand?"

Serral did not. But it seemed important to play along. "Why are you telling me all this?"

Callia handed her a towel. "Wipe your chin. If he doesn't become Heir, he is doomed. And so are you. Understand? We all are, though Riellen doesn't understand that. Our only protection is Hal remaining legal. Understand?" Callia's dark eyes met Serral's in the mirror. "Do not screw things up for him with the other men. Do not make him look foolish. If that happens, all of us are less safe."

"Okay," Serral smiled, hoping to put Callia at ease. Her whole body felt tired. Her head ached from the overlapping voices outside speaking her language, but so quickly and loudly she could hardly understand anything they said. "When can I go to my bunk?"

Callia laughed, but not unkindly. "Oh, Sweetheart," she said. "There is the Xalavria talent search tonight, and your presence is required."

"The what?"

"Whatever you need to do to pass this test, do it. It's important." Callia pushed her out the door, her shoulders back, expression triumphant. Serral tried to emulate her fierce energy.

"That's right. Smile. Remember, don't let Riellen decide anything for you."

Serral allowed herself to be escorted to a well-lit amphitheater where she felt the presence of Harb stewards. They did not try to auger with her and, except for uniformed Helpers passing tall drinks, taking away empty glasses, and offering small pieces of food, they stayed out of sight. Serral scarfed down two or three snacks before noticing the other women staring at her.

Those in the audience took their places on curved benches. Riellen dragged on her smoke. "We've got standards," she said. "You should know that you won't make it as a visual artist, Hon, because everyone here," she waved a long-finger-nailed hand toward the crowd, "is the crème-de-la-creme of artistry and stage craft." She turned to her ladies. "Am I right?"

The women hooted and cheered.

"Hallenander likes my drawing," Serral said softly.

Riellen scoffed. "You'll see. Get up there. Go on."

Serral felt Riellen's eyes on her while she walked the stone steps up to the stage. There had been an amphitheater on Chlore, carved from the ground and wet half the year, but she had never been alone there. The only songs she knew were the kind kids sang around the crescent fire. Inoa had directed them in the Story of the Ascension, but Serral could tell a religious play wasn't what the crowd here was waiting for.

Riellen gestured from her place in the first row of the amphitheater. "Sing?"

Serral shook her head.

"No, I didn't think so. How about dancing?"

She shook her head again.

"Magic? Fortune Telling? Animal tricks? Circus? Instrumental? What can you do?"

Serral knew her skills were not meant for the stage. She could contrive, draft, repair machines, and kill Harbs. This audience of captive women, who didn't even know they were prisoners of war, did not understand, or care, about any of that. Riellen came closer, her face looking painted on, red lips, spiky lashes, thick black liner around her small blue eyes. "Are you going to be useful to your Master? Or make him look like a fool in front of his uncle and the other seven? Can you handle this job?"

"Sure, I can," Serral said, picturing the star ship she shot down, the smoke pouring from every side, the Thrill of such a huge kill almost too much, before darkness took hold and her new Master gave her a new life. "I'll figure something out."

Riellen motioned to a few people in the back row. "Zeds, you can have the honor of bringing Hallenander's toy to her pretty new cage."

A handful of women moved down the steps, their outfits plainer than the rest, their expressions hesitant. Riellen directed them to stand closer. Serral crossed her arms protectively, then thought better of it. She would show no fear. The other women in the amphitheater sat motionless and silent.

"That's right, Zeds. You never have that much to do, and even less now you have lost one level of seniority. But no matter. We live to serve." Riellen stamped her smoking butt out on the ground and spoke to the crowd, theatrically, a person used to being listened to. "Hallenander's new girlie needs to go now, and get ready for her master's attentions. It's important that she prepare herself to represent him in the proper way. He has so many liabilities, it astonishes me that he would choose such a one to consort with. But here we are. We must help her. As much as she can be helped."

There was undisguised aggression in Riellen's tone, obviously meant to frighten Serral. But something in the way she was speaking led Serral to the conclusion that Riellen didn't really know Hallenander. Riellen reminded Serral of Inoa. Both wanted to contain her, keep her under their control. Whatever her agenda, Riellen had chosen the wrong tactic. Serral had only spoken to Hallenander briefly, but he didn't seem to be as vulnerable as Riellen implied. No matter. She smiled. She was a strong flier and a born soldier. The Harbs had rebuilt her body, but even they couldn't undo the white of her hair. This was wartime. Petty squabbles in a prison camp, albeit a strange one, seemed the least of Serral's problems.

The Zeds led Serral out of the amphitheater into manicured gardens. Through a haze of exhaustion, Serral marveled at the Xalavria. The women called it The Resort. They marched her past a forested glade then past a mansion with awnings and chimneys that they called The Clubhouse. Ahead she saw large, brick warehouses and a wide, paved road leading to a grassy village circle. Serral was charmed by the many Imsethan touches: a gazebo occupied by Harb musicians, several store fronts and a sidewalk cafe with umbrellas out front. Beyond the square, she saw low, balconied housing units, a row of townhouses, and then, a long lawn leading toward pools surrounded by a large open space lit with strings of lights. She sensed more buildings off in the dark, by way of a north road that they did not take. They passed purposeless, ornate structures that looked as if they'd been lifted out of period strippies. And then, finally, Serral saw a tall building, shining out above the rest.

"Your house," said a Zed named Alysse, smiling.

Serral stumbled up the rest of the road alone. *Her building*, as they call it, was a seven storied structure, black and gold, a series of interlocking rectangles with smooth edges lined in textured gilt swags, narrow windows shining with yellow light. Serral had never seen anything as intricately beautiful. The reassuring feeling of Harb protection came over her. Tall, girded glass doors swung open to reveal uniformed Helpers. She augered.

*Is this my place?*

*Yes! You are meant to be here. Good evening, Mistress.*

*Thanks.*

She let the Helpers in her mind lead her into a beautiful lobby, past an elegant elevator, and then into a wide room with passages leading several directions. A table bore a large, sweet-smelling flower arrangement under a chandelier. The room sparkled with light. New Helpers bowed.

*Welcome, Mistress! Your place has been readied to his specifications! We hope you will find them satisfactory!*

The thought river here was narrow, occupied by her crew and a handful of other crews in the resort. Her helpers were genuinely happy to have her there.

*What kind of specifications?*

She saw flashes of the building's construction, from a hole in the ground, to a girded skeleton, to a shiny black edifice cross-hatched with golden metal, decorated like a jewel. There was a flash of Hallenander in a white shirt with his sleeves rolled, directing Harbs, pointing, speaking words that came to her as ideas: *the very best quality, the highest, the most private.*

The Harbs' head domes swelled pridefully.

Her apartments were as impressive as the rest of the building. High-ceilinged rooms, plush furniture, gold and topaz decking the walls. She asked for her bunk, and the Harbs directed her to a bedroom hung with embroidered white linen. She surrendered to the softness of the bed.

She augered. *What does he want from me?*

Laughter, a sense of mischief and adventure. Flashes of Hallenander fencing in a white suit with a mesh face mask, a boy that must have been a younger Hallenander racing in circles on a small red Bisbee, and finally Hallenander speaking at a lone table occupied by the stone men and wiping sweat from his forehead.

*Yes, but what am I expected to do now? Am I some kind of concubine? What is the price of my life?*

She tried not to let her consternation show up in her augering. The memory of kissing Rafe flashed through her mind. How long ago was that? Where was he now? Had he and Brume made their trips to the cities safely? Did she even still exist in their same universe? She had accepted that she would likely never see them again. No doubt they considered her dead. But she couldn't let go of the idea that she was there, with an intact memory and a healthy body, for a reason. She could still be who she had been raised to be, a soldier, a killer. But if she had to allow herself to be physically available to an overlord, even a part-Imset one, would she even still be able to consider herself a soldier? The idea was impossible. She couldn't let herself be used that way. Even if it was potentially useful to the Cause.

*You are to be a Companion, Mistress! You are to play your role, as your Master must play his!*

*Ugh.*

Her helpers began to cry with disappointment and astonishment throughout the thought river. Was she not aware of the honor that had been bestowed upon her? How lucky she was to have a man such as Hallenander for her Master?

*Never mind. I'm too tired to care right now. When will I encounter the Master again?* She didn't think she would ever get used to using that word.

*In the morning, Mistress. In the morning. But now, you must rest. You must rest and prepare.*

**32**

C hapter Thirty-One

Serral woke before dawn to explore her building. The Harbs didn't want her on the first six floors where they kept all their necessary equipment, but agreed to quickly show her around the racks of linens, food stores, and the strange, red, tent-like structures they used for sleep. And there was plenty to see on the seventh floor, which was *all hers*. There were closets of clothing, spacious hygiene areas, a large show kitchen flanked by a Harb service kitchen, dining and lounge area, and multiple spare bedrooms. But her favorite place was the wide terrace where she could see the whole resort, the jungle and mountains, and far away across the valley, the gleaming towers. Her terrace held two hot pools and a swimming pool, a covered lounge area, and open-air dining areas from where she could watch silver ships rise from the horizon.

She sensed, from the map she and her medic helpers had worked on while she was healing, that the palace complex, village and bay where she crashed lay below them. She augered with her helpers, who confirmed that a high cliff separated the Xalavria from what they called "the regular world." Everything she saw was carefully manicured, seemingly designed and executed by Harbingers for the sake of beauty and harmony. But for the two gleaming buildings across a wide valley, covered in glass. She had never seen anything like them in books or strippies. She augered. *What are those towers that you call Reykos?*

Serral sensed the begrudging cooperation in the Helpers' answer.

*Mistress, they are in the style of the magnificent architecture of Natolyo.* The Harbs went on to lecture her about the seventh Volterran World, a single planet created by the Ancient Navigators for a tribe Serral had never heard of, with a proud history of mining and silver smithing. But deep in the thought river, Serral heard faint echoes of a different purpose. She detected the notion of a project, a use that she wasn't supposed to worry her head over.

*Excuse me, but what is inside them?*

*Mistress! There are preparations to be made! He is coming!*

She sighed. She would try again later. Something about the towers felt familiar, which was odd. She didn't know where she could have encountered anything like the gleaming, reflective structures.

*When is he arriving?*

*He is here!*

The sun was only halfway up, and Serral was still in a soft robe. She hadn't had time to look for weapons.

*Can you stall? I need a minute to dress.*

Her skin crawled. If only she had armor, or a space suit.

*Yes, Mistress!*

Serral went into a closet. To her relief, a full, yellow flowered dress with coordinating sweater lay on an ottoman. Red leather shoes sat neatly on the floor. Two Harbs stood by solicitously while she dressed, and then took her hands in their soft gray ones and guided her to another room with many mirrors and a padded chair.

*Sit, Mistress! We will make you beautiful.*

*You will? What are your names?*

They laughed. *We are the Harbingers, Mistress! We do not need names!*

She couldn't help smiling. *I'll call you Click and Clack.*

Their head domes puffed with satisfaction, and they tugged combs through her tangled white hair. They augered compliments while they piled the smooth mass into a hive atop her head and decorated it with yellow-jeweled pins. They placed strings of pearls around her neck and fastened her shoes. The woman in the mirror was starting to resemble the ones Serral had met the night before. Click handed her a tube of red pigment and showed her how to rub it onto her lips. She looked like a lady in a strippy, theatrically regal and decorative. A Companion. Whatever that meant.

*Can I go now?*

*Yes, you look lovely.*

Serral stuck her tongue out. Lovely is as lovely does, she figured.

Hallenander stood with his back to her, gazing out at a garden materializing in the morning light. He turned. "Good morning," he said.

He wore dark clothes, though this time Serral understood the costume. He was fitted out like an old Imsethan man, complete with suit, vest, and tie. But the period effect was interrupted by the tattoos peeking out from his sleeves and collar and by the silver crown encircling his head dome. His hands glittered with rings in a way she'd never seen in any strippy. His face brightened as he took her in.

"Eighty-eight gods, were you this beautiful before your accident?" He motioned for her to join him at a table set with tea service. "Because you certainly are now."

Serral sensed he wasn't flattering her, but merely stating fact. "No," she said. "My looks were considered average."

He nodded, eyes reluctant to meet hers. "You don't regret," he hesitated, "being brought back to life?"

"Not so far." She shivered. "Did I actually die?"

"Yes, for a moment," Hallenander said. He leaned closer to her. "You are to pour tea for me now, and then for yourself."

She complied. "So, it was you that told them to reanimate me."

"Yes," he said. He looked to be gathering his thoughts, to be deciding what exactly to say. "I was under pressure to take a Companion. Do you know what that is?"

She shook her head.

"My uncle and the other Volterran men keep Imset women here as," he searched his mind for the right word, "as pets."

Serral did not move.

"Each of them, each of the Eight of the Volettu, has a special friend. Those Lady Companions, as they call themselves, are entitled to special privileges."

"So, this whole situation," she gestured at the room around her, "is to show the privileges afforded to me because I have been deemed, because you have declared me, your Lady Companion?"

Hallenander looked into his cup. "It's shameful, I know."

"What am I supposed to call you? How am I to address you?"

He smiled and Serral realized that he was as crafted by Harb science as she was, maybe more so. His chiseled face was perfect as a god's. "You may call me Hallenander. Or if you see fit, Hal."

"Not sire, or Your Highness, or something regal?"

He closed his large eyes wearily. "Please no."

"So, I'm here, in this fancy building, looking down on everyone..."

"For two reasons. The first," he said, his face animated, "is that the building is beautiful because it took ages to build, which was purposeful.  I wanted to stall. I wanted more time before I was forced to take a Companion."

"You don't want me?"

He looked at her with confusion, startled.

"I'm joking," she said.

He looked uncertain. "The second reason for the building's placement and design is that I will—we will—have privacy here." He looked back into his teacup. "I'm sure you already noticed."

"The Xalavria women are a loud bunch."

"More than loud. They are powerful with their masters." Hallenander pointed to the gardens below the balcony. "They will watch you and look for an excuse to complain. You may have noticed that my entourage doesn't approve of you, does not approve of my choice. If you show yourself to be unfit in any way..."

She raised her hands to interrupt him. "Listen," she tried to catch his direct sight, "Hal. I'll never do anything to betray my own kind. And I will try. But I am unfit. I can declare that before we even begin."

"To be someone else's Companion, perhaps. But you are ideal to be mine. Please, come inside."

She followed him to the first large lounge. Hallenander sat on a wide sofa and indicated for Serral to join him there. She hesitated.

"I'm not going to hurt you." He looked embarrassed. "I just want to explain why I went to so much trouble bringing you here."

Serral sat and tucked her dress tight around her legs, hoping her smile concealed her nerves. She hadn't misread him. He was a soldier in his own war. She sensed Harbs hiding in distant rooms, leaving the two of them alone. She smelled Hallenander's not-unpleasant, green-wooded scent. His hands knit nervously, his rings clicking.

"Yes," she said. "I think I understand. You brought me here to be your Companion. For your own reasons." Keeping her face expressionless and her body still while she wanted to flee made her feel nauseous. "I was hoping to spend some time with the other Imset."

"Of course, if you feel confident, you may come and go freely."

"Only in the Xalavria, though."

"Of course, only in the Xalavria. Nowhere is safe for you, unless I am close. Please understand. This is very important." He leaned toward her, intense. "There is more to this Companionship than you know."

She looked around the room until her eyes came to rest on a large silver candlestick that sat on a table behind his long, brown-skinned head. "I see," she said.

"How should I explain. I wish I could show you, as the Helpers can so easily show one another." He swallowed and struggled for words. "I have anticipated this moment a long time."

Serral turned her body to face him. "Yes?"

"I am amazed that we would meet again, after our random contact in your colony. Are you?"

"A coincidence?" she said.

"If I believed in such things, I would thank providence." He shook his head gently, "For I have a particularly acute need. Of you."

Serral forced a smile and moved her hand to rest on the back of the sofa, within inches of the candle stick. "Really?"

"There is something," he moved closer, "something only you can satisfy. And I hope your being given your life back will engender the appropriate recompense."

She closed her hand around the cold metal of the candlestick. "I don't know, Hallenander."

"But I do." He turned and looked out the window to the sky. "I've never seen anyone so brave as you."

"What?" She gripped the candlestick tighter. "You want my bravery? Just, close my eyes, and let it happen?"

"No, definitely not with your eyes closed." He sat forward. "First, I saw you on your planet, when you stood there refusing to let the Xaff cut you down."

She had the candlestick in her grip, but his head was out of reach. "I didn't refuse anything. You did. That much I saw. You sort of ordered them not to kill me, didn't you?"

He laughed, still leaning forward, not turning. "No. It was you. I admonished the Helpers, the Xaff in particular, but they had already made the decision to spare your life. I believe they were impressed by your lack of fear." The room fell silent. "As was I."

Serral thought back to the encounter, remembered the scratching of Harb augering on her brain. "Well, thank you."

He sat back, now within range. She calculated which spot would incapacitate him. She decided on the space behind his ear and raised her arm high.

"And then when you fought the ship. Your flying, so intense. Such skill, speed beyond anything I thought could be reached."

"Thank you," she said again.

He turned, and grabbed her arm as she brought it down, his hand hot on her wrist, which he twisted until the candlestick fell heavily onto the floor. He heaved a sad breath.

"You are a warrior," he said. "I understand that. But before you do me the kind of violence you did to the Harbingers, would you listen fully?"

"You think they would have killed me if I'd bashed your head in?"

His lips pursed into a small smile. "I know they would have. And you would have had no Arrow to escape in." He let go of her arm.

She picked up the candlestick and rested it back on the table. "What do you expect? I've been fished out of my ship and turned into," she picked up the hem of her skirts, "this. And you talk about Companions and Imset captives, like I am here only to serve you? Like I should let you do whatever you want to me? As if this is normal conversation and by the way, pour me some tea?"

"Not anything." Hallenander rested his hands in his lap. "I told them not to wipe you."

"*I* told them not to wipe me."

Their eyes met.

"Did you?" He nodded and said, "I know they respect you. Probably more than they respect me."

"What do you want, Hallenander? You want me to be your special friend, to pretend I willingly choose to be intimate with you, to spend my days performing for your amusement?"

His teeth flashed white. "No." He shook his head.

"No?"

"Absolutely not. The idea of that makes me ill." He frowned.

"Really?" She felt confused.

He made a wry face. "Not to hurt your feelings."

"Of course not." Relief washed over her, but she remained wary. "I'm very sensitive, you know."

"I understand your assumptions. This place is horrible. Yes, it allows a hundred Imset women to stay living. But what is a life without memories, a life as a pet? I do not want such a life for any person of any species. But I do need you."

"I'm not... I don't want..." Serral thought of her one night with Rafe.

He whispered, "I need you to teach me to fly."

Serral choked, her face flushed. "To what?"

He knelt before her with a desperate look. He took her hand in his. It felt cool and smooth.

"Dearest Serral Brook of the Imset Military and the planet 30258, you are the bravest pilot I have ever seen. And for reasons I will explain, I have a need to know how to operate a spaceship. And you are the only one on this entire planet who is positioned to teach me. Will you? Will you teach me to fly, Serral Brook?"

Serral sat close by Hallenander's side while they paraded through the resort grounds in a shining Bisbee. "So everyone can see I hold you in high favor," he said, "and will not question our disappearing together."

Serral smiled and waved at Riellen, who gaped as the couple passed by.

"What really happens in the Xalavria?"

He scowled. "Primarily parties and shows. The women are skilled performers, and in all honesty, their efforts are entertaining. There are rules to prevent the men from taking advantage of their Companions, but the women are free to choose their own behaviors.

How free is a woman, Serral thought, if her mind has been wiped?

"I find it horrifying," he said.

Serral studied the side of his face and wondered if he were telling her the truth.

"But what about Overlord women?" she said. "Why aren't they here to amuse their men?"

They passed through the village. Serral noticed the delightful striped umbrellas in front of a shop labeled "Ice Cream," a wide awning over dainty cafe tables at a "Bistro," and a beautiful buttressed Yskeon in white stone. All belied the reality of the place. Along the route, women looked up at the Bisbee with fascination.

"They're Volterrans. Not Overlords. For many years I had to be held in secret, so my father gathered men, one from each of the Worlds, and exiled them here to educate me. So the Harbingers created for them a place of relaxation and fun. But now that my father's people are sullied by their association with Imset slaves, the men's Volterran wives would never degrade themselves by appearing on Evincio."

"I see."

"You didn't think the Volterrans saw your kind as their equals, did you? Though, in truth, they enjoy visiting your culture, so long as they are in complete control."

Serral's eye was caught by a herd of small deer running into a copse of trees.

"All of this because you are a Hybrid? A Rakki?"

He turned. "Where did you learn that word?"

"The Harbs, I guess. Though they didn't say where you came from."

"I am from here. Evincio is my prison, except for the one trip I took to visit your planet."

"So, did someone accidentally make a child with their Companion?" Serral asked, watching his face darken.

"Far from accidental," Hallenander said. "The Harbingers created me as a potential solution to a problem, nothing more. The Volterrans are no longer capable of producing more than a handful of babies each year."

"Why not?" Serral had an urge to auger her question to her medics, but they were absent to her now that she was out of the palace complex.

"They call it the Emptiness." He leaned over and whispered in her ear, which caused women on the road to gape. "I am sure it is an illness caused by the Harbinger scientists, but it wouldn't help my cause to say so."

Serral played along, laughing giddily as if he'd said something delightful. She saw Callia in the crowd. Serral winked, and Hal gave her a small nod. Callia did not visibly respond, but Serral sensed approval in her gaze.

"So," Serral said, "they wanted to create you, so they had someone to inherit their war. But why? Why insure a perpetual conflict?"

"You are quick to understand. I will explain more later. We must be quiet now until we pass through the Xaff patrols."

When they arrived at the final road to the airfield, Hal spoke more about his dilemma.

"So, you want to learn to fly because you might need to escape. If politics don't go your way?"

"Yes. As a potential Syxarit, a role you might call Emperor or King, I have tasked myself with studying the Law."

"Because you think you can find a legal basis to exist?" The only policy and law Serral knew was from listening to the Air Guards talk to Whit about bending rules.

Hallenander turned his head slightly. They were passing through a farming area where Imset people in white coveralls worked the fields. They waved. He waved back. Serral lifted her hand in a colonial salute, but no one noticed.

"The universe is defined by law."

"Sure. But whose law? Not the Imset."

"No, not the Imset. The Alliance dictates the law."

"I've heard of the Alliance." She didn't say from where, that she'd heard mention of it during augering. "Explain the Alliance to me?"

"In a moment."

They passed another guard gate, this one staffed with Xaff warriors. Serral counted twelve. She felt a hard, physical shock in her psyche. It knocked the breath out of her, like being punched.

"Are you alright?" Hallenander asked.

"They don't like me," she nodded toward the guards. "And I admit, I actively hate them."

"As do I." He faked a smile.

"You do?" She too smiled through gritted teeth.

"Yes. And I am aware that they seek to fight you. My Helpers have shared with me that you have a special appeal for their people."

"Really?" Suspicion prickled her spine. "What exactly did they say?"

Hal passed the guard tower and eased the craft around a bend. The landscape was a flat, cleared scrub land, and at fifty meters or so on either side, the bushy ground rose suddenly in high walls of sheer jungle. The effect was of gliding down a sunny corridor in a darkened, green room. Bird and animal sounds carried through the corridor and with them, a scent of rotting fruit and warm leaves.

"Ordinary Helpers seem almost in love with you, which is very strange. But the Harbs are the strangest of folk. And their affection for you, if you'll forgive me for being so crass, works in my favor."

"Of course it does." She turned away from him, trying to find anything in the landscape that would help her understand where they were.

"They have an incentive to protect you from my uncle, his friends in the Volettu, and the women, who are ten times as dangerous."

"You'll need to explain that."

"Of course. But first let me tell you where we are going."

He told Serral about his life and his long interest in flight, about his collection of planes, Bisbees, gear and paraphernalia. "You will believe my flight center to be a museum, and that impression is intentional.

The Harbingers are hoarders, and I have convinced them to provide me with all manner of salvaged craft so that I can hoard flying machines."

"Really? You're taking me to a contriving bay?" Her heart beat faster.

"More than only a bay. There are multiple bays, and hangars, and what I believe you refer to as a bone yard. The Harbingers serve me by adding to my various collections. I own this planet, you understand."

"Not the Harbingers?"

He grimaced. "No, for the moment it is mine."

They entered an area of tarmac so large that Serral strained to see the end of it. Far to the north, Harb ships glimmered like a sun-dappled lake. The black paving of the road gave way to cracked concrete, filigreed with weeds.

"What is this place?" she asked.

"We are in the southwest quadrant of Evincio's airfield. The Harbingers use most of the field. But I have reserved this section. They stay away from it. They say it is haunted." He shrugged, "I don't believe in their nonsense."

But Serral did. She felt the shadowy presence of a deep vibration like a far-distant mind dreaming. "How old is Evincio?" she asked.

"I don't know. But I do know that the Harbingers have been here since long before I was born. Whatever medical magic they know how to perform, they learned it long ago."

"Yes. They've been stealing our genetic material for generations. Since before the war, even."

"I know. I have studied Imset history," he said.

"Really? They made you learn about us?" She felt almost dizzy with the realization that while her people had needed to limit her knowledge of almost anything going on in the larger universe, his did not. She felt intensely frustrated and at a disadvantage, not knowing or understanding the war, the reason for her family's exile, for Chlore, the cities, any of it.

He spoke slowly like he was choosing his words carefully. "I was required to learn about my father's people. And I chose to learn of my mother's."

"You might join us in our fight?" He said nothing so she continued, "That would be hard, Hallenander. The Imset wouldn't accept you."

"I know," he said. "But that is not my fantasy."

"I'm sorry," Serral said. "The regulations regarding enemy contact are brutal. They'd shoot me on sight for having spoken to you."

"I have heard of the First Directive, this business of stamping out any possibility of Harbinger augury. I think it is a sensible approach, in most cases. When you do not understand your enemy, it is easier to believe they can be beaten." He looked off into the distance. "We must focus on flight craft now. My time, our time, may be short."

They left the Bisbee and walked towards a swirl of parts, tiny pieces at the edge that grew into larger and larger piles. A classic boneyard.

"Who created this?" she asked.

"I can't tell you that. I can tell you that I do know that the Helpers and you communicate. By augering."

Serral gasped. "You know about that?"

He picked up a piece of side wing and then threw it back on the pile. "As I said, I don't think the First Directive is completely misguided. I must refrain from telling you things I don't want the Harbingers to learn."

"But you're showing me your plane collection."

"They know all about this."

"So, you think there's no way for the Imset to win the war, but you're not going to tell me why?"

"I don't think the Imset can win. Of course I don't. But that doesn't mean I want you to lose. I have a plan, but to carry it out, I must be careful. I am surrounded by enemies. I know you understand this."

She wanted to trust him. She wanted to explore ways they could follow his impulse to challenge the law. There was so much he could teach her. The desire to keep talking to him was like the Thrill, addictive and dizzying. "Am I one of those enemies?"

"No," Hallenander said. "I am planning to put my life in your hands, flight instructor. I hope you will endeavor to convince me that you are trustworthy."

"Do you believe that saving my life means I'm obligated to keep you alive?"

He thought before he answered. "I'll say this, I don't believe loyalty to your cause requires that you murder me. Your people aren't aware I exist. Therefore, you break no laws by allowing me to live. And, as you know, I am half Imset. So, technically, letting me live ensures at least a small part of your kind will survive."

"It's cold comfort," she said.

"That is the only kind I know."

"I can keep my mind closed. They don't suck information out of me. That's not how augering works."

"We shall see."

"Oh, shall we?"

"Come now. We are here. To fly."

She jumped down out of the Bisbee before he could help her and followed him to a huge, well-maintained hangar, the first in a row of five. "I must caution you never to linger outdoors anywhere but in the Xalavria. The Xaff will not bother you here when you are in these hangars, but there are dangerous Imset in the jungle. We call them Wilter. Many of them consider themselves soldiers."

"I consider myself a soldier."

"They won't. Look at you."

She looked down at the red leather shoes, the yellow-flowered silk dress that hung gaily to her knees, and the soft sweater embroidered with arrow designs and pearls. "You did this," she said. "It wasn't my choice."

"And you have already said you accept it as necessary."

"That's not what I said," she countered. "I said I was glad to be alive."

His face reddened. "You will not live long if the Wilter get hold of you. They will apply the First Directive, most likely after a prolonged interrogation that I will not be able to prevent. Am I clear?"

"Yes," she said. If they saw her now, no Imset alive would hesitate to shoot her, or worse. Except possibly Slook. But Slook was in another world, and as far as she knew, her friend Serral was dead.

They moved further into the cold, dark hangar. Hallenander paused at a wall and turned on lights. Serral gasped. The place was littered with shining, perfect Arrows of every conceivable model and configuration. Some were built to hold two pilots, others four. Most were fighter planes, but a few were outfitted with seats like old-fashioned airplanes.

Serral put her hand on a fuselage, the metal cold, and tears spilled onto the floor. "What is this place?"

Hallenander held out a handkerchief. Serral hesitated, then took it, and blew her nose.

"It is a collection of planes, obviously. But if you are asking me where they all came from, I do not know. As I said, the Harbingers delight in the material lives of others."

Serral walked away from him, her hand trailing over surfaces, taking comfort in the cool metal and taut power of the machines. They felt like friends. "What is in the other buildings?"

"More ships. Tekkus mostly, some Halos and other Harbinger models. Bisbees. Equipment. Suits."

"Ectos?"

"Yes of course. I have a collection of Ectos."

Serral rounded on him. "So, this is what's going to happen. I'm going to teach you to fly."

His eyebrows shot up. "Good."

"And you are going to tell me about the Law and the Alliance, The Emptiness, what goes on in those towers, and why you were created. Because you know they had a reason for concocting a replacement emperor. It wasn't because of some mysterious, incurable disease. And you know it."

She moved to put her hand on an Ecto, thinking about all the empty tubes on the recruitment Portainer, the final resting place of the escape pods someone had sold off. There was so much about the war she didn't understand. But she wanted to.

He took off his coat and hung it on a peg. "You feel the war is being fought on shaky terms, a misinterpretation of its original justification? Or something else?"

"I know nothing about that. But you do. You study Law because you suspect as much. This whole situation, the end of the Imset, the rise of the Rakki, all goes back to some Alliance agreement. Before I died, I learned that there is something changing in Harbinger tactics. They attacked us in space, where they're not supposed to. They're begging me to kill them. Almost like, the war doesn't mean anything to them now, if it ever did. It is just a pretext to die in glory and get to the afterlife. Their hearts aren't in it. The Harbs are itching to let it go, I know they are. I can feel it."

She opened the Ecto hatch. The inside was pristine and new, like a time capsule from before the war. She looked for some indication of who built it but found nothing. If she checked its programming, would it tell her where the pod was supposed to go, in case it was jettisoned into deep space? The idea of it made her sad. Wherever it was, she wouldn't be safe there. There was only one way for her to be a soldier now. Only one path forward. Through this man.

Hallenander gently closed the hatch. "I was hoping we would work on planes, today. Not escape pods."

"Please." She met his eyes. "Help me figure out what they're really doing, so the world can contain everyone in peace. Be the emperor that sets us all free."

He regarded her. "You want me to end the war?"

"At the very least, I want to convince you that you should."

He held out his large, bejeweled hand for her to shake. "Deal. You turn me into a pilot, a real one who can escape danger and defeat attack, and I will speak with you about the state of the war, the empire, everything. But I warn you. Right now, I am most concerned with survival. Becoming Emperor and negotiating some kind of different arrangement with," he lowered his voice, "The Helpers, is a best-case scenario. I do not expect to be so lucky."

"I never expected to be lucky either. But here we are."

They shook hands.

## 33

C hapter Thirty-Two

Serral and Hal finished at sundown.

He explained his side of the war, and she taught him the basics of flight craft. They spoke in near whispers on their drive back to the Xalavria.

"I still don't understand why the Imset must be exiled. You don't think they do, do you?"

"Of course not," he said. "I have had nothing to do in my life but read books. From them I have gathered a theory. I will tell it to you. I believe the Ancient Navigators were Imset."

"Imset? Are you serious?" Serral laughed. "We didn't get space travel until recently, Hal. Only a few generations before the Harb Invasion. If it weren't for stealing their tech, no one would have gotten off Imseth in time."

"The Harbingers are thieves and hoarders. That includes species. They have had interstellar travel for many thousands of years. But they are not inventors. The Ancient Navigators must have been the source of their tech. Who knows what happened to them. But I believe that the Helpers created a new set of people to serve, because they require lives of servitude."

"The Ancients are our common ancestors? That is a bold theory. But it crossed my mind," Serral said. "The helpers told me that we are all cousins. They said that we separated a thousand generations ago."

"Related we may be. But the Harbingers don't seem to want to breed with us," he smiled. "Maybe we have evolved past where the strains can interbreed."

"You're half Imset and half Volterran, I think that is proof enough that having common ancestors doesn't leave us able to mate," she shuddered. "Ugh. Not that anyone would want to be with a Harb."

Hal laughed. "I'm going to try to forget the image that you just conjured in my mind. Besides, they do everything in a lab, I believe."

"Are you sure?"

He flashed her an irritated look. "No. I'm not sure. Nor do I know if I am the first or only Rakki they made. If you ever find out, please do let me know. Because they want to use me in their game, but they have no intention of sharing its rules."

They glided on. Serral thought he had slowed them down, but she wasn't sure. The jungle seemed to have eyes, but she saw no one. Even the sky was empty of ships. It was pleasant there, next to him. He smelled good, even after a day's hard work under the hood of several planes. She had never spent so much time with any man other than her brother, and he hardly counted. Rafe had been handsome. But Hallenander's face was perfect, his cheekbones and lips pronounced, his green eyes large and intense. He seemed to notice her staring. She looked straight ahead.

"So, did we auger, back in the times of the Ancients? Or did the Harbs once use spoken language?"

She thought of the mural in the cave, the space craft carved into the wall. It was impossible to know what species the pilots depicted there were, Imset, Volterran, or Harb.

"Another mystery." Hallenander wheeled the Bisbee as the road turned. "Did you know that about five thousand years ago, with no historical precedent, the Imsethans began worshiping a single deity? Suddenly it was one god, Ysk, and the old gods were all relegated to the scrap heap."

"I've heard a little about that." She pulled her sweater around her against a jungle breeze. "But your father's people didn't jump on the Ysk train?"

He laughed, "Oh, no. The people of the Eight Worlds are absolute in their adherence to tradition. No servant would have their attention long enough to convince them to change a brick in their temple, not to speak of whom they worshipped there."

"Nice."

"I've read about your people's history extensively. Somehow, monotheism sprang forth seemingly out of nowhere. The old Imsethan rulers told the people about the Ousians and the Astulia and how they were able to earn a better life in their next incarnation. They simply had to serve their kings well, with endless sacrifice and perfect obedience. Being Imset, of course, that level of blind trust didn't happen. Too many regime changes, wars, disasters and mayhem. But still. Tell me the shift to a previously unknown diety doesn't sound like typical Harbinger nonsense to you?"

"We had strict limits on personal research. And too much work to do even if they had let us read what we wanted. But yes. I know what you're talking about. The *Imsetamid times* we call them. The only reason they showed up in our history lessons at all is because of the rock carvings left by the Ancient Navigators. I've seen these some. They're incredible. I assume our authorities were afraid that we would stumble upon them and forget our identity as mindless soldiers. Which, to be honest, is what exactly happened, because as soon as they suspected me of looking beyond their teachings, I was thrown out of my colony."

The carvings had been more than incredible. They had been alive, somehow. But she didn't tell him that. She already felt exposed and vulnerable, like he was her closest friend rather than a stranger with the power to force her to do anything.

"Shortsighted of them not to see your potential. Though even so, here you are, where no Imset soldier has been before." He made a faint smile. "Have you really seen the Ancient carvings? You're not lying to please me?"

Serral fixed him with an angry glare. "Yes. Why would I want to please you? Are you my master or something?"

He stared at her. "I have seen pictures. The carvings are ubiquitous. Whoever the Ancients were, they seemed simultaneously obsessed with life on planets, of which they created thousands, and the afterlife, with its winged Thantons. Very strange people."

"Maybe it was only the same Thanton, over and over," she said.

"You mean, the same story represented on carvings everywhere? So the Ancients became obsessed with spreading their version of truth. Could they have trained the Harbingers to insist on the rightness of their religion? In perpetuity?"

"Ugh. You think the Ancient Navigators were in league with the Harbs? How depressing. Make sure there is never any evolution, even after you are long gone."

"Perhaps. But I believe it was stranger than that. The Harbingers, I think, enslaved themselves to the Volterrans. To serve Ysk. Evolution of thought or species would threaten the meaning of their lives."

"Something is changing, though. You can see it in how they're fighting the war. They have started breaking the rules." She rubbed her eyes, the rightness of his theory clicking into place alongside things she'd heard on the Harb thought river. "This alliance started before there were Volterrans?"

"Volterran civilization is only metaphorically a hundred generations old, not a thousand, like the Harbingers."

"The Imset don't know how many metaphorical generations we have supposedly had. But we know we weren't the first creatures to live on Imseth. The planet was littered with fossilized remains of species that predated us. Maybe the Ancients planted us there. And the Harbs came, stole genetic material from us, created the Volterrans, and placed them in some special paradise, like this one." She waved at the scene around them, the green wall studded with colorful flowers.

"They seem to feel they have power over life and death. In a sense, they contrived you."

"Sure, they grew my body again in their special goo. They are miracle workers when they want to be."

"Maybe it is not miraculous. Maybe this is how they earn their next, better life."

"Next life?" Serral ran a hand through her hair. "We did not learn about next lives in our Yskeon. It was never mentioned at all. Maybe we share Ysk. But I don't think we worship like the Harbingers do."

"They believe in the afterlife utterly. Or, so my research tells me."

"They do," she said faintly. "Uh, that is, I think I heard them say something about that when I was hesitating to come aboard for all this.

He stared at her. "I'm sorry. I didn't think about how it would impact you, to be brought back to life. Of course, I assumed that anyone would be glad for more time to live. But perhaps you are not."

"No. I am," she wrapped her arms around herself, shivering. "I want to make the most of this second chance."

They drove in silence. The landscape changed from jungle to rolling fields filled with long shadows.

"I wonder if it is coincidence that you are here on Evincio, my Companion, my flight instructor."

"I don't know." She sighed. "The times they almost killed me are as real as the times they decided to spare my life."

"Or so they want you to believe. Or they want someone to believe."

"Why would they go to such lengths to get me here? Just so you can learn to fly a plane?" She thought of the choice her medics had given her, to remain alive or become a Thanton. Maybe she had hallucinated that exchange. Maybe they had drugged her as part of her healing.

"We are both pawns in their plan."

"Sure. To make you Emperor." She gestured out at the landscape. The Palace was coming into view, overlooking the shimmering bay. "Look at how much they've done, just so you have a nice place to grow up, and learn courtly manners, and romance girls."

"Yes, they work very hard." He snapped his long, brown fingers so his rings flashed. " "It provides an opportunity for us. You being my Companion is even more advantageous than I appreciated."

"An opportunity? How? I can teach you to fly. I can play the political game in the Xalavria, and stay alive. But the only way for me to help my people would be to strip the Harbs of whatever insane rationale they have for murdering my people."

"They don't think it's murder. They see it as retribution for malfeasance. The threat of planetary death violated Alliance law, you see."

"The Imsethans didn't know they were part of an interstellar Alliance. They didn't know they were subject to some absolute law that meant losing their planet if they missed certain health milestones."

"Imseth was on its way to dying, did they not teach you that?"

"They did. Did you read how they treated us during the time when they expected us to obey their commands about our planet?" Her voice grew hard.

"Only that the Imsethans were aggressive and stubborn and refused to take their warnings seriously."

A flock of yellow birds scattered as the Bisbee crossed the perimeter gate.

"Look at it from the Imsethans' point of view. Harbs used to abduct people randomly. They'd suck them into a Halo, tie them down, tell them that Imseth was dying, and order them to spread the alarm. All while helping themselves to our genetic material in a degrading and terrifying violation of our bodies."

Hal grimaced. "They don't understand bodily autonomy."

"Yeah. No kidding. Anyway, no one believed them. In those days, Imsethans didn't think the Harbs were real. They thought the stories were made up."

"Even though people returned from captivity?"

"With stories of sexual violation and telepathic conversations about laws no one had heard of and war with people the Imsettans didn't believe were real. The carvings of the Ancients were believed to represent old Imset civilizations. No one thought they were proof of ancient astronauts. The abductees went crazy or started denying they had ever been abducted. Maybe they were wiped. Who is to say? It was two hundred years ago on a planet that last anyone checked was a smoking husk. To this day, the Imset believe anyone who has contact is a spy for the Harbs with an altered brain, guilty of treason at best, leading the Harbs to more targets at worst. Anyone who has been in contact with Harbs will be killed on sight."

They sat in silence.

Hal said in a soft voice, "So, you can never return to your people. You are like me. A non-entity."

"Yes." Tears rose, but Serral made no move to dry them. They did not fall. "Why do they want you as Emperor?"

He scowled. They passed over black road, jungle casting long shadows on the scrubby corridor like skyscrapers in an old Imsethan city. Pools of water ruffled in the gnarled, root-encrusted dirt, glinting periwinkle.

hTo save the Eight Worlds from their falling population."

"But you're one person."

"They could make more. I often wonder why they have not."

"Maybe they have."

"Why do you want me to become Emperor? Or do you? Perhaps you want to hit me in the head with a candlestick and be done with all this. You will have died doing your duty. Ysk will be pleased."

She smiled. "It's my duty to convince you to overturn the law that says the Imset have to be exiled. If we don't get a planet within this generation, we will lose the ability to ever adapt to gravity again."

He scowled. "I thought you were safe in your space cities."

"Technically we are. But you don't know what space does to people. It takes away... I don't know exactly how to put it into words. It weakens us physically. But that isn't the real issue. We need what you have here, for the same reason that you need it, the reason the Harbs aren't raising you in a space station somewhere.  The Imseth can't survive without a planet. We maybe can live on, but we won't be Imset anymore. I have never been to the Cities. But from what I've heard, they're a degraded way to live."

The wind kicked up, making the fields ripple like fabric all around them. The road crossed into orchards. The trees were in shadow, but a smell of delicious blossoms met Serral's nose. "We need a planet."

"Thank you for believing I could wield such power successfully. It has been clear to me for some time that the game being played is between the Harbingers and my father's people, with the Imset simply an example to demonstrate that the Harbingers alone know how to build, to create, to fight. The Imset never gave up their vitality. Perhaps the Harbingers, in their twisted way, are trying to keep the Imset alive, by blending them with Volterrans. But whatever their intensions," he said, replaceing his crown. "If I become Emperor, all of this, all will be subject to review."

"And will you be the one to review it, once you are safe?"

"I'll never be safe." He looked up. A row of silver ships was flying toward the airfield behind them. "Not unless the entire legal structure is subjected to the same fate as the lost planet."

Serral took in her new master. "Melted down," she said, a slow smile lighting her face. "I like that."

They drove on in silence.

The next day they arrived to the flight center early. Hallenander was already book-knowledgeable about planes and quick to regurgitate facts. Serral tried to provide a thorough lesson, but Hal said, "There is no time to waste on review. I don't know when the Eloxiture will rule on my fate. If they do before I am flight ready, I am likely to perish."

"I understand," she said. "The Harbs can go from being your friends to gunning you down in an instant."

Hal smiled. "You're an exemplary Companion."

They ate a picnic lunch in a back room that reminded Serral of Whit's lair from a hamper they'd packed into the Bisbee.

"Whose office is this? Don't say yours."

"It is mine. Everything here is." He looked at her intently. "And I protect what is mine."

"That means you're not going to tell me?" Serral worked on her sandwich. It was obvious to her that someone else used the place. But he didn't want her to know who.

"I won't share your secrets with anyone either. I'll help keep you alive. I want to."

"And when you can fly? What then?"

His green eyes flashed. "Do you imagine me a monster?"

Serral looked at the floor, which was too dusty to be under the care of Harbs. Hallenander must be keeping other Imset around, at least a contriver who maintained his collection. "No. But you are my master now. I belong to you. How do you expect I feel about that? How much can I trust in someone who controls my fate?"

"I don't know." He stood and paced. "Perhaps you can tell me how I am supposed to feel about my predicament? I am neither Volterran, nor Imset, nor legal, nor yet illegal. I am nothing. I may become everything. And yet. Even if you do not call me monster, I know the Imset consider me such. And my father's people, the Volterrans, are worse. Though you may resent the power I have over you, do not doubt that it is the only thing keeping you alive."

Serral nodded, saying nothing about the Harbs who called her *Thanton*. It was only a hunch, but she suspected that between her and Hallenander, the Harbingers would prove more loyal to her, the one they saw as a Thanton sent to dispatch them to the afterlife. "The Imset are proud. We may have no reason to be. But we are."

"I know. And I'm sorry. Please realize also that you are one of the only people in the universe who could be a friend to me. Unfortunately, to gain an ally, a teacher and a skilled tactician, I must lock you in a cage and force you to wear pretty frocks. I wish it were not so."

She said nothing.

Hallenander turned to her. "Do you trust me?"

"Why do you care?"

"Because I am not a monster, you must understand that." He paced, his eyebrows knitting. "Do you not see that I am also in a cage? That I must also stay within the boundaries of my protectors or be hunted like a criminal? Because of being born, same as you."

Serral's face flushed. "You're right. I'm sorry."

"No, I am sorry. Please help me."

"I will. But I am curious, is there no one else like you? No siblings? They only made one hybrid son of the emperor?"

He sat down, calmer. "You can auger. Put that on your list of questions."

"Your father wouldn't tell you? Your uncle?"

Hallenander smiled. His teeth were blinding. "The Harbingers, the Volettu of Eight, and my father, none of them would like my asking. But they must have made others before me that did not thrive. It stands to reason. The palace is not new. The village, either."

"What happened to those hybrids?"

"Rakki is a more polite term. I am called a Rakki." He peeled an orange. "Do you think they would tell me? I am the last person they would want to know. Whatever fate became of my predecessors, if there were any... I would be next."

"Death. The Harbs are pretty into it. They have ideas about duty."

"Yes, that it is the highest form of worship, and the only way into the Ouserium."

"Right. Into the very best afterlife."

"And when the Harbingers' duty shifts from raising and educating me to hunting and killing me—well, I suppose they believe that I shall join the others in glory, that is if the Thantons deem me worthy."

"No. You're wrong."

He looked stunned. "What do you mean?"

She shook her head. "Harb thoughts aren't easy to translate. But the feeling they have about you, it's not that neutral. You are important to them."

"I understand that they care passionately about their work," he waved his hand, "but they only care about me until they are given their next assignment. They are unstoppable. I am sure about this. I have seen the Xaff shooting down Arrows all my life."

Serral flinched.

"I'm sorry to pain you," he said, "but it's true. I have watched from my window. The Xaff live only to fight."

She nodded, her voice breaking. "I'm aware."

"I want my freedom, Serral. I want to be able to fight and we both know who my real enemies are." He touched her wrist with one finger, meeting her eyes. "I ask you again, will you help me? Freely? Because you trust that I will protect you, and give you the answers you seek to the very best of my ability?"

Serral expected to feel disgust at his touch, but none came. "I will. But I don't believe the Xaff will ever be tasked with killing you. I think you'll become, what do you call it? Syxarit? And when you do, I expect you to end the Alliance. I need this promise from you."

"My mother was Imset." He dropped his hand from her arm. "You can be sure that regardless of anything I say to you, I have no intention of allowing the Imset to suffer further." His voice lowered such that it was barely audible. "So yes, though it is no sacrifice for me to say so, I do promise."

Serral smiled. "As masters go, you're not half bad."

"Flatterer." His large eyes rolled. "At least you understand why it is in your interest to help me."

Serral wrapped up the remains of her food, feeling lighter than she had since waking. She kissed her finger and held it aloft, a greeting to Zaphia. "Thank you for the destiny."

"What are you doing?"

She shrugged. "Just thanking the Thantons for sending me here. Don't worry, I'm done."

The second hangar held so many Harb spaceships, it took Serral's breath. Tekkus, Halos, and other craft she didn't know, littered the floor, gleaming like cartoonishly large pewter saucers, wheels and helmets. For the first time since arriving in the southeast quadrant, she augered. The only vibration was a far-distant electric hum, the Xaff. But something else dark and angry hovered in the ethos, like a forgotten animal in a cellar, almost too weak to scratch at the door. She shut her mind. Hal watched.

"That's what it looks like when you speak to them? Like you're in a trance?"

She pushed her braid behind her shoulder, embarrassed. She hadn't thought about what she looked like when augering. "I suppose, yes. There are no Harbs around right now."

His face lit up. "You can tell?"

"Yes. For the most part. But I felt other things just now. Dark things. What happened here, Hal? What is this place, really?"

He went and checked the locks on the door.

"I can only tell you that Evincio is more than a planet to grow a hybrid Minsyx,  a half breed Heir apparent, though what more I don't know definitively. Around the time you crashed, there was an escalation in the conflict. Those are downed pilots hiding out in the jungle, more than have ever been there before. So, unless and until the Xaff clean them out, you and I are surrounded by Imset enemies."

Serral ran through the bounty of Harb ships, from one to the next like a child in a playground, climbing in and jumping out, asking too many questions. But she quickly overcame her breathlessness.

"You're not going to fly all these ships."

Hal looked amused. "Really, why not?"

She laughed, "I don't know how. I only know how to fly Arrows."

He crossed his arms. "You'll teach yourself. Look at you."

"You're insane."

Serral determined that the many planes and spaceships in his collection were made of components, just like the ones she had used to build her Bolt. They had strange controls she didn't recognize or know the purpose for. But if they went out to a remote location where nothing could get damaged, Serral reckoned they could figure out what each did. The Harb cockpits were cramped, and since the pilots sat in chairs configured to their alien bodies, they felt strange to sit in. But the challenge appealed to her.

"Okay. I'll try. But an Arrow first?"

"Fine. Armed or unarmed?"

"Thantons in air. You have weapons?"

He glared. "Of course. But I don't want the Wilter finding out, so tell no one."

"The jungle soldiers." She understood.

"They would love to get their hands on a cache of weapons."

"Ah. And how do you think I would I tell them?"

"You wouldn't. But you may slip and mention something to one of the ladies."

"I don't talk much to the ladies. They're wiped." She scrunched her face. "And they're prisoners."

He touched one of the knobs and powered up the Tekku they sat in. The engines whispered for Serral to take them out and push them to their limit.

"Imset are resourceful, clever people. I'm sure you have your ways."

"Is there a resistance movement?" She watched as he showed her how to operate the lights. She laughed. "These lights are diabolical. They used to scare us so much. Turns out they don't do anything but frighten people."

"The resistance likewise isn't positioned to do much, and if they tried much of anything, it would be their last act."

"Because the Xaff would wipe them out?"

"I don't know why the Xaff have not killed them yet."

"Hmm... Because they're waiting."

"Did they tell you that?"

She ran her hand over the curved control panel, guessing what each section covered. "I think this panel must be for life support. Here, give it a try."

He flipped a switch and the Tekku jumped, hovering up above the floor. They clapped with the thrill of it. Hal flipped the switch again. They landed gently, the saucer-shaped fuselage perfectly level.

"No," she said. "Talking to them is painful. Plus, I hate them."

"We agree on that."

"It makes no sense for the Xaff to swoop in and hunt Imset while you and your uncle are here. They've worked so hard to make Evincio amusing and pretty for you and your advisors. They're not going to spoil it now."

He put his face in his hands. "Once I leave here, I fear, the hunting will begin."

She unstrapped herself from the seat. "If the Wilter, those wayward pilots in the jungle, are becoming as bold as you say, then the Harbs are probably starting to feel the pressure. They seem pretty keyed up. I don't know why. But I think it has to do with politics."

"Ah. Politics. There is no resolution in sight. The Houses of Eloxiture and Jalophians will follow their own timetable in the capital. They will discuss, dispute, test public sentiment, repair to their summer villas to play games on the lawn, and talk some more until there are only two old Volterrans left if they so choose. The feelings of their slaves matter naught. If I die of old age, they would rather risk that than be rushed to a decision they can be blamed for later."

"The Volterrans don't control the Xaff. Not really. Though I'm sure they're meant to think they do. The Harbingers are nothing if not duplicitous." She jumped out of the Tekku. "What other reasons could the Xaff have for holding off hunting Imset? Because they seem to enjoy it."

She thought of her mother, alone with Brume in the mud, Halos landing all around, Xaff swarming around, baby her in their gray arms. Had they hurt her mother? Sent her to a quick, painless death? Was there anyone she could ask, who would remember?

Hal climbed out after her. "Serral."

When she turned to look at him, his face was streaked in kohl.

"Are you crying?"

"You don't know how much it means to me to meet someone," he laughed desperately, "Someone as completely paranoid about the infernal Harbingers as I am. It truly means the world. I am grateful."

"Settle down, Your Highness." Serral smiled. "We have so much work to do."

He made a grim face and sat straight.

They didn't speak much in the Bisbee on their way back to the Resort. She stifled the urge to put her hand on his arm, to comfort him. But they were passing through Xaff controlled areas, and she didn't want either of them to let their guard down. Her finger inched toward his leg. He looked down and saw it. They exchanged a brief look, which she hoped showed that she was touched by his feelings. Then she withdrew her hand.

In the hangar, she knew just what her duty consisted of. But alone with Hallenander, everything became murky. She had never felt as close to Brume or Rafe as she did to this alien man, passing along a blank stretch of road on an enemy-controlled planet, dreaming of toppling an empire. A guilty pang ran through her. She would never be able to explain this comfortable connection to her brother, or to Rafe, or even to the craziest person she knew, Whit. She missed them all.

Had any Imset soldier come this deep into Overlord terrain, un-wiped as she was, and been able to auger? Serral knew in her gut that no one had, and that no one ever would again. She alone had to make this opportunity benefit the Imset. She looked at her master, at Hallenander who seemed lost in his own thoughts, a faintly satisfied look on his face. Despite his strange half-alien-half-Imset-dandy appearance, she decided she trusted him.

"What are you smiling about?" Hal said.

"Do you think we can pull this off?"

He shrugged his wide-lapelled shoulders. "No, of course not. But we must try. Agreed?"

"Thank you for making the Harbs save me." She brushed at her dress. "I mean that."

"You're quite welcome." He turned the shiny carriage to the north.

They drove inside the silver gates, and Hallenander signaled to a group of Helpers who then rushed forward with a large bouquet of white roses. Serral felt the eyes of the Imset women who milled around.

Hal handed her the flowers and spoke quietly. "Walk through the resort with these, and act like you and I have had a very romantic day. You're giddy. You can't believe how lucky you are."

The roses smelled sweet. "Thanks. Master."

"Ugh." He made a pained expression. "There's a party in our honor tonight. Expect trouble. However stunning you can look, do it." He handed her a scarf. "Shouldn't be hard."

"Aw," she laughed. "The Harbs are good at their jobs."

He leaned down, looked into her eyes, and quickly kissed her on the lips.

Her hand flew to her mouth.

"You've just been kissed by your master." He said into her ear, then hovered away in the Bisbee.

Serral stood on the platform clutching the flowers, feeling very alone. She began the long walk through the resort to her building and its seventh floor where she would collect herself and prepare for the night ahead.

## 34

C hapter Thirty-Three

Hallenander switched on his liquid portal. "Hello my father."

"Late, you arrive late to your only real obligation of the day."

The accusation was untrue. Hallenander was just on time. But he was expected to always be waiting when his father appeared, ready to talk.

'You have had alone time with your new friend, I am told," Taurellio said, his deeply lined face animated. "My brother is unhappy. Which delights me. Because I am a terrible person. His need to control everything that happens in your life didn't disappear with your coming of age. I expect he wants to feel safely useful. Or else, he likes his life there and desires to infantilize you and continue his present comforts. In any case. A good day?"

"I shall be glad to report to you all about it, Father. Though I rather prefer no women be present when I do." Hallenander kept his face serene so his father wouldn't see through the lie.

Taurellio laughed. Behind him candles illuminated rich tapestries, though no women were visible. He was in the Capital. People were always around him, there.

"Of course, you may keep that joy private, if you wish. You have lived such a solitary life, my boy. I know the Eight are not enough to provide the entirety of your education. For all that you will need a wide variety of understanding when you return triumphant to the Worlds." He winked one of his fiery white eyes.

"I hope one day to travel there, of course, father, but remember, one may not return to a place one has never visited."

His father waved a large hand. "No, certainly not. But the people think of you as belonging. And you will feel that way instantly, when you come."

"I know, the people think of my return as the return of their noble legacy."

"Exactly so."

His father then spoke to someone else in the room, and his face changed from genial to angry at some news delivered out of earshot "Hallenander. What would you say to a visit from your father to your own pretty world of Evincio?"

"What would I say? Are you joking with me? Your last visit was fully half my lifetime ago."

"Don't whine."

"Then don't tease. Of course, I would be overjoyed to have you here. I can imagine nothing more wonderful."

"Nothing?" Taurellio was back to twinkling.

"Oh, of course a decision of rightful citizenship and legal status as your Heir and a triumphal parade down the fields of victory would suit me. But if this visit helps our cause, then I guess I can settle."

"And your coronation. Do not leave that off the list."

Hal darkened. To speak of his own coronation was to acknowledge Taurellio's mortality. He did not want to lose his father. "It will be so long from now, sire. I can hardly imagine such a thing."

Taurellio looked pleased. "You have a princely way of speaking. It will serve you well in your future."

"Will you come to visit, really? When will it be?"

His father looked off into the distance, where someone was speaking. "Soon, son. But there are matters I must attend to first." He turned his attention back to Hallenander. "Boy, enjoy your Imset wench while you can. She must be quite a creature, to have riled my brother Mimmelio so."

Hal waited to see how he was expected to respond. Finally, he said, "You shall see her for yourself, when you come."

The Syxarit's face grew blank, a look Hallenander knew well. It meant his father did not want his feelings known.

Hal's muscles tensed, though the older man was millions of rimeters distant. "I am delighted to anticipate your arrival," he said.

"Good."

The liquid portal went blank

Hal scrawled a note and stuffed it into an envelope.

"Helper," he called. A pair of Harbingers came into his chamber. "Get this to my Companion, immediately."

C hapter Thirty-Four

The note was on heavy card stock and Hal's handwriting was a work of art.

*Dearest Companion, as discussed today, all care and discretion is advised. Keep those you trust close. We shall be tested but I will not fail you. Whatever occurs, keep your head high. -H.*

Serral closed the note and studied the gilt crest on its cover. The design was repeated throughout her apartment; a kite, a sheaf of wheat, and eight spheres connected by single, short lines, a celebration of the Eight worlds, the harvest. Serral put the card on one of her dressing tables.

Click and Clack had selected for the evening an embroidered gown beaded in shades of gold and silver, a matching headband, and a fussy little bag. The dress hung heavy on her frame but looked ethereal like a foggy dawn. Her Helpers hid her long hair inside a tight cap, and then stretched over it a gold wig shaped in sharp angles. They painted Serrals face, and then they opened her jewel trunks.

*May we suggest these?*

They held up gleaming diamond bracelets and long earrings. Serral had noticed at the Medotel that her ears had been pierced while she slept. Now she knew why.

*Fine, fine.*

She slipped the baubles on and then chose several large rings.

*What do I do with this fancy bag?*

The helpers laughed.

*It holds whatever you choose to bring to the parties, Mistress. May we offer these?*

They showed her a tube of lip pigment, a mirror, a tin of candies, and a small pad of paper in a metal case with pencil attached.

*What do I use the paper for?*

*We do not know, dear one, but the other ladies scratch upon one while gaming.*

*Oh, alright.*

In the mirror, she looked like a stranger in an old-timey strippy. The clothing she wore felt cumbersome and made her feel like she was playing a part instead of going undefended into battle. She looked like a beautiful woman, rich and powerful, and Hal would be pleased. Serral blushed. She realized that she wanted to please him, and the emotion surprised her. She had to remember that her part was not to impress a paramour, only to look as if she did. She felt silly. Was it possible she was beginning to enjoy dressing up, and being fussed over, like a girl in a strippy? If so, what did that say about her? Chlore felt so far away. Then she remembered Hal's warning to stay focused and play her part.

*And this!*

Click held up a long strip of satin-lined white fur with long, silky tassels.

*Really?*

*The evenings sometimes grow cold.*

She wrapped the soft fur around her shoulders. It felt delicious. She was a strange woman, living a very odd life. But who could say what service to the cause was supposed to look like?

*I have questions.*

*Yes, Mistress?*

*Who can I trust down there, in the Village?*

The thought river bubbled in confusion.

*Why, all of us, Mistress. All the Harbingers are your humble and devoted servants.*

*And if the Volterran men try to harm me, what then?*

More confusion, tinges of horror.

*No one shall harm you, Mistress!*

*I see. Okay. What happens to Imset ladies who are not liked by the men?*

This question yielded results. She saw a strip of jungle-lined ground covered in low shrubs and puddles and felt a strong sensation of sorrow and pain.

*They are exiled?*

*Put out, yes.*

*And the Xaff hunt them?*

More sorrow and shame. Agreement.

*And do the Xaff always win?*

*We do not know, Mistress. But you are under the protection of the Minsyx! Surely nothing like that will ever happen to you!*

*Calm yourselves, friends.* She said into the river. *All is well.*

They threw themselves onto the floor in supplication, head domes roiling. *I am going now.*

*Oh!* They rose immediately. *We shall let the door guardians know.*

When Serral got to the ground floor, two Helpers were waiting for her outside in a hovering black Bisbee. She noticed its gold stripes and Hal's family crest. She climbed in and the Bisbee rolled down the drive. They were only halfway to the gates when Callia emerged on the side of the road, holding out a thumb. She wore a flowing gown in a colorful, sheer fabric, and a wide-brimmed hat. Serral didn't know the name of her era, but the style seemed familiar.

*Helpers. We will stop and give her a ride.*

The Bisbee slowed. Serral motioned for Callia to get in. The girl smiled, breathless. The carriage floated on.

"Let me out before we get there, okay?"

"Why?" Serral asked.

"You know. I'm low status. You can't afford the ding on your reputation."

"No, no. You're giving me a tour of the resort."

"Indeed I am." Callia brightened. "Who are you?"

"Hallenander's beloved, of course. And nothing could besmirch my... whatever."

Serral straightened her bracelets. Callia wore no jewels, though her long, dark hair, heart-shaped face and light brown eyes were ornament enough. It was obvious why people had thought she and Hallenander would make a good physical match.

Callia smiled. "How are things going? You seem to really be winning Hallenander over. People are noticing."

"I think my main appeal is that I'm young." Serral chose her words carefully. "You know, if you're a half Imset like Hallenander, you want to avoid accidentally taking your mother on as Companion."

Callia laughed, "You're too clever. I already told you. You're saving me from a situation. I like him. I don't want to be his Companion. No need for an apology. But tell me, does he not know who his mother is?"

Serral shrugged. "I don't know. But why else would he choose me? I'm not half as beautiful as you are."

A new feeling crept through her. She was lying. The Harbs had made her just as physically attractive, only in a different way. Callia looked natural. Serral was more dramatic.

"Stop," Callia said. "I already have a paramour. And Hal knows about it. But if the men did... I'd be put out immediately."

"I see."

"We're going to be late."

"I thought I was on my way to meet Hal. What are we late for?"

Callia hesitated. "I'm sorry. I'm not allowed to say anything. But thumbing a ride is acceptable. Just. I think you should tell the drivers to hurry."

She did. Their head domes undulated in agreement, and the Bisbee turned to the east and entered the gardens Serral had seen from her balcony.

"If you can't tell me what is happening tonight, at least help me understand what is happening in general. Please."

Callia eased back in her seat. "Fine. These are the pleasure gardens," she narrated. "There is the reflecting pool, the carriage track, and over there is the kissing maze."

They hovered over perfectly manicured tracks that wound through green gardens decorated periodically by small alcoves housing benches or swings or little tables. Callia pointed out party pavilions, outdoor gaming grounds, a large, flat esplanade resplendent with bathing pools. She pointed to a balustraded cliff edge she called "Lover's Point" where the view was magnificent. First, she saw the white palace, then the royal gardens, the white village, the harbor with its tall, masted ships, and the wide sea beyond. And finally, above all, the two blue-green glass towers twinkled.

"Those towers. What happens inside of them?"

"I am so sorry." Callia shook her head. "But I could be put out if I say too much."

"You've been inside?"

"You must be careful." Callia motioned to the drivers inside the front of the carriage. "They're crafty Dantons."

"I know," Serral whispered. "But I don't have time to discover for myself. If the Harbs get a chance they'll," she almost said 'wipe me' but caught herself in time. "They'll put me out."

Callia hid behind her hat and whispered back, "They're called The Project. And as a Lady Companion, you'll be working on it, working within them. But that's all I can say. We need to go now. Okay?"

"Why are you here, Callia?"

Callia met her eyes, her face wry. "I don't want to be with him, please understand. But I want him to succeed. Hallenander is the future. And we desperately need one."

"I see," Serral said.

"Please, can we go?" Callia said. "The sun is ready to set."

"And that means what?"

"You really don't know anything." Callia looked amazed. "Sunset is when the amusements begin."

They jumped back into the carriage, and as they rolled away, Serral stared at the perfect replication of so many things she'd only seen in images: gazebos, shops, and game courts. It made her ache, the sense that old Imseth had been like this. "So," she said, "the Harbs made a theme park for Volterran men to visit because the men of Volterra are easily bored?"

"That's right," Callia said. "Each of these built environments are based on one of the Great Imsethan Eras. The men like it that way."

"Of course they do. Like visiting a zoo." Serral noticed a daisy pattern on Callia's long, flowing dress. "So, you're from the Flower Children Daze?"

"Right." Callia smiled. "And you must already know you're from the Skyscraper Time."

"And the others?"

"Riellen is from Swing Time. Cheloa is from Graffiti Glamour." Callia blushed.

"Let me guess. I saw Lord and Lady Ages, and Romantic Interlude..." Serral thought about the different costumes she'd noticed. "City of Lights, Peasant Village, and what else?"

"You know your eras."

"Nah. Seen a lot of strippies is all."

As they neared the resort village, Callia pointed out residential buildings. "There's our dormitory. We live like the lower levels of the Lord and Ladies, very plain. We still have Helpers, luckily, and we get to go to most events. No kitchens, though. We eat in the Clubhouse."

"The Clubhouse?"

"See the little building across from the station? If you want to make friends, get out of your penthouse and come be a regular girl with us. We're served three times a day."

"When can I start?" The idea of eating in a community of her own kind made her want to jump out of the Bisbee right there.

The carriage moved slowly down a street of attached houses, each with a manicured garden inside a fence. "Who lives here?" Serral asked.

"Other Lady Companions."

"And those two?" Serral nodded to a pair of villas that stood dark, their gardens bare, their outdoor furniture stacked.

"That's where," Callia's voice lowered, "those are the homes of friends who went missing. But it's been a while now. Before my time."

A chill shot through Serral. She thought about the iron fence, the pain Click and Clack had communicated but not named.

"Listen. I have a warning," Callia whispered. "Riellen is coming after you tonight."

"Coming after me?" Serral said. "What is she going to do, challenge me to hand-to-hand combat?"

"This is serious."

"Is it?"

"She'll seek to humiliate you in front of the men. She'll try to show them, especially Mimellio, that you are a fraud. If that happens..."

"I know. I'll be put out."

"Is that what you want?" Callia breathed in quick and quiet breaths. "Because I don't think you'd last long with the Xaff after you."

Serral paused, then said, "I'm not prepared to escape. And it seems to me, we are all in the same boat when it comes to the Xaff."

"There's a lot you don't know."

"I'm sure there is. Thank you for the warning, Callia. What do you think I should do?"

Her mind raced. She felt foolish. Hallenander had warned her to be careful, but she had forgotten all about Riellen's admonishment to come up with a way to entertain them all.

"Pretend you're one of us; pretend you belong here."

Serral flinched. "I am one of you."

Callia shook her head. "Don't patronize. We both know all Companions except you have our brains rearranged. Half of what we once knew is gone. You are obviously a whole woman."

"A whole woman?"

"You haven't been wiped." The carriage approached the village square. "Serral, look. I have no idea what you're doing, but I do know

Hal is a good man, the only good man in our world. And I'm not alone in that understanding."

Serral put her hand on Callia's wrist. "I know. And from what I've experienced, I agree with you."

"Good. So, we can trust you're looking out for him?"

"You can," Serral said. "Though, I think you overestimate my importance."

"Now, regarding tonight," Callia said while they pulled up and stopped next to the theater. "To impress the men, act entitled. The men are tourists, and just as you said, they look at us like animals in a zoo. They won't be able to tell if you are a real artist or not. The women might, but they aren't the ones who rule here, none of them, no matter how they delude themselves. Make sense?"

Serral laughed. "Not at all."

Callia jumped down. "Good luck."

*Mistress, the orchestra is almost ready for you.*

*The orchestra?*                     .

Chapter Thirty-Five

The white bulbs of the theater's marquee were on and spelled out, *The Evincion.* The glass box office stood empty. The front door didn't open when Serral tugged on it.

Serral augered. Helpers told her to go around to a side door.

*They are waiting for the show to begin!*

*What show?*

*The men are so excited to hear your music!*

Serral let out a string of every curse she could think of. She had no music. She had no talent for performing. She felt like she was in a terrible dream.

*Your place, Mistress! It is time!*

Four helpers dressed in usher's uniforms met her inside and brought her to a wide, dark wooden stage. The curtains remained closed. On the other side, sounds of a tuning orchestra rose from the pit and then silenced. The theater smelled of old wood and hot dust. Serral knew without any evidence that it was old Imseth, built in the time before the Calamity. It might be three hundred years old, moved here by Harbingers from the lost planet. A piece of her ancestors' history. It was a time when they didn't live in big tin cans in deep space, but presided over their own green, beautiful planet. She wanted them to have that again. The thought calmed her.

Helpers showed her where to stand. The curtain hung in front of her like folds of black water. In the center, a narrow slice of light revealed the scene in the auditorium. Women chatted in their seats, their murmurs sounding like a rushing stream. A tall Overlord's head moved to the side as if annoyed. It made Serral think of a bobbing fish, a rock sticking out of a lake. Did they have brains under there? Or just thick, rocky protuberances with no discernible purpose? Her body began trembling with nerves.

The people were waiting. Waiting for her to fail.

Nausea spun in her gut. What would Zaphia, the angelic lady from her dreams in the Medotel, advise her to do? *She didn't prepare me for the traps my own people would set.* Serral took a breath and remembered the promises she and Hal had made. It was too soon to be defeated. She had to do something to succeed.

# 36

Serral and the Harbs in the orchestra augered until they found a tune they both knew, an old ballad from Imseth. It was a field-worker song, sad and low, but beautiful enough that Serral thought it might pass as entertainment. Her stomach threatened to bring back her dinner. She told herself this was less dangerous than a raid but didn't fully believe it. She took measured breaths to calm herself.

*All right,* she augered. *I am ready.*

The curtain rolled open to blinding lights, and beyond those, the glittering throats of hundreds of Imset. On either side of the theatre, rising high above her, Serral saw box seats and in them, the stone men from her previous test in the Medotel, uproarious women, and to her far right, the stoic face of Hallenander.

The music started.

Serral recognized Riellen in a box next to White Dress. She wore a towering red wig and peered through a pair of small binoculars on a stick. She leaned up to Hal's uncle and whispered in his ear. The man smirked.

Serral reminded herself of her first sortie. If she could lie strapped in a harness inside a fighter plane and allow herself to be shot into a raging air battle, she could do this. Her cue passed and the audience tittered. The Harbs played the introduction again, slower this time, and Serral caught her cue, her voice a rusty, quavering vibration that barely rose loud enough to reach the first row.

*I am an Imset, an Imset of Imseth...*

The audience strained to hear. Laughter bubbled.

*Working the soil, tilling the rich earth...*

A tomato fell onto the stage, and then another. Serral didn't look. Harbs scurried across the stage to remove them. One of the helpers was hit by a flying object, and the audience roared.

*And when the whistle blows...*

*And when the Thanton calls...*

*We farmers prepare a day for Myrth.*

The Harb fled the stage, leaving a trail of ooze from an exploded tomato

Serral kept singing, holding her head high and watching Riellen's box. Anger made her louder. The song built in power.

*I am a child, a child of Ysk.*

*Alive or dead, none dispute this.*

*And when for her the stars align...*

*She'll make the heavens mine...*

Suddenly, the audience gasped. Serral blinked, and continued singing as the auditorium grew quiet.

*I will know peace, and joy, and love.*

*Thantons assembling far above.*

*The good will find sweet rebirth.*

The eyes of her audience shifted to her right. She felt a nudge and then someone grasping her right hand. Hallenander, in a black swallowtail tuxedo opened his mouth and sang along. His face was grave, but Serral saw a gleam of mischief in his eyes.

*Sweet rebirth.*

*Sweet rebirth.*

*The good will find sweet rebirth.*

*Right here, here on good green Imseth.*

The orchestra finished with a flourish. The audience didn't move. Hal and Serral reached to the sky, then bowed deeply as if they had pleased their audience entirely. Serral bit back laughter, though she couldn't have said what was funny.

Far off clapping echoed in the room. Where had it begun? Serral couldn't see, except it was high in the back seats in the furthest balcony. Riellen lowered her spectacles and scowled. People began applauding, mechanically at first. Hallenander smiled, a prince, accepting the respect that was his due. He bowed his head in mock protest. Serral was impressed by his ability to command the crowd, to play his part. His hand trembled in hers, but to the world he looked as calm and resolute as a statue. The stone men stood together, smiling and clapping for their prince. Next to them, their Companions offered the same.

Serral held tight to her master's hand, and then took another bow.

Hallenander hovered them away from the theater, rocks kicking up as he gunned the Bisbee.

"You are the thing, master."

He pushed his top hat further down on his head. It was cleverly devised to hide his head dome, making him look more than ever like a Imsethan man of old. "What thing?"

"The Minsyx, the future king, ruler of all Volterra and the Alliance and all that. I'm serious. You're good."

"You're paid to say that."

"Ha!" she said. "There's not a fancy enough prison camp anywhere to make me lie."

"You cunning flirt, you."

She tried to grab the wheel. "Can I drive?"

He pushed her away, "No. We've just narrowly averted having you voided from my service. Let's not tempt fate."

"Bleh," she said and sat back.

They left the village square and buzzed down a road she hadn't seen before.

"And now we have to go to a party? Seriously?"

"That is the purpose of this place. Entertainment venue, then party, then after-party."

"And what happens at these things?"

"Dancing, gossip, gambling. Nothing too debauched. Volterrans pride themselves on their upright morals."

Serral laughed long and hard. Hal smiled.

"The evening is far from over. You did an admirable job back there. I think the Harbingers want you to stay. But danger has not yet passed."

"Was my complete lack of talent that obvious?"

"Only to me."

"So, what's next?"

"I told you. A festive ball."

"No, I mean how are Riellen and your uncle going to try and undermine me now?"

In the lights of the passing streetlights, he looked older and more confident. His face broke into a grin.

"We shall see," he said. "But you did well at the theater. Riellen looked frustrated, which is a sure sign of victory. Your choice of song was irresistible. Volterrans love that kind of old Imsethan music."

Across the village, people traveled on foot away from the theater, chattering like birds calling in the night.

"I can't get over the notion that our two civilizations, your two civilizations, have been so closely linked all these years. I thought only the Harbs took an interest in the Imset."

"Harbinger theft benefited their masters' need for novelty. During my father's youth. Volterrans avidly consumed Imsethan culture."

"And that was during the Cataclysm?"

"Father was a child. But yes. Volterrans live to be well over 100 years old, and many alive today remember the tragic time when Imseth was lost."

Serral sat back. "So, your father is nearing the end of his life span. Imseth died 125 years ago, give or take. Though maybe time is different on Volterra?"

"Not significantly. The Worlds and Evincio all rotate in the same way and use the same calendar."

"Harb work."

"Yes. The Harbingers are nothing if not precise. When and if I move to the Worlds, I will have no significant time adjustments to make."

"Same for me and other Colonials. That is, if we ever get a planet again."

"But the people in space... your Civicians. Will not be able to take part."

The air carried a bitter-sweet scent of flowers. "Civicians who've lived their lives for long periods of time in space can't adjust to gravity on the ground; they die within five years. The whole colonial program was meant to preserve a population of Imset who could live on surface, kids like me with both strong bones and skills. The Harbs, of course, have made that difficult. Rumor is the Imset are about ready to give up."

Hal abruptly stopped the Bisbee. They were near the entrance to the maze, and across from it lay a gravel path along a tree-lined reflecting pool as long as a landing pad, a wide ribbon of rippling moonlight.

"The Imset cannot surrender. It would scuttle my chance to appeal alliance law."

"The Imset don't look at this as a legal fight. They think it's a war. And they think that they've lost, that we've lost."

"The Imset have not given up yet though, or you yourself would not be here." He looked around nervously.

"Sure, technically we're still fighting. But our resources are tapped. Scrap rats like me were grown to be soldiers with the thought that we would colonize the new Imseth. Countless capital was put into the colonies, into the Air Guard, and into the war effort. For generations. But the Harbs have started a new bunch of dirty tricks, which may mean they're tired of playing with their prey. Who can say? I would love to ask the Xaff, but they'd hurt me if I so much as came near. All I know is, if we fail to find a new planet, rumor is the cities won't absorb us all. They're too crowded. And they hate colonials, anyway. We're garbage to them."

Hal scowled. "Good Gods. Was the real purpose of this last battle to rid the Imset of excess children?"

Serral shook her head. "We're not children. We're soldiers. It is our duty to fight and die for our cause. It's our only purpose. Unless we get a planet."

"And you are truly unwelcome in your own cities?"

She pulled the shawl tighter. "So they say. You and I have a lot in common in that way." Her wig itched, her ears rang, and she was hungry. "In truth, no one in their right mind wants to live in the cities. Stories of life there are awful."

"The tales they tell you, before sending you off to die."

"Maybe. But people I trust have told me about how bad the cities are. People who love me and want me to live."

Serral pictured Miss Pune and Whit, Rafe and Brume. Her heart squeezed with the knowledge that none of them would be able to accept the person she was now, in her shimmering evening gown and half-overlord master. She pushed those thoughts aside.

He looked melancholy. "I envy you that."

"What? That people love me? Your father must love you."

"Of course he does. But if I become a political liability, I'm not so sure."

"You're making good progress, Hal. You'll be flying soon."

"Good. Because there is no one I can trust."

"Sire?" she made a face. "You'd best trust your flight instructor."

"As long as I control your enemies, the Xaff, I have complete faith in you."

Serral laughed. "You're smooth."

The party took place in a large crystal house, its clear panes set in iron. The ceilings were strung with elaborate chandeliers that sparkled with light. Serral's heart caught at the magnificence. The Harb orchestra played dance music, but the place felt dreary. Women stood in groups around the perimeter: Riellen and a clutch of bejeweled ladies, then another large tangle with elegant ennui, and further beyond them, a smaller group of more plainly dressed, more nervous-seeming younger girls. Callia stood in that group, gaze averted.

Serral left her wrap and bag with a servant. Hallenander led her onto the polished wooden floor, and they began a swirling, dizzying dance. She willed herself not to fall or be caught under his feet. But he was strong enough to do all the work, and in a few whirls, she relaxed enough to let him lead. The room let out its breath, and the overlord men took up dancing with their ladies, then pairs of women joined in.

Chatter erupted. People smiled. If Hallenander hadn't been holding her, Serral would have tripped, careening off through one of the large panes into the gardens beyond. But he had a firm grip. She couldn't tell if he was enjoying himself or just well-practiced at performing his role.

Finally, the music paused. "I need a drink of water," she said.

They went outside to a wide stone veranda that looked out over the lawn, beyond which the cliff dropped into nothingness. The Reykos towers winked sapphire and emerald in the low light. A Helper approached with crystal goblets of water. Serral gulped.

"What did you call yourself? A scrap rat?"

"Sorry," she wiped water from her chin. "Manners aren't important for the survival of our species."

"At this moment, they are." He looked bemused.

She sipped her glass slowly. "Better?"

He nodded. "Try to keep liquids from dribbling down your face."

"Got it," she said, wiping the front of her dress. "Any other instructions?"

"Too many to mention." He leaned on a barrier. "First things first. You'll need to meet all the Lady Companions."

"Anything for you, master."

The Lady Companions made Serral's task easy by gathering her up in a pack and frog marching her into an adjoining room full of low furniture and tall potted palms.

"Darling, how did you make him fall so deeply in love with you so quickly?" asked a woman in a shiny, white cocktail dress. "Not that you aren't charming, of course."

"Thanks for the compliment?"

"I'm Cheloa, and my master is Lord Kleitwan."

The tall woman pulled Serral into an air kiss. "Serral."

"Sit here." Cheloa patted a deep velvet couch near the fireplace. "I'll perform the rites of the Leading Lady, since Riellen is busy with her man." Cheloa winked a long-lashed eye.

"You mean she's avoiding me?" Serral said.

"I like this one." Cheloa laughed. "Lady Serral, this is Lady Midrey." She nodded to an old, lavender-haired woman. "Beloved of Lord Tuss."

"Lady Serral." Midrey curtsied gracefully. "It is my great honor."

Serral curtsied. "Oh no, the honor is mine."

"Lady Shanno," Cheloa gestured to another tall, deep-voiced woman in a glittering gold evening gown. "Of the house of Lord Maurdoy."

Shanno had an elegant, serene face. Her arched brows lifted. "I offer sincere friendship, little one."

Serral grinned. "Accepted, thank you."

"Mistake," Cheloa murmured, and everyone laughed.

Cheloa continued to introduce Serral around the group. Lady Zella kept her eyes down, which struck Serral as odd. Lady Irie looked uncomfortable in her long, tight-waisted gown, but her face blazed with good humor. Lady Jinima wore an embroidered get-up equal to any of the men, and she curtsied theatrically. Lady Latrice had comically wide red lips and bouncing fuchsia curls that threatened to fall into her tintorello ash. She held out her hand to shake.

"Nice to know you."

Harbs came around the corner with hors d'oeuvres and refreshments. Serral realized after a long pause that she was expected to serve herself first.

"Please," she met Lady Midrey's eyes, "Let us partake of our Mast ers'..."

Several of the women made pained faces.

"Let's eat."

They snacked and sipped sweet, sparkling wine. Serral couldn't think of anything to say. The others started chatting Companionably. Serral bathed in the sound of Imset. She felt almost happy. Then she noticed that the women were speaking in polite code.

"There is talk of rain."

"So early in the season?"

"I hope you're ready for tomorrow."

"Oh, of course I am. And I know you are too, sister."

"What I don't know is, why have they kept us out for ten days."

"It must have to do with…"

The women suddenly fell silent.

"Candid bitches will get stitches," Riellen said from the doorway.

Lady Irie swiftly vacated her seat. Riellen held a brown tintorello in a small holder, brought it to her lips, and sucked in smoke. She sat and crossed her legs, leveling her gaze at Serral. No one moved.

"Where did you get your training?" she asked, curling her red lips. "And I don't mean your singing and dancing, unbelievable as they are."

Cheloa jumped in, "Darling, the girl is seventeen at best. Be nice."

Riellen sat back, blowing smoke. "Evidently that is quite old enough to know how to take advantage of a needy boy."

Serral smoothed her dress. She could tell Hal she'd met all the Lady Companions. There was no need to tangle.

"No answer?" Riellen leaned toward her.

Serral noticed her eyes were bloodshot. She wondered how old Riellen was, how long she'd been stuck in the Xalavria.

"What are you asking me, exactly?"

"*What are you asking me, exactly?*" Riellen sneered. "Mimellio is on to you. You're not worthy of this place. Everyone can see that."

Serral felt a bubble of anger rising in her chest. "What do you want?" she said. "Do you want me to say that Hallenander is too stupid to know his own mind? Is that it? Does his uncle think Hallenander is a child who needs trained concubines to help him with his homework?"

Riellen's face filled with rage. The others tensed, though Serral sensed both enjoyment and fear.

Serral stood. "This can go one of two ways. Either you realize that we are all Imset," a look passed between Cheloa and Shanno, "and therefore on the same side. Or," Shanno made a nonverbal signal, and Cheloa looked away. "Or you and I can go to war. But I caution you."

"Do you now?" Riellen said loudly. She was drunk.

"I do. I caution you. You're queen rat on a ship that isn't built to last. You have no power in the grand scheme of things."

Riellen hissed, "What do you know, little miss No Talent? Sashay in here, start lecturing people about their place."

Serral stood tall. "I'm not your enemy."

"The hell you're not." Riellen reached for a drink from a tray.

"I'm here to remind you of who you really are. Who we are. And what we are truly capable of. Because some of you have... forgotten."

Pain flashed across faces. People exchanged glances. Serral became aware that the women knew their memories were gone. And it hurt to be reminded.

She went on. "If that's a problem, if you are so deeply involved in the schemes of people who will never accept you, it may be time to consider your loyalties. I for one encourage you to look within. And remember yourselves."

The other Companions shifted, now visibly uncomfortable.

Cheloa held up a long-nailed hand. "Don't underestimate our understanding, little one. You're very new. The complexity of our situation may come as a surprise. Our... importance in the grand scheme."

"Fair enough. I hope over time, you will find a way to teach me that doesn't involve jeopardizing my Lord's position."

Women gasped. Some laughed. Others looked ashamed.

"It's good you're thinking about your Lord's wellbeing," Lady Midrey said gently. "We cannot fault you for that."

"I will do anything to solidify my Lord's position. And as you can see." Serral tossed her long, white hair. "I have more important skills than entertainment."

Some faces looked baffled by her words. But Riellen stepped back, face drained of color.

Serral took the fur a Helper held out and wrapped herself in it. "Good night. Lovely meeting you all." She turned and walked back out into the dancehall. Hal was in shirtsleeves, surrounded by the stone men. He looked happy. When he saw the look on her face, he excused himself.

"You're still standing."

"For now," she said. "There's real fear here. I don't know what's at stake, but it's more than just making master happy."

He grinned. "They still hate you?"

"I think they hate themselves," she laughed. "But there's more going on than just being party girls. They are protecting something. I don't know what we've disrupted."

"Nor do I. But the Volettu is watching us now, so let's be idiotic young people for them. Safer that way."

Serral began giggling moronically, and he joined in.

"And now," he put his hand on her elbow. "You must meet my advisors."

"Oh no." She stopped walking. "I met them already. In the Medo-tel."

He gave her a look. "Really meet them. Ingratiate yourself."

"You are a terrible master."

"And you have no notion of duty."

Serral forced a smile, and they went to greet the stone men. Their names swirled together in her mind; Tuss, Maurdoy, Klietwan, Eltu, Lollio, Zinnerit, and Kettu. Each wore a tunic with elaborate detailing. Some had braided beards, others ceremonial weapons, and everything glittered with jewels. The most alien thing about them wasn't their long, oiled head domes, but their eyes, huge, heavily lidded, framed by thick smudges of kohl. When they looked at her, she felt the depth of their condescension, their foreignness and their huge self-regard. It wasn't that they hated her, or she them, but more that they were from such different worlds that nothing she did could appear to them to be anything but novel. The big eyes that watched her were stranger than the black orbs Harbingers had, because the Harbs understood that Serral was a living being, Thanton or not, and therefore their equal. The Volterran men would never understand that. They were incapable of seeing her as more than an animal available for their service.

By the time Hallenander dropped her at her doorstep, Serral was so tired she practically melted out of the carriage. The Helpers held the tall glass doors open, and she kicked herself for feeling the sense of home the place already gave her. Had the Harbs engineered that, somehow?

She turned to Hallenander, who looked relaxed. He was enjoying all this. Why wouldn't he? Being hunted was an abstraction for him, something he was preparing for but not convinced would ever really happen. Serral had no way to know how much danger he was in. But his paranoia was her reason for being alive, so she decided to trust in it.

"What time for lessons tomorrow?" she said.

"Sadly, I will be with the Volettu all day." Hallenander tapped the steering column, distracted. "It's a good sign. It means they have turned their attention away from controlling my Companion choice and toward the future of my family's legal case."

Serral felt unaccountably disappointed. "Okay, your Highness."

Hallenander gave her a long look.

"Oops. I almost forgot my role in life." She came close to the carriage, and he leaned down. Their lips met lightly, and she inhaled his fine, complicated cologne.

She straightened. "Master, what a delightful day! Please don't delay in bestowing your manly attentions on unworthy little me again soon. It's what I live for."

He cracked a smile. "You're an ungrateful, crude barbarian."

"And you're an entitled, conniving freak." She used her palm to wipe her lips. "Seriously though. Come back soon."

He drove away down the drive.

Thoughts of a warm soak pulled at her. If only the elevators weren't so far away. Serral stooped to remove her shoes, which seemed to have shrunk in the hours since she put them on.

"Serral," came a sharp whisper.

Callia, wearing dungarees and a simple shirt, appeared from behind some bushes.

Serral motioned for her to come closer. "Hi. Bit late, don't you think??"

"Can I come in?"

"Sure. But I'm getting in a tub. With or without you."

Callia smiled.

When the two girls had soaked in warm bubbles, compared notes on the strange stars above them, wrapped themselves up in thick robes and shared most of a chocolate sprinkle cake, Callia got around to why she'd come. They each sat on a long velvet couch, and while the night was just barely cool, Serral had the Harbs light a fire.

"They really take care of you, don't they?"

"It's because of Hal. All of it. I'm sorry. Is that bad for me to say?"

"No, of course not. Hal and I are friends. I have an idea about what's going on."

"Yes?" Serral touched the silver candle stick, smiling. "Care to enlighten me?"

"He wants someone who's not on the project."

There was that word again. "You mean the project of getting him ready to be his father's heir?"

Callia put a hand to her mouth, dark eyes widening. "Uh oh. Forget I said anything."

"Nope." Serral sat up. "Spill."

"If it gets back to Riellen..." Callia looked fearful.

"Let me handle that witch." Serral flopped comfortably sideways. "The thing is, I'm a bit of a spy for Hal. And if I can figure out some of what his uncle is really up to, you know, it helps him."

"Sure you are." Callia rubbed her temples. "Listen. It's risky." Her eyes traveled to the door. "They could have Xaff auger me, and then I'd have to betray people's trust."

Serral leaned on an elbow. "Then don't speak. What if I just happened to follow you to the thing? Sneaky upstart that I am?"

Callia's teeth gleamed in the firelight. "Well, that would be on you. It wouldn't be my fault if you just happened to be curious and stalked me, at say, dawn tomorrow morning?"

Serral lay back. "Is that why you came here tonight? Because you wanted to not invite me to follow you to whatever this mysterious project is?"

"No." Callia shifted nervously. "I need a favor."

"Could we consider it an exchange? I needed information. You need, what?"

Callia looked grateful. "M'Ysk, you are such a breath of air."

"Is that code for something not at all flattering?"

"Nope." Callia had a desperate edge in her voice. "I need jewels."

"What?" Serral sat up. "What is the deal with jewels in this place?"

"Before Hal chose you, everyone thought I'd be gifted with his wealth. Like you are, here." Callia waved at the opulent room with its high, medallioned ceiling that reflected light from the pools, its gold-paneled walls gleaming with crystal sconces.

"This was supposed to be your penthouse," Serral said.

"It was meant to look that way. I have had an understanding with Hal since he came of age. He knows I'm with someone else, and he used me as a convenient distraction to stall while he waited for you. I don't know where he found you and I don't want to know." Callia held up her hand. "No offense, but you must have something that he needs. And it must be more than charm and talent."

"True." Serral nodded.

"I played along with his plans, because he asked me to, and because I hate the men and the Helpers, all of them. And" her voice dropped, "because he's Rakki. He's half us, and that means something to me. But during the time I pretended that I was going to become his Companion, I incurred," Callia flinched, "gambling debts."

"Gambling debts?" Serral tried to soothe Callia with a smile, but her friend looked downcast. "Jewels are money here?"

Callia nodded. "The price for playing the game at all."

"And if you are in debt, you don't get to go to the ball?"

"Right. And if I don't show up at the parties, and the men start to notice..."

"You'll be punished."

"Yes. And not only me, but all those who depend on me."

Serral snapped her fingers, calling out loudly. "Click, fetch my jewelry cases."

Click tried to auger, what Serral assumed would be a reminder that all her property belonged to Hal.

*I know that the Minsyx owns them. They won't leave the grounds. It's okay.*

Click and Clack scurried in with two other Helpers Serral had named Spoons and Phava. Callia's eyes bugged at the dozen leather-bound chests they brought.

"What do you need?" Serral held up handfuls of glittering baubles.

Callia dug into the closest box of jewelry. "He is really rich."

"Help yourself." Serral itched with fatigue. "We outsiders need to stick together."

"Serral," Callia tried a rope of colored gems on her wrist, "you don't have to tell me what you and Hal are up to. But whatever it is, if you need me, I'm here."

Serral smiled. "I like a girl who pays her debts."

Serral walked to Xalavria Station by the light of breaking dawn. She wore overalls, a plain shirt, and a pair of work boots. As she moved toward Callia's common building, conversation reached her ears, women speaking in hushed tones. The rising sun illuminated a streetscape as different from the evening before as Serral could imagine. Callia moved toward the outer gates. She showed no sign of noticing Serral. Once at the station, they joined dozens of resort ladies, unpainted and wigless, wearing simple day clothes and holding baskets or cloth bags. Callia stood in the back of the cue and looked straight ahead, waiting.

"What are you doing here?" a voice from over Serral's shoulder said.

She turned and recognized the handsome, slender person, Cheloa.

"You know," she said. "The project."

Cheloa clucked their tongue. "There's no one available right now."

"Oh. I know. But I'm still here," Serral said woodenly.

"He must just want you to observe and report, right?"

Serral let out her breath. "Those were his exact words."

"All right then, sweetheart. Here comes the bus now."

A long, shining black vehicle approached. Its side door opened revealing two Harb drivers. Accustomed to routine, the orderly line filed aboard. Serral was the last. She took a seat in the front where she could see out.

The doors hissed closed, and the bus passed swiftly out the silver gates and onto the road leading to the airfield, the same road she and Hal had traveled. But at the second Xaff checkpoint, the bus turned abruptly westward. They headed to the south side of the village. Toward the towers.

Serral leaned her head on the smoked glass window and pretended to sleep.

*Hello friends. Where are we going?*

*Oh, Mistress! You honor us unworthy servants. Safety is our primary concern. But uniting special friends is so important.*

She sensed their yearning for approval.

*Yes, uniting special friends is very nice. And I see you are hard at work. Where are you taking us?*

When they had finished basking in the glow of her acknowledgement, the drivers explained that they were going to The Reykos.

*Tell me why.*

*The reunion of special friends!*

She felt warmth and excitement. Chaos. Laughter. Children.

*The Reykos is a school?*

Or is it more like Chlore? A colony?

The driving Helpers hesitated, unsure how to explain. The ideas of other Harbs flowed into the thought river, twenty or more new minds.

*We are almost there. You shall see.*

Serral opened her eyes. They entered a bright tunnel. The others on the bus gathered their baskets and bags, speaking quietly. A small woman in a white dress caught Serral's eye. It took her a moment to recognize Riellen. Before Serral had a chance to greet her, the bus stopped.

Serral now understood the images from the thought river. Noise rose deafeningly, squeals of delight, shrieks of recognition. They exited the bus into a cavernous landing and saw forty or more Rakki children of varying ages. Each child was greeted by a companion with an enormous hug and joyful noise. There seemed no other point to the meeting than the reunion of special friends.

Serral found a bench and sat to watch. Groups moved across the stone atrium to a set of escalators. Blue light bathed the space. Plants full of flowers and butterflies draped over the sides of the escalators. Fountains splashed. The place felt less like a colony and more like an indoor nature park but carefully supervised like the Xalavria. The scene unfolded like a well-practiced ritual. The smallest children, none younger than five, led women by hand. These duos were followed by clusters of older children. They held paintings, stuffed dolls, or other small gifts. They chattered non-stop in Volterran. Serral was astonished to see Cheloa, Riellen, and the others answering fluently. Did the men know they spoke their language? When in the Xalavria, the men all spoke Imseth. She looked for someone to auger, but decided she didn't want to make a spectacle of herself. On the edges of the room, Harb helpers watched intently.

The children lead the women up the escalators. The atrium began to clear, and Serral noticed that not all the special friend reunions were entirely happy. Some of the Companions were relaxed, but others seemed to barely endure the arm tugs and pleas for attention. Callia passed a shouting girl of around seven pulling on her arm. Callia reached into her bag and handed the girl a rag doll. The girl took it, made a face, and threw the toy on the ground. Callia's stony expression failed to hide her misery. She clearly didn't want to be here. Several others looked just as unwilling.

Riellen walked arm in arm with a stammering teenager whose feet pointed inward like a bird. His skin and eyes resembled Hallenander, though he was younger. A brother maybe, or a cousin. Riellen looked at the boy tenderly, betraying no impatience with his slow gait.

Serral followed them up the escalator. They reached a room full of play structures, plants and trees, a facsimile of nature encased in the tower's glass walls. More children stood on the balconies of higher floors and watched the loud romping below. Play time began in earnest, and groups moved to swings, or sand, or picnic areas. Baskets and bags opened for gift exchange. Sound disappeared into the towering space, and everyone settled into a happy rumble. The place felt like the part of Chlore colony where small children were housed. Except here, Harbs roamed the periphery observing and all the children were Rakki. They were bigger than Imset kids, with their long, bald head crests and large eyes, but their energy was the same as the children's on Chlore. They all reminded Serral of Hal. She wished he could see the scene around her. Words couldn't convey its exuberance, the life force of these energetic bodies.

Serral found a hygiene area, and when she'd secured some privacy, she augered. The thought river bubbled over with happy vibrations; these helpers were much more alive than the ones in the Xalavria. They delighted in the children and held the women in high regard. Serral understood that this place was the reason the Imset women were here. They were not solely for entertainment; they were here for this nurturing tumble of joy. Were these special friendships for kids like Hal who maybe had parents on the Volterran side, but no place in the world?

*Friends, what can you share with me about what is happening here?*

*Mistress! We are so deeply honored that you have come to see our work!*

*These are all Rakki children, yes?*

*They are. This generation benefits from Imset nurturing, which helps them thrive. Are they not the most intelligent, beautiful, most blessed beings in all creation?*

*Oh yes. They are wonderful. Are they meant to replace the unborn children of Volterra?*

*If all goes well. They are meant to be children, strong and kind and good. We serve them and those who love them.*

*What if things don't go well?*

The thought river darkened. Serral felt her chest implode with worry.

*Things will go well! Surely they will. Surely they will.*

*Of course, the children will be all you hope for. You have worked hard*

*Oh, yes, very hard. But to be tasked with raising and educating the blessed ones, the future of the universe, is not work, it is pleasure. The Rakki are the chosen of Ysk, and shall inherit all the fruits of life, Ysk willing. And we do our duty, because any of us could be reborn as Rakki one day. Even you, Thanton Mistress.*

Serral sighed heavily.

*Right. The chosen of Ysk. And only Imset women can raise them. Am I getting this right? Not men. Only women?*

*There are few men in the Xalavria. Shall we show you more?*

*Not now, friends. But I am very impressed with your beautiful work.*

They shimmered with gratitude.

*Could you tell me though, only one more thing?*

*Yes, Mistress?*

*Are these women the children's biological mothers? Is that why they're here?*

The helpers laughed.

*Each child is the best of all the mothers. That is why the children are so special, you see?*

She didn't see.

*And their fathers?*

Fog appeared in her mind, a blankness that was so full of images and thoughts it could only mean the Harbs weren't comfortable with the question. Before they cut her off completely, she changed the subject.

*So. The other Reyko, the green one, what is that tower for?*

The connection went even duller, and there was a sense of agony.

*Never mind, friends. You don't have to tell me.*

The thought river settled into a polite transmission of dutiful hospitality.

*Are you hungry or thirsty, Mistress?*

*No, I am fine. Thank you for your kindness. May Ysk bless you.*

*Good day, dear Thanton!*

*I am not a Thanton right now, friends.*

*We know! Perhaps we shall meet in the next life. If Ysk is good and we are fit to live in her grace.*

Again, she sensed need.

*I am sure she is pleased with your hard work.*

Why did she say that? She grimaced as the thought river rose in a cacophony of ecstatic screaming. The more she augered with these Helpers, the weirder her responses became. It was as if she were losing herself to the thought river. She closed the connection.

Serral stood behind Callia while in line for the afternoon return bus, and Callia whispered, "When we board, sit next to me. Conflict is coming. You don't want to be sitting near the front."

"What kind of conflict?" Serral asked. But Callia didn't answer. They took their seats.

Riellen climbed up the bus's entry steps, openly sobbing. Lady Midrey and Lady Irie followed, both stone faced. The three stood motionless near the front as the doors closed and the bus began to move. Riellen cursed through tears.

"Why are they so upset?" Serral whispered. Callia's expression warned her to be quiet.

"Happy now, you impostor?" Riellen called to Serral, wiping her eyes with the sleeve of her dress. "And the rest of you? Glad you let her win, are you?"

Serral didn't know how to respond. The other women shrank into their seats, avoiding Riellen's gaze. The bus got underway and drove back through the wide shoulders of scrub land flanked by sheer walls of jungle.

"You arrogant white-haired bitch. You think you're superior because you're a soldier."

The bus stopped. Serral felt an electric charge. Xaff fighters. "I don't know what you're talking about," she said.

Riellen laughed maniacally. "That's right. You know nothing. You're a talentless nobody. And you waltz in here, acting like you own the place just because that spoiled boy decided to rile his poor uncle.

So many jewels, and flowers, and trips to wherever it is you let him have his way with you. No effort to turn your situation into something with dignity. Or grace."

Serral felt alarmed by the insult. It didn't surprise her—she and Hallenander had intended to create that impression—but the scorn Riellen spewed felt dangerous. More than a drama about pecking order. Life or death.

"Riellen. What is happening here?" Serral measured her voice.

"You don't even know, do you?"

Serral looked around. No one met her eyes. "I don't know. Please enlighten me."

Riellen said bitterly, "I'm going to be sent off like an animal, to be hunted. And I'll never see my kids And who's going to explain that to them?" She broke down, sobbing.

The doors hissed open. An automated voice said, "Those of you who have arrived at your destination, please exit the vehicle."

Serral turned to Callia, "What have you got in your bag?"

Callia opened the cloth satchel on her lap. "Yarn art, three clay pots, my knitting needles."

"Give me the needles."

Serral tucked the knitting needles up the sleeve of her shirt.

No one made a sound. Riellen pressed on her mouth with her hands, trying to stop the emotional pain. A Xaff warrior entered the bus and waved a pistol at the three standing women. Riellen choked on her tears.

Serral got up and stood behind her. She whispered into the back of her hand, "When I give the signal, run deep into the jungle as fast as you can."

Riellen squeaked, "I don't want to go."

"You have no choice."

The older woman sobbed. "He loves me. He doesn't want to do this."

The three women stepped off the bus. Serral followed. She counted four warriors, all helmeted, all heavily armed, riding two armored Bisbees.

She closed her eyes. She asked the drivers, *Helpers, what happens now?*

An electric Xaff shock ran through her, but she kept a tenuous connection to the thought river anyway.

*The ladies must run, and the Xaff will hunt them. They shall die in glory. May the Thantons bless them.* They hummed prayerfully.

Serral turned to the open bus, speaking aloud in Imset to the drivers, "Go now. The others don't need to see this."

The doors closed immediately. The bus moved down the road, leaving Serral and the others alone with the Xaff.

Serral hissed, "Run now. Do not stop. Get to the jungle."

Lady Midrey's eyes were calm. "There is a life for us? Out there? With the Wilter?"

"Only one way to find out."

"Who are you?" asked Lady Irie. "You're not one of us."

Serral stepped back. "I am. You just don't know it. Go. Now."

The Bisbees eased toward them. Serral slipped a knitting needle into each hand. The three women ran. Their skirts flew. They tumbled and grabbed and ripped through the scrubby field. Serral jumped up onto one of the Bisbees, knocking the other off course. She felt three things simultaneously; the harsh energy of Xaff trying to bore into her brain, the report from several rounds of bullets fired from a mounted rifle, and the warm gush of blood from the necks of the two Xaff where she'd buried the knitting needles. She threw each foundering body off the craft and commandeered the controls.

The second Bisbee speed toward the women. Lady Irie was the fastest. Midrey followed close behind. They vaulted across tree roots, bushes and puddles. One of Riellen's feet had lodged in a tangle of tree roots. She screamed, frantic. Shots rang out.

Serral flattened the throttle, leveled her craft's rifle, and squeezed off ten shots. One of the Xaff went down. The other pointed a side arm at Riellen, who finally freed her foot and staggered toward the steep wall of jungle. Serral stopped shooting for fear of hitting her.

"You don't want her," Serral yelled to the remaining Xaff. "I am here!"

The Xaff looked at his partner bleeding out on the seat. He pointed his pistol at Serral, uncertain. Serral felt the throb of his mind, trying to confront her. Callia had said the Xaff could wipe her with a single auger. She feared opening her mind, feared responding to him and risking the wipe.

Riellen screamed, "This is your fault!"

Serral and the Xaff stood frozen in standoff.

"You're being put out, Riellen," Serral said while her eyes stayed locked on the panting Xaff. "I had nothing to do with that. I am trying to save your life."

"You have everything to do with it! If you'd stayed away from Hallenander, he would have been able to go on for months, years even, without any problems. If he weren't so selfish, he could have bought time to get those babies ready for the Fullness. It's too soon for them! You are stupid brats, the both of you."

The Xaff warrior pushed his mind at her, a maddening thud. She forced herself to focus. If Riellen would just move a few meters, Serral would have a clear shot.

"Hal didn't know about the Rakki kids."

Riellen stared, her face draining of color. "Taurellio is such a bastard. He knows his brother loves me. But nothing matters except his ambition. Even the children. He would kill them all in a heartbeat if it suited his purpose."

"Run, Riellen. Now."

"There's nothing for me in that jungle. I'm not a Wilter. I won't eat dirt and live in caves."

Irie and Midrey ran into the wall of trees.

"There's life for you there."

"You don't get it!" her voice rang through the canyon. "Stupid child. My life is back there. In the Reykos."

A single shot echoed.

Riellen slumped and fell to the ground.

Serral spun around. The Xaff lowered his side arm, ready for Serral to kill him. She lifted her gun and squeezed the trigger. Her sense of the warrior's mind dissolved into smoke and dissipated into silence. Thrill entered her. But the energy infused with anger. Instead of vibrance, Serral felt violation.

She hollered into empty air, "I don't want to be your liberator! I'm not your Thanton."

She ran to Riellen. Blood soaked her white dress, mixed with dirt, and turned to oozing red mud. She had a wound in her torso and one on her upper arm. Serral gripped Riellen's arm while ripping a piece from her sleeve to fashion a tourniquet.

"I'm going to get you to help," she said.

The older woman's bright eyes gazed up at the sky. "I don't want help." Her voice drifted. "All I ever wanted was what I had. And you took it from me."

"You were a slave." Serral worked the tourniquet tight.

"Everyone is a slave, sweetheart. Even the men doing their emperor's bidding. Even Hallenander. Especially Hallenander."

"Shhhh... tell me later."

"One day he was a needy little monster, and then he found you. Now he's just like his father, crafty, full of schemes. Only thinking of himself."

"That's not true. Stop talking now. You need your strength."

"Why are you fighting so hard, girl?" Riellen said in breathy fits. "He'll put you out, too, you know. As soon as he's gotten what he wants."

"Please stop moving."

"Mimellio sees what you're up to. He's going to make sure the Xaff hunt you dead, make sure his precious nephew knows his little rebellion is meaningless. Hallenander is the real killer. He won't care what the Xaff do to you. He'll be Syxarit of the Eight Worlds. He'll forget he ever knew you."

"Shut up, now, Riellen."

"Serves you right." Her voice was almost too weak to hear.

Serral wrapped her arms under the older woman to carry her. But it was too late. Riellen's eyes ceased to see.

Serral passed two Xaff patrols on her way back to the resort, but neither stopped her. The uniformed Harbingers stood impassively, as if waiting for her to shoot them, too. She muttered old prayers from Inoa's lessons to keep the dull pressure of their minds from entering hers.

When she arrived at the silver gates, Callia's friend Alysse let her in, saying, "We've been watching for you. Something's wrong."

"I know," Serral said wearily. "Did the project ladies get home all right?"

"Yup." Alysse closed the gates carefully. "And they're saying a lot of crazy stuff about you."

"No kidding."

"Someone said they saw you standing over Riellen's body."

Serral nodded. "I stood over her body, all right. But I didn't kill her."

Alysse looked relieved. "Of course not. The Xaff would have executed you."

Serral walked to the Clubhouse. She augered and determined that the Harb Helpers were in the back kitchens. In the large, front common room, in front of a massive fireplace, Serral helped herself to water and sat, shaking. Several women nodded politely, then disappeared.

Callia stalked in, out of breath. "Rumors are flying." She sat next to Serral. "Tell me what happened."

Serral told her but left out how the Xaff tried to get her to kill them. She kept the Thrill coursing through her like a nasty fever to herself.

"Damned Harbs," Callia said. "You look terrible."

"The rest of the girls really think I killed Riellen?"

"No one wants to believe Mimellio would do something so cold." Callia looked haggard. "We thought he loved her. She thought so too."

"It wasn't Mimellio that killed Riellen. It was the Harbs."

Callia sat back. "How do you know that?"

"I can't prove it, but," Serral sighed. "Riellen's boy, her Rakki child in the tower."

"Piettu. What about him?"

"He's one of the oldest kids in the place."

"Right. She'd been with him since he was tiny. She was so proud of him."

"Because he's of Sevenni blood. Can't you see that?"

Callia gasped. "Taurellio's? Or Mimellio's?"

"Does it matter? Isn't Piettu in line for the throne, either way?"

"So, for the Helpers anyway, your appearance at The Project wrecked Riellen's status as foster-mother to the Heir. Because, if you were to be placed on the project, you would be the most highly placed foster mother. She lost her place."

"Ah." Serral put the cool water glass against her forehead. "Piettu was her safety. He was the reason the Harbs kept her around."

"But that only makes sense if the Harbs believe you're more than temporary. Otherwise, they wouldn't place you with any Rakki kids. The Project is too important. They must think Hal is destined to become legal ruler, the Syxarit."

"I don't know." Serral shook her head. "Maybe the Harbs think he's going to be put out himself. Piettu is almost old enough to take his place. But Hal had eighteen years of the Volettu of Eight guiding and molding him; wouldn't they give Piettu at least a couple of years of the same?"

"Who knows. For all we know, half those kids could be in line for the throne," Callia said.

"Half. Or all."

"This is all going to end soon. Isn't it? We'll all be put out."

Serral was not sure. "Maybe. But the men don't seem to understand that. They think the Xalavria is for them. For their amusement, their entertainment. No one has told them it's really a front for foster mothers to nurture a new breed of people."

"None of us would have told them. It's a completely taboo subject." Callia bit a cuticle. "Like... empty townhouse kind of taboo. Like speaking of the women who once lived here, and once did our work as Companions. And now have mysteriously disappeared."

"Sure. Because if the Volettu knew, they wouldn't work so hard to help Hal. They'd have moved on to Piettu who is not as difficult."

"Do you think the Syxarit knows? The Harbingers wouldn't do something like this under his nose, would they?"

"He must know," Serral said. "Maybe their secrecy has a dual purpose. What if it's to keep the people of Volterra from understanding that Hal is just a way to legally allow Rakki to take over the whole eight worlds? If they accept one Rakki, wouldn't eventually there *only* be Rakki in Volterra?"

The two women sat in silence. First Serral broke into a small smile, then Callia did.

"Oh, it's good."

Callia giggled. "If it didn't involve the death of the Imset, it would be perfect."

"Just one thing I don't understand. Who is Hal's foster mother?"

"I heard," Callia bit the end of a piece of dark hair, "he didn't have one. He was fostered by the men and an Imset tutor named Geddon. Rumor is, Hal helped Geddon run away before the Xaff had a chance to murder him."

"Poor Hal. What a terrible life. Not a single person you can trust."

Callia looked sideways at her friend. "Are you falling in love with your Master?"

Serral ignored her. She thought about the immaculate collection of planes in the flight center, the lived-in office off the contriving bay, Hal's secrecy about who had compiled the bone yard. "Don't you ever wonder what happened to the women who came first? To the people who lived here before it became Hallenander's finishing school?"

Callia laughed. "I have enough to worry about. I can only hope they moved on to a better place."

"That seems to be the best any of the people around here can hope for."

She and Callia moved on to other topics, then Serral bid her friend goodnight.

Serral walked back to her building, feeling as shunned as she had when cinched. When she stepped off the elevator Hallenander was sitting on a hard-back chair, handsome face full of rage.

"Oh, hello master."

He spoke with a dangerous edge. "You are not to leave here again."

She studied him. He was neither trustworthy nor untrustworthy, she decided. He was just a man trying to stay alive, trying to end a war. Like her.

"I found The Project. It's impressive."

"As is your handiwork, I'm told."

"What handiwork? You mean, my pretty dress?" She looked down at her bloody shirt. "Attractive, I know."

Hal rubbed the sides of his nose as if trying to hold his temper in. "What were you thinking?"

Serral felt the Thrill leave her body, the last rush of air from a balloon.

"I have been hunted." She closed her eyes. "I have hidden in holes in the ground while bombs exploded. I have seen the adults I love lose their senses from strain. I have seen kids I've known all my life blown out of the sky for no reason other than being born an Imset."

"So, you are sorry you're not wiped?"

She snapped, "No. I am sorry to be on the wrong end of a terrible war."

"Oh? I had no idea there was a war on." Hallenander's words dripped with sarcasm. "If only I were in a position to do something about that. Oh wait! Perhaps I am, but my Companion is threatening to derail my efforts with her unauthorized, Imset barbarism."

"Imset barbarism?" Serral straightened. "Imset barbarism is nothing in comparison to what your father's servants do in the name of your people. Wake up, Prince."

They fell into silence.

Hal rose and walked to the door, then said, "You have not left this property. You have been here all day, doing small tasks I assigned to you for my pleasure. Your hair will be freshly washed, those bloody clothes burned. You will look immaculate and well groomed. You will smile and greet everyone you meet with polite grace." His voice again grew sarcastic. "Such a performance is a great stretch for the likes of you, I know." He smoothed his tunic. "As my Companion, it would never occur to you to engage in mortal combat with Xaff fighters. You are but a weak girl with no particular talents. Whatever rumors the ladies are currently spreading amount to nothing but idle gossip meant to undermine your status."

His body was rigid with anger. She did not like it. She did not understand it, until with a moment's pain, she did. She had acted rashly. She had failed to trust him.

"I'm sorry. You told me to get information, and I did." Serral blinked back tears. She stood up, but black dots swarmed around her eyes, holes of energy where the Thrill had been.

"Wait," he said quickly. "Are you hurt?"

She looked at her arms, scratched and bruised. "Nothing your servants can't repair, Sevenni Highness."

"That's right. I'm the master here. Do not forget that."

She looked deep into his eyes. "If you ever say anything like that again, I swear I'll let the Xaff wipe me clean. See how much you enjoy my flying lessons then."

His face flashed with annoyance. He took her wrist in his and hissed, "It's easy to act rashly."

"Don't touch me." She tried to twist away, but he was much stronger than she.

"You are a soldier. You have only one solution to every problem. Violence. But unlike you and your kind..."

"My kind? You mean half of you?"

He pinned her arms behind her. "I mean the kind of person who crashes into a starship and thinks that it makes her some kind of hero. When that kind of sacrifice is cheap."

She squirmed. "Oh yeah? Let's see you sacrifice something, your Sevenni Highness."

His voice was low. "I have. Among other things, my credibility, by taking you as my Companion."

"I will always defend my people. Get that through your thick skull. You don't know..."

He flung her arms away. "Be smarter. I command it. Think through the consequences of your actions."

"So they don't embarrass you?"

He spun toward her. "So they don't jeopardize our agreement, you savage."

Serral stepped back. "Get out."

"I am your master."

"You're your father's plaything."

He moved away from her. "This is your only warning."

She drew breath to say more. But Hallenander was gone.

Chapter Thirty-Seven

Only Callia, Alysse and a couple of their lower status friends acknowledged Serral's existence. Hallenander sent huge bouquets of flowers every day, had them carried through the resort by Harb delivery Helpers for all to see. Enormous, heart-shaped boxes of chocolates arrived. Velvet cases spilling jewels that Serral fastened over her ladylike outfits. She spent time sketching and augering, but nothing interesting presented itself. And from her window, every day, silver glimmers against blue sky reminded her of the world she had left behind. She felt restless and frustrated.

On the third day Serral put on the blue-and-white frock that Click and Clack had laid out for her. She put on the gloves and the matching shoes, picked up the small frame purse that felt like something Hal would approve of, and went to the row of Lady Companion town houses. Hal had said she had to stay in the Resort. He could not fault her for taking a walk. And she would make sure he did not find out. Because sitting on her terrace watching starships land and take off in the distance was driving her mad.

There she found Cheloa sitting in their garden, reading a paper magazine and smoking a tintorello. The table in front of them held a tea service and pastel cakes.

"You're missing your man, aren't you," Cheloa said in a honeyed voice. They were wearing a pair of tight, cropped pants, a shimmery tunic, and a sparkling turban. "Come tell mama all about it, sweetheart."

Serral sat on a flowered chaise. "Things are awfully quiet around here."

"Riellen was in charge of performances. Without her organizing, it's tough to pull much together."

"Who's next in line to take charge?"

"Well, technically you, darling."

"Oh."

"Don't worry, Shanno is going to fix it. We'll be up and running by Friday night. And then, you'll be reunited with your paramour."

"Okay. Good to know."

Cheloa tipped their head to one side. "What? Trouble in paradise?"

Serral smiled, "He's annoyed with me."

"Can't imagine why." Cheloa put a slice of pretty cake on a plate in front of Serral. "I don't believe for a moment that you killed Riellen. But if you had, there are plenty of people here who felt she had it coming."

"I didn't kill her. I tried to save her."

"Be that as it may, you frighten people here."

Serral took a polite bite of cake. It was sweetly tart and delicious. She wished she could carry it to Chlore and share it with whoever was left there. If anyone was left there. "People here need to be frightened."

"Shhh," Cheloa called out to her servants, four Harbs decked out in silly, short white pants and pink short-sleeved shirts. They came to the table. "Creatures, I need all of you to go to the village and get me some fresh fish for tonight's supper."

Their head domes roiled. "I'll be fine here with little white hair. Go on. We have all we need. The sooner you skedaddle the sooner you'll be back to give me my massage. And get me some of those apples I like, you know the green ones?"

Serral giggled as The Helpers, baskets and straw hats in tow, trooped down the narrow road between rows of houses. "Why didn't I think of dressing my servants like living dolls?"

"About the purge of Riellen and the others." Cheloa became serious. "How long do you think the rest of us have?"

Serral swallowed. "I'm trying to find out."

"What do you know about the Wilter in the jungle?"

"They're soldiers. Still fighting the war."

"Like you, Hon." Cheloa winked. "What about Geddon?"

"Hal's old tutor? No one knows. He's disappeared."

"Well, where else would he to run, but back into the jungle? I think he still has friends out there."

"Friends?"

Cheloa spoke softly. "I met Geddon a number of times. He was a good man. No memory, but free access to the jungle. He spoke to people. He pieced together a story of what happened here. He tried to give Hallenander as much of a chance as possible. Which leads me to believe that Hal has a real shot at upsetting this whole... whatever it is that the Lords are trying to pull off. Geddon was like you. Still a soldier. Never a slave."

"Thank you. I'm touched by the comparison."

Cheloa sipped tea. "Don't be silly. The key to everything is your master. Geddon knew that. I'm sure you do, too. It may be that the Lords' biggest error was trusting Geddon to oversee Hallenander's education. The Harbingers know that they can't raise a Rakki kid in any kind of meaningful way. That much they admitted freely to Geddon. Ysk only knows how many failed attempts they made. And where those flawed Rakki wound up. I would rather not know. Not that the Harbingers would admit any of this. But they were desperate when Hallenander was a boy. I came in a few years ago, after Geddon agreed to help. They begged him. I don't know what they promised, but it was his life. They respected him for his warcraft. Maybe they wanted Hallenander to learn something. I tend to think so because, suddenly you arrive. A wild, feral, smug little soldier. *Little Geddon.*"

Serral put sugar in her teacup and stirred. "Smug? Really?"

"Don't be angry. I mean it as a compliment."

"You think Hallenander chose me because I remind him of his tutor?"

"Why else?"

Serral laughed. "He sounds like my kind of guy. Still fighting."

"Always. Geddon's crew supposedly swamped his starship so none of their members could escape and tell the Imset authority. Because if the authority knew, they'd be obliged to hunt them down and kill them, something called the *First Directive*?"

"Right." Sadness welled up. "We're considered traitors. Anyone who has had contact with the enemy."

"It must take a lot to destroy a starship."

Serral sighed. "Not to speak of what it does to space lifer's bodies to be stuck on planet. An excruciating death."

They shared a look.

"So, when their commander was captured, they sacrificed their ship? They decided never to return to the Imset, even though they have nothing to do with the Harbs here? That is..." Serral sat back, thinking.

Cheloa studied her. "A big deal?"

"It was murder. Understandable, though. We Imset are so afraid of having our brains turned to jelly by the enemy's telepathy, we would rather destroy our means of escape than risk being caught by our own."

The two sat listening to the rustle of trees and chatter of birds.

"And here we thought the Imset were such nice folks." Cheloa kicked off their low-heeled shoes.

"You mentioned a purge. Do you think the others are as convinced as you are?"

"Oh, yes. While we aren't performing, we are talking. Who will be put out next? It could be any of us. Or all."

"Are the Companions up for a rebellion?"

"How could we refuse?" Cheloa smiled ruefully. "It seems the war has finally found us."

A colorful, little bird landed on the walk, looking up with expectation. Cheloa flicked crumbs to the ground. Several tiny birds joined the first, bobbing up and down like toys.

Cheloa sighed theatrically. "So, we need a plan."

"You and Shanno are the leaders of the Companions now. Do you think the rest would follow you to freedom?"

Cheloa closed her eyes and laid back. "Yes. I do think they would, but we'd have to start telling a lot of hard truths that they won't want to hear." She opened one eye. "And you would need to appear uninvolved. Trust issues."

"Easy enough. But I need to find you someplace safe to hide."

"And how do you intend to do that?"

Serral smiled. "See who else is ready to rise up."

Friday dragged. Serral invited both Callia and Alysse to visit, but both said they would not sully her apartment with their low status. Callia had only come in the dead of night. Serral suspected they feared Hallenander arriving unexpectedly.

"I hate you both," Serral said, smiling.

Instead, Serral took a long soak in the tub, had a massage and an application of sweet-smelling lotions. Then, Click and Clack put her in a pink-and-gold frock that resembled an old-timey bottle of cologne.

*Mistress, you look beautiful.*

*If you say so.*

She wrapped herself in a cape of golden fur, then paced the lobby, waiting for Hallenander to arrive.

*Mistress, it is unbecoming for you to be seen here.*

*Why?*

*It is not for us to criticize, but some might consider a lady desperate.*

Serral returned to her apartment. Why had she assumed Hallenander would drive there with her? He had never said so.

At sundown, Helpers augered that she needed to hurry to the party, or she would be late. She trotted down the hill and across the wide lawn next to the reflecting pool, until she saw lights and heard voices.

She missed a rise where the gravel path turned to lawn, tripped, and went down hard. It took a full minute to get herself and her crazy dress back up again. Ahead, people flocked to a large, black-and-white striped circus tent. She did not see Hal or any of the stone men.

Serral ducked behind the door of the tent and augered.

*The men have not yet arrived, Mistress.*

*Do you know why not?* She pushed herself into a corner so no one could see her augering.

*They are in a meeting.*

*Will they come soon?*

*Mistress is missing her Master. He is in the meeting. Speaking on liquid. Very busy.*

She moved into the party. Few people greeted her, and those who did seemed to be forcing themselves. Serral thought about the day she got cinched on Chlore. This night felt the same.

It smelled glorious inside of the tent, like sawdust, and animals, and perfume. Serral joined Cheloa, Zella, Jinima, and Latrice in a section of seats at the front of the audience. The lights went down, a spotlight came on, and a cadre of women including Shanno in spangled tutus rode into the main ring on the backs of beautiful horses. They rounded the ring continuously until Hallenander and the other men came through the door and took their seats.

Harbs passed boxes of nuts and popcorn, and bottles of sparkling wine. The women on horseback performed a wildly daring set of tricks, the horses traipsing proudly. They paraded while standing, rounded barrels in the center of the ring, stood on their hands while the horses galloped, then leapt from one horse to another. Serral watched Hal through the act, though he did not look her way.

Next came a sequence of twelve Harbs dressed like clowns with painted white faces and black crosses over their eyes, wearing onesies in checkered patterns with ruffs at their necks and pointed caps over their domed heads. Serral thought how strange it was that she accepted the Harbs taking on Imset costumes immediately, laughing as the dozen Harb clowns walked into one another in mock clumsiness, then tried to jam their way into a small Bisbee, falling out onto the floor, making the audience roar with laughter. She laughed, too. She felt no fear.

After that, women swung on the high trapeze, leaping and catching one another so the tent filled with gasps. It was all so distracting, Serral hardly noticed when the men filed out again. Hal did not look her way. She was surprised at how hurt she felt. The worst part was not knowing if he was ignoring her because he was still angry, or because she was no longer of any interest to him. Cheloa's revelations about Hal's past made her wonder if being abandoned by his tutor made Hal bitter. If his lonely life had predisposed him to think of Imset as cruel.

The lights went up, to everyone's consternation, and the evening was over.

Cheloa muttered in passing, "Find out what is going on, could you?"

"He's giving me the cold shoulder," Serral said softly, "We need more parties. He won't come here without them."

The next day, Shanno called a general meeting of the Xalavria ladies in the amphitheater. Serral sat in the front row with Cheloa and Shanno who were visibly upset and discussed "the situation with our productions in light of the loss of Riellen" and "our obligation to be extraordinary for our Lords."

"In other words, no men means no safety," Callia whispered into Serral's ear. She was sitting in the row behind.

"What?" Serral kept her face toward the speakers. "Is that why everyone is so stressed? Because of attendance at their shows?"

"It's not about the shows, it's about where the men are. If Hal rises, our time is up. If Hal falls, same. With Riellen gone, and Hal not speaking to you, the only way we have of knowing that something has been decided is if attendance slips. Do you understand?"

Serral half turned. "You think the Volterrans have ruled on Hal's future? Because the Masters have been distant lately?"

"Maybe. Have you noticed the Helpers working less up here and more down in the Village?"

She had not noticed. Everything seemed normal at her apartment, except Hal's absence.

"You really think they would let the Xaff come purge the Xalavria?"

"Why wouldn't they? Twice we've waited to go on the project and the buses never came. Something's up. If you see Hal, try to find out."

Serral turned to say more, but Callia was darting out of sight.

Serral studied the complicated smocking on her red dress, her green jade and red coral bracelets, and the clever clasp on her small bag. No one called on her, or referred to her at all, as women volunteered their ideas for new and exciting acts designed to entice the men back to the resort. She did not follow all their plans for dancing and music, comedy acts and a complicated tumbling routine involving *fliers* and *sparklers*. Serral excused herself and wandered to the village square. She sat under an umbrella until Harbs brought her cold, sweet ice cream. They poured sauce and placed a cherry on top, their heads roiling with satisfaction in their service.

She entered the thought river and gasped, it was so sparsely populated.

*Thank you!* she communicated. *This is delightful.*

*Yes! We offer only the finest treats.*

*And what are the future plans, friends?*

*Our future plans are to take care of you, Mistress, to take care of whatever you might need.*

*I need to know when my true love is returning.*

*Ah. Of course! Let us ask our colleagues in the Palace.*

They closed the connection.

Serral ate a few bites of the sweet treat and wondered how the Harbs knew how to make old Imsethan ice cream, or if what she had was just a facsimile, like the resort itself, too perfect to be real.

*We have sent word to your paramour of your desire to see him.*

*You did what?*

*We have told the palace Helpers of your desire, and they are pleased to help.*

Serral imagined Hal's reaction to a summons from her via the servants.

*Well, you certainly are remarkable people.*

Beneath their paper caps, the ice cream Helpers puffed with pride.

*Is there nothing else you can share with me about what is planned?*

The thought river seemed genuinely baffled by her question.

*The ladies are planning parties! Perhaps you would like to join them?*

Serral walked to a small store and perused the shelves. Not only did they have grooming essentials, but they also had old and real Imseth books, magazines, and stationery. There were purses, wigs, and stockings. Glass cases held jewels and little glasses like Riellen had used at the Evincio.

*Where did these things come from, friends?*

Two clerks stood behind the counter, their long-fingered, gray hands moving along rows of merchandise, seeking those she desired.

*Which, Mistress? Does something please you?*

*All pleases me. But I am curious of the source?*

*Ah, each treasure has its own story. Several came from Lady Companions.*

*What about those opera glasses?*

*From Lady Elva.*

*And that feather fan?*

*From Lady Elva.*

*And... those paper valentines?*

*From Lady...*

*Elva?*

*Yes, Mistress.*

*Did anything here NOT come from Lady Elva?*

*Why yes. Over here are some things from Lady Riellen...*

Serral thanked them and left.

Piles of neglected leaves gathered against an ornate iron fence down the street, in front of The Lady Companion townhouses. Once the Harbs would have kept up appearances, she was sure, but now the homes looked haunted. Something was wrong. She augered, but the only voices were back in the village.

Serral pushed open the gate. The house was locked, but she had seen enough strippies to know where to run her hand to find a key. Three minutes later, she stood in a darkened living room, its draped furniture like undersea creatures, its air infused with mildew and rainwater.

Upstairs in an abandoned bedroom, Serral found silk brocade drapery blackened with mold hanging in front of open balcony doors. She closed the doors and opened the curtains. Sunlight poured in and revealed a posted bed, comfortable chairs, and a carved fireplace. This was the chamber of a splendid lady. Serral perused the bookshelves, unsure what she was looking for. She needed a way out of the resort, and whoever had lived in this house had found one, for better, or for worse. Wind beat against the glass balcony doors, leaves pressed like hands, then whipped away.

Serral continued snooping, opening tintorello boxes, drawers filled with playing cards, envelopes with notes in Volterran she could not read, and books in the same language. With concentrated effort, the strange shapes on the page formed patterns and repetition, but nothing more. She put them back on the shelves. Reading was not going to get her a meeting with Geddon.

Finally, she came across a silver frame lying face down. It was a photo of a Volterran man. Its inscription read: Taurellio, the Emperor. Hallenander's father. His broad smile and half-closed eyes spoke of great entitlement and power. Next to him sat an exquisite lady in a high, powdered wig, plunging gown, and masses of jewels. It could only be Elva, the Companion whose fate no one knew. They did not look like a master and his slave. Serral imagined them as two people who truly enjoyed one another's company, relaxed and happy, maybe in love. Serral wished for Hal's insight. On her own, she could only guess. What had Taurellio done to this woman? And was he planning to do the same to the others?

Serral removed the photo from the frame and put it in her bag. She opened closets and wardrobes. They were empty but for scented paper and a few lonely silk stockings. Harbs would not have left detritus like this lying around. Other ladies must have emptied this house of its finery. Callia had said Elva left when Hal was small. It seemed like a waste of resources to leave this house empty for so long unless someone thought its inhabitant would return some day. Serral augered again, but there were no Helpers nearby. Far off, she could hear talk of lunch preparation for the women's meeting. She received a visual of Alysse, on stage, balancing on a wheeled contraption and juggling small pins. No one would miss Serral yet.

She explored the kitchen, which was empty but for a couple of wine bottles in a cobwebbed cabinet. She moved on to the service kitchen, the Harb kitchen, down a narrow flight of stairs. A neat row of copper pots, shelves still laden with gilded porcelain, and crystal glasses etched with the Chi'irea family crest still laid about. Judging by the green patina on the pots, it had been at least a decade since they had been used. Wherever Lady Elva was, she did not seem to be in a rush to return. Serral pushed on wall panels and discovered secret storerooms holding folded linens, racks of wine, and party supplies. Finally, she pulled open a hidden doorway that revealed another narrow staircase, this one angling steeply down into darkness. Warm air floated up, carrying the smell of old stone.

Serral slipped out of her dress and hung it carefully on the storeroom door. She removed her jewelry and stashed it in her bag. She found a length of string and tied her hair in a knot atop her head. What she had left were a pair of brown day shoes, underclothes, and a red lace slip. After rummaging in the party supplies, she found a candle which she lit with an ornate silver lighter. The staircase was just wide enough that she could descend without scraping the walls. She was entering, she knew, the world of the Harbingers.

The stairway led down to a low gate which opened onto a much wider passage. Her small flame lit only what was immediately around her, but the cooler, less dense air told her that she stood at a crossroads. If she turned to the left, she would follow a path that led to the rest of the townhouses. She augered for guidance. But, in the near distance, she felt Xaff energy, so she closed her mind immediately. She must be near the palace complex. She turned to the right instead. After a few paces, she reached a wide, circular staircase, big enough to hold ten Harbs shoulder to shoulder. After dozens of revolutions down, and down, and down, with a couple of stops to regain her equilibrium,

Serral arrived at a flat space, and a puff of air blew out her candle. Serral sensed warm moisture. She sensed more openings, two sets of stairs on her right leading downward, two on her left leading up. Using her hands to feel her way along the walls, she chose a level, middle path. It opened onto a large open space, its walls dripping with moisture. The stench of Harbs was overwhelming, their scent unmistakable, a mixture of iron and musk like the sweaty blood of butchered animals.

The floor sloped down to her left where the smell was strongest. Instead, she walked to her right, on and on, and the atmosphere grew ever fresher. At one point, she felt the presence of Harbs in the dark, a group passing behind her. They shuffled along together, she imagined, holding hands. To her surprise, the Harbs did not knock at her mind, asking to auger. She opened the tiniest bit to the thought river, but no one greeted her. They seemed pre-occupied, engrossed in a task she did not know the name for. She guessed they did not even notice she was there and would have been astonished to find her so deep in their territory. She closed the connection and walked on, following tendrils of fresh air.

Finally, she saw a narrow slice of green light at the far end of a long passage. She came to another gate, this one a simple mesh door that opened onto the jungle. It was locked. Serral guessed the earthen walls around it were unreinforced. With tools or a few more hands, she could defeat it, she was sure. Beyond her, on the other side of the door, a dirt path stretched a few meters, then was lost in leafy undergrowth. Serral must have passed below the palace complex, gone beyond the white townhouses, and come to the village's southern perimeter. Part of her wanted to hurl herself at the gate until the ground around it gave way, to run and keep running until she was far from this constructed world. It might be weeks before the Xaff came after her. If she could find Geddon, he might be willing to hide her. She imagined his band of former crewmembers and the escaped women sitting around a fire.

But if Serral bolted, what would become of her agreement with Hal? If she were caught by Imset soldiers, she might be able to survive interrogation, maybe convince them to help the Companions escape, but she would have to betray Hal. Was it worth it?

Xaff energy abruptly pushed on her mind, paralyzing her. Black dots swam in the corners of her vision, coaxing her to give in, to surrender, to come out and play. She struggled to breathe, to stay standing. She rummaged through her brain for a counter image, something opposite Xaff aggression. Zaphia appeared in her mind, but not as an imagined being, as an augered voice. The white lady vibrated love and wholeness, and other magnetic concepts that folded themselves into words: *destiny, duty, need.*

Serral broke free of the paralysis. She bolted back the way she came, running as fast as she could. She emerged into the empty house and slammed closed the door to the passageway. She wriggled her dress back on just in time to receive the message, *Mistress, Your Master has received your message and is on his way to your penthouse.*

Serral heard a familiar sound when she stepped off her elevator, but it took a few seconds to place it. Hal's laughter. He sat at the table in her show kitchen, a liquid portal open, deep in conversation. She called Click and Clack to smooth her hair, apply lip pigment, and wipe the dirt from her arms. Then she approached her master.

"Was not Elonyi'i a monster before the fire?"

A deep voice replied in Volterran, saying something Serral did not fully understand about *friends.* Hal looked relaxed and happy. But his face shifted when he saw her.

He stood, and then pretended to kiss her cheek. "You made it sound like an emergency. I've been stalling him for ten minutes."

*Him?*

"Master! Thank you for favoring me with your presence," she said loudly. "It's all I live for."

"Is she finally there? Ah, young Serral, come to me now," Taurellio spoke in a heavy accent, with an erudite flair that betrayed many previous conversations in the Imset language. "I want to see you, dear girl. They have told me much about you, but can it all be true?"

Hal sat back down and motioned for her to join him at the portal, pointing to a place on the banquette. Serral pushed herself defiantly onto his lap. There, in the center of the liquid, was the man from the photograph. He looked more lined and tired with age but was just as cheerful as the picture. Taurellio's large eyes were alive with pale flames, like opals.

She bowed her head. "It is my great pleasure to meet you, your Sevenni Highness."

His white, fire eyes narrowed. "So, you are the girl who has my boy wrapped around her finger, eh?"

Serral turned to assess Hal who smiled woodenly. He poked her in the back.

"Did he say that? Or did someone else?" She turned back to the Syxarit, "To be very honest with you, sire, I am the least of your son's concerns."

Hal made an impatient noise behind her neck.

"Please don't be too hard on him. It is my fault, you see. I have him running this way and that, preparing legal arguments, speeches and," he paused to gather his words, "other plans you needn't worry about."

Serral tried to look pleasant. "Of course. He is a very important man. I am the most fortunate of girls to be a Companion to one such as him. Whenever it is that he can spare a moment for me."

Hal leaned in. "So. All is well. You can see she is real, father."

Serral started to get up. "Shall I go? You men have things to discuss?"

"Yes," Hal said. "We are very..."

"Not yet!" Taurellio interrupted. "We have only just met."

Hal cursed under his breath. She sat back down, though Hal's knees were beginning to feel uncomfortable.

"Father?"

"She certainly looks charming, but the servants have done much of that, with their medicine and curation," the older man said. Hal's body tensed. "They made you lovely, child. To be sure."

"Thank you," Serral squeaked, fear rising.

"But. My son has bent the rules for his own pleasure, Serral, and it simply will not do," the old man said pleasantly.

"Oh, no?" Her voice refused to rise higher than a whisper. She felt cold.

He laughed, "No! You are a Companion. And not only that, but a Lady Companion."

"Yes sir," she said meekly. "Lucky me."

"But you are hiding some skill, then, some talent, to fit the requirement." The old man motioned with his large hands, "Out with it, then. What is your act? The charm you are too shy to share?"

Hal made a small noise of objection, but she clamped her hand on his knee to silence him.

"Oh, sire," she looked shamefully at the table. "You got me."

"Oh ho. So you are ready to confess?" He smiled broadly, eyebrows raising.

"Yes. I am, though you're the one who is going to be punished," Serral sighed. "You see, my performance area is comedy."

Hal cursed again.

His father clasped his hands in glee, "No! I love a good joke. Pray tell me one, right now. Son, I do not know why you have been nervous about this. We haven't enjoyed any good Imset humor in ages."

"I suppose I wanted to keep it to myself," Hal said without emotion.

"Greedy boy," Taurellio said. "Proceed then, girl."

"All right, though I warn you it's not very good."

"Don't be modest. Only the most gifted ladies come to our humble resort. It is a zealously guarded standard."

"I'm sure I don't live up. But if you insist, I'll tell you a joke." Serral spoke over small suffocating noises coming from Hal's throat. "Once there was a Xaff warrior who grew tired of hunting Imset."

Taurellio's face lost its smile. Hal sat very still.

"So, this Xaff warrior took off his armor and pretended to be a kitchen Helper."

The Syxarit's opaline eyes broadened.

"It was the day of a great banquet. The warrior felt delighted to be so far from the war and tried very hard to do his duty. He was relieved that all went well throughout the meal and that the Masters did not recognize him. He felt sure he could keep hiding this way forever."

"And this is funny?"

Serral continued, "The meal ended."

Hal whispered something but Serral ignored it. "Then one of the Masters came and said, 'Slave, where is my whiskey?' And the warrior ran to get a glass of whiskey. The Master tasted it and said, 'Slave, where is the ice?' And the warrior ran to get ice. The Master took his whiskey now filled with ice and went to smoke with the men."

Taurellio tried to interrupt.

"So. The Master's Lady Companion spoke to the warrior, believing him to be a kitchen helper, and said, 'Slave, where is my whiskey?' And the Xaff warrior reached down, took a knife, and sliced off her head."

The Syxarit stared, unblinking, into the liquid. Hal made no sound but nervous breathing.

"The Master returned, and said, 'Slave, what have you done?' And the Xaff warrior said, 'Why Master, I have done what Harbinger slaves always do, and given you the thing you most desire.'"

There was a slight pause, then the sound of Taurellio roaring, slapping the table. He laughed so hard that he started to choke and bent his long head out of the frame.

Hal whispered, "Go now. Do not reappear until after this report is over."

Serral moved out of sight of the liquid and took up a chair on the other side of the room where she could observe Hallenander.

Taurellio was animated and merry, "Oh, my brother is a fool. Let us move on, because the topic of your Companion is finished. She is delightful."

Hal looked at Serral through the corner of his eye, his green eyes widening ever so slightly. She gazed at him steadily, and he continued to speak to his father for another quarter of an hour. Women's voices carried through the transmission, though Hal seemed reluctant to laugh along with them. They spoke on and on in Volterran, and Serral caught snatches of meaning here and there, things about a *coming visit*, *plans*, and the word *Evincio*.

When at length the King shut down the communication, Serral got up and stalked out of the room. Hal followed.

They sat in the living room, and Serral augered her Helpers to bring food.

"You have dirt on your shoes," Hal said. "Good gods, you have dirt on your legs, too."

Serral bit into a sandwich. "When do they arrive?"

Hal poured himself a glass of wine. Then he poured her one.

"It is not yet decided. But my father is convinced something important will happen soon."

"What does the word *soon* mean in Volterran? A week, a month?"

Hal regarded her with a neutral expression. "I am asked to convey my good wishes to you from Lord Maurdoy and Lord Zinnerit."

"Oh? You came to visit me because the men told you to?"

"The Xaff commanders explained what happened in the jungle. So, while it is true that you were in grave breach of obedience, it is also true that you helped their Companions escape imminent danger."

"Are you saying the Lords wanted their women to escape?"

He blinked his eyes with painful slowness. "We are caught in a situation not of our making. You just received a taste of that in the kitchen while under genteel interrogation, but interrogation, nevertheless. You handled it admirably, I must acknowledge. I was sure you were the Companion soon to lose your head."

"Please tell Maurdoy and Zinnerit that there is an easy way to help their women: end the war."

Hal took a sip of wine. "Nothing has changed on that front. The only way to end the war is to renegotiate the Alliance, and you can be sure the Eight of the Volettu are not authorized to do such a thing."

"Politics."

"Politics." He loosened his tie. "We will begin flying tomorrow."

"Flying? You're ready to actually fly?" She speared a pickle. "Isn't that my decision?"

"There's no time."

"I need to meet Geddon."

Hal stared. "Give me a reason to put him in such peril."

"So, he is alive. You know he is safe?"

"I apologize for my bluntness. But given your recent actions, why should I trust you?"

They stood face to face. Serral felt her skin warm, She turned to straighten a painting. "Because, your highness, I went someplace you will be very interested in, and I learned about what you are very much caught up in. And in doing so—which, by the way, is what you asked me to do—I saved the lives of two innocent people."

"Of course. You acted heroically." He paced. "Always the hero. Regardless of the larger task."

A wave of cold crossed the skin of Serral's neck, traveling slowly up her face and scalp. He seemed different. Something new was animating his muscles. For the first time, she feared him. But she could not show it. Impressing the Emperor had bought her time. But looking at Hallenander in his fine suit with his expression of lofty calculation, she wondered how much.

"The larger task. You mean, making you look good? Helping you with politics?  What task is the most important? Ensuring your path to power? Or smashing the Harbinger's control over the universe?"

"I don't know. Maybe start with surviving. You speak as if I personally created the trap we are both caught in. They are not MY politics." Hallenander turned, face flushed. "They are my attempt to make something good out of this infernal conflict, that just like you, noble Imset savage, I was born into. You knew all this. But yet, you put yourself in mortal danger and risked losing your position as my Companion."

"My position as your Companion? Don't you know I am more than your stupid Companion?"

He took her hand in his. "Of course you are. But Serral, if you lose your place here, in this building, in this resort, then you will quickly die."

"I think I have proven that I am not so easy to kill." He let her hand drop.

"They did not try to kill you because you are my Companion. If that were to change, how long do you think you would last?"

Serral called out to her servants. "Out. We want privacy now."

He took off his golden circlet and placed it on the table. "I am the proposed Minsyx, the Heir-in-waiting. Being made to look as if my judgment is lacking puts my future in peril. Do you not see that, you selfish child?"

"What I see is someone trying to play both sides against the middle."

His eyes flashed. "What is wrong with that?"

"Sooner or later, you're going to have to take a side and fight."

He sat heavily on one of the velvet sofas. "Spoken like a thoughtless barbarian."

"I know. You think you'll come to power, and then everything will be easy."

"I think many things, but not that." He rubbed his eyes. "You know nothing about it."

"But it won't get easier."

"How would you know?"

Serral took her shoes off and threw them across the room. She sat near him, curling her feet under her. "I'm going to tell you about a choice I made. And you're going to believe I'm insane. And I don't care if you do."

"I already think you're insane."

"I've made hard choices. I am here for a reason."

"Ah. So, crashing your Arrow into the side of a ship was all part of your plan, was it?"

"It was part of *a* plan."

"Please. Go on. You are telling me that you meant to die fighting. I admire that. But it helps no one if I do the same."

"No, that's not why I came. I have a spirit guide, Hallenander. A Thanton."

His handsome face fell. "Oh, come on."

"And the Harbingers call me Thanton, because not only can I auger with them, but because I have this person, this woman, who appears to me sometimes to advise me. I know it sounds crazy. But the Harbs feel it. And that is what protects me, not you. And when I came to this place, I had a choice, Hallenander. I could have..."

"Don't say any more." He held up his large hand.

"I could have chosen to be a Thanton myself, if I'd wanted that. But I decided instead to come here, and join forces with you, and try and do what is right. Not only for my people and the Volterrans, but for the entire universe."

"I said, stop talking."

She paused. "But there's a third side to consider in all this, Hal. That's why I asked you here."

He glared, "Oh ho? You think after all the nonsense you just spewed, I need to hear more?"

Serral walked closer to him and took his hand. "You have siblings, cousins, subjects—whatever you want to call them. At least a hundred children."

"Cousins?" He dropped his hand, his face thunderstruck. "What are you talking about?"

"I'm talking about the real reason there is a slave colony here on Evincio. I'm talking about the project."

Chapter Thirty-Eight

The day dawned cold and clear. Serral had been up for two hours drinking hot tea on her terrace and watching air traffic across the valley. No silver ships had risen or descended in the time she had been there. Since the Tuval had left the area, it seemed the Harbs on Evincio were not flying much. She had a sheaf of papers in front of her, a set of drawings and a long, handwritten note. When she heard morning shuffling coming from inside, she stuffed the pages into a cloth bag and hid it beneath her chair.

Hal rubbed his eyes in the morning light, in striped pajamas, a plush robe, and embroidered velvet slippers. His feet looked ludicrously large. Serral had already braided her hair and donned the simple leggings and tunic that she could fit under a flight suit. Hal appeared strangely youthful absent the kohl around his eyes, tailored suit and gold crown. He seemed ordinary, albeit finely made, and she could not help smiling at his vulnerable self.

"Come on out." Serral pointed to heat lamps in the awning over her head. "It's cozy."

He poured himself a cup of tea. Two kitchen Helpers offered him a plate of food.

"The gray menace is back."

"They're so excited you stayed overnight."

He shooed the Harbs away, "Leave us."

Their heads shimmering, the two servants bowed and reluctantly re-entered the apartment.

Hal bit into a pastry. "I still intend to fly. You understand, right?"

"Of course," she said brightly. "You don't have to explain to me why it is you want to be master of your own fate."

The previous night, Hallenander had watched with curiosity while she built a fire. The hours passed and she prepared more wine and food she had fetched from the Harb pantry. Hal had been impressed by her skill, impressed that she felt empowered to enter Harb spaces. She replied tartly that it was his building, and he needed to get out of his comfort zone more often.

"You're referring to your ill-fated trip to the project? If we are talking about comfort, it seems you've become rather comfortable with murder, I must say."

"It was self-defense; you know that." She washed her hands in the kitchen sink. The soap smelled like sunlight. "Is that why you have been ignoring me? Discomfort?"

"I have been attempting to deflect attention away from rumors that you killed Riellen. It seems that my uncle did not want her put out, and he feels enraged that the Harbingers chose to do so despite his wishes. He believes you capable of chasing her down and murdering her. What would motivate you to do so when she was already being hunted by Xaff is irrelevant to him. Riellen was working against you in the Xalavria. You are the darling of the Harbingers. He would never admit that Riellen was acting on his behalf, and her recklessness in front of the servants caused her own demise. Such a thought would never occur to him. Nor would he show any grief or remorse, only rage toward you, an outsider, a convenient scapegoat. In fact, his Companion died because of his scheming. There is no proof you murdered her. Only a report of you with her body."

She paused, chewing a piece of toast. "Who reported seeing me?"

"A Xaff pilot."

"There were no craft in the area."

"Then my uncle is either misinformed or lying."

"And what about the project? Did that come up at all, while Mimellio was asking for my head?"

"Never once." He made a noise of disbelief. "All this time, I have had a hundred relations living within my purview."

"I think I figured something out, Hal. It's important for your future."

"My future?"

"Yes. I think the Reykos towers are more than nurseries for Rakki kids. I think they are starships."

He looked perplexed. "That makes sense actually. They would be convenient if the Xaff decide to clean house and exterminate the Wilter," he glowered. "They could easily remove the children until Evincio became again safe for them. Or simply take them to another planet."

"All this time, all these resources devoted to your care. You never suspected it wasn't only for you?"

He paused, considering. "Those things seem normal when they tell you you're the great hope of an entire civilization. And yet, obviously, the reason you are here is because I do have suspicions."

"You suspected that you were one of many heirs?"

"No, I didn't, stupid as that makes me sound." He studied the high, coffered ceiling. "I have entertained many notions about my situation, but it never occurred to me that my father would," his voice had dropped, "...that my father would create a hundred new lives, knowing that I might not make it to the throne. It was bad enough when that threat hung over me. His cruelty toward the others is monstrous. He has tried to tell me many times that the powerful must see life differently. To be emperor is to lose the luxury of kindness and intimacy. But I never understood what he meant. Until this."

"You're absolutely sure Taurellio knows about them, about the children, the other heirs? No chance the Harbs have fooled him too?"

He smiled tightly. "I am not planning to ask. But this looks like his work. He is, after all, its beneficiary."

"How's so?"

"Let's not be naive. I have not seen the children, but I can guess at their parentage. Did they or did they not appear related to me? Not only the same race. But the same family?"

Serral gasped. "You think Taurellio is the father of them all?"

He spun a small globe on a low table. "It explains many things. First, his determination to have my case decided as soon as possible. He never intended to wait for a new generation of Rakki. He planned to populate the new world with his offspring immediately. I am sure he plans to make everything legal so that the Harbingers must continue to serve. Nothing in the Worlds will change, but the genetic makeup of its citizens. The Imset will perish but live on in this way. The Volterrans will simply morph into a new version—that happens to resemble him."

Hallenander closed his eyes.

Serral hung a dishtowel on a peg. "Strategic of him to keep these plans to himself. Keep you from feeling the pressure."

"Yes, to keep me from knowing he has replacements should I fail."

"But you're the first born, aren't you? Isn't the throne your birthright?"

"Is it?" Hal's eyes flashed. "Didn't Riellen say that the kids don't grow without Imset foster parents? How many failed experiments did they try before they took me public?"

She grew somber. "Do you want me to go back to the Reykos and find out? I will."

He shook his head no. "Right now, I'd rather not know."

"None of this explains why you'd not be allowed to meet the children. If you're all joined together in this cause, why not allow you your siblings?"

He thought for a moment. "Separate me from friends or family outside of Father's sphere of influence and," Hal struggled, his eyes darting around the room, his one foot tapping nervously, "...a lonely, isolated person is easier to manipulate."

"Screw that. When are you going to see them? Maybe the Helpers at the project will answer your origin questions."

Hal looked startled. "See them? You think I could go into the Reykos towers without my uncle finding out?"

"And what if he does?"

"They lose the ability to easily replace me. It is bad enough they forced me to take a Companion." He gave her a friendly nudge. "But seriously. When the Eloxiture and Jalophians render their verdict, tell the world who will be the next ruler of Volterra, the time may come to act. And I want the element of surprise."

"You really don't trust your father or uncle, do you?"

"How I feel is not important. What matters is destroying the hold the law has on the Imset and ending the war. I must concretize my strategy." He paused. "You said Riellen was devoted to a Rakki boy named Piettu."

"Each Companion had at least one child assigned to them. But not all of them seemed as passionate as Riellen."

"Of course, they have to appear to care. But you think some of them really do? Fear of consequences is incentive enough to force them into their roles and to keep them silent. To insist others follow suit."

"You're being paranoid, even by my standards."

"Reasons for secrecy:" He held up a finger. "One, my father must appear to control the Rakki's fate without interference or consequences. Two, for all we know, the Harbingers insist upon it. They created the Rakki. Do not believe for a second they did so because of the Emptiness. They could cure the Emptiness in a heartbeat if they wanted to. No. This is their project. The Harbingers decide who benefits. Three, father does not want me to know because it is so dark and cynical, because keeping me isolated forces me to interact only with those of his choosing, and because it forces me to yearn for his approval. If the Eight know, they must pretend not to. Because they are here for me, and only me. To confront Taurellio about the others puts their value in jeopardy. And whatever else Volterrans are, they are obedient to the hierarchy. Class status is everything to them. The Volettu of Eight yearn to go home to the Worlds and live as heroic close advisors to the emperor, whoever he is. They will not risk that by throwing open the doors to spare Heirs in their dozens. That is not their way, especially after they have invested so much in me. I could go on."

"Do you love your father?" Her voice was pinched.

He spun the globe, so it rolled across the rug and disappeared under a table. "Of course I do. But I also understand that he is an emperor and has responsibilities beyond what I can fathom."

"And he can use ruthless methods to meet those responsibilities."

Hal rubbed his eyes. "He is Volterran. He follows the law."

"Alliance law."

His hands flew away from his face, leaving his eyes streaked with black. "Yes, Alliance law. It is the only law currently applicable. We are in Alliance territory."

"The entire known universe is Alliance territory," Serral said dryly.

The fire cracked and shifted. Serral had always thought Imseth must have looked like a molten piece of organic matter when it imploded. Later she learned that the planet of her ancestors had been nearly barren, covered in ash and pocked with craters, when it finally died. By then, the great space cities were built and gone, and the left-behinders dead of starvation.

"If all habitable planets belong to the Alliance, whose fault is that?" Hal said irritably.

Her heart hardened. "Really? You of all people blame the Imset for the Calamity and for the war? When you've seen firsthand how the Xaff treat us, how happy they are to kill us, to take our genetic material and leave us to slowly go mad out in space?"

She realized she was shouting. She turned to stoke the fire.

"You're right. There are two explanations for the death of Imseth. I have only heard the Alliance's."

"It doesn't matter." She made a dismissive motion with her hands. "As you told me, unless you renegotiate the Alliance while there are still enough legal citizens to ratify a new Law, we won't ever be absolved of our crime, our planet murder."

"Time is running out." Firelight danced over his face, creating dark and flickering shadows. "For the Imset. For the Rakki. For me."

He did not mention her.

"There's a major piece of the puzzle we don't have," she said.

"You mean the part the infernal gray Harbs play? I think we can count on them to be up to no good."

Serral flopped down on the sofa and took a long swig of wine to take the edge off her rage. "Okay, I'm going to tell you this one more time. And I want it to sink in."

"Uh oh." He feigned helplessness.

"The Helper Harbs love you and all the Rakki. They worship you in this tender way that makes me nowhere near as concerned about their safety as you are. Believe it or not, I am more worried about what the Xaff will do to your father's people if they switch their loyalties to the Rakki, as the universe's great hope Then the Volterrans would lose everything, do you see?"

"No."

"The Harbs have had access to Volterran genetic material for centuries. And we know they have been taking genetic material from the Imset for at least two hundred years. They probably have enough stockpiled to breed thousands if not millions of Rakki."

"You're saying this whole war is a front for Harb genetic meddling? That it is not a response to the Emptiness crisis? That they are simply using my father as a puppet for their plans?" Hal ran his hands over his long head. "They do service work. It is what they live for. Being of good service is how they get to their glorious afterlife. Why do the Harbingers care whom they serve?"

"Spoken like someone who has never had to do any kind of service work."

"My whole life is service, woman."

"They want to serve you, and only you. That is their goal. Your father's people are as expendable to them as the Imset. Because they created you, they believe you are perfect."

"I do believe you're flirting with me."

She rolled her eyes. "I'm serious. What the Harbs really want is for you to take over, and for the Rakki to inherit all of the great and beautiful Worlds. But they can never admit that, of course. It would be disloyal. I think you can play along, and rise to power, and they will protect you. Unless the Volterrans say you're a non-entity and prevent you from taking the throne. The Harbs, you realize, must accept whatever the Volterran authorities decide, whether they like it or not. The Xaff would be obliged to hunt you, if given the order. Let's just say you're wise to want to learn to fly."

"Volterra must decide to accept me. Or all is lost."

She grabbed his arm. "The Harbingers desperately want the law to include you. It is what they are working toward. But as faithful servants they could never admit as much. They make it look like the emperor's individual idea, his project, just a way to serve Volterra. But they created the crisis. They want change. You must see that."

Hal looked horrified. "So, the Harbingers have perpetrated the project so they can replace one race with another? Like dolls in a doll house."

She ate candy from a dish. She was exhausted, and wanted to sleep, but the buzz of sugar would have to suffice.

"I think the Harbs have convinced themselves that interfering in the order of things is necessary, that they are preserving what is best in the universe. The Rakki are half Volterran. So, the Harbs justify their actions by giving the Volterran people a legacy through the Rakki."

"Hardly a consolation."

"Welcome to Harb social engineering. I wonder if your father hasn't made the only deal he could. I wonder if from his vantage point, the end of Volterra is inevitable. But his children can live on, if he plays things right with the Harbs."

"You don't think my father is the driving force behind the war?"

"No. But the Harbs, yes." Serral mulled her answer. "Long before the Cataclysm, there were tales of Tekku saucers kidnapping Imset people for experimentation—wiping them, leaving them traumatized and full of warnings about how the Imsethans needed to awaken to their folly in not saving the planet from imminent destruction. Sadly, very few listened. This was before Contact, when the Imset thought they were alone in the universe. Anyone who ran around spewing about gray aliens was written off as insane, especially because they had memory problems. So, unless your father is a thousand years old, the Harbs started this long before his time."

"If this is true," he said, "why would the most powerful man in the universe bargain with his slaves?"

"Because he's no fool. Everything is coming to a head. Once the issue of your legacy is settled and the Volterrans accept you and the Rakki as their heirs, the Imset die out, and the Xaff have no purpose. And that is fueling their violence."

"You base this theory on what?"

"Things I've seen," she swallowed. Her head hurt, and the dots in her vision were dancing, waiting for a moment to fill her with black exhaustion. "Since the war began, Harbs obeyed Alliance battlefield rules. They engaged in combat only below the exosphere, never in space itself. Which seemed logical since it's inefficient to fight in zero gravity. But all that changed around the time I got recruited, the same time you were coming of age, yes?"

His eyes narrowed. "Six months ago."

"Right. Finally, you stood as a real candidate to take the throne and usher in a new Rakki age. What that meant for the Imset was that suddenly the Xaff would attack anywhere, even on ships in space that had no means of fighting back. It must hurt the Xaff. They love to die in battle, as martyrs. Space attacks are dirty tricks, no nobility in them. They are against the rules, which as you know Harbs usually follow to the point of madness. The Xaff are being deprived of their identity as great warriors."

"Stick to facts, please."

"I am. Martyrdom is what motivates the Harbinger Xaff to fight. It's why the Helpers work so hard, it's why sacrifice is so absurdly sacred to them. Because if they do their duty well and with good heart, they will be rewarded."

"Yes, according to their religion." He waved a hand dismissively. "In the afterlife."

"You're missing the point."

He glared. "Come on. It's superstitious nonsense."

"Maybe. But look at it from their point of view. They want to be born into the next life as higher people than lowly Harbs."

He nodded. "Yes. I understand."

She rubbed her hands together, trying to fend off a creeping numbness. "So, ask yourself, what would motivate a creature who believed that their next level of evolution was into people they hate?"

He stared. "So evolving into Volterran lives isn't good enough for Harbinger slaves? That is hard to believe."

"It's about being proper and righteous. Eighty-eight tribal gods and all that. They do not want to be Volterrans because Volterrans live in darkness. They do not believe in Ysk. Not in Astulia, or Ouserium. They do not believe in rebirth into the next higher life form."

Hallenander flopped onto his back. "Just a descent into hell, and eternal suffering amongst the Dantons."

"That's right," she yawned. "I have to go to bed."

"Serral, somewhere in all this speculation, I believe there is a thread to the truth."

"It's not a thread, it's a fuse," she said, stretching. "I believe you lit it when you rescued me."

"Just like the Harbingers wanted me to."

She smiled. "Let's get some sleep, master."

"I feel like a pawn in everyone's game." He stood. "At least in yours, I know what you want from me."

"And I in yours."

"Do you really want to sleep?" He smiled.

She laughed. He moved toward her and took her hands in his. "Could we continue my flight training, like we did last lesson?"

They didn't sleep for hours.

"Do the Xaff speak Volterran?" she asked Hallenander as they glided in the Bisbee from the village gates out onto the road to the airfield.

Xaff patrols stood in their armored Bisbees, straining to get a glimpse of her. They rattled at her brain at each checkpoint, but she refused entry. Did they want to challenge her to a fight or auger all wits out of her? Whichever it was, she did not want to risk it. Hal could not help her on the thought river.

"I have never heard a Xaff speak," he said, looking around suspiciously. "I suppose they must accept orders from someone, but when my uncle has commanded them, he tells liaison servants in the palace, and they convey his orders to the Xaff."

Serral shivered as they passed by the turnoff to the Reykos. The section where Riellen died was out of sight, down a deep bend to the right. How far had Lady Midrey and Lady Irie gone since that day? And had the Wilter captured and harassed them? She tried to imagine how she might have felt toward enemy collaborators when she was an Air Guard.

The Reykos towered like sharp, faceted emerald-and-sapphire sword hilts buried deep in the ground as Serral and Hal traveled the curving road south. She watched the buildings recede and said nothing. The day's warming breeze crept in from the jungle. The wide strips of scrubby ground on either side of the road were wet from recent rain and the trees and vines in the canopy sparkled with water droplets. The Imset living on the other side of the green wall were well concealed.

"I know you're anxious to get flying," Serral said carefully. "But don't you have a SIM in that machine collection of yours?"

Hal eyed her warily. "I have used the SIM many times, and my scores are well beyond passing. Though I appreciate your apparent concern."

"What concern?" she smiled innocently.

"Your attempt to stall my piloting. It's not going to work. We fly today."

"Yes, master."

"That's better."

She socked him playfully on his arm, but he did not flinch.

"In the air, you follow my orders. Understand?"

"Of course," he said. "I have seen you fly. You are just the pilot to teach me how to crash."

He grimaced as she hit him harder.

The southwest quadrant's sick vibration started well before they reached the component field. A tendril of darkness tugged at her mind, it was not Harb, but was akin to the scent of an old photograph, and it called out fretfully. It reminded her of something. She fumbled in her cloth bag.

"I want to give you this," she held out the image of Taurellio and Elva. "I thought you'd probably prefer to keep it out here at the airfield, where you have privacy."

Hal looked at the smiling faces in the picture. "Is that Elva? I never knew her. I appreciate the gesture, but this is not my mother."

"How do you know?"

"Because Rakki are created through artificial means."

Serral did not point out that this did not mean Elva could not have donated her eggs to the effort. But Elva had very light hair, like a soldier, and was thereby, perhaps, sterile.

"Do you know what happened to her?"

"To Elva?" He slowed the Bisbee. "They say she hated life here without my father."

"Wait. Your father lived here at some point?"

"Oh yes, at the beginning. At least, he visited several times a year just like he visited his estate." The Bisbee stopped. "But he has not been here since I was ten years old. And during that visit, he brought press along, so I was obliged to perform like a trained animal, posing for pictures meant to win public acceptance. I am happy to not go through that again."

"Did it work?"

Hal shook his head, scowling. "Oh, quite the contrary. He has not heard the end of people's vile hatred of the monster planet of Evincio. He has not risked the people's wrath by returning."

"The Volterrans really hate you?"

"Most do. Some don't. My understanding is that the people of Volterra are unable to agree upon whether I exist, by their definition anyway, and if I do, whether or not I truly share blood with my father. If I do exist, and I am of his blood, whether I am a violent, half-Imset brute."

He parked the craft gently next to the hangars. Serral looked at the components stacked around his flight center. Hallenander stepped onto the tarmac and tucked the photograph into his pocket.

"Get out of the Bisbee," he said. "You're not safe out in the open."

She could not bring herself to move. "I'm starting to understand why the Harbs hate the Volterrans."

"I'm sorry. I shouldn't have burdened you with my problems."

"Don't be silly," her voice cracked. "I don't care what those lazy hypocrites think of the Imset. At least my people are honest, and we do our own work. We fight our own wars, bleed for our own cause."

He held his hand out to her and said, "Regardless of my genetics, I am tired of being pushed around by the powers that be. We share that much, you and I."

Serral took his hand and stepped out of the Bisbee.

They argued for twenty minutes about which type of craft to fly. Hallenander wanted to take a Tekku. "The Xaff won't shoot us down if they think we are one of them."

Serral scoffed. "The Xaff know where we are at all times, believe me. If we fly an Arrow, they won't be fooled into thinking we're Imset military."

"So, you auger with the Xaff as well as the Helpers? Is that why you asked if the Xaff spoke Volterran?"

She shook her head. "I can auger with them. But it's unpleasant and they have this fetish for fighting me. I wish I could speak to them in words. They communicate with some sort of chain of command, but I don't understand who is in charge. I just really don't trust them."

"Good. I don't either."

Finally, they agreed on a two-person Arrow. Unlike single-occupant fighter planes or the Bolt, these fighter craft held a pilot and co-pilot side by side much like a Tekku did, but with roomier seats.

"I can fit in a Tekku seat easily enough, but you'd be a bit squished," Serral said.

He crossed his arms and looked at her sideways. "Yes. I have experienced the discomfort of squeezing myself into the narrow confines of a Harbinger seat. But in a Halo. Remember?"

"When you were over Chlore? No wonder you looked so grumpy."

"And you looked fierce as a lion." He motioned toward a door. "Little did I know that's how you always look."

"Do I?"

He brightened. "No. Right now, you look like a hungry eagle."

"I like that better. You look like a lost rooster. Better remedy that."

He laughed.

They chose flight suits from the stock room. "These are all custom made?"

"Imset workers in the village do most of the manufacturing, though they have workshops in the Xalavria as well. They work with the Helpers, of course. It takes a lot of sewing and printing to keep things going around here."

Serral gazed at the collection of equipment and supplies. "I will never get used to the amount of wasted resources in the Volterran world."

"That is what Geddon says," Hal replied. "Or, what he used to say."

Once they were suited up, Serral went over safety procedures, then system checks.  Hallenander listened patiently.

"Very well. Number one," he read from a card and looked at her suspiciously. "Are we not going to check the systems again?"

"No, I just wanted to see if you'd agree to do it for a fourth time. And you did. You're very good at hiding your true feelings."

He looked at her quizzically. "My true feelings?"

"I know how impatient you are to get out there, but you're acting as if there's nothing you'd rather be doing than safety checks."

"I don't think your analysis is correct. The truth is, I am enjoying your presentation. Not only is it informative, but," he stammered, "you are so full of confidence. I feel a bit in awe."

"Eagles are like that." Serral tucked the safety card away. "You'll understand soon."

Serral and Hal pushed the Arrow out onto the tarmac, past the junk piles, and onto a large square marked with reflective paint. He tried to jump into the plane as easily as she had but wound up hitting his head dome on the cockpit shield and making her roar with laughter. Then, they tested their coms.

He closed the shield. "We cannot stay here on the tarmac long."

She agreed. A sick feeling that emanated from the ground beneath the rubbish spirals set her on edge. "Straps clicked in," she said. "Hatch closed. Power up. Shell hardened."

"Check. Check. Check. Check."

"Let's go." Serral could not help squealing with delight as they hovered off the ground and lifted into the atmosphere.

Hal made no sound, but his face beamed.

"What?"

"Nothing." He checked the floor window. "Only. We are flying. Flying, in the air."

She gunned it over the palace complex which spun below like an ivory toy. Then they flew high over the jungle-clad continent and its lazy brown river flowing away from the high black-and-white mountains.

They screamed with delight.

"Safer if we head over the ocean now," she commed.

"Safer, how? Because if we crash, we wind up in the water?"

"We're not going to crash." She pulled them into a steeply banking turn, then said in a mock-dramatic voice, "I'm utterly bored of crashing. Much more fun to thread the needle."

"To what?"

"Hang on tight."

The shield flashed murky green as they dove into the waves, then blue again when they emerged. To Hal's surprise, the ocean's drag did not slow them down at all. Serral took them under and over the surface three times before she lifted the craft high over the water. Sunlight glinted on condensation.

"You are either trying to impress me or make me sick."

"Is it working?"

"Both," he laughed. "Yes."

She began explaining the technical marvel that was a Imset Arrow.

By mid-morning, Hallenander was flying the Arrow by himself. Serral taught him how to evade different kinds of attack. He was a quick study, eager to learn, happy to work at mastering the skills. The Arrow was even more nimble and impressive than he expected. At one point, Serral had him retract the wings and fly through a narrow chasm. When they emerged alive on the other side, he screamed himself hoarse.

"This is the most fun I have ever had," he croaked.

She pretended to be frustrated. "Fun? Fun? You think this is fun?"

He bit back his smile.

"Well, you're right. It is. I'd be worried if you didn't think so."

When Hal had mastered maneuvering, Serral showed him how to hit targets with bullets and rockets. He practiced a few dozen times, then said, "Let us not waste ammunition."

A craggy rock they were using for target practice exploded.

"I get the impression you have plenty."

"I do. I've been collecting it for a special occasion. Like this."

"Yes. A festive day out with your Companion." She looked starboard. Below, the sea glimmered. They had orbited the planet, getting a sense of the place. Hallenander knew the names of all the land masses, their properties, and resources. Beyond a few burned crash sites, the Imset were all but undetectable. But they were, Serral knew, alive and down there, like mice hiding beneath a well-tended farmstead.

"One of many more, I hope."

Her chest felt heavy. "Oh, Hal. I think we both know that my war is almost over."

"What do you mean, your war is *almost over*?"

"I only mean you're getting to be a competent pilot. Landing, take-off, navigation. Those are your last three subjects before you graduate."

"I've taught myself navigation already, using books and the liquid portal; it was the easiest part of this."

"The easiest part?" She looked at him, "I'm going to say something, and I don't want you to think I'm being a Companion about it."

"Oh no, what?"

"You are amazing. Seriously. I've never met anyone as brilliant as you, and that includes my brother, who is a genius. There is nothing you aren't good at. Is there?"

He did not answer.

"It must be frustrating, to be worthy. For a group of people who don't value you."

He bowed his head. Finally, he whispered, "Thank you, Serral. I don't want to sound like a master about this, but you are a better friend than I could have ever hoped for."

Whisps of clouds raced past below them.

"Where would you say we are, right now?" she asked. "Longitudinally?"

"As far from the palace as we can be."

"On the opposite side of the planet from the Harb operation center?"

"Yes. If you dug through Evincio, you'd come out somewhere around here."

"Take the controls, Hal."

"What?"

She pointed to a set of islands, dark splotches in the silver sea. "We're landing. Over there."

Serral spotted a brilliant green lagoon, with hard-pack sand on a long, tree-lined spit of land. Hallenander's first two attempts left deep, architectural-looking circles. But finally, he touched down, leveled off, and yelped with satisfaction.

He was about to open the shield when Serral said, "Hold on for one second, okay? I warn you, I might look a little weird."

Serral augered. No one answered. She and Hal were alone. The freedom felt sweet and fresh, like breathing again after a long dive underwater. "No Harbs, no Helpers, no Xaff, anywhere I can reach."

He made a quizzical face. "Can you detect the presence of malevolent animals as well?"

"Nah," Serral said. "The price of freedom is risk, don't you agree?"

"It is. Though I doubt the Volettu will leave us alone for long. As soon as word reaches them that we are off having fun, someone will come ruin it."

She threw her helmet on her seat. "So, I guess, this is your chance to find out what freedom is all about."

The lagoon was surrounded by high rocks and sand. It had a narrow passage to the sea that was held in place by deeply rooted trees with leaves the size of a Bisbee. Dried-out shells littered the ground alongside old components, white resin and black wires, all bleached by salt. The water on their toes felt cool and refreshing.

"We're going in," she stated emphatically.

"It's either that or get heat stroke."

They stripped to underclothes and swam. Then, they climbed high rocks and jumped into the cool blue. Serral stepped on a mysterious ooze that made her squeal. Hallenander laughed.

When they had enough sun, they found thick roots to lean on in the shade and sipped hydration fluid. Tiny, bright white birds emerged from the underbrush and combed wavelets with their beaks.

"I don't ever want to leave this place," Hal said.

"The planet belongs to you, doesn't it?"

"You're a bit more optimistic than I am. But, if in the end, I do wind up in charge of Evincio, this place will become a sanctuary."

She nodded. "The birds will appreciate that. Look how happy they are."

"What's wrong?" he asked.

Sadness and worry crept into her limbs. "You're a pilot, Hallenander. You're ready for whatever they throw at you."

"Am I?"

She swallowed. "Your plan worked. I got another year of life. Thank you."

He sat up. "What are you talking about?"

She touched him lightly on the wrist, "Thank you for reviving me, and giving me a chance to fly again. I am grateful for everything. For this day." She gestured toward the water. "Thank you."

He scowled. "What's gotten into you?"

"My contract is up," she said quietly, "I can't feel whoever is going to come for me yet, but they'll come. Your future is about to start."

"My future," Hallenander said.

"I don't have a lot of options," she said. "But one thing I'm sure of. When I'm no longer needed by you, the Xaff will find a different use for me. And I don't think I'm interested in letting that happen."

"Then it's good they don't know that I've learned all this." He took her face in her hands and touched her forehead with his. "Because you are my Companion. I will decide when your contract ends."

"Yes master." She smiled to hide her sadness. If she had Slook to talk to, she was sure she could come up with a reasonable explanation for everything she had done since crashing onto Evincio. All she had learned, which felt like a puzzle no one else had all the pieces for. But while Serral felt proud of the steps she had taken since meeting Hallenander, the stronger emotion just then was deep, aching sorrow.

"I really can't bear it when you get sad like this. I am going to become Emperor. If only so I can cheer you up."

She laughed through her tears. Then his lips were on hers. Her pain disappeared into the jolt of his arms around her.

"You don't have to do this," he said. "Please don't pretend, I couldn't stand it."

She ran her hand down the length of his skull, It felt surprisingly smooth. "Kiss me."

He did. A long time later, they swam again.

Almost as soon as they were airborne, a Tekku squadron flanked their plane and accompanied them all the way back to the airfield. The blue sky flashed with Tekkus and Halos, like a scattering of silver confetti.

"The Xaff are in a panic," Serral said. "I would have expected them to know where we were."

"They may have put tracking devices into my collection of ships," Hal said. "And I may have removed them."

Serral hated being surrounded, but the Xaff peeled off as soon as the landing pad came into view.

Covered in salt and sweat, she was glad the hangar had a shower. While Hal washed, she took out her cloth bag and removed a large envelope marked "Captain Geddon," and placed it in the Arrow.

"What are you doing?" Hal called out.

"Just worrying about what happens to the Companions when your verdict is rendered."

He dried his brown head dome with a small cloth. "They are important to the Rakki. And you said the Rakki are important to the Harbingers. Would they not keep the ladies on the project?"

"I think it depends on if the Harbs want to take Evincio for Rakki only. Dispose of the Imset here or let them die out."

He scowled. "I want Evincio to for my friends. I include the Imset in that. Perhaps it could be their new home."

Serral imagined squadron upon squadron of Tekkus swarming, the orange flames of explosions, ships crashing into the sea. "Sure, that sounds nice."

His scowl lifted.

At the silver gates, he leaned down so she could kiss him goodbye, but her aim was bad and she smacked the air next to his ear. He whispered, "Are you all right?"

"Of course." Then she said loudly, for show, "What a divinely romantic day, Your Sevenni Highness."

"Here." He handed her a box. "If you want to reach me, you needn't use the servants."

The box contained thick cards with his gold-embossed crest, and matching envelopes.

She smiled. "Thanks."

"What's wrong?" he said again, quietly. "Are you still worried about the future?"

She shook her head. "I have total confidence in you."

"Ah. You are worried. And nothing I can say will override your knowledge of the Harbingers. I know. But have faith. And now I've got reasons to succeed."

He sat up again and drove off.

**38**

C hapter Thirty-Nine

"You there," Hallenander called to one of the Harbingers in the cobbled yard between the wide, stone palace stairs and the outbuildings where the travel Bisbees were stored.

The Gray bowed, her black eyes turning toward him and her small mouth upturned. "Yes, Your Sevenni Highness?"

Hal regarded her crossed arms. Her partner soon joined her, and they both stood at attention in their gray uniforms, black and gold detailing glinting in the sunlight. Their head domes puffed respectfully. They stared straight ahead.

"Do you go to school to become... what is your specialty?"

They spoke as one person with two mouths, "Transportation maintenance, sire."

"Transportation maintenance?"

Their heads ruffled ever so slightly as they conferred without speaking. "Sire, we do not attend school. We are given knowledge and understanding from our team."

"And where is your team?"

They communicated silently to one another, their heads now pulsing with vehemence.

"Our team is all around, always advising and offering correction."

"All around you? Where? Tell me, specifically where?"

"We do not know that. They could be anywhere in the palace complex, your highness. They are always with us, to guide and help us."

He could see they were becoming agitated, though they stood rigid. It was a hot afternoon, and Hal was in a hurry. "Fetch me my small, armed Bisbee, the one with rocket launchers and automatic rifles."

They ran in obedience. He suspected they were glad to get away from his questions. When they brought the Bisbee out, it hovered between two uniformed Helpers. Were they the same ones? He did not know. Few Harbingers bore distinguishing features. He had known a few with a wrinkle where their bulbous head joined their face and some with slightly darker skin, but they all refused to use individual names.

"Are you the same Helpers I spoke to a moment ago?"

They stood stock still. "Of course, your highness. We are all one."

Hal gave up his inquiry. "Thank you for your service."

Their domes roiled. He noticed that one of them bore a slight quib lubricant stain between one of his four long fingers. Not the same creature as before.

Hallenander mounted the machine. He checked that the guns were loaded and drove out the gates and down the drive, exiting the complex. He nodded to the Xaff patrols, who stared impassively with their twelve black pairs of eyes. Their armored Bisbees outweighed his by thousands of kilos, he noted. He took comfort knowing that their machines were slower than his.

But soon, the warriors disappeared behind a bend in the road, and the jungle shimmered with heat. Waves rose too from the concrete and combined with the air of the jungle until a fetid, green tar smell filled his nose. Hal noticed holes in some of the giant, glossy leaves. He left the road.

The ground below the Bisbee snaked with tree roots that curled around deep puddles. Venomous-looking bushes had long thorns protruding in all angles. When the wall of trees was fifty meters behind him, he noticed signs of violence: huge stalks snapped in two, bark torn and ragged, small punctures riddling waxy green fans. He was amazed that two women had made it this far. He only had to hover for a few minutes to find a place where rusty stains had dried around one empty white shoe wedged in a hole beneath a root.

He had turned back to the road when the first bullet pinged out from the dark forest. Imset voices called out tauntingly. He whipped his craft around but saw nothing.

"I have no desire to fight you," he called out. "Geddon, is that you?"

He gunned the Bisbee away, and the place he had been exploded.

Hal fired back into the trees; his guns felt foreign. He had never shot at anyone. His hands felt damp. His knees jangled with nerves. Birds flew, leaves scattering violently. He hovered to the tree line. If he moved carefully, he could see both above and below his craft.

"Please tell Geddon," he hollered into the green void. "This is no longer a good area for Imset. Best let me leave peacefully. If you fire on me, you will be killed."

A ragged, high pitched man's voice called out in Imset, "Then take your chances and leave, you disgusting alien. See what happens."

"Who are you?" Hal yelled. He twisted his Bisbee carefully back into the trees and vines. The jungle thickened around him. He had to ascend.

"Not Captain Geddon, that traitor! We're your worst nightmare," came a powerful second voice.

Bullets pitted a nearby tree trunk.

Hal turned and took his craft high, back out toward the road. There was a flash of silver, and two armored Bisbees exploded into the forest, guns blazing, shooting so fast he had to scream to be heard.

"Cease fire," he commed to the Harbingers.

Someone in the forest screamed. The Xaff stared at him silently from their Bisbees, their guns poised.

Hal spoke sternly. "We are leaving now."

There was no movement.

"Now!" Hal shouted. He maneuvered his Bisbee so he was facing off with the armored carriers. Two Xaff on each vehicle stood, motionless. They did not wear their customary silver helmets.

"I see what you want. Luckily for you, I'm in a mood to give it to you."

He squeezed off a barrage of shots, and the four Xaff went down, falling out of their Bisbees onto the harsh ground below. Their crafts switched into automatic mode, and hovered away toward the airfield. Hal felt a small sense of power enter him. The Thrill. But he did not like it.

He called back into the jungle. "They will send more. Get away from this area. It is no longer safe for you here."

Cursing his vulnerability, he hovered away. He was sweating; tears coursed involuntarily from his eyes. But within, he felt a steel he had never known. He was no longer an observer of the war. He had become one of its soldiers, tangled though his loyalties might be.

He would never let anyone fight his battles again.

When he arrived at the checkpoint near the airfield, the two empty Bisbees butted gently against an abandoned kiosk. They looked like animals trying to return to the barn. Hal left, turned his craft to the east, and in two minutes, the gate was out of sight. Ten minutes later, the Reykos gleamed into view. The green tower loomed closest, but the road led to the further, blue tower, which stood coolly like a defiant trophy.

He slowed as the road curved downward under the building into darkness. His eyes adjusted in the large receiving area. It appeared deserted, but when he had powered down his machine, and stepped out, a pair of Helpers in green coveralls stood bowing.

They said in Volterran, "Hallenander, our most beloved benefactor! We are honored by your visit!"

He unzipped the top of his flight suit. "You do not feel the need to acknowledge my rank?"

"Oh, Your Sevenni Highness," their domes pulsed. "We are unworthy subjects! And you are Minsyx! But we have known you always. We were your loving caregivers."

"My caregivers?" he said carefully. His chief memories of childhood were times the Volettu instructed him in the law, or individual men gave him lessons in different subjects, or the long, lazy days spent with Geddon, which were the best of all. It had not occurred to him that he had ever lived outside the walls of the palace. "Well then I thank you for your good service."

"Please ignore our impudence. We are only nursery helpers and have no real knowledge of the world."

"But you knew me when I was a baby?"

Their heads erupted in violent heaves. "We did. We did. We tended you."

"And your team is how large?"

"Oh, we are many. There is no need we do not provide. We love the babies. The boys, their energy, the girls, their fierceness. The imaginations of the older children! And you, you were such a beautiful one, so bright and bestowed of the powers." They bowed once more.

Hallenander felt an odd feeling of recognition in his gut. His body seemed to know these Harbs. Or their predecessors. But childhood was so long ago, before he could think, when all he had was fear, hunger, and yearning. He must have come from this place, been created here.

"You said *children...*"

"Oh yes! We forget your purpose. You have come to approve your father's plans, of course."

Hal hesitated. "Yes. Of course. Where are they?"

The two helpers took him up a set of escalators, talking all the time about their preparations. Hal felt strong emotion coming from his core, and only half listened to their chatter about where the Syxarit would stand when he arrived alone, before the others were off the star ship. "He must see for himself, of course. He must witness."

"See?" Hallenander asked idly, a strange prickle moving over his skin. "Witness what?"

They reached the top of the escalator, and Hal's mouth went dry with emotions he could not name. Sound hit him first. Children squealing, laughing, calling out to one another. Voices, unlike anything he remembered consciously, layers of cheerful yelps. Twenty or more Rakki kids played under blue skylights and among plants and brightly colored play equipment. They were watched over by dozens of Helpers all dressed in green coveralls.

His two Helpers led him forward. "The children have prepared a special song for the Syxarit. They shall perform it here, and then we shall show him our gardens."

"I want to meet Piettu."

"Piettu?" They stood still for a moment, heads in motion.

"Yes. He is closest to me in age, correct?"

Their slit mouths gaped open, an expression he had not seen on a Harbinger before. In fact, he realized, these helpers were altogether different, more talkative and emotional than any he had known.

"Please follow us."

Hallenander tried to take in the faces and forms of all the children they passed, but soon doors were opening and streams of young Rakki were gathering around him, too many to remember. The youngest was five, he reckoned, and the eldest, a likeness of himself moved toward him with a pigeon-toed gate. The broad, brown face and thick lips were close copies of his own. Only the boy's green eyes were different, deeper and wilder, like a mountain lake.

"Hello," the boy said in Volterran, extending his hand in the Imset fashion, "I am Piettu."

Hallenander wrapped his arms around his brother. But it was no use. Everyone could see he was crying. Then his legs were tangled in small arms, his torso pushed inward by larger people, and soon both he and Piettu were laughing on the ground. As if trained to do so, the others sat in concentric circles.

They said, a hundred voices ringing in tandem, "Welcome, Hallenander. Welcome, brother!"

## 39

C hapter Forty

Hallenander became fuzzy after the forty-eighth child stood and recited her name. By the time the one-hundred-and-third Rakki, a boy of about seven, had chirped out "I am Dellum," the prince was overwhelmed, though he smiled and nodded politely. So many names, so many different personalities and faces, each staring with large eyes, their bodies animated with repressed energy. He dismissed them, and they ran away, back to classrooms and play.

"Go now," he called to a group of teenagers who milled around whispering and curious. "We will meet again. I must speak with only Piettu now."

Piettu motioned for one of the girls to stay. "Dear brother, this is Subuii."

A young woman of sixteen smiled broadly and extended her hand. Her eyes glowed with pale fire, like his father's, though hers were pale turquoise and sparkled with laughter. "Many thought you would never come. But I always believed."

"Believed?"

They walked back toward the escalator. Subuii took his arm. She was nearly as tall as he, though Piettu was taller than both. Hallenander struggled once more to contain his feelings.

"We waited and waited for you to come see us, of course!" she said. "Some people said you didn't care, and some people said..."

"Shut up, Subbie." Piettu said, moving in his stiff way to keep up. "You're being rude."

"What did people say?" Hal asked, smiling at his brother to signal it was all right for Subbie to speak freely.

Subuii tossed her long, bronze head, "That you were too stuck up. That you were an Overlord, not a hybrid freak like us."

Hallenander stopped. Piettu and Subuii watched him expectantly.

"I don't know how to tell you this. And I fear it may endanger you if I tell you too much, since my—our—Father is counting on us not knowing about one another."

"Why would he want that?" Piettu scoffed. "Are we not well controlled enough for him? Locked in a tower? Unable to even walk outside?"

Hal put his hand on his brother's forearm. "We have much to discuss. But believe me, there is danger to us, all of us. And for now, meeting and talking must be enough. Agreed?"

"We trust you," Piettu said. "You are our brother. And you will help us, we know it."

Hal rubbed the golden circlet around his head. "I will," he said, his voice dropping to near nothing. "Whatever comes. I will not abandon you."

An ancient-looking Harbinger Helper approached. She held her long, gray arms toward Hallenander. It was the first time in his life that he had thought of a Harbinger as having gender. Yet, for reasons he could not name, he was sure this one was female.

"Ah, good afternoon, dear Uniaah." Subuii said, leading Hal by the arm toward the creature.

"We kneel," Piettu whispered, "or else she can't hear us."

"Kneel? Me?" Hallenander asked in amazement as the two teenagers dropped to the level of the old Harbinger.

They touched their fingers to hers and spoke words of greeting. Hal lowered to the level of the wrinkled gray lady. She regarded him with black eyes that narrowed affectionately in a way he did not expect.

"Oh, Hallenander," the old Harbinger said in a wavering voice. "At last, you are back to us."

He played along. "Yes, Uniaah. I am back."

"My child. How strong you have grown. The Masters must love you well. I am glad."

She held a narrow, gray hand out to him, and feeling very self-conscious, Hallenander stretched out his own. They met in the space between them, fingertips touching, in a gentle greeting. Tears came to his eyes as he was flooded with realization.

"You were my mother," Hallenander said quietly.

"In almost every way, child," Uniaah said. "I became like the Imset, because you needed your Imset mother. And now, I am changed. For the better."

"You did your work well. Thank you."

Uniaah's eyes closed and her head dome puffed with gratification. "You were always so special. I see that has not changed."

"Uniaah was the one who invented the program of Imset surrogate mothers," Subuii said.

"The Project?"

"Yes." Piettu sat on his haunches. "It was too hard for most Helpers to change in the way she did."

"It came at a cost, you see," Uniaah said. "Not many are willing to pay it."

"The Harbingers no longer accept you?" Hal asked. "Is loneliness the price?"

"You are perceptive. Like your father."

Hallenander did not know how to reply. He turned to Piettu. "Your Imset mother was Riellen, yes?"

The boy's eyes darkened. "I know she was murdered. She told me last time I saw her that she expected to be."

"I am so sorry," Hallenander said. "I didn't know her well, but I met her many times. She loved you powerfully."

Subuii snorted, "All of the Imset moms are in danger from those monsters."

"Which monsters to you mean?" he asked.

"The Xaff. They're the killers, right?"

Hal and Uniaah exchanged a look. The woman's black eyes gleamed as if to say, *she does not understand.*

"The Xaff are tasked with killing the Imset," Hal said, nodding.

"I will avenge her," Piettu said quietly, wiping away a tear. "Someday."

Hal turned to the old Harbinger. "Mother, is there a place the four of us can meet privately, somewhere we won't be overheard?"

Uniaah took them to an elevator that led to the top of the tower. They stepped into a large room under a faceted, blue glass dome. The view of the valley and bay below was breathtaking. The palace, the whitewashed village, even the lofty Xalavria winked brightly in the setting sun. Serral's black-gold edifice gleamed. Hal imagined her sitting on her terrace worrying, or drawing pictures, or quizzing the servants. Serral, who prompted him to do what he had never thought of before; rebelling. Taking control. Questioning. And she had been right. She had insisted the Reykos towers were more than they seemed.

Hallenander turned his back to the others. "Tell me, Uniaah, you have confirmed that these towers are in fact star ships, and that is the important thing, but I need to know if there are any specifications for this ship."

The old woman bowed her head, and her dome rippled stiffly. "Yes, dear. But they are in the hands of the warriors. And the warriors are not friends to us." She sniffed. "These towers are wondrous prisons, child. And I suppose they are ships as well."

The elevator doors opened and Helpers brought chairs and refreshments. Uniaah shooed them away, and the four sat huddled together.

"We must talk through plans for the future," Hallenander began. "There are several possible paths, and I do not know which course history will take. But I do know that all the children must be kept safe."

The others agreed.

"Most important," he continued, "when Taurellio arrives, he must not learn I have been here."

"Father must not know?" Subuii said. "Is his love for us wavering?" She and Piettu laughed comfortably.

"What is funny?"

Uniaah explained to Hallenander, "The girls have never seen their father. None of the children have, save you."

"Ah. And I, not very much." Hallenander thought about how to explain his request for secrecy. "Father does not know that I am here. He has never told me about you."

"What?" Piettu said. "Do you mean you came here without permission?"

He and his sister gripped each other, delighted.

"I did. And I am glad I did. But I believe that I will be of more help to you if father does not discover my disobedience."

Subuii's turquoise eyes glowed. "You want to be a double agent! Oh yes, we will help you."

"Good. Let me begin by telling you what I know about the current situation. I do not think the timing of Father's visit is an accident. We must prepare in other ways than plans to show him your progress."

Several hours later, Helpers came back up the elevator to inform Hallenander that an army of Xaff fighters had gathered around the entrance to the tower, and the children were terrified.

Hallenander stood. "I will return."

Uniaah held her hand out for a goodbye touch. She said, "And why have you not brought the Thanton to meet me, dear Hallenander?"

He took her hand fully into his. It was warm and soft, the slick gray skin worn down by age. "She is busy. But tell me. I have always wanted to understand, why do your people refer to my friend as *Thanton*? Aren't Thantons divine deputies of Ysk?"

"Yes, that is correct. I know you are not a believer, not if you are being groomed to be the ruler of the Volterra and their many gods." Her lids looked heavy. "We who believe in Ysk believe the Thantons can select our souls for the Ouserium. They can bestow eternal life and love upon those they deem worthy."

"Yes, I understand that." Hal spoke quickly knowing he had to protect the children from the gathering Xaff. "But Serral is a person, flesh and blood. Not a Thanton."

Uniaah folder her slender gray arms. "No. She is more than that. She is caught between life and death. She hangs between, like a spider on a thread."

"How do you know that?"

"She has shown us. Her divinity allows her to speak our language, and we listen. She is not alive. She is not dead. Spirits ride on her shoulder. Thantons speak to her as their equal. She is a beloved of

Ysk. She is endowed by Ysk. You are an unbeliever, so you do not understand. But she does. She knows what she is."

Hallenander stood, speechless, unsure how to respond without showing disrespect. "I see. Thank you."

"You're obviously in deep with this girl, Hal." Subuii tugged on his arm. "Better get back to her."

"Come back soon. Please do not bring the Xaff with you." Piettu clapped Hal on the back. "We will invent the sorts of silly myths and legends every tribe needs. A thousand years from now, children will repeat our tales and try to live up to our legends."

"We will play gods?"

His brother leaned on his arm. "Who better? Are we not Rakki?"

Hallenander felt lighter than he had in years, and he gunned his Bisbee away from the Reykos through a gathering of a hundred armored Xaff, back toward the palace.

"Not today. No more killing today," he said to himself as the group disappeared in his mirror, the glimmering of their silver carriages and armor faint under a full moon. "You will make it to the afterlife when you have done something to deserve it."

When he returned to the palace, his helpers handed him an invitation from Serral to a party that night. He rushed to dress, sensing for the first time that his rooms were temporary, a place he was soon to outgrow.

**40**

— • —

Chapter Forty-One

When she got inside the silver gates, Serral pulled her cloth bag over her shoulder and went straight to the Clubhouse. The Caf was busy with casually dressed women eating and chatting. Most greeted her. Her stomach reminded her she had not eaten yet, so she helped herself to some of the old-Imsetthan food on the buffet. Helpers rushed over to heap her plate high. A couple of women further along in line muttered about how it must be good to be paired with Hallenander. Serral was relieved when Cheloa and Shanno called her over. They were at a table with Alysse, who took notes on a pad of paper. Serral sat down, discreetly reached into her bag, and passed an envelope across the table. Cheloa quickly pocketed it.

"It's all happening, Hon," Cheloa purred. "The components are snapping together nicely."

"Good," Serral said. "What a lovely afternoon for ladies to meet to exchange gossip."

Alysse said, "Yes. Lots of juicy happenings here at the resort."

"We have much to plan for," Shanno said. "As you know."

"I've just given you the information you need. I am waiting for final confirmation of the time and day."

"Wonderful," Cheloa said. "We will be ready."

Callia appeared, breathless. Serral smiled, relieved to see her. Callia said over loud: "Serral, do you know how to sew?"

The workshops in the industrial buildings between the Clubhouse and the town square held sewing facilities, and Callia took Serral to a room full of worktables, sewing equipment, and bolt after bolt of fabric.

"I'm supposed to finish these today," Callia said. "It's not possible. I'm panicking."

"Hand them over." Serral took stock of the sewing machine, started it up, and began pinning. "These are nicer." She almost added, *than anything I wore as a girl*, but stopped herself. "These are sweet."

"You think a spoiled six-year-old girl would like one?" Callia paced anxiously.

"Don't hold back your real feelings."

"Sorry," she whispered. "I don't like kids."

"But what about your little girl in the project?"

Callia flipped her dark hair back. "Bettiu. I really wish I could love her. But she's awful." Callia looked down at the floor. "I never asked to be her foster mother."

"I understand," Serral said, remembering when she had childcare duty back in Warren Falla. She had loved the scrap rats with all their energy and neediness, but when the bell had rung at the end of her shift, she had run off to the bone yard without looking back.

"You're doing a nice thing, though, making these frocks." Serral held up the frilly dress Callia had set down. "Or trying to make them."

Serral knew how to sew flight suits, harness straps, and safety shelters, almost anything a colonist might need in the wilderness, or a pilot might need for flight. The only clothing she had owned before recruitment had been her graying, patched colonial coveralls. She had never even dreamed of finery like the colorful dress passing through her hands.

"Holy hell, can you sew," Callia said gratefully. "You're a life saver."

"You don't have lay it on that thick." Serral laughed.

Serral rested in the knowledge that she had successfully passed the catacomb map to Cheloa, and that the women were actively planning their escape. But why didn't she feel less worried? She focused on the seam in front of her, the metal foot hammering up and down. There was so little time left to help the all-important Rakki, and the subservient women of the planet. If Serral was able to pull off her plan for the children, she could finally let go of her worry. But she also needed a final plan for herself. And then, with a jolt of pain, she realized the needle had run over her finger.

Callia got serious. "We trade little gifts to give the children, so it looks like we care. Not that everyone hates the project as much as I do. Most are fine with it. But the Helpers expect us to come up with a new gift every time we go. We're punished if we don't."

"How often do you go?" Serral bit thread and handed over two finished dresses. "Here, run an iron over these."

Callia looked impressed. "It used to be three times a week, whatever days we weren't putting on a show."

Serral stopped sewing. "The Xalavria gives performances four nights a week?"

Callia shook out a dress and draped it over a chair. It looked like a frothy pink-and-yellow flower. "Yes. We used to go to the project on the three remaining days but now, it's once or twice a week. We have to keep amusing the men, since that's why they keep us here."

"But they want you on the project too?"

"We are strictly forbidden to mention the project to the men. They threaten us."

"Who threatens you?"

"The Helpers, of course." She reached for some colorful paper and began wrapping the dresses up in packages. "They hate us. But they need us. Whenever we get back from the project, they show us a little strippy to remind us that talking about the you-know-what is grounds to be put out."

Serral paused the sewing machine. "Is there enough talent in this place to still perform four nights? How is that even possible? Where did you all come from?"

"Well, I'm wiped, so I can only guess," Callia replied lightly, tying a glossy pink bow.

"I am so sorry." Serral's mind went to the girls from the Transport 'Tainer, the deaths of her class of recruits, and the two girls who had made it out alive. Had Captain Thrish planned to use them in some way, like the stone men were using the Companions here? Was there a connection between these two different parts of the war?

"Don't worry about it," Callia said. "Maybe the Harbs put our talents in us. Maybe we were grown to have special gifts. Or maybe there's an academy somewhere missing a whole lot of students. We don't know. All we can say for sure is we're Imset, we're fabulous, and we know how to put on a show."

Serral thought for a few minutes, happy to be making something with her hands again. "So, it was Riellen that created this whole resort idea?"

"I guess. She was here from the beginning, they say. She knew what the men liked, what they wanted to see. For all we know, she did it to save us from the war. Or maybe to please Mimellio. Or both. Everyone knew she was in love with him. And they thought he loved her, too. But the Volterrans are evil and decided she was expendable. Maybe because you came. Maybe because Riellen was no longer fun. I don't know." Callia flipped a lilac-and-ultramarine dress onto her ironing board.

"Do you believe Hallenander will make it all the way to Volterra, and onto the throne?"

"If he doesn't, Thantons in air, have they wasted a lot of resources here. Those bastards." Callia shifted in her seat. "It's going to be hard on you, isn't it?"

Serral met her friend's brown eyes. "Me?"

"Oh, please. It's obvious what's going on between you and Hallenander."

"We're putting on our own show." Serral snipped thread. "It's all intentional."

"You are both terrible actors, no offense."

Serral started stitching again. "It's a much larger game, my friend. And my part is almost finished."

Serral augered to see if they would be overheard, but the closest helpers were across the village setting up the amphitheater.

"Are you all right?" Callia asked. "You looked like you were going to pass out."

Serral nodded. "I'm fine. But listen. About Hallenander—"

Callia slid close to Serral on the bench. "He's not a bad man. Not like the rest of them. He's worth fighting for."

"I agree." Serral's eyes stung. "But Hal and I are partners, not lovers."

"Can I give you some advice?" Callia said, smoothing white hair away from her friend's face. Serral nodded.

"All we really have is now. My lover and I take advantage of every moment we can. That way, being wiped, being a prisoner, everything they have done to us—at least I know what joy feels like. They'll take it eventually, like they take everything. But think about it. You're alive. He's alive. Why not just be happy, if you can?"

"It's a nice thought. But happiness is a luxury I can't afford right now."

"You know what's happening next. Don't you?"

"No. But whatever the Volterrans decide to do, this place won't last forever." Serral handed off the last dress. "I'm working closely with Cheloa and Shanno. They'll give you the signal. Be ready to run."

"What? Give up all this?" Callia's beautiful face dimpled in a smile. "Live free? Are you joking?"

Serral used her hands to quiet Callia. "The Imset have their own factions. I'm working on getting you to Geddon."

"Hallenander's teacher?"

"Have you met him?"

Callia shook her head. "No, but I know he's a good man. Are you not coming, Serral?"

She found it hard to speak. "The Xaff will pursue me. They want to fight me, and there are many of them. They'll never stop. Anyplace I go, they'll pursue me. Forever."

Callia's dark brows furrowed. "Because of Riellen?"

"No. It's hard to explain." Serral put away the scissors and turned off the sewing machine. "And if I did, you would think I'm insane."

"Now I'm worried."

"If you want to help me, offer Cheloa and Shanno your assistance. When the time comes, everyone here will need to move quickly."

"But how are we going to avoid the Xaff? It's not like they love us either."

Serral felt tired. "Leave that to me."

"I don't like the sound of that." Callia took the wrapped presents and dropped them into a hand basket. "You're taking on more than any one person can do."

"I know," Serral said. "But I told you. I'm part of a team. And my partner is pretty powerful."

They turned to leave, and Callia whispered, "Please don't put yourself at risk. Not for people who've done nothing for you."

The sun was low in the sky and a cool breeze had set in.

"You had best get ready for your show. It's getting late," Serral replied.

When Serral got back to her building, Click and Clack were fretting. They wrung their slender gray hands, their little slit mouths open like black rectangles of stress.

*A Lord came looking for you. You were not here! He was displeased.*

Their grief pulled down in the river, sinking deeper until Serral pushed it away.

*Which Lord?*

*Distinguished Lord Zinnerit, Mistress. He was angry. He called us despicable worms.*

*He sounds unpleasant. I wonder what he wanted.*

She tried to conjure an image of him. The river showed her a Volterran face with ritualistic scars, dots in straight lines across his high cheekbones. His light topaz eyes were smeared heavily with black. He was both handsome and cruel looking. A realization crept in. Zinnerit was the Master of Lady Irie, one of the women who had been put out when Riellen died. Serral had never spoken to him, but he often sat at Mimellio's side.

*What did you tell the Lord, friends?*

*That you were busy doing tasks for your Master, of course.*

Their fear was like a cold rain pouring onto Serral's mind.

*That's good. I was in the workshops making dresses for the project.*

*Yes! We knew you were behaving with virtue, dear Mistress.*

*You did right, friends. I will fix things with the Lord.*

They bowed, head domes roiling, but with her approval, their anxiety had given way to a measure of calm.

*Come, let us prepare me for the party.*

The Helpers sprang into action, and guided Serral into a closet where they explained the evening's costume.

*Could I not choose my own gown? I have been here long enough to understand.*

Click and Clack looked horrified at her suggestion, their head domes sucked in, making them look like slender, flat headed monsters. *Never mind. Your expertise is very appreciated. Show me your selections.*

Serral was getting help with the finishing touches on her ensemble—a layered, frothy concoction of white mesh beaded in gold—when her helpers announced that her master was at the door.

"We haven't done my hair," she said, accepting his kiss on her cheek and a huge tin of sweets. "We want me to look like the proper Companion, don't we?"

Hallenander placed the sweets on a table already piled high. "You look fantastic right now. But I can wait while the Helpers work. I have something I'd like to talk to you about."

Serral blinked. "While they do my hair?"

His green eyes gleamed. "I have much to tell you." His face was different. He seemed to have both aged and become younger at the same time.

"Why not relax for a minute?" She called to her Helpers. "Whiskey for my master.""Argh. No amount of liquor will get me off topic," he said. "I need you."

"Come on then. A quick hair styling won't take long."

They moved into a mirrored dressing room. While Click and Clack worked, other Helpers brought trays of pre-show snacks. Hal sat in a frilly slipper chair, looking ridiculous in his dark suit and watch chain.

He scowled and sipped his amber drink, stating in code that she had been *absolutely correct in her predictions for the weather,* until Serral's hair had been piled into a jeweled hive atop her head.

"Thank you, Helpers," he said, patting Click and Clack on their shoulders. "Your work is truly stunning."

The helpers' heads puffed and turned a shade of red Serral had never seen. They ran from the room.

"I went there," he whispered, eyes glistening. "You were right about the Rykos towers. I owe you an enormous debt of gratitude. You've changed the course of my life."

The setting sun turned her mirrors dark gold. She felt overwhelmed by his emotions. He had never revealed his feelings so starkly. She wanted to grab him and hold him to her.

"We're going to be late," she said.

In the elevator, Hallenander leaned toward her. "I wish we were back on the island."

Serral watched the floors, counting as they passed. It was strange to her how quickly she had fallen into thinking of this place as her home.

They walked down the road, her heels clicking, the trees above blowing loudly in the rising wind.

"May I hold your hand, Companion?"

She held it out to him but could not look at his face. Was it because of his obvious happiness? Or the fact that it contrasted with her own inner emptiness? He expected her to share his joy. She felt like a Danton, evil and selfish. But all she saw in her own future was a blank hole, like a port worm leading nowhere. His large hand around hers made her want to kick something, to hurl one of the metal chairs in the village square into the fountain. But she forced a smile, and they walked on. Soft music started up, and the sounds of clinking ice and voices.

The party pavilion was decorated with tiny white lights sparkling beneath a silk tent. The air was thick with perfume and tension. The Volettu of Eight men were already surrounded by knots of sparkling women, all flirting and laughing uproariously in the usual Xalavria manner. Silence fell as Serral and Hallenander walked in. The men's faces appeared strained beneath a veneer of elegant detachment. The women looked amused and curious.

"Wine?" Hallenander passed Serral a fizzy pink drink. "My uncle beckons. I am sorry. We must be courteous."

Mimellio sat with four men draped on low chaises, sipping from crystal snifters and puffing on wide, black Tintos that smelled like smoky poison. The men seemed far more like Overlords than Serral had ever seen before. They barely listened to the women and looked only at one another. Their demeanor had a tribal edge with more accessories: blacker kohl liner, and head crests tipped dismissively to the side.

"Come, boy," Mimellio rasped in his high voice. Serral felt the rage and disappointment in his tone. Something had changed.

"Uncle," Hallenander said forcefully in Volterran,."Lords Tuss, Kleitwan, Eltu and Kettu, you all remember my Companion, Serral."

They raised their cheeks her way absently. Serral curtsied. They resumed talking among themselves, quickly, impatiently, straining against the need to listen to one another. Serral could almost follow the conversation. Perhaps because the men's voices were so uncharacteristically emotional, their meaning rang clearer. Lord Eltu, with his deep red-brown eyes and sober, dark clothing, took a conciliatory tone, while Lord Kleitwan, who seemed drunk and sweaty under his shimmering caftan, badgered everyone. His point had to do with the futility of their attempts to gain advantage on Volterra. Old Lord Tuss, who appeared smaller without Lady Midrey by his side, hoarsely counseled the others to calm down and remain open-minded. Serral felt a wave of hostility emanating from Lord Zinnerit, who watched the proceedings with a sneer. He pulled at a white lace collar that flopped over his green velvet smock.

Mimellio, wearing his usual pleated white linen and heavy gold collar, veered back and forth between hysteria and despair. He tugged at one of his massive, carved cuff bracelets anxiously, and Serral could not help wondering if the death of Riellen had not affected him more than he wanted to admit. Her suspicion seemed reinforced when he glared at her, his blue eyes icy. She kept her gaze on Hallenander's ornate, carved shoes, his dark suit and satin waistcoat, the colorful gemstones that flashed on his fingers. He held his own in the conversation, refusing to be interrupted, keeping his voice controlled and level. He held forth for several minutes, saying Volterran words Serral recognized having to do with *the law*, and *patience*, and *respect*. He mentioned *Taurellio* a handful of times. Within a few minutes, calm fell over the men, and Hallenander put his hand on the small of her back, as if to reassure her that everything was fine.

The conversation continued until Cheloa and Shanno arrived, two gorgeous tall creatures in platform shoes who beckoned the men into the theater. Serral avoided Zinnerit's gaze as he passed, but his hand brushed against her back gruffly, and he hissed a word in her ear she did not recognize. His meaning was easy to guess at. He hated her. He blamed her for the loss of Lady Irie. Serral had not known Irie well, only from her staged, fairy-tale-princess story, her tight-waisted dresses and high, pointed hats. Which bothered Zinnerit more, Serral wondered, that he had lost her, or that she was now free? Free for a while. Either Hallenander became Syxarit, and ended the war, or he did not, and then the Xaff would hunt the Imset on Evincio to extinction.

She breathed deeply, thinking about the first time she had flown into space and how excited she had been. She had wanted to help the Imset. And that hope was still alive, though now she had no giant Thanton to whisper in her ear how to make it happen. All she had was faith that once in power, Hallenander would remember his mother's people. And, if she were honest, that he would keep his promise to her.

"Move it, Syxaritta," laughed a voice in her ear. Alysse, in a lavender wig and purple gown. "We're waiting."

"Watch your insults," Serral said.

*Syxaritta* was Volterran for Princess.

In the auditorium, red velvet seats filled fast. Helpers led Serral down side hallways and up into the box seats. Hallenander was at the far end of the Sevenni box, past Zinnerit and Mimellio. Serral squeezed past them. Mimellio glared, but shifted his long knees to one side. She caught Hal's eye. He placed a hand on Zinnerit's shoulder, and Serral quickly slipped by the older man. Hallenander had seen her intention, and moved deftly, so that instead of being forced to sit between the two men, Serral was on Hal's far side, closest to the stage. Zinnerit growled something. Hal smiled, replied lightly, then grabbed Serral's hand, kissing it, and saying Volterran words Serral knew were intended to convey infatuation.

The lights went down, and Serral took her hand back. It tingled, as if not fully her own. Hal's forearm sat on the arm rest between them. She did not know what to do with her own arms. Finally, she crossed them and rested her hands on her lap, though that felt awkward too.

Silence fell, and a spotlight illuminated a tall stool in the middle of an empty stage. Callia walked into the light, barefoot in a long gown, her dark hair falling loosely down her back, and bowed her head to the audience. Women cheered and clapped. The men did not move or make a sound. Callia said something in Volterran, which made everyone titter, then touched her guitar. Music blossomed forth with as much warmth and light as the dawn.

Callia picked and strummed with such dexterity, Serral could hardly believe she was the same inept girl from the sewing shop. The auditorium changed into a different dimension, its atmosphere more tender and earthy than seemed possible, some kind of molecular shift in the space between the bodies in their seats and the gilded, carved ceiling. The sound reached deep into Serral's chest and held her; a memory, a feeling of something lost or broken returning to life. It was as if the spirit of the Imset people were speaking through Callia's fingers, through the strings of her instrument. The girl's hair fell onto her face, and she began to sing in a deep, clear voice. The song was an ancient Imsethan ballad about love and abandonment, simple and beautiful. Time and space fell away. Serral looked to see if others felt as moved as she did. Every face, Imset and Volterran, was mesmerized. She felt Hal's hand on her wrist. He placed a handkerchief into her grasp, and she realized she was in tears. She smiled in thanks and dabbed at her eyes. The show continued, the audience as still as sleeping children, bursting into applause and calls for more at the end of each song. Only Hallenander seemed unmoved, watching Serral instead of the stage.

When the music ended, and the cheering began, Serral ran up the aisle and out of the theater. She went to the hygiene area to fix her makeup while she struggled to calm herself with breathing techniques. She thought about the plight of the Imsethans, and how they had built cities out of technology stolen by their Harbinger invaders, how they insisted on surviving no matter what happened. She had to be like them. She had to think of a way out, a way to get back to the Imset and to Slook, to tell them not to forsake the colonies, not to give up hope. Women came in and out, asking if she was okay. Serral splashed water on her face, borrowed a lip tint, and fixed her hair pins.

She found Hallenander standing alone under the marquee. The other men were nowhere to be seen.

"Are you all right?"

"I'm fine. Sorry to keep you waiting."

"Come on," he took her arm. "We need to talk."

They crossed the village to the entrance to the maze.

"Why is it called the kissing maze?" Serral said, instantly regretting it.

"I have no idea," Hal said, his white teeth glinting in the moonlight.

They walked on and on through twists and turns, the high hedges making deep black rectangular and triangular shadows. The wind had died, and warm air rose from the grass beneath their feet.

"Are you sure you know where we're going?"

"Yes. Turn right."

The hedges opened onto a large open square, barely visible in the evening light. In the center stood a small stone building, like the skeleton of a Yskeon, a series of high columns set in a circle. It was elaborately carved, though Serral could not make out much detail beyond the curving shapes of flowering vines. The structure had a stepped shape, but the roof consisted only of a circular piece of stone that capped all the columns but left the sides open to the air. In the center stood a carved bench with two reclining seats that faced one another. Serral and Hallenander settled there and looked out at the stars. Serral closed her eyes and augered for a moment. No helpers about, just the bubbling enthusiasm of cleaners in the theater speculating about the Minsyx and his Companion. There were other threads, but now was not the time to dive into the thought river.

"Are we alone?" Hallenander asked.

"Yes."

"They call this place the kissing maze because it is off limits to Harbingers at night. I have been here only once before, with Callia. She said she often meets her lover here, because they will not be disturbed."

"Brilliant. I'm pretty awestruck by Callia at the moment."

"She is gifted." His hand grasped her wrist loosely. "Are you feeling homesick?"

She was glad he recognized the reason for her dark mood but did not want him to know. How could she be homesick for a planet that had been dead for over a hundred years?

"No. Can you tell me about the constellations we see from here?" She tried to steady her voice.

"The constellations over Evincio?"

"Never mind." She blinked. "I just know so little about this place."

He leaned in toward her and spoke. "I found out so much more about it, today."

"You went to the Reykos," she said, moving her face so that their foreheads were nearly touching.

"I did. I met my brother and sister. And a strange little Harbinger woman who was my foster mother."

"What?" Serral said. "Tell me everything."

"First, I killed four Xaff today."

"I knew there was something different about you."

"At first, I felt nothing. But then a feeling of satisfaction and then one of shame came over me, but I suppose an Emperor must be ruthless, so I am not certain what to think. I wish it had not happened. But I had no choice."

"Start at the beginning."

"It was after we arrived back from the island. He paused, passing his hand over his temple. "I suppose I was so happy to have flown and so angry waiting to learn the truth that I went to see for myself what happens on my planet."

He told her about his trip to the jungle, about being fired at by Imset, and then defending them against the Xaff. Then he shared his feelings of awe and astonishment in the Reykos. He confirmed that her hunch was right, that the towers are star ships, off-line but capable. It took longer for him to find words for his joy at having Rakki family and about the old Harbinger woman who had known him since he was a baby. When he was finished, he sat back and rested in the darkness. "And I have you to thank for all of it."

"Me?""Yes, you, thick, Imset savage. I would never have thought to confront the Imset, or to fight the Xaff, or to force my way into meeting my people, had you not crashed into my life. You have taught me to fly. In every way."

She did not respond. His cut-wood smell was giving her a headache.

Finally, she squeaked, "That's what you get for reanimating a burnt-up barbarian."

She leaned back in her chair. The sky was a glittering black blanket of suns, of solar systems and nebulae. Was Zaphia up there in the miasma of white dots, somewhere beyond the membrane of one of the port worms? Would Serral ever join her there? The sky had never been so clear or the click of Hallenander's rings so crisp. Evincio must be the most beautiful planet of all the Harbinger's hundreds, its atmosphere so sweet it made her want to hold her breath and never exhale. But she could not stop thinking about leaving.

"Hello? Companion?" For the first time that night, he sounded annoyed. "Care to tell me what is bothering you?"

She felt his gaze. "I suppose I'm nervous." She tried to sound casual. "Now that you know how to fly, I'm a bit unclear what happens next."

"Ah, so many milestones reached. You are worried I have no more use for you." His hand found hers. "We continue our charade. We must. Imagine what we have yet to do."

Her hand tingled. "You will become Syxarit. It's in motion now. I see how ready you are, and I'm betting they see it too. You are all set. And if it goes south, you have ships in which to sail away. You have your real family. You are so lucky." Her voice ran out.

There was a pause, "Have I used you? Did you do all of this for me because I made you a slave? Do you regret helping me?"

She hesitated. "No. No, I entered into our agreement willingly. In a way, I am the one who used you," her voice dwindled to a whisper. "I would have done anything to help end the war. I still would. You know that. But if I have helped you find reasons of your own to follow through and end the Alliance, then I am glad. You have found the Rakki. I have found the women here who have their needs, their limitations. But also, even if the Harbs gifted them with talent, they are incredible. I have learned so much about my own people, about myself. It is only that I worry—I know things are going to change. I don't know if the Imset are going to survive, and even if they do survive, I don't know if it will be long enough to find a new planet."

The two sat silently.

Hal's voice was formal and tinged with anger. "You are frustrated. Of course. You are wondering when this agreement between the two of us will pay off for you."

"Pay off for me?"

"You were hoping to help the Imset, but the Rakki are not your kind. They are not a consolation for you. I understand. You are too young to be the genetic contributor for the children."

"For the Rakki children? No, that is not true. I could have given my genes to any of them."

"I don't understand." Hal hesitated. "Were you not culled when you came of age?"

"I have not come of age yet, Hal. I am sixteen." She covered her face with her hands. "Anyway, it doesn't matter. The Harbs culled me at birth."

"I see."

"So technically, I could be the mother of most any of those kids."

"But not of me."

"You are of age. So no."

"Thank the Eighty-Eight."

"Why?" She touched the smooth stone embedded in her armrest. The texture felt Imset, not Harb. Someone, some time, had carved this little temple. Had they intended it for aliens? Serral felt her hatred for the Harbs rushing back.

"Well, I suppose I would feel awkward calling you mommy."

She laughed. "Hal?"

"Yes?"

"Can we fly again tomorrow?" She felt his smile in the dark.

"Nothing would please me more."

They walked silently back through the maze, past the reflecting pond, to her building. The darkness was full of the low voices of lovers. In her lobby, Hallenander pulled her close, the elevator Helper standing ready, the doormen stiffly staring straight ahead.

"Do you not want me to come upstairs? We could start early tomorrow."

"No." Her muscles were stuck, no matter how hard she tried to look animated and happy. "If you're there, I won't be able to sleep."

His face turned into the expressionless mask he got when he wanted to hide his feelings. "Yes. Clearly you are exhausted."

"Good night then, darling," she said.

Serral did not look back down at him as the elevator whisked her up.

But before they reached the third level, her elevator operator stopped the car. Serral stffened.

*Friend, what is happening?*

*Gracious and honorable Lord Zinnerit is in your house, Mistress. Would you like to prepare yourself first? We can go in the back entrance.*

*Zinnerit? Yes, take me back down. Quickly.*

When she ran out into the night, Hallenander was gone. She augered, but the gate helpers told her he had driven down toward the Palace and could be anywhere.

*We would be pleased to bring him a note if she cared to write one.*

*Please tell his Helpers that Lord Zinnerit is in my building.*

*Mistress, I am afraid we are not allowed to report the movements of any of the Lords to one another.*

*It's a rule?*

*Yes.*

She cursed under her breath.

*The Xaff are still not allowed onto Xalavria grounds, correct?*

*Correct, Mistress.*

She cursed again and headed back to the elevator. She would have to take care of this herself. But then, halfway up, she had an idea.

*Friends, what is the back entrance?*

*It is for the Helpers, Mistress. But as Thanton you are allowed to enter.*

*Let's go.*

The operator stopped the car at the fifth floor.

*We will lead you there.*

Serral followed the operator out into an unfinished part of the building. The space was raw, without walls, but stacked with 'Tainers of various sizes. She followed the Harb through the semi-darkness. They passed shelves of boxes, and machines, and an organic looking shape that loomed like an insect cocoon. The musky, pungent Harb smell that came off it told her it was a sleeping place for helpers. It throbbed gently.

"Yuck." She whispered to herself.

They came to an interior barrier which she assumed housed structural support. The Elevator Harb led her into a stairwell and switched on lights so she could see that the stairs were shallow and the walls close, that they were scaled for Harbs. They climbed to the seventh floor, and the elevator helper opened the door.

*He is in the sitting room, Mistress.*

*Has he told anyone what he wants?* She called out to the whole thought river. Click and Clack and two food helpers responded.

*He says he knows you are not a good girl and he wants to explain to you.*

*Explain to me?*

*We do not understand what he wants to explain.*

*Thank you, friends. Please tell him I will be there shortly.*

Relief poured through the river.

*Who will serve as translator for us?*

*Translator?*

*When I speak to the man?*

Fear and anxiety blossomed. The Helpers reminded themselves of their sacred duty to serve. The river rippled incomprehensibly.

*Clack said heavily, I shall speak for you, Thanton.*

*Thank you.*

*Helpers, please put your sharpest knife on the kitchen counter.*

*Oh, Thanton, we are not allowed to give Companions sharp things while men are present.*

*Of course, you are not. My mistake.*

She went to the dressing room and changed out of her filmy dress into a pair of slacks and a blouse. She missed her coveralls. None of her drawers or cases of jewels contained anything that could be used as a weapon. There was still the silver candle stick in the living room, but Zinnerit was taller than Hal, and she was not sure she could land a blow on his arrogant, scarred head. Anyway, what would happen to Hal if she attacked a Lord?

Serral put her hair into a ponytail. She looked young, casual, and non-threatening. All she could think of to disarm the unpleasant man was what she had seen Hal do in the party pavilion, speak reasonably and calmly. The warrior in her wanted more. But she either had to run away, and wait in the dark resort until morning, or see what Lord Zinnerit meant by "explaining." Curiosity won.

The sitting room crackled with negative energy. The big man sat with his legs wide, taking up most of one of the large couches. He had unbuttoned the top buttons on his green velvet smock. His white lace collar contrasted oddly with his stiff leather boots. He looked at her sullenly when she walked in, large topaz eyes following her closely.

"Good evening, my Lord," Serral said, curtsying. "To what do I owe this honor?"

Clack spoke hastily in Volterran.

"It is not necessary to use the Helper," Lord Zinnerit said. "I will speak Imset."

"Wonderful. Helper," she waved to Clack, "please wait in the kitchen. Wine, my lord?"

"Dismiss your Harbingers." Zinnerit sipped from the goblet she offered. "They are terrible gossips, you know."

Serral smiled with what she hoped was a serene expression. "Of course. I have no doubt my master would want me to protect your secrets."

She walked to the formal kitchen, quickly augering while her back was turned.

*I am about to instruct you in Imset that I want you to leave. But let what I am communicating here in the thought river now take precedence: do not leave. Wait in the kitchen. Do you understand?*

*Yes, Mistress.*

"Go on now. Bye-bye." Serral knew the Harbs would be useless in a fight. But they might be able to bear witness if something happened to her. She knelt and poured more ruby wine into his goblet. He smelled of acrid smoke and old dust. "What brings you to my humble apartment?"

He bent toward her, his scarifications darker in the low light, like angry bites on his high, caramel-colored cheeks. "It is not my secrets to be discussed now. It is yours that are troubling us."

"Us?" She poured wine for herself and pretended to drink. "Who is 'us'?"

He ignored her question. "We want to know who you really are. Why have you come, and why do the servants make an exception of you?"

"Ah, you are trying to have me killed." She kept her voice light. "And the Xaff refuse. Is that it?"

Zinnerit's lips parted, shocked, and moved the dots on his cheeks closer together. "You think a Sevenni Companion can be assassinated so easily without trial or protection of law?"

"Of course, I do."

He tipped his head crest back and laughed, a deep, resounding cackle like an echoing cave. "You are right. You have no protection under the law. Imset are nothing. Imset are not people."

"I've heard this before."

"Have you? But perhaps not here. There is a rumor that you have not had your memory wiped."

"Hmmm." She tried to keep the panic rising in her from showing. "Did the Xaff tell you that?"

Zinnerit sat back, one hand absently preening his lace collar. "Your only protection is the Minsyx, and he is but a boy."

She pretended to drink again, trying to get a feel for what the large man intended to do next. He was not young, but like all the stone men, he was over a head taller than she, and strongly built. She missed her armed Arrow, the reassurance of her weapons. All she had were her wits, and they would have to be enough.

"He is not a boy. He has come of age. He has taken a Companion."

The Lord licked his thick lips. "Has he really? Or is he pretending, trying to fool his father into believing that he is more mature than he really is?"

"Fool his father? I cannot know." She straightened her goblet on the table. "But if he were falsely accused of a crime as grave as deceiving the Emperor of all Volterra, surely his accuser would be considered to be a traitor? Or perhaps I don't understand enough about Volterran Law."

Zinnerit showed his teeth again, his thick brows curling angrily. "Imset women. You hold such high opinions of yourselves. And yet, here you are." His hand circled the apartment. "A cat in a cage. I can smell your fear. It is," he breathed in luxuriantly, "rather enticing."

"You are a very powerful man," Serral replied, rising to open the doors to the balcony. "Your Companion Irie must have respected you a great deal."

She returned to her seat.

He loosened the collar on his green velvet coat. "She was a simpleton. The only time she held my interest was when she did her little water tricks. Then she was a goddess. But the rest of the time," he made a dismissive face. "Nothing."

"Women with no memories are not very interesting, I suppose," Serral said evenly. "Perhaps you should instruct your servants to stop wiping the Companions."

"Bah," he waved her away. "They do as they please. But you, you are not like the others."

"What makes you say that?"

"Hallenander. Of course."

"Hallenander?" She could not hide her surprise.

"He spent so long finding excuses. All the while spending long periods talking to Callia. Quizzing others. Pretending to want a Companion. But he was wasting time. All knew. Even the ladies knew."

"He came of age only a few months ago."

"Yes, but he could have had a woman much sooner. If only he would lower himself, you see. In comparison to Imset barbarism, our ladies are refined, clever, educated. There is only one thing Hallenander could have learned from you lot. And he claims to have learned it. Thus seasoned, he is now ready for women of quality. Thank you very much. Now we are equal, we men who have insulted Volterran sensibilities with our descent into this little folly of Taurellio's. Clever. A bit of debauchery to bond us, to keep us amused. But secret, now and forever," Zinnerit said, with a self-satisfied sneer.

Serral did her best to look bored. "And yet, here I am. A disgusting Imset."

"Yes. You are here, coming from out of nowhere. Something is off about you. You show no sign of humiliation at colluding with your enemies. Which is odd. And the boy is not acting right. He is not ashamed, or degraded. He behaves as if he respects you, which obviously, he cannot."

Serral did not respond. She tried to think of another reason to get up and walk around, maybe run down the stairs and out into the park. Zinnerit held his glass out for her to pour him more wine. She did so, and he grabbed her wrist and forced her to sit on the table at his knees. "You are Imset. Do you understand the meaning of that?"

"What is your point, sir?" She wrenched her hand back painfully and moved out of his reach. "I know I'm Imset, and I know who he is."

"Who he is?" The man's voice rose angrily. "You don't begin to know who he is. How could you possibly understand what awaits him in his life? The tradition, the responsibility. The heavy weight of his position in the Empire. He must be more than great; he must be the greatest of men." Zinnerit looked at her through kohl-smeared slits. "You know nothing. You offer him nothing."

"Agreed," she said, noting that Zinnerit was no longer watching her, but seemed more interested in the chandeliers. "I am his Companion here on Evincio. I know he is leaving soon. Do you think I expect anything more than that?" His topaz eyes blazed. "Do you not?"

Serral looked back at him, a realization dawning. "I'm sorry?"

"Oh, you pretend not to know."

She did not answer. A cool breeze reminded her they were still far from the night's midpoint.

Zinnerit stood, looming over her. His shirt was partly unbuttoned, and he had stuffed his collar into a pocket. But he did not touch her. Instead, he sat again and crossed his legs. "So, you mean to say that you have not been wheedling to go with him?"

"Go with him?" She did not have to try to make her voice sound incredulous.

Zinnerit's face calmed. "When he returns home to rule."

"He is going to rule? Truly?"

"Yes," the man spat. "But he cannot sully himself with a Imset whore in Volterra."

"But he is going to become legal heir? Yes?"

The big man waved her away. "I did not say that. It is rumor only."

"Ah. Like the rumor that I am planning to go with him to the Eight Volterran Worlds?"

"Are you not begging for that?" He made a high, mocking voice, "Oh, master, I would be such a fine girl for you."

"Is that what Irie said, before you put her out?" The words tumbled from her mouth. She regretted them instantly.

"What?" he tensed. "Before I what?"

Serral sprinted to the foyer. "Let me share some of these exquisite sweets, My Lord." She augered. Her helpers were huddled in their kitchen, worried.

*Do Volterran men beat women? Do they fight?*

*No, Mistress. The men do not hurt. Only the Xaff hurt. But a Lord can tell them to do so.*

*Thank you.*

She opened a huge, heart-shaped velvet box and swooped back into the sitting room. "Chocolates. An Imset delicacy."

Zinnerit swiped the box from her hand. Candies flew all over the room and the box sailed to the floor. "You will never come to Volterra. If you try to accompany Hallenander into his new life, I will personally see to it that you are executed in such a way that the Imset will know that you have helped him, that you have given yourself to him and shamed your people."

"What?" She lost her patience. Her voice grew cold. "You think the Xaff will do something terrible to me."

His face took on a frustrated look. She had called his bluff. "It is not to you the terrible thing happens. No. It is to him that bad occurs."

"What do you mean, 'bad occurs'?"

"Do you not imagine it? A new Rakki prince in Volterra? Short, with a stubby head, and from a nothing planet? And he has a Imset whore at his side?" Zinnerit shook his long head crest forcefully. "He will be made a laughingstock. A bitter joke. And the efforts his father the Syxarit has made, all the work and care, all for nothing. Time lost, chances lost. All in order that the boy have a female! In Volterra he does not need a Companion. There, a Companion makes him a dirty criminal. There are true women in Volterra. Not many, it is true. The Emptiness has prevented more than a few new babies each year. But there are still marriageable, noble girls. And they are very proud, very refined. They would have to accept the Imset blood abomination in him. But they would do it, for the good of the Empire." He looked around the floor in distress.

The tension in the room flowed out with his words.

"Have some more wine, my lord." Serral filled his goblet, and he settled back on the couch. "Tell me more about Hallenander's challenges in Volterra."

"They are many, the challenges. Already, the people do not like him. He is a stranger. Despised by the ruling families. He is permanently stinking of his Imset blood."

She spoke quietly, calmly. "But he is the Syxarit's son."

Zinnerit shook his head. "Not yet, not yet. He is still like you. Still nothing. Until the houses of Eloxiture and Jalophian rule him a Volterran citizen."

"I see." Her mind raced. "What do you want him to be, Lord? Do you want him to become Syxarit?"

"Of course we do, idiot child," Zinnerit said grimly, "We have been exiled here these twenty years. Educating him, being with him, trying against all hope to make a decent man of him."

"And? How do you men think you've done?"

"As well as we could, but he is still only half."

If Zinnerit said one more insulting thing about Hallenander, she might have to kill him with her bare hands. "It is time for you to leave, Lord Zinnerit."

"Me? Leave?" he said incredulously. "You are telling *me* to leave?"

"I believe you have learned all you can from me. You have delivered the warning. I've received it. You can go back to Mimellio and the others and tell them you scared the Dantons out of me."

"And you promise not to try to come to Volterra?"

"Come to Volterra?" She rolled her eyes, "Lord, do not mock a poor girl in a slave colony."

"Good. You know your place. We thought you were confused."

"I'm definitely not confused. Thank you for your visit."

She walked into the foyer and poised her finger over the elevator call button. But Zinnerit hovered over the round table, looking coldly at the many boxes gathered there. He crossed his green velvet arms.

"I don't care what the women say," Zinnerit lowered his head crest and growled. "You do not really love him. You do not open his gifts."

"Did Irie not love you?"

He laughed harshly. "Of course not. The Imset hate us. But she was not an animal for a cage. I tried to get Irie to leave long ago. I do not know why, but she wanted to stay."

The project, Serral thought to herself. She cared about the project.

"Perhaps she was wiped such that she had no choice."

"There is always a choice, even for the Helpers, though they pretend that is not the case. They pretend not to cure the Emptiness, so they can have their pet Hallenander on the throne."

"Their pet?"

"He is the servants' Syxarit, not ours. Not the people's." He tossed another box of candy onto the floor. "Not the Imset's. My only hope is that once he is on the throne and they have achieved their desire, the cursed Harbingers will cure the Emptiness disease allowing us children and hope for our future. That is the rumor I cling to."

She swallowed. "The plan is for the Harbs to cure the Emptiness once you've gotten their choice of Syxarit on the throne?"

He huffed with impatience. "That is what I said. Stupid girl. But no one knows."

Serral pushed the button for the elevator. "Raising Hallenander has been a huge sacrifice for you."

"It has," he scowled, the dots on his cheeks undulating.

"I don't know anything about the people in Volterra. But I know him. And you could not have a better man to offer up to the critics and princesses. He will be magnificent. You will see. He will."

"Bah," Zinnerit growled and got on the elevator. "The Imset understand nothing, and no one will miss you when you are all dead."

"Good night, Lord Zinnerit."

**41**

— • —

C hapter Forty-Two

Hallenander took his Bisbee to the village and parked by the docks. Serral was back in her apartment, the Imset were asleep in their white villas, and any Helpers seemed to be underground for the night. The moon was just rising, and it illuminated the still waters of the bay. The hulls of his two sailing ships rocked along with the waves of the incoming tide, the sound of their riggings pinging across the water and the wood of their hulls straining against the fenders of the dock. Hallenander climbed aboard his brig the Neoterra and took a seat in the stern. The ship's solidity and the smell of its pitch and varnish comforted him. The stars had faded somewhat, and he could not help wondering why Serral had developed a fascination for them. He made a note to ask the servants to find her a telescope for her apartment. He watched the towers of the Reykos gleam on the hill above the bay.

He thought she had been worried ever since she had realized he knew how to navigate. It cut short, he realized, the amount of time she thought she had in the relative safety of the Xalavria. He would have to try to comfort her, to convince her that there would be a place for her even after he left. Her ability to auger was far too valuable an asset to waste. There was more to his feelings for her, but he decided to focus on his duty. The water below him glimmered. He stripped off this clothing and dove in.

Hallenander still was not tired when he arrived back at the palace. When his helpers told him of a summons to the liquid portal by his cousin Bellex, he was glad for the distraction. Bellex always made him smile, and her cheer despite her physical challenges impressed him. She never complained about her halting gate and her bent skeleton, nor did she explain why she had not let the Medic Harbingers regrow her body. She was five years older than he was, someone he had always looked up to, and he had never pressed her. All she had ever said was, "I'd miss too much."

Her pouting brown face materialized in the liquid, the elegant blue-and-gold carved walls of her chamber gleaming behind her. "Oh dear, Hallenander, I have to tell you something bad."

He smiled. "No. You? Bad? The two don't go together."

She made a face, turning away so her long head crest hid her blush. Hallenander was used to such courtly Volterran gestures. The more highborn the person, the more embarrassed they were meant to feel about any kind of natural impulse. Bellex was Mimellio's child. But though she was Sevenni, her life had been difficult.

"I need a moment, to compose myself," she said, breathily.

Hallenander knew that Bellex's husband, Lord Mephi Zhokkerit, whom Hal had never met, rarely left his estate on Torl. When Bellex had been disfigured during childbirth, rendered lame and barren, the man had simply left her. Bellex professed not to care. She claimed that in her weakened state, she needed the comforts of the Sevenni Palace and her family more than her husband's provincial tribe.

"I'm a superficial creature," Bellex had once said. "Since my body has betrayed me, I need stimulation for my mind. Lest you compare me to an intellectual like yourself, Hallenander, please understand that by stimulation, I mean feasts, and gambling, and delicious conversation. And, of course slandering everyone behind their backs." Her face had been bright. "Except for my noble cousin, of course," she winked. "You need no help in that department."

Hallenander spoke into the portal. "Dear Bellex, I see that you are truly remorseful. Tell me why?"

She tipped her head in shame. "This is so embarrassing, my darling." Her pupils looked tiny in her heavily-painted eyes. "But perhaps the last conversation we had, when we discussed that subject of importance, it may have been overheard."

Dread passed through him. He clapped his hand to his head. "Oh."

"You must know I would never, ever compromise your privacy. Ever! I thought we were on a secure connection," Bellex said, her eyes beseeching. "It must have been the servants, those sneaky listeners."

Hallenander nodded. They need not say aloud who might order the servants to listen, or to request a report of what had been said. "Never mind. Nothing will change."

Dread coursed through his body. But he kept it hidden. Bellex smiled, her high cheeks glistening with tears Hallenander knew to be sympathetic, albeit a bit dramatic, in keeping with Volterran style. "Oh, Cousin, I'm glad. Nothing would distress me more than to trouble you or to cause a rift somehow."

"A rift?" he smiled, to conceal his mounting terror. "What rift?"

"Oh, nothing." Bellex busied herself dusting a compass on her table. "Only that your notion, of," her voice dropped, "of bringing an Imset girl to Volterra, even if only to your father's furthest and most obscure estate is causing much consternation here."

There was a pause. Hallenander made his expression into a mask, willing the color not to rise in his face, though heat exploded within him.

"The idea was a joke, of course," he said. "Naturally I wouldn't seriously propose to do anything so brash. I know you understood my humor, cousin."

Her dark eyes narrowed with pleasure. "Of course, how hilarious. The very idea. An Imset woman here, in the presence of real women."

"Of," he said haltingly. "Of real..."

Bellex caught herself and brought her hands to her chest. "I didn't mean real, that's not the right word. I meant ladies. People such as myself, people of quality."

Hallenander swallowed, the numbness that he relied upon to get him through difficult moments serving him well, creating the illusion of control. "I understand. There was nothing to it. I was pleased to find an able instructor and Companion."

Bellex made a face of mock disgust. "Pray do not feel the need to offer details!"

He seethed. But his face remained stoic.

"But I have shared too much. I am a fool, and I thank all eighty-eight gods for the indulgent friendship of my cousin." Bellex's eyes traveled away from the portal, deeper into her room, her face changing in reaction to something he could not see.

"Of course," she spoke to the other presence in the room. She bowed her head. She moved out of the frame. Another face appeared, one Hallenander knew from journals and strippies. Though older and more reserved than in pictures, the visage was unmistakable, beautiful, haughty and cold, with limpid pond-green eyes and diamond-studded nostrils, earlobes, and cartilage. His father's wife, the High Syxarim of the Volterran Empire, Miranxis Chi'igypp. The queen of all. His oldest and most devoted enemy.

He bowed low. "Why, your Sevenni Highness. What an unexpected honor and pleasure."

The woman reared back in an insolent posture. She put a long, green-and-white candy stick to her thick-lipped, unsmiling mouth. She regarded Hallenander for a long while, then leaned forward.

"You have a princely way of speaking, Hal. I will grant you that." She observed him through the portal. "You are fine to look at. Considering what you are."

"You are all courtesy," he said, meeting her gaze.

"I am not. I'm a bitter old woman with little to give me pleasure."

He said nothing. She was not old, and the candy in her mouth gave her evident pleasure.

"To that end, your father has presented me with a challenge, which as you probably know, benefits me in one way only."

"Pray say more, Madame. I am overcome with curiosity." He unconsciously adopted the speaking patterns of his father's people. It was not his preference to be catty and cunning, but long years of speaking to his father and the Eight made matching Miranxis' taunting tone second nature.

The queen broke off a piece of candy and chewed slowly. "You see, it is my aim to lose no more of what comprises my happiness than I already have. Grief is a bore, and I need some way to offer my gifts to the people, since I can give no Heir. Am I clear, boy?"

She looked across the room to someone who had entered. Then she looked back at Hal. "You shall be my special project."

"What new honor is this?"

She waved him away and spoke to someone else in the room, hidden in the background. "It is as you say, Rel," she said. "He is truly your son, with your silver tongue and false courtesy. What a task your brother has accomplished for you, really. Bravo."

She clapped her hands. Hallenander wondered if she were drunk, or so angry that her movements were overwrought. He stopped wondering when his father's large, bronze face appeared next to hers in the liquid.

"My boy, do not listen to your stepmother's abuse."

Miranxis protested, but the older man pursed his wide lips and nodded her out of frame. Miranxis continued speaking but her words trailed off, as she exited the room.

"I can see she is impressed with you, by her offer to help us in our cause."

"Is that what she meant by a special project?"

Did Taurellio stiffen, or was it Hallenander's imagination?

"Son, your Companion is still ruffling feathers, I am told."

Hallenander sensed danger. "I suppose. She has taught me to fly, which is what I intended her to do."

"Oh, is that all?"

He weighed his words carefully. "Sire, I believe I have conducted myself in a fashion no man of the world would find fault with. I have adhered to my uncle's wishes, as well as those of the Eight."

Taurellio rubbed the sides of his domed head. "Relax. I have no doubt you are a man now, and no one can question that. All agree that you are in love with this girl," he winked one opal eye. "Or you pretend to be, which is almost as good."

Hallenander felt his instincts in a jumble. "In the grand scheme of things, what is the significance of my Imset Companion, father?"

"Oh, who knows," Taurellio said. "Perhaps she has some use, I don't know."

"Help me understand."

"I have heard many rumors about your girl. And they have me curious. So, I would like to meet her as soon as possible."

"Meet her?" Hallenander pretended to be surprised, though his siblings on his trip to the Reykos had forewarned him that his father was coming, "As soon as possible?"

"Yes, son. I am thrilled to offer you this happy news before you hear it from another source. We are all coming to Evincio, the whole family. Very soon." Taurellio's pale-fire eyes glowed with excitement.

"So, you plan to make good on your threat to visit. How wonderful." Hallenander did not have to coax his delighted smile. Having his father come to visit had been his most painfully impossible dream for nine long years. But knowing about the Rakki, and not understanding or being able to ask his father's plans for them, filled him with a swirling stew of emotions. Many were unpleasant. Some were angry. He pushed them all aside, for now. He was learning. "Father, there are no words for how I feel in this moment."

"I can imagine well enough, boy. You have dwelt alone for so long with eight, stodgy old men, that even a wretched prisoner of war seems like good company. But as I say, all will be resolved soon enough."

"And my case for recognition before the Eloxiture and the House of Jalophians? It remains locked in stalling tactics?"

Taurellio waved his hands dismissively. "What does it matter? We are masters of our own fate, are we not, my son?"

Hallenander reveled in his good feelings and agreed. But a sneaking dread climbed up his spine so that when he finally closed the liquid, fatigue moved in like sudden fog. How would he navigate his family here, in person?

When morning came, he found Serral pacing in her foyer, dressed in simple clothes with her white hair braided down her back. Her amber-green eyes looked odd, but he could not say what was different about them. She looked past him, over his shoulder.

"Are you fit to fly?" he asked. He had requested food and drink from his Helpers for a long day on the island. Now he wondered if Serral had other intentions.

She nodded. "Sure. But first I need to speak to your Geddon."

Hallenander looked at her quizzically. "You understand that he lives outside of my command now, don't you? I cannot simply summon him."

Serral folded her arms. "I'm hoping he'll be at the meeting I requested because I summoned him. It is important that I speak with him. If he doesn't show, we'll need to look for him during our flight."

Hallenander summoned the elevator. "He comes to the boneyard often. I leave supplies and food for him there. I am sure you already assumed as much."

"No. I did not assume. That's nice of you, Hallenander."

The elevator doors opened. "I can be very nice. Just like you can. If you so choose."

He felt unaccountably gloomy for the rest of their journey to the airfield. He had Serral drive the Bisbee while he manned guns, but the jungle remained quiet, and no Xaff stirred to bother them.

Serral began breathing unevenly when they approached the Imset scrap piles. She refused to explain what bothered her, except to say "allergies."

He implored her to get out of the open air and into the hangar quickly. Once inside, she turned on lights in one building after the next, finally entering the last hangar where he kept his collection of Ectos. There she walked from pod to pod, her hand passing across each metal skin as if caressing a loved one.

"What are you looking for?"

She shrugged. "Just wondering why nobody has stolen any of these. Ectos are the perfect space craft."

"The perfect craft? Perhaps if you are escaping a broken station. Otherwise, is not a small pod adrift in deep space a form of coffin?"

"That's what's so perfect. Being in stasis is almost like being dead, only you can be woken up again. If you're inert, no one knows you're there. They can't detect your consciousness. At least, I don't think they can. The Xaff would be blind." Her hand dropped from the silver Ecto, voice trailing off. "In theory. Unless they saw you right in front of them, they would fly right by you, like you were space debris, not a person. It would be a perfect way to hide."

"I don't think it would be useful to spend a hundred years in stasis, but I suppose someone might."

"No, for you it wouldn't make sense," she smiled for the first time that day. "You have things to do. Don't think I've forgotten your promise."

"Nor have I forgotten yours. But can we discuss this in flight?"

She picked a piece of dust off the Ecto. "Of course."

When they got back to the contriving bay, Hallenander smelled pipe smoke. "He's here. Whatever you did to summon Geddon, it worked."

Geddon sat at a desk looking at drawings, his white head lowered in concentration. He bit on his pipe stem. He looked thin, his clothes tattered, but healthy enough. The man rose, his eyes similar in color to Serral's, wrinkling with pleasure. "Hal, my boy," he said.

Hallenander embraced his friend and former tutor. He still had not gotten used to being taller than the man. "Geddon, this is Serral Brook."

Serral and Geddon looked intently at one another, the sameness of their eye color proof they once belonged to the same tribe. Serral made a kind of salute, which Geddon returned. Hallenander felt he was witnessing a secret part of Imset society, a piece of their military which, in his mind, had always been represented by sparks in the sky more than actual people. Serral and Geddon stood at attention, both still considering themselves soldiers.

"Commander," Serral said. "You got my specs."

Hallenander flushed with annoyance but said nothing. Of course, Serral had been working on an agenda of her own. He should have guessed as much. She was seeking members of her own kind, and had been, even after she had found his siblings in the Reykos. He could not blame her, and yet he did not like what was happening. Serral and Geddon teaming up, while he prepared to move on toward the Eight Worlds of Volterra. It felt like an inevitable loss.

"I was Commander of the S.S. Vetulis, Osprey Class II War Intelligence Por'Tainer. To be brutally honest, I don't know if we can somehow get her up and running again. She's ditched in a bog about fifty clicks from here."

Serral looked delighted, but Hallenander felt somber, left out.

"What remains of my crew still seems willing to work with me."

"Sir, anyone who knows you values your wisdom. Surely that cannot come as a surprise," Hallenander said.

"Thank you, son. I am learning more and more who I was and what I went through before the Harbs took Evincio and made it your home. Though, I admit, having so much of my memory wiped makes understanding tricky at times." The old man held one of Serral's hands and one of Hallenander's. "Our people have mobilized. Since the Wilter have been coming at us, we've lost ten good friends to vigilante justice; at this point, we need help and more resources."

Serral understood. "The ladies are capable of more than you might think, sir. Don't underestimate them."

"Ah." Hallenander took his hand back from Geddon. "I see what you two are up to."

"You don't mind?" Geddon asked. "Serral here believes there is change afoot, and the two women she helped run across the line agree. They say their masters told them to get as far away from the resort as possible."

Serral moved to the drawings on the table. "We'll need some kind of signal."

The two Imset put their white heads together and spoke intently. Hallenander listened to them, half paying attention to their scheme for the Companions to follow a series of tunnels out into the jungle, and half noticing how alert and focused Serral appeared. She did not smile, yet it was apparent to Hallenander that she was as happy as he had ever seen her.

"I can continue drawing this map, giving coordinates all the way to the flight center." The old man pointed to the paper. "The Harbs who built this place never bothered to close up their passageways."

"That's great," Serral said.

"But what about the Xaff?" Geddon asked.

"I've got that."

Geddon straightened. "You're taking on too much. If Hal here shares his arsenal, we can have five or six top fighters take position..."

Serral shook her head, "No. There's no point engaging in the tunnel, you'd be outgunned and have no place to run."

"What about you?"

Hallenander did not see her face, but Geddon's expression changed. "I see. Are you sure?"

Serral nodded.

"You are welcome to my arsenal, of course," Hallenander said. "But I trust you to be aware that once armed, the Xaff will find reasons to fight you."

Serral and Geddon parted with a degree of hugging and warmth that Hallenander found baffling for two people who had only just met.

They boarded a four-person Tekku, heavily armed. Serral soon forgot her gloom and fascination took over. She was in awe of the Harbinger craft, of its simple console, and its foreign weapons systems.

"Ah, I see," she purred, firing a rocket at a shard of rock sticking out from a cliff's side. The red rock exploded. "Nice."

When Serral was satisfied that Hallenander could fly the plane and fight effectively, she had him shift course to the small island. Serral augered when they got close, to check for enemies, "I sense that the Xaff came and investigated."

"You can feel that?" Hal said, trying to land the craft on his first attempt. The Tekku landed on hard sand. The day was windy, but clear and sunny.

"I can feel a lot. More than I want to," she replied, jumping out onto the beach. They stripped and waded into the cool lagoon. "I felt a lot of vibrations at the flight center and they weren't Harb. I don't know what they were. But I guess that doesn't matter now."

"No?"

"Why should it? We did it. We completed our contract." She treaded water, "You're a pilot, Hal. Congratulations."

He felt uncomfortable at her change of subject. He paddled around her. "You're an excellent instructor. I can't imagine how I became so lucky as to have you crash onto the beach right in front of me."

"Yes. Very lucky."

"I didn't mean it that way."

"I'm glad we met. Both times. I have faith in you, Hallenander. I believe that you are going to do all you can to bring peace."

He treaded water and noticed that Serral was as comfortable in the water of the lagoon as she was in a fighter craft in the sky. "What happened to *our* working together to end the war?"

She floated, her face in profile. "Hey, we're here together now, aren't we?"

He floated beside her. The water was buoyant and refreshing, just cool enough to mitigate the day's heat.

"Have you ever looked for Tekku crabs?" he asked.

"Crabs shaped like Tekkus?"

He showed her how to dive to the sandy bottom of the lagoon where patterns in the sand, when touched with a stick, revealed circle-shaped crustaceans skittering out of their hiding places like tiny, vibrant, prehistoric monsters.

Serral and Hallenander played and dove for half an hour, then rested in the buttresses of the lagoon's trees, leaning against their solid bark. Two Tekkus passed overhead, very high, silver lozenges against flat blue sky. Hallenander wondered if his Companion could auger up to such a great distance.

"Can you speak to them?"

She closed her eyes but did not appear to slip into an augering trance. "I can try, but the Xaff usually shake me off their thought river with a vibration that feels like an electric shock. It's nasty."

"So, you reserve your information gathering for servants and helpers."

"The Xaff believe that being killed by me is a great honor that will get them into the afterlife," Serral said.

"Ah, Serral the Thanton. I remember when we came to your planet. The pilots would not have fired upon you, even had I not urged them to desist." He remembered the many months before, flying above her green planet. "So, the Xaff wait for the opportunity to be killed by you?"

She wound her braid around her finger. "For now they wait. They won't wait forever."

"When you're with me, they don't bother you."

"True. But the time will come when I have to confront them."

"Are you worried about this?"

She thought for a moment. "Not really."

"But you are worried about getting the women out of the Xalavria," Hallenander said. "Even with Geddon's help."

"I've got a plan," she said. "I'll get them out."

Hallenander took the braid from her hand, so she would look at him. "Then what? They are hardly going to be safe from the Xaff, even in Geddon's caves, and caverns, and even with the protection of his former crew. They can have all my weapons to fight the Wilter, but it won't be easy to survive outside the resort."

"They're Imset. They'll figure it out."

"You're not as confident as you want me to believe."

She turned, her shoulder pressing against the comforting, soft bark of a tree. "I think as long as you move forward as ruler of Volterra, the Harbs will leave the women alive, because they might need them in the future, if they decide to breed more Rakki."

He took her braid in his fingers, amazed at its thickness. "Hedge their bets."

"Yes. That's what I would do. If I were trying to raise children with Imset caregivers."

"And yet, you're not sure."

"No," her expression turned thoughtful. "The Rakki teenagers could take over the project, now. They're old enough. But it will take some time for the Harbs to see if it works. I don't think the Xaff will go hunting on Evincio until the Rakkis' future is decided. I think the Harbs will wait for instructions, and those will come from Volterra. From the Empire. From you, if things go the right way."

"Which I will make sure they do." Hallenander opened the hamper the servants had packed and handed her a hydration cannister.

She gulped it down.

"Your insight into the Helpers' thought process is invaluable, you know that."

She wiped juice from her cheek. "I'm counting on it."

He watched her tear into a sandwich hungrily.

She looked embarrassed. "What?"

"You must not allow them to hurt you."

"And you think that's up to me?"

"I'm serious." He handed her a napkin. "I want you to come to Volterra with me."

She looked skeptical. "Am I invited?"

"No. In fact, officially such a thing is out of the question."

Serral shook her head, chewing. "Sounds fun."

"Think about it." He pushed his foot through the water, causing tiny fish to scatter. "Everywhere we go, you have immediate insights about the movement of the Helpers, of the Xaff. You know how they think, and you can predict better than anyone what they will do."

"What they will do depends on your father, and on you, and on whoever runs the Alliance."

"And that is why I need you, so I can get to whomever runs the Alliance." He drank his juice. "You have the ability to listen to their concerns, do you not? To hear their reflections, their insights, and the things they see and understand?"

She stopped chewing. "You're asking if I can eavesdrop, report what's being said about you behind your back? Spy on your enemies and the like?"

"Could you?"

"Probably. But what you're talking about could backfire. The Harbs are good at presenting what they want someone to know and not presenting what they do not want someone to know. I might come to Volterra and auger all day long and find out nothing more than what you are being served for supper. They might know I was sniffing around for information, and make sure what they want kept secret is well hidden."

He thought of his conversation with Bellex, how she had been unable to keep his family from knowing about his wish to bring Serral to Volterra. Hallenander watched a cloud's shadow cut across the turquoise water of the lagoon. The sun was high, the air humid and close, but something was changing in it, the pressure building. A storm.

"I don't care if no one agrees with me. No one thought it would be a good idea for me to learn to fly, either. But it was the best decision I ever made." He reached for her hand. "I want you to come."

Serral smiled kindly, then removed her hand, using it to brush sand off her damp undershorts. "I'd be more trouble than I'm worth."

"I will be the one to decide that."

"Yes, master. Whatever you say." She stood, stepped over him, and splashed back into the water.

He followed, trying to grasp her arm in a joking attempt to show her who was boss, but she darted out of his grasp.

"I am your Syxarit. You must show me respect!"

She laughed. He grabbed her hand beneath the water. A larger shadow covered them in dark blue.

"I don't want to be parted from you," he said.

She turned away from him. But he kissed the side of her face, and she turned back and returned his kiss with an eagerness that at once surprised and did not surprise him. They moved into an embrace that lasted long enough and was intense enough, that only the falling rain convinced them it was time to get back to the Tekku. They plodded through the splattering storm, the landscape muted and gray. Hallenander wondered how long they had been on the island, their ship having moved several meters down the beach, rising and falling with the waves.

"The tide!" Serral yelled.

Hallenander ran to the aircraft, partially submerged and swiftly sinking. "I'm an idiot," he said.

They pushed together, and after several tries, emptied the craft of enough water to climb in. Serral started the engine and cruised it inland a few meters until it sputtered and lost altitude.

"It's okay," she called. "I think I can fix it."

Her understanding of machines, even those unfamiliar to her, amazed him. In half an hour they were back in their flight suits, the Tekku functional again.

"Are you sure you want to risk this?" she said, wet and shivering in the now late afternoon overcast. "I could try sending a signal out to the Xaff, maybe they'd come pick us up."

"Please don't do that," he said.

"You've been bitten by the flight bug."

"Among others."

The Tekku appeared to function perfectly. By unspoken agreement, they delayed their return as long as possible, chasing the day across Evincio. They spent hours flying, taking turns maneuvering and shooting off weapons, swooping through canyons, following a lazy brown river past evidence of Imset settlement, seemingly uninhabited but more likely housing a hidden population. They explored mountain ranges, and wide, empty valleys dotted with herds of brown beasts. They saw volcanic craters bubbling with toxic orange goo and rolling green hills studded with leafy trees. Hallenander had never considered the great beauty of his planet, but now he was forced to understand the irony of his position. All he saw belonged to him, but none of it did. The desire to resolve his situation roared forth, and he complained about it to Serral, who listened patiently. She made no comment except to assure him that all would be well, that he had the gifts needed to become a legal Volterran, his father's heir, and eventually, a great and just Emperor. But she said nothing about her own dilemma. Though he sought to assure her that she would one day have a fair and legitimate place in the universe, as would all the Imset, Serral only smiled sadly. They kissed again. Hallenander felt he had never been so happy, or so afraid.

With the early evening, the storm moved to the village and palace complex, bringing great slashes of lightning that illuminated the Reykos towers in massive pulses of green and blue. Then the Tekku seemed to explode with sound. They had been hit.

"Okay, flight's over." Serral pushed the steering lever down and turned the aircraft toward the southwest. Warning lights flashed. The Tekku's regular glide changed to more of a rattle.

As they neared the airfield, they saw a cleared section of the forest where Imset were burning trees and creating a column of smoke that rose into the sky like an angry smudge.

"What are the Wilter up to?" Hal asked.

Serral turned the observation bubble so they could see better. "Probably trying to signal the military. They don't seem to understand that the Imset have given up the offensive for Evincio."

"They are stubborn people. I see why Geddon is worried about them."

"They're just like all people. They are at war, they think their side is right, and nothing will stop them from doing their duty," she said.

"Are people really all the same?"

"Aren't they?"

"The Harbingers clearly disagree."

"Yes, but they're deluded. That is going to be a problem. But they don't know it yet."

"What do you mean?"

She hesitated. "Nothing. It's just that they are behaving as if they're Ysk herself. Engineering races of people in the name of duty. It is not what they think it is. They're confused."

They were still outside the perimeter. The Tekku's shudder increased to a rollicking wobble.

"Propulsion is compromised. Dammit." Serral pulled open a console which spit salt water back at her. "Just a bit further, sweet machine."

The Tekku lost altitude. The airfield loomed a thousand meters distant, the main hangar and cluster of Harbinger craft like a silver city in the near distance. The jungle was only a few meters below them, so close Hallenander could make out paths and platforms in the canopy.

"Hal, be prepared to take fire. Grab the guns."

As she said it, bullets hit, a series of sharp pings.

"Who am I firing on?"

"I don't know. Wilter, probably. Cover us as best you can. We need to get past the perimeter, then the Xaff will drive them off."

"Why aren't the Xaff protecting us now?"

"They think I'm a great warrior." She worked the controls. "Go on, buy us at least a few more seconds."

He fired two rockets. Behind them, the jungle erupted into twin orange fireballs.

Four Tekkus appeared. The southeast quadrants' curling scrap piles grew closer like spirals on a beach. Their Tekku wobbled, still hovering but just barely. Treetops brushed the window.

"Only a bit further," she coaxed. "Come on, beauty."

The Tekku lost power, and they fell, hitting branches and lurching violently. The ground crunched beneath them, and the ship went silent.

Hallenander had his harness off in a flash. Serral had not been wearing hers, and she lay flopped like a fish on her seat.

"Are you hurt?"

Her amber-green eyes looked up, past him. "It's okay. Everything's going to work out."

That was when he saw the blood.

He slammed the wind shell open and carried her out, disoriented by a blast of heat from explosions in the jungle. Above him, four Tekkus fired repeatedly into the trees, rocket after rocket. The noise was deafening. Smoke, and a smoldering green, blew over the top of them. Hallenander shouted for the Xaff to stop, to help him with Serral, but they were enclosed in their silver saucers, and could not hear.

The Tekkus rolled out their secondary guns and rapid-fired bullets. Hallenander cradled Serral to his chest, blood soaking the front of his flight suit, and ran for the southwest quadrant. She whispered, trying to get his attention, but he ignored her words, trying to find the wound on her left shoulder so he could stop the bleeding with pressure. But the hole in her torn flesh was larger than his hand. He ran faster, pleading with her to stop talking and hang on.

By the time he raced Serral onto his Bisbee and back to the palace Medotel, she was hallucinating, muttering about *spirits*, and *Thantons*, and repeating his name. His hands shook as he delivered her to the team of medics who had run out to the courtyard to receive her. Summoned by the Xaff, no doubt. They swept her onto a stretcher and sprinted into the building.

"Wait," he called. Two medics returned, their black eyes unblinking, gray head domes moving into a series of cubic shapes he had never seen them make before. "What will happen to her?"

They lowered their blue surgical masks, slit mouths moving in unison. "Your Highness, she is weak but alive. We will tend to her."

He followed them. "You will heal her. She will recover fully. That is your duty; that is my order to you.?"

"Yes, sire. You are no longer needed here. We will send Helpers with updates."

They closed a set of heavy doors in his face. He pounded on them, but the medics did not respond. He sat with his back against an exterior wall, struggling to breathe, enraged at his own stupidity, his willful ignorance.

Hours later, Hallenander walked to the palace in a daze. He would clean up, prepare himself for dinner and his uncle's inevitable questions. He tried to calm himself. He walked into the building holding his helmet over the worst of the blood stains. But he passed only servants. No one noticed as he slipped into his private rooms to change back into the well-groomed, pampered, and sweet-scented prince.

## 42

C hapter Forty-Three

Serral floated in the familiar black of the Medotel. With total concentration, she pushed shut the door in her mind to keep her free from the endless bubble of thoughts and feelings, images and imperatives that moved ceaselessly forward, never stopping; the language of the Harbingers.

But silence amplified the pain which seared like the bite of shark's teeth, radiating from her left shoulder, bringing desperate tears. Her medics drugged her so she could neither feel, nor move. It was an improvement but left her feeling vulnerable there in the white bed, in the white room, where the Xaff knew to find her. She distracted herself with thoughts of astronauts in stasis, inert but holding onto a thin thread of life.

*Oh, soldiers of the Alliance, have you not been looking for me?*

No electric buzz answered. But was she safe? Or were the Xaff just otherwise engaged?

Serral explored the reaches of what she could not see. Her body lay motionless, throbbing with the effort to regrow. But her mind went wandering, drawn by the vibrations of the planet itself. It quivered like a hillside she had once seen on Chlore, dirt suddenly giving way to a million baby ladybugs, which flew crazily into the air and disappeared.

Who was hatching, now?

What was Evincio giving birth to?

She did not know. But she could feel something, both tender-new and ancient, a presence below the ground, permeating the soil. She sensed deep sorrow, need, and frustration. An impossibly powerful force was stirring, and she understood by its force that it was waiting for her.

She cursed it. Why must she be the one to release this thing? And could she survive its unleashing?

Serral moved away, like an underwater swimmer, moving toward a surface only she could feel. The Xaff were there, but far distant. Their harsh buzz sounded like cracklings in a fire across the room. A sweet breeze came to her from nowhere, and she gave up the struggle.

*Oh, you are finally here!*

Zaphia. The large white lady was a bubble of happiness, a presence of both nothing and everything combined. She filled Serral's head with white light and words in every language that meant the same thing. Safety, home, to be loved and held close. The area all around them was stars, a million sweet voices in harmony, impossibly beautiful.

Zaphia asked, *Beloved, do you want to stay with me now? Your task in this place is done.*

Serral burrowed into the feeling of safety, of home. *My task is not done, Lady. Not yet.*

*Ah, you will see all who love you again. Do not fear.*

*It's not that.* Serral realized with clarity that she was not afraid of loneliness, of being separated. *I have to save my people, don't I?*

*You are not a Thanton yet.*

*I know!* Serral said, music wafting past her like clouds, *But you made me like this, didn't you?*

*Yes. We... and they.*

*Didn't you think I was going to see things through?*

*You have completed the task, dearest one. You may rest.*

*I have not completed the task! Are the Imset free? Are the Harbs at peace? And Hallenander, is he crowned now?*

*The universe is set in motion.*

*What about the vibration I feel in this planet?*

Zaphia took in a breath, a pause of glacial slowness.

*You are only a person, and so many have been lost.*

*You cannot abandon that situation, Zaphia. It is... I do not know what it is. But it is alive, too.*

A different voice came then, that of the man, Woseth. Serral did not see him, but his sharp, aching presence pierced her comfort. *You are a miracle, child. We cannot let a thing like you loose in the world.*

*I'm not loose, am I? Look at me, I'm a prisoner twice over.*

Woseth's breath changed to soft waves, placing her back in peace, *All will be well.*

Serral felt disagreement between the pair. Woseth desiring her to stay and finish her work, Zaphia afraid... of what? Serral wanted to cry. She felt the lady slipping away, the lights fading, music losing its strength. The black dots crowded her eyes.

*So, you have made your choice, Beloved?* Zaphia coaxed.

*She has,* Woseth said. *It was always thus.*

Serral felt her own tears, the itching in her shoulder, the memory of Hallenander's arms. She said, *I am fine being mortal. I can die like everyone else.*

The white lady's gentle laughter was like rain on leaves. *You are not like everyone else. But you will come to us, if not this time, then another.*

*Do you promise?* Serral asked, realizing she was afraid.

Woseth rumbled impatiently, *She is on her path. Do not make it harder.*

*Of course, we will be there,* the lady said. *We wait for all souls.*

Then she touched Serral's forehead, and Serral fell deep into darkness.

**43**

Chapter Forty-Four

Hallenander emerged from his chambers in a gray tweed suit and a caramel silk vest that complemented his skin. His watch chain swayed heavily as he walked. His hands were scrubbed clean of blood and glittered with gems. He traversed the bridge of ancestral busts to his uncle's chambers and waited as always in the foyer.

When Mimellio emerged, his blue eyes were smiling.

"What amuses you, uncle?"

The older man accepted a golden belt from a Harbinger helper and strapped it over his pleated white linen tunic. "Oh, something wonderful."

"Something to do with my father, perhaps?"

Mimellio's haughty, ebony face froze with patient indulgence. "In a way, yes. Your ridiculous obsession with flying and taking that savage girl for companion has exposed a pocket of Imset resistance in the jungle. That would ordinarily give me great consternation. You are aware of that."

Hallenander was struck by a deep impulse to grab hold of his uncle's jeweled collar and shake him with it. "All is well, sir. Why would you think otherwise?"

Mimellio's expression flared. "You have had your whims indulged for far too long. No more flying, no more of that rude girl, and no more lying to me!"

"What are you saying, uncle? I can make nothing of your nonsense."

Mimellio stared down at his nephew from a half-head's height above him. "Your father is coming. He will tend to your education now, as you are a man and are ungovernable."

"I am delighted."

They walked together back over the bridge, its magnificent view down the valley spread below.

Mimellio's voice dripped with venom: "Will you tell the ladies that fifty of their brothers and sisters died in the jungle today? Because of you?"

"Uncle, as their memories are wiped, I cannot imagine it means much of anything that the Xaff chose to defend our colonial perimeter. But if you think the ladies would benefit from knowing that their military has left so many former pilots behind in the jungle, and that those pilots died fighting the war in the only way they could, of course I shall tell them."

Mimellio stepped past Hallenander toward the huge front doors of the palace. "What ridiculous fantasies are you spewing? The war is over, and whoever remains of the Imset will die off. The former pilots are already dead. If only you had not taken it upon yourself to venture out into the jungle, they might have enjoyed a life there before disease and age took them. But no matter. The necessary was accomplished."

"Of course. It is my fault we are, or should I say were, at war," Hallenander said , waiting for Mimellio to climb onto a large Bisbee outfitted for the entire Volettu.

"We were never at war. The Harbingers were at war. You must stop lumping yourself together with the Imset. Was that not the very first lesson I taught you?"

Hallenander climbed in beside his uncle. "You did."

"Honestly. I have done my duty with you. More than my duty. I have spent decades on this backwater planet, allowed myself to be caught up in its petty dramas. Suffered from lost friendship. It is too much for your father to ask. I am done. Live, die, ascend, fly away in disgrace, I do not care."

"It is all the same to you, Uncle?"

The Bisbee moved toward the Xalavria.

Mimellio picked lint off his tunic. "Look to the future, boy. Your only path is to Volterra. All else is death and darkness. If you have any further questions, for the love of the eighty-eight gods direct them to the emperor."

They drove on in silence. Reaching the party pavilion, the lords greeted Hallenander and exchanged anticipatory opinions about Taurellio's visit. "Just think, dear Lords. Your sentence here on this provincial planet is almost at an end."

Every one of the Volettu grinned with relief.

The Xalavria showed signs of neglect. Flower beds were overgrown, fallen leaves choked a drainage grate, white stains from bird waste splattered the platform. But the lights of the party pavilion shone brightly, and the wine flowed as freely as ever. The women were especially glamorous, their eyes clearer than Hallenander was used to, their posture more alert. The building he had contrived for Serral was reasonably safe even without guards, should the Harbingers abandon the place altogether. But he hurried. As soon as the men had disbursed to their fawning companions, Hal found Callia and Alysse.

"Where are Cheloa and Shanno?" he asked, feigning polite conversation. "I must speak with your leaders."

Callia looked sideways, "They're in the dressing room."

Helpers showed him to a back passage, and he knocked, his knuckles rapping loudly on the wood.

"Entree!" came Cheloa's rich voice.

The dressing room was a riot of sparkles, feathers, and mirrors. Cheloa's lithe muscles and dark skin were nearly entirely exposed. and Shanno's pale limbs and chest were barely concealed by her satin robe.

Hallenander felt instantly self-conscious. "I have news," he said.

"Your father is coming. We heard." Cheloa smiled blindingly and returned her attention to the mirror. "We are preparing, as you can see."

"Where is Serral?" purred Shanno, blinking her long lashes. "Does she mind your coming in here to see us like this?"

"She's in the Medotel."

Cheloa and Shanno spun away from the mirror.

"We were shot down by the Wilter today before the Xaff bombed the hell out of them."

"Are you alright?" Cheloa asked, concern shining through heavy stage makeup.

"Sit down." Shanno brushed props from a chair to make room for him. "You must be stressed."

"The good news is, the Wilter are less of a threat now. But Serral," his voice faded. "I don't know."

"Good Ysk, darling." Shanno pulled his hand, forcing him to sit. "You actually do care about her."

"Is that surprising?" He looked at the floor, which was covered in ridiculous high-heeled shoes.

"Who knew?" Cheloa leaned toward him. "We've been taking bets all month about you two. The odds were against you falling for a girl like that."

Hallenander's mouth opened but no sound came out.

"Oh, no disrespect." Shanno said breathily. "We think she's the bees' knees. But you and her? Really? You're so different."

"Poor sweetie." Cheloa made a sympathetic face.

He shook off the long-nailed hands that tried to grasp his own. "That's not what I came to talk to you about."

"Oh no?" Shanno's brows lifted.

"The plan. You know which plan I'm referring to?"

Cheloa's mouth dropped open. "She has you working for us? My god. We underestimated you, honey. And her. Yes, do spill. Hold on, let me grab some of the others."

The audience was as glittering and enthusiastic as usual, almost giddy, though Hallenander felt ill at ease in the royal box. Cheloa and Shanno performed a dance with huge, feathered fans that struck Hallenander as shockingly risqué. Mimellio and Zinnerit gaped, their distaste evident. The Xalavria women in the seats below, however, screamed and applauded as if they had only just discovered they could.

In the party pavilion, a mild voice approached Hallenander from behind. "Did you enjoy that wanton display, son?" It was Lord Tuss.

Hallenander allowed the old man to catch up to him. He had always enjoyed Tuss' contributions to his law lessons. The ancient Katylman was brilliantly intelligent, and dependably kind. "My lord, I think the women were dancing for one another tonight. So, beautiful as they are, I felt a bit of a voyeur. What about you?"

"The companions are distracting themselves, no doubt. But I confess I yearn for the more tasteful refinements of our own culture."

Hallenander said nothing. Tuss no doubt knew that Hal wanted Serral to come to Volterra. But the topic was off limits for conversation, or so he hoped.

"Would you like a smoke, my boy?" Tuff asked.

"No, thank you."

"I understand you've learned to pilot a space craft." Tuss lit a wide, brown tintorello with a metal lighter. "Whatever good that will do you. If your father fails in his efforts to make you his heir, such a skill will prove superfluous."

"Why is that my Lord?"

The old man turned to look at him. "Where would you run?"

"I see," Hallenander said. "Do you believe me to be a non-entity? With no property rights?"

"It is of course not for me to decide such things." Tuss waved to several passing women, who giggled agreeably. "And our good Syxarit Taurellio has undoubtedly indulged your whims, for some reason."

"I suppose my father has a clear understanding of innovation, at least for the purpose of entertainment."

"Ha, quite so." Tuss laughed. "You've changed, Hallenander."

"Have I?"

They approached the party pavilion, which shone with masses of tiny colored lights. Hal found them a table and held a chair out for the older lord before sitting beside him.

"Yes, you are more confident, dare I say, more cunningly like your father's family, the famously duplicitous house of Chi'irea. It's clear your little Imset vixen has done you good."

"In what way? Causing me to care if I live or die?"

Tuss smiled. "Causing you to look for enemies, probe for the game being played beneath the game itself. You will need all that and more, whatever comes next."

Hallenander paused to breathe. He kept his face from showing how frustrated he felt to be there, at a party, while Serral was in the hands of Harbinger medics, vulnerable to intrusion by Xaff or worse, his advisors.

He put on a smile. "You feel an Imset can take credit for making me more like my father's family?" Hallenander took a glass of wine, straining to keep his worry from showing on his face.

Tuss brushed ash off his heavy, ceremonial breastplate, enameled and colorful in the Katylm style. "You're a changed man, anyone can see it. The girl has served her purpose and given you confidence. And just in time, as you will be introduced to several appropriate potential wives soon."

"You heard the rumor, did you?"

Tuss puffed smoke, gazing at the scene before them, ladies laughing and removing outer layers of clothing, revealing bathing costumes. "A man in your position is subject to no end of rumors. But if you refer to the rumor about you seeking to bring your little white-haired friend to the Worlds, I assumed that was simply your enemies seeking to taint your reputation with the stench of Imset."

Hallenander knew he should feel anger at the old man's words, but he saw the kindness in them. Tuss was warning him. He knew what was coming. He had seen it far enough in advance to send Lady Midrey into hiding.

"I have enemies, Lord Tuss?"

The old man tipped back his long head crest. "More enemies than friends, though I hope to be included in the latter category."

"As of course you are." Hallenander sipped his wine. "So, answer me honestly, if you will. Do you believe that I will become a legal citizen?"

"If it were up to me, of course, you would be made Heir this instant. But I have dwelt so far from the Worlds for these last years, the journals and gossip mills of liquid do not give me clarity. I will say, the betting is mostly against you."

"What are the odds?"

Tuss shrugged, causing his armored plates to clink together softly, "Sad to say, two to one."

"And yet you tell me not to prepare myself for flight?"

"Flight will do you no good. But the act of preparing yourself seems to have. I believe in your present condition, if you are as lively and courteous as it seems you are capable of being, the people of Volterra may yet be won over."

"Well, thank you for your honesty."

"Ah, I have offended you."

"Quite the contrary. I appreciate your frankness. As you know, I have spent enough time in the company of the Imset that brash confessions seem downright ordinary to me now."

They watched six or seven women plunge into the largest of the pools, lit from below. They looked like jolly, mythological Imset mermaids.

Several Harbingers set a juke box to play old Imsethan recordings. A handful of women began to dance. Volterran men stood in groups, watching. Mimellio sat at his table alone, an image of consternation.

"What are the worst pitfalls you see in my path, sir?"

Lord Tuss listed a variety of political and cultural obstacles. Hallenander listened, accustomed to the old man using the clarity of history to predict murky events of the future. "...but that was a tribal conflict. Not the same, exactly. Though the law is unclear, of course. In those days, it was taken as a given that all Minsyxes were full blooded, of course..."

"Did the Volterrans not originally come from Imseth?"

Tuss stamped out his tintorello on an ash tray. "That is the story, but since the cursed Harbingers write nothing down, and we had only stone tablets to understand them by."

"I suppose my question is of blood."

"Ah, the so-called servants have tampered with our blood for millennia. Concocting, experimenting. They take the plants and animals and transport them throughout the universe. But we bipeds alone seem to matter enough to breed and craft. We are their creation, as I believe are these little Imset cousins."

"I see. The Harbingers create the very people they serve. I am just one more of their attempts to manage the order of things."

"Just so. Do not believe that the question of bloodlines is in some way clear or well defined. It is a fabrication, as I dare say you are."

"A fabrication. Do not worry," Hallenander said. "I am not offended. But tell me this, if you will. Who sees after Alliance business?"

Tuss grew serious, the lines between his cheeks and jaw deepening. "The Alliance is all around us; it is the very air we breathe. But if you want to know who rules over the gray Harbinger people, I am afraid that secret is closed even to me. Your father may know more. But even he is at their mercy, I'm afraid."

"Is he not their trusted partner?"

"What need have the slaves to trust him, to trust us? We have no power over them."

The two sat like that for another hour. Other members of the Eight joined them for periods but sensed the somber mood and soon moved off again. The women screeched and danced, but the men did not join them.

When the sky was fully dark, Hallenander thanked his counselor, and bid the others good night. He took an empty Bisbee from the row at the station and proceeded to the Medotel. Two Helpers met him at the doors. They stood in the light of a pair of palace sconces, which threw ominous shadows over their bulbous heads. They pulled down their surgical masks to speak.

"Please, I want a full report," Hallenander said.

Two blue-clad Harbingers blinked shining black eyes in unison. "She is out of danger, your Highness."

Hal leaned a hand against the wall, suddenly exhausted. "How long until she is healed?"

"Soon, soon," they said. "But there is not enough time to perfect her, sir."

"Perfect her? Do you mean her memory?"

Their head domes moved, like worms under their skin. "No. Her shoulder is very damaged, and the skin will have scars, my Lord."

He sighed with relief, "Scars? Do you think a person of Serral's value could be made imperfect by the presence of a few scars?"

They did not answer.

"I'm sorry. Thank you for your work healing her." He bowed with gratitude. "Why is time so short then, Helpers?"

They hesitated, spoke softly together, and then replied, "The Syxarit is in transit, and will bring with him all authority."

"Authority?"

"The Imset are not to be here in the palace complex or the Medotel, Lord. All is to be prepared for the guests."

He looked through the wide, wood doors to the Medotel. "May I see her?"

"We are your unworthy servants, Lord. But she is asleep and dreaming."

"Dreaming?" Hal scoffed. But he understood the medics to mean she was in a healing coma like she had been when he had brought her in from the first crash. "Very well. I will return."

They bowed.

The next morning, Hallenander watched out the window he had looked out most all his life, the white village, his ships, the green-and-blue glass towers, and the sea beyond. It had once seemed mysterious and full of danger. He had wished for adventure, for action, and most of all for understanding. Now, the safety of those years had vanished. He no longer yearned. The education Evincio had offered him was soon to be tested in ways he dreaded. But he had come this far. He worried about Serral, and beyond that a great flood of joy waited to be unleashed when he was finally put to the task for which he had been born.

He was buttoning a shirt when he heard a knock.

"Hello?"

His uncle, flustered, came through the door. "Ah," Mimellio took in the room. "Apologies for the disturbance."

"Sit," Hal gestured. "Helpers, something warm for my uncle."

Mimellio sat heavily on a leather chair. Harbingers brought tea.

"Thank you, boy." Mimellio passed a large hand over his dark eyes, which looked weak without their usual painting of kohl. "I have had a message from your father."

Footsteps carried down the hall. Zinnerit, then Tuss, and then the rest of the Eight, came through the door.

"Is it true?" Zinnerit asked, as the men took up places around the room.

"Is what true?" Hallenander asked. A meeting of the Volettu of Eight in his chambers was odd indeed, but he was determined to stay collected.

Mimellio nodded his long crest in affirmation. "Yes, it is true. The Syxarit has made the boldest possible gambit."

The men scoffed and growled.

"What gambit?" Hallenander shouted. "What has my father done?"

Silence fell. Mimellio breathed, "Why boy, he has threatened to abdicate."

The men howled again. Hallenander forced himself to keep breathing. The end of his father's gambit was coming, very soon. Hallenander might be in his final hours.

"Gentlemen. We have work to do to make our humble planet ready for a visit by the court. I suggest we meet in the Volettu Chamber tomorrow, and all can be discussed at length."

"Tomorrow? Why not today?" Zinnerit demanded.

Hallenander buttoned his cuff. "I have something I need to attend to today."

"Not more explorations I expect?" Mimellio said.

Hallenander forced a grim smile. "You tell me we are to expect important visitors, accompanied no doubt by others whom we seek to impress, is that not so?"

Tuss smiled, "It is so."

"Then I, as owner and proprietor of this planet, am obliged to secure its readiness, if for no other reason than to avoid embarrassment. Am I wrong to want to make the best possible impression?"

To his surprise, the men muttered and agreed. Within five minutes, Hallenander was again alone. He went immediately to the courtyard and took out a Bisbee.

**44**

— • —

C hapter Forty-Five

Serral became aware of cool sheets against her skin. She was alive, no longer floating. Complete. But as soon as she moved, she understood how badly she had been hurt. Her shoulder itched and ached, the worst pain she had ever felt. The familiar bite, too much for now. She slept.

Later, she woke hungry, opening her eyes to the white room she knew so well. Her medics assured her they were the same as before, and she sensed their truth in the thought river. They spoke with concern, offering her food, which she ate with her good hand. They encouraged her to stand, to move her injured arm which caused her to cry out. Serral told the medics she did not want medicine, but to her surprise, they told her she was not to be offered any. She saw images of a golden kite, a silver ship in black space, and a face she knew. The Syxarit.

Serral cast her mind out into the thought river. *Was it time?*

Not yet, but preparations were in full swing. The Helpers buzzed with activity, with plans and requirements, *clean linens here, fresh flowers for this room and by all means, more crystal must be procured from storage immediately.* Beneath that, the atmosphere was heavy with a ship throbbing with Xaff energy, unpleasant, but more pro-fessionally focused than she had felt before. Various soldiers milled around. They had a sense of purpose she had not noticed in the Xaff on Evincio. These Harbs reminded her of her own time soldiering, of her brief forays to the front. They did not immediately reach out to shock her, and she had no desire to commune with their hard, sharp, minds. She withdrew her presence and slept.

When she opened her eyes, Hallenander stood in simple clothing looking out the window with a scowl. Mist fell in the midday overcast. Her master's half-crested skull was all that kept him from looking like an ordinary Imset youth, until he turned, and his large, chiseled features came into view, his thick brows and lips pursed in worry.

She spoke her first words in days. "What are you looking at?"

His face brightened. "The arrival of another legion of Xaff." He dragged a stool to her bedside.

"Oh, yes. I've heard."

"So, you know what is happening."

She nodded and her shoulder flared with pain. "I know the Xaff are massing. I assume it's because your father and his guests are coming soon."

"Yes." Hallenander took her hand in his. "I met with the companions. They are ready."

"Okay." She sat up slowly, painfully.

"No, rest easy. The Wilter used some kind of exploding bullet on you. The damage was deep." He touched her side. "I will be the one to give the signal."

"Are you sure?"

"The Wilter won't fire on me in an Arrow. What is left of them. Probably not a lot. I'm sorry."

"You can't be sure that some survived. They're like me, former pilots. Trained to fight to the very last, never to let themselves be captured and augered," she flinched, pain making every word an effort. "Be careful."

"Of course," he said. "I would think hearing that the Wilter had been beaten back would be good news to you. The women have a much better chance now, if they're not to be hunted as collaborators."

"The Wilter were my people, trying to obey the law as they understood it. I'd have done the same, before I met you."

He kissed her cheek and whispered. "I'll come collect you when it's finished."

"I won't be safe here."

"Serral." He brushed hair out of her face. "You have to trust me. You can't do everything on your own."

She closed her eyes. He kissed each lid and left the room. Minutes passed. Four medics came and checked Serral's vital signs. She feigned sleep. They tried to gain access to her mind, but she resisted. Even so, she sensed deep concern and conflicted feelings, because she was there.

When she was alone again, Serral rose painfully and pushed the stool to the window just in time to see an Arrow rise from the southeast quadrant, a silver cross flashing below the clouds. It flew low over the palace complex toward the cliff and the Xalavria above. She leaned out, listened for shots, but heard nothing. Then she lost her balance and bumped her wounded shoulder. Pain seared down her arm. She tore off the wide gauze bandage from across her chest. Mottled red tissue ran from her chest to her elbow. Clearly, the damage had been deep and wide, a fatal wound if not for the skill of her medic friends. Pulling her robe closed, Serral shut her eyes and reached into the thought river. The dimension was so noisy she quickly became overwhelmed. Had she once been able to handle that level of unseen conversation, or was something different now, the volume and sheer emotion more extreme? She waited for the chaos to settle into familiar streams of team conversation. She moved from the medics, who were talking about her delicate state, to palace helpers deep in panicked preparations, to the distant squeaks of servants above in the Resort.

She found the information she sought. Hallenander had landed an Arrow on the game courts of the Xalavria. The Harbingers found his activity odd, but Serral understood its meaning. The signal had been given. Cheloa and Shanno and the others were poised to escape. Things would happen quickly now.

Then their voices turned in a direction Serral had difficulty following, happy anticipation of someplace red and warm, which felt important. Their cocoon. With great effort, Serral closed her mind. She sat panting for a few minutes, catching her breath. The quality of her connection to the thought river was stronger than ever, but so was a newly seductive feeling that she ought to remain there, that removing her mind was futile. The Harbs knew everything about her.

Serral felt her sanity was fragile, like a raindrop, as the membrane between her mind and the thought river thinned. She had best hurry. She donned a pair of slippers, tied a flimsy robe over her white gown, and crept out into the hallway. She knew where the stairs were by smell if not augering. She opened a narrow Harbinger door disguised as a paneled wall and descended quietly into the catacombs. There she felt vibrations all around, a feeling like being under a floor covered with dancing people. She opened her mind, and this time the overwhelming number of voices and minds did not shock her. She leaned weakly against a stone wall, gathering her bearings.

When she knew which way to go, Serral began walking, turning and descending as she went. At times, she needed to stop and rest or gently detach from the thought river when her presence was noted. The harsh feeling of Xaff, like an unpleasant scraping noise, drew her ever down and to the east, until eventually she came to a dripping cavity permeated with Harbinger essence. It made her gag. There was little light, but what she saw was red, and alive.

She rushed through, stopping only to drink from a spring. It tasted fresh enough. She tried to run, but her shoulder ached and throbbed. She found staircases, and more staircases, and still more. As she climbed, the deep vibrations grew stronger. She was on the right track. But too slow, she was too slow.

She forced herself to climb faster, noticing a familiar sensation, the southwest quadrant's thrum of spirits. Their timbre was so Imset, so homelike and friendly, Serral did not know what to make of it. There was more than just space between her and the potent earth-bound energy. It felt like a forgotten part of her. Tears ran down her cheeks in the dark, her slippers wet and heavy, stumbling on the stone stairs. The presence reached out to help her, with a sorrowful calm. It reminded her of the Thrill, but without any sense of euphoria. Rather, the spirits of the airfield felt like stubborn, tenacious will, without form or substance, but real, nonetheless. They were the essence of Imset, reduced to one strand of power that rose inside her, animating her tired muscles. She felt the embrace of an energy loving, welcoming and clear; she was one with them, and they wanted her to succeed.

Breathing easier, Serral came to a flat alcove she knew to be beneath the airfield itself. The space was lit by lanterns, which her eyes adjusted to slowly. Here were wide, arched halls able to hold legions, and leading away them, many staircases and closed doors. Soon she came upon rows of armored Harbs running military-style drills. Their stench was overpowering, the sounds of their movements precise and terrifying.

She risked opening her mind. The expected jolt fell harmlessly through her, as if she no longer grounded electricity, so it could find no purchase. She sat on a stone, allowing the Imset vibration to course through her body. It felt like cool fire, numbing her shoulder, her exhaustion and thirst. The Xaff, adapting to their new impotence, spoke to her as an equal. The changed politics seemed to soften the electric edge of their voices. Or perhaps she was different, now, closer to them and thus immune to their boundaries.

*We are preparing for our duty, Mistress Imset. It is not your place to interfere with us.*

Serral felt genuine curiosity. *What is your duty, soldiers?*

There was a strange, angry sound.

Serral saw the flash of guns firing, of women falling dead. The women were like strippy characters, not actual people. These Xaff had never seen a real Imset woman.

*No. You are mistaken in your goals. That is not your duty to Ysk, only to yourselves. You shall not harm the women. You shall not harm anyone on this planet.*

The harsh sound rose again, like a rearing cobra. Something rose inside Serral too, like a hundred birds of prey, snapping at the snake, screeching with rage. The Imset energy suddenly roared through her, like water through a pipe, screaming with silent rage in the thought river. Sick, sweating and off balance, Serral fell to the floor, her shoulder jolting painfully. The battle raged on within her, power surging through her chest. She could not have quit the scene if she wanted to. The Xaff became confused, then angry, then panicked. Strands of thought called out, small groups of minds grappling with their situation.

*We are beloved of Ysk, we are the Harbingers of Doom, and we are charged with enforcing the law,* called one group of voices,

*But she is the Thanton,* came a chorus, almost as loud.

*We are doing our duty,* came a competing refrain. *As was given to us by the Ancients!*

*Your duty is not to behave as Ysk!* Serral said, her voice in the thought river magnified, dark and horrible. *I am Thanton! And I tell you, Xaff, you are out of grace with Ysk!*

Silence fell. Serral detected the minds of a thousand or more soldiers. They scrambled to make sense of her words. Then, creeping chaos began to ripple through the Xaff. Like a looming earthquake, it ricocheted around the thought river.

Serral heard the visceral sounds of an immensely heavy force alighting over their heads. Something landed on the tarmac. It groaned under the unfamiliar mass. Soldiers rolled on the ground, cradling their head domes in pain, whimpering. Some ripped off helmets, others grabbed their neighbors as if fighting an enemy. The Xaff had gone mad. With great difficulty, Serral extricated herself from the battle. She willed herself to come to her senses and not succumb to the morass of pain. Her mind returned to her with a harsh snap, and she was wide awake again, in a cavern below the airfield, the stench of hundreds of Xaff warriors choking her breath. The Imset energy was nearly expended, leaving her light and empty. She turned and ran. Tears sprang into her eyes, her strength running out, the drama of what she had just witnessed making her reel. She thought about her sorties from the Tuval, her training. When outnumbered, lose your pursuers, and get back to your ship.

She hobbled as far as the red cavern. Here, she drank again and reached out her mind. Nearby Harbingers puttered on, helpers and servants buzzing happily with thoughts of the coming work. There was no connection to the Xaff or the recent confrontation. All thought was on the Syxarit, who was now in the Reykos. Soon the rest of the courtiers would arrive, and all would require sparkling wine, and fresh candles, and cakes. Everything in order.

Serral felt a breeze in her mind. The spirits of the southeast quadrant, spent, like the last few drops of rain giving way to empty sky.

*Thank you for your help,* she called out to the spirits, aloud, in Imset.

They tapped her with a final, weak finger of friendship. Then something flashed and was extinguished, the last of their trapped energy released back into the air. She almost wished she could go with them. It was all she could do to stand and begin moving again.

When she reached the Medotel, Serral augered for a micro-second before withdrawing her mind. Something was wrong. She stood inside the hidden door, processing what she had learned. Her medics were all gone. In their place appeared a group of six Xaff, with some sort of large machine on wheels, talking loudly on the thought river about how she would *cease to be a nuisance once they had wiped her mind completely blank.* Their visual of her was correct; these were local soldiers, and they knew her face. They speculated whether their master's instructions had included Serral's death. Their master was a familiar face as well; Lord Kettu, a man she had barely spoken to. He always wore an archaic green-and-gold military-style uniform, and his Companion Lady Zella never spoke in his presence, hovering in low-cut satin gowns with a pained smile that fell as soon as his back was turned. The Xaff discussed Zella's rage that the women of the Xalavria had made a clean escape, how the Lord had wanted the satisfaction of humiliating them in front of the visitors. Zinnerit's face came into their minds, along with a plan to parade the Imset ladies like animals before the Xaff euthanized them with more compassion than Zella thought they deserved.

Serral had never known a Volterran to be so overtly bloodthirsty, but of course it was only the Harbs talking, and Zella no doubt thought he would never be known for his true colors by the Volterrans, or by Hallenander. Serral pulled herself off the thought river, controlled her rage, and began to descend back into the catacombs. But there were more Xaff below. Serral leaned back in the dark stairwell. Whatever happened next, the women had escaped. She had accomplished that much. She hoped Hal had enough sense to return the Arrow and feign ignorance. He could say he had gone in search of his Companion, but that she was not there. He could be as vexed about it as the others, though he probably wouldn't be. He might still hold out hope that Serral was coming with him on his journey to the Worlds. She leaned against the wall in the darkness of the stone stairwell.

She did not want to expose herself by augering. But even without it, she could tell that the electric barrier between herself and the warriors was eroding. That open void was a danger. But she had to get word to Hal that she was not in the jungle, or he would risk his reputation looking for her there.

The Volterrans had to believe Hal fully accepted their culture continuing just as it was. His future, the future of the Imset, hinged on his father's people believing he was grateful to be their Syxarit's heir, and that he wanted nothing more than to end the Emptiness so they could go on being the supreme beings in the universe. They were just vain enough to believe it would work.

She slipped out a side door into a dark night. The cobblestones were soaked with rain, so she kicked off her ruined slippers and picked her way carefully around the side of the Medotel to the courtyard next to the palace. There were a hundred armored Bisbees parked, and even without augering she knew all exits would be blocked by Xaff.

Her shoulder throbbed without mercy. Serral walked toward the palace property with its manicured grounds and the high cliff beyond. The palace sparkled with light and the sound of music, voices, and laughter rang in the night. The noises burbled together like a distant brook, like bird song, melodious but devoid of meaning.

Serral walked slowly, stopping to dip her hand into a frigid fountain to drink. The sky was red and copper and striated with black clouds, windless and cool. Her feet soon grew numb with cold, so she stumbled and fell from a barrier onto a gravel curlicue. She picked herself up and hobbled over to rest against a clipped, cone-shaped tree. Suddenly, a white explosion sent her back onto the ground, breathing hard, feeling panicked. But it was only fireworks, explosions of sparks that trailed harmlessly in the night sky. Serral forced her breathing to return to normal. Peals of laughter erupted from balconies above, foreign voices, the tinkle of Volterran in higher registers. Volterran woman, the Lords, other voices. More fireworks flew, chrysanthemums of fire, so close she wondered if the Helpers were using her as a target. Eventually, the show ended. It seemed like the only part of her body she could feel was the flames of her shoulder. She moved on, slowly, agonizingly, expecting Xaff to appear and arrest her. Click and Clack had told her that the palace grounds and the resort itself were off limits to Xaff. Perhaps the rules continued to apply.

At moonrise, she skirted a wide fishpond and came to a stand of pines rooted in a deep pile of shale that made up the side of the cliff that hid the Xalavria. Serral had climbed cliffs many times on Chlore. She always started with the lower tree branches. Then, using her good hand to grasp roots dangling from the cliff, she moved up, and up, refusing to look down, smelling the wet earth and an essence of bat holes that she grasped with her bare toes. She made it three quarters of the way to the top before the root she held snapped, sending her crashing back down. Branches broke her fall, but her numbingly cold fingers could not grasp them. Something hit her head, and she fell into blackness.

Serral felt sun on her skin and opened her eyes. She was lying on a pile of old tree needles and rubbish between large pieces of rock.

Her clothes were torn and stained with dried blood, her head and her shoulder ached, but she was able to sit up. The sky was a sweet blue with pink clouds, Tekkus hovering like a line of silver beads far to the south. The Reykos winked blue, green and coral in the rising sun, rooted in the planet like bright sword hilts. She took stock of her body; a broken wine glass no doubt thrown from the lookout above had cut her knees. But the cuts were shallow, and the bleeding had stopped. Her shoulder looked like fresh lava beneath her white Medotel gown. She rotated her arm and cried out. The joint seared with heat, but it seemed functional.

In the new light, Serral looked for Harb doors in the side of the cliff. But she knew it made no sense to put them so far from the palace, and she found nothing but moss, rocks, and old broken kites. She drank water from the tops of leaves, causing a frog to croak away angrily. Mushrooms grew between cracks, but she decided hunger was preferable to making herself sick. She began the climb again. The tree roots were drier now, and while the sun shone in her eyes painfully, Serral was better able to grip those roots now.With a final painful heave, she flopped over the edge onto flat ground, gasping. Below her stretched the white palace and village, the sea and islands, the Reykos above all. Serral drew herself up, climbed over the balustrade and onto cold, dew soaked grass.She walked slowly, weaving a bit, then course correcting. If she fell, no one would be there to help her up, and she would be too weak to get up on her own.

She felt anger, passing by the kissing maze, which already looked untended and shaggy. The Imset women were all gone. The Volterrans below carried on with their parties and fireworks, laughter and amusements, their plans to make Hallenander heir to the throne and take him far away across the universe. She forced herself to breathe through the pain and hobble to her building. The building he had built, for her.

No Harbs stood ready to let her in, and the large cross-hatched portals were locked. But a small door around the side pushed open, unlocked. It smelled unused. Serral climbed the Harb stairs up and up, finally arriving on the seventh floor, where she found the passage that opened into the Harb kitchen adjoining her apartment. She pawed through the shelves of supplies there, then sat on the floor forcing herself not to gobble the dried cakes and sparkling water, while she listened for sounds within the apartment.

It was silent. Her nose told her the Harbs had fled. Now that her immediate hunger and thirst were assuaged, Serral took stock of herself in her white, Medotel gown covered in dried mud and blood, of the matte of stick-infested hair falling over her scratched and lacerated skin. A sudden desperate desire to be clean and asleep, not necessarily in that order, overwhelmed her. She had grown used to being a pampered pet. The comforting silence of her own apartment was far more powerful than she wanted to admit.

As secure as she could be without augering, Serral pushed open the Harb door and entered her show kitchen, which was spotless as always, lit only by metal-girded windows. Fruit sat in bowls, overripe, a sure sign Click and Clack were gone. She risked a silent walk through the rest of the penthouse's rooms. The place smelled of rotting flowers drooping sadly in their vases. Serral opened one of the foyer's velvet chocolate boxes and greedily stuffed a sweet into her mouth. It tasted like sugared almonds, like the Xalavria's many temptations. Serral carried the box with her as she checked every corner of the place. No one seemed to have been there since the day she was shot. Click and Clack had obviously been ordered to leave. What had the Lords expected would happen to her? Had Kettu been involved with the

Wilter attack? It seemed unlikely. If Imset soldiers had been in contact with either Harbs or Volterrans, Serral did not think they would plan to sabotage Hallenander. No, it was more likely the Lords saw an opportunity to get rid of her and took it. No doubt they were congratulating themselves on a job well done, believing she had run off into the jungle with the other Companions.

And what were their plans for the women? Would the reality of the Reykos mean the Xaff would be instructed to let them be, to let them live out their lives in the jungle, a potential source of help for the Rakki children if such help were needed?

And what about the children? Would the Lords clean Evincio of threats, making it a perfect place for the children to come off the Reykos and inhabit? Would they take Hal's place in the palace, occupy the villas and behave like real colonials?

She knew what she would do.

She looked out her kitchen window toward the east, toward the Reykos. Where was Hallenander? She did not dare auger to find out.

Serral forced herself to bathe in the hottest water she could bear, adding salts to clean her cuts though it stung so much she cried. When she was dry, she painted her wounds with sealer from a first aid kit she had found in the Harb supply closet. She tried moving her shoulder again, which brought more tears. The many bottles and packages in the kit were marked with Volterran symbols Serral did not understand.

She made a syringe with what she hoped were healing and pain meds, then injected them into the muscle. The sharp stab made her grimace, but within moments, the shoulder numbed, her body relaxed, and her breath slowed. Taking shears, Serral cut the tangles out of her hair and fashioned it into a chin-length bob. She tied that back in a ponytail, balled the severed hair up into wrappers from the kit, and hid that under layers of supplies in the closet. She swept the floor, rinsed the tub, and replaced the box of first aid. She dressed in simple clothing, then went over the space again, so the apartment looked just as she had found it. Cursing, she put the chocolate box back on the pile, silently thanking Hallenander for his showy generosity. The apartment was full of so many miraculous delicacies that no scrap rat could dream of the richness of it. She was not sorry she had gotten to experience such decadence, if only for a matter of weeks.

She looked at the silver candlestick she had once used to try and hit Hallenander with. The memory unaccountably cut into her mood, making her feel weak and weepy again. She pushed the feelings away and tried to get her fuzzy brain to focus.

Using the Harb stairs, Serral descended to the next level. The sixth floor was partially finished and had closets and storage shelves stacked with spare bedding, food, and supplies. She awkwardly dragged a mattress to a window that had a view of the circular drive and road to the village. She found a sharp knife, which she placed on the windowsill. Then, on a bed she made up behind a stack of storage totes, she covered herself with spare quilts, and she slept.

When she woke, the sun was low in the sky. Her shoulder felt much better, but she fetched the first aid kit and took what she figured were pain pills and washed them down with a tangy juice. She looked through a closet and found a warm sweater, some thick socks, and a pair of opera glasses she had used to watch the scene outside. Trees danced in the wind. Leaves skittered across the distant square. A toppled cafe umbrella rolled toward the gazebo. The Xalavria had become a ghost town.

Serral fought the feeling of being trapped. It seemed the Xaff were not coming after her, for the moment. No doubt their priority now was the comfort of their Volterran visitors, their cakes and linens and introduction to the new heir. The Xaff were probably waiting to attack until the evenings of parties and festivities calmed down, when the courtiers would not notice some loud explosions on the plateau above the palace. It was possible that by not augering, she was invisible to Xaff, but she doubted it. They had found her in space, and they would find her now. She rotated her shoulder again, relieved that the fire in it had gone out. It throbbed, but at least the joint was healing, and she no longer felt like a fish gasping for air.

Serral tried the tiniest possible micro-second of augering, on and off. As she suspected, no Harbs appeared in the Xalavria. But the day wore on, and nothing happened. She ate a dinner of canned fish and hard crackers while watching the sun set. More fireworks exploded. More Tekkus took off and landed. She slept dreamlessly.

The next morning, she woke to a body without pain. She stretched, did exercises, relieved to find her energy returning. At sunset she crept out into the resort. A herd of small deer ran away as she walked across the lawn. She stood at the lookout, trying to get a sense of what was happening below in the palace. A pair of masted sailing ships, Hallenander's, he had told her once, was pulling away from the docks. The palace stood in silence. Serral wondered what had happened to the captive Imset in the village.

She cursed softly to herself. What would Slook make of what had happened to Serral? Did the military have the faintest inkling of what happened to the Imset people they had abandoned? The Wilter had been soldiers, left behind, trying to do what they could for the good of their people. Just like Serral. And now they were dead. But the women of the Xalavria, the talented and beautiful Companions, where had the Harbs gotten them? Were they acquired somehow from the colonial diaspora, from Captain Thrish or others like him? Serral wished she knew more. If she were able to find Slook, to explain to her some of the complexity of the war and the fact that they had a potential ally in Volterra, she might be able to make a difference in people's lives. But it was such a long shot. It seemed less risky to Serral than Hallenander's plan. Her eyes rested on the Reykos, the two towers shining brightly in the sun like reflective holiday ornaments from a surreal strippy. Were there alternatives Serral was not considering? Miss Pune had always told her that her greatest strength was her ability to see not only what was intended, but what was really there.

Satisfied that no one was imminently coming to shoot her, she began exploring the resort. She returned to the Lady Companion townhouses. Cheloa's doors hung half-open, clothing and bedding lay abandoned in the yard. A raven hopped by with a resentful glare, in its mouth a sparkling earring. Serral called out, "Don't worry, friend. She won't be needing that now."

Serral descended the stairs in Elva's house, but was met by such a strong Harb stench, she wondered if they had retreated and were now living under the Xalavria. She went to the workshops, which were unlocked. She found secret passageways easily, but none led underground, only to other parts of the Resort, to storage rooms and Harb sleeping nests, the deep-red, cottony cocoons, their viscous coating drying fast.

Then she tried the Clubhouse. Opossums waddled away, unafraid. They had eaten through the coverings of several food bins. But the freezer was untouched. Serral warmed herself a lunch from within it. She missed the people who had once inhabited the empty tables. She hoped they were all right.

There were large catacombs under the Clubhouse, but they smelled warningly of Harb legions. She had let them know of her use of the catacombs, and obviously, they had no plans to let her travel that way again.

Giving up hope of escaping the Xalavria in the light of day, Serral found a way into the theater. The old building had no windows, so she risked turning on the lights. The auditorium echoed with the music of its many performances. Serral's feet made quiet creaks as she walked the wood floor where she and Hal had sung their awful duet. She crept up into his box and sat on his velvet seat, realizing that she missed him terribly. She felt left behind and useless. She leaned back in the comfortable seat, snapping awake hours later in a panic. But the room was still. The ornate ceiling and enormous crystal chandeliers sparkled down at her. Serral stood and inhaled the scent of the dead planet, realizing how rare and incredible it was to be so close to the craftspeople of her ancestors, to their idea of beauty and hope for the future. She could not give up.

Serral wandered by the darkened store fronts in the Companion village. She did not want to spend another night alone in her building. She was sure the Xaff knew exactly where she was and were biding their time before they came to kill her. Trees rippled in the wind against a pale gold, sunset sky, and carried the scent of the northern fields. Life was a greater gift than she had ever let herself know. She thought of the spirits of the airfield, and how they had flowed out of their trap and into the universe. What was going to happen to her? How long would she be in this empty and lonely place?

Realizing she had been avoiding it, she made her way to the hexagonal, redbrick Yskeon. It looked like a tall, stark tower, a star that had been stretched and hardened. The interior was dark and smelled like mold. Serral tried to summon a prayer to Ysk but felt foolish. She thought about the Imset; rumor was that the people trapped in the cities had become religious fanatics, convinced that Ysk desired them to live out their lives in space.

Serral went back to the lookout. The wooden ships had returned.

When the sun was fully down, Serral crept to the silver gates. Ten armored Xaff hovered, silent but for the faint purring of their Bisbees, looking out toward the road and jungle. Ten. Serral wasn't ready to face ten Xaff, especially as they would no doubt have a hundred more on her within seconds.

She was looking for Harb doors out of the station when she heard a larger Bisbee approaching the gates. A covered carriage entered the resort, passed her, and proceeded toward the square. It moved swiftly away from her, and toward her building which stood like a gleaming black-and-gold beacon, the windows on the seventh floor, dark. The vehicle moved fast and went quiet.

Minutes later, Serral stood in a clump of bushes, watching. The shiny black carriage was parked in her building's drive. Lights were on inside the foyer. Stepping back, she saw the lights had been turned on up on the seventh floor.

If her visitor were one of the Lords, he would no doubt become impatient, and leave soon. She found an overgrown mass of shrubs, and sat on the ground among their branches, watching. The sky turned from purple to indigo to black, and stars came out. The air grew cool. When she was satisfied that whoever had come to see her was planning to wait, Serral brushed the dirt from her legs and climbed the Harb stairs to the sixth floor.

A voice spoke in the darkness. "I don't think this knife will do you much good, unless you carry it.

She squeezed her eyes closed, waiting to be attacked.

"They're using bullets these days." Hallenander wrapped her in his arms. "But not on you. Not anymore."

She pressed her face into his warm chest, unable to stop the tears.

**45**

—·—

C hapter Forty-Six

They sat in front of a proper fire, Serral and Hallenander, wine open and a hamper of dinner half consumed at their feet. He told her about his father's arrival. A staff of helpers had come along with Hallenander, bustling about in a show of hard work.

He told her about the moment he killed the four Xaff, the Thrill rising in him, his green eyes aglow.

"I had just witnessed the Xaff brutality against the Wilter," he scowled. "I was soaking from the rain, wearing my flight suit. The courtiers looked at me as if I were an animal in a menagerie."

Serral tucked her bare feet under his leg on the giant couch, feeling comfortable and safe for the first time since before being shot. "Tell me about them."

"Of course. I expect you'll learn as much from the Helpers as I can tell you."

"I want to hear your point of view," she said. But she did not say that she was afraid to auger because her contact with the Xaff had brought her so close to the edge of sanity. She did not say that Lord Kettu had plotted to have her wiped. She was unsure what to say. What if Hallenander demanded justice for her? It would not help his cause, not when the court was still deciding his citizenship status.

"Very well. I came into a dining room full of people, me looking quite the brash alien, my father at the head of the table, everyone staring as I entered. The Syxarim," he said rolling his eyes.

"Miranxis," Serral finished his thought. "Your father's wife, your enemy, maybe."

"Yes, dressed in her silks with a filigree face crown." He touched his own face. "Looking like quite the Sevenni Highness, unimpressed with our little Imset kingdom here."

"Remember, she's lost so much."

"Yes, and she is trying to keep at least the appearance of dignity, for the sake of her legacy."

"How many others were there?"

Hallenander went on to say how the sixty guests stared, silently gaping at him while the Syxarit Taurellio rose to greet him. His father wrapped him in a warm hug, making a show of his affection, and Hallenander spoke the correct words, made the visitors welcome, disarmed them so that within the hour he felt their affection and growing loyalty. He spent an exhausting three days speaking at length to each person. They played games, danced, and sailed, he said. He had formal meetings of the sort Volterrans practiced daily, made sacrifices to their gods, and watched artistic performances that deviated so far from what she knew, Serral could only nod and try to understand.

"Is this boring?" he said, "because I can certainly see how it would be."

"Oh no," she chuckled, "it helps me understand why the men filled a resort full of entertainment. Volterran life sounds like one intense group experience after another."

"Exactly," he continued, "and I focused on behaving like a proper gentleman in order to discern where everyone's political interests lay. So, it was not boring at all."

"And what have you learned?"

He told her about the shifting sands of allegiance among the nobles, their connections to the house of Jalophians and to the elected commoners of the Eloxiture who were easier to win over with favors and riches and seemed to be leaning in his favor. The governmental bodies give the courts an opportunity to rule, which involves speeches and lobbying.

"At the moment," he said, "it appears I have a decent chance at citizenship and the crown."

"And you're just getting started." Serral made a smile, though her heart felt heavy. She forced herself to focus on his words.

"Syxarim Miranxis has taken up my cause and is busily accruing favors for me. Meeting my cousin Bellex in person has been empowering," he said, making two plates of dessert and offering her one. "She alone seems to understand the depth of the game at hand. She and my father."

Serral sat up on her knees. "You and Bellex are natural allies. She is a good friend to have."

Hallenander did not answer. His expression went blank. Serral realized that while Bellex might be a friend to her Master, the Volterran princess did not extend that friendship to his Companion. Bellex was no fool, Serral decided. "I'm glad you have her. She'll be able to feed you information about your enemies."

He regarded her quietly, the crackling fire the only noise. "I hope you will do that for me too. You are the person I trust most."

"But I can only talk to the servants, and they are sometimes oblivious to nuance," she trailed off, feeling trapped. She yearned to be honest with him, feel his arms around her in a comforting embrace. But her shoulder was raw, and tears were close to the surface. "Tell me more about your father. You said he wanted to meet with me?"

Hallenander accepted the subject change. "Yes. You must become a professional Companion once more, I am afraid. Though he knows my feelings for you."

"And what are those?" she moved closer.

He took her in his arms, and they did not speak for a long time.

Serral missed Click and Clack fiercely. The sky grew pink, and she had to make herself look glamorous. A staff of Harbs had appeared as Hallenander left, but even without entering the thought river, she knew they were not Click and Clack, but new helpers sent to aid her with her presentation to the emperor. She chose a high-necked deep green frock that covered her wounded shoulder and arm. She chose a pale wig not far from her white hair color, colored her lips red, and lined her eyes with black. She wondered if she ought to wear Hallenander's family jewels, but instead settled on a string of pearls and a jade ring. With stockings and a pair of pointy black pumps, she looked like an old Imsethan librarian, which suited her fine.

For the first time since creeping back to her home, she took the elevator down to the lobby where fresh flowers now filled all the vases. A pair of Harbs held open the tall glass doors and stood attentively as she climbed next to Hallenander in his carriage.

"You didn't have to come get me," she said, remembering how she had arrived, panting and bloody, flopping over the cliff edge in exhaustion.

"I am aware that you have your own ways of getting from place to place," he said, flashing a grin. He wore a beautiful tweed suit, new gold jewels, and an ornate crown that made him look like an epic hero. "But the only way I know to keep you safe is to keep you close."

"It's still risky to be seen with me," she said.

Hal steered them down the road toward the silver gates. "It may be, but our guests are all asleep. Volterrans don't believe in mornings."

"So why are you taking me to the palace now?"

"My father is awake."

She controlled her breathing, fighting her fear as they entered the palace courtyard. Hallenander helped her down. What looked like a hundred Xaff stood guard around the place, armored and helmeted. She half expected them to challenge her to a fight. She did not auger, and they did not react. Was she invisible to them now? Their large black eyes followed her as she passed. She had never seen Xaff do that before. She figured that they were aware of her identity and her role, but that they were unwilling to move against her while Hallenander was present.

He was right. She was safe, so long as he kept her close.

They entered through a pair of massive, carved doors and into an echoing hall draped in long banners and smelling of exotic spices. Awe-inspiring. Her feet trotted across the soft carpets. Hallenander led her up a set of wide stairs and into a further series of halls, on into a narrower passage with arched windows overlooking the valley, and then finally, into a wood-paneled chamber.

He kissed her hand and whispered, "Just be yourself."

Then she was alone. It was the most magnificent place she had ever seen. The walls were masterpieces of carving, the fireplace made of shining stone, and a ceiling gilded and painted until every square foot was decorated, each slightly different than the next. A peaked window looked to the east, out to the colorful Reykos which, from this angle, looked more than ever like pieces of technology, like intentional works of contriving rather than cubistic monuments. Serral lost herself in imagining how they worked, where their various systems might be located, and how deeply they were buried. She was startled when a voice behind her spoke.

"Well, dear Tseeroolk, Companion of my son. Come and have some wine with me."

Taurellio towered over her, wearing what looked like black silk brocade pajamas, his brown face craggy in the morning light, his smile white and broad.

Serral reflexively curtsied, and he laughed a deep, rich laugh. "Oh, there is no need to put on airs for me, Miss Tseeroolk. I am well acquainted with the Imset. I know what you are."

He waved a massive hand and sat on an armchair. She sat opposite him, behind his head a painting of a boy who looked like Hallenander, a grave-faced furry animal in one hand, and in the other, eight globular jewels dangling on thin chains. The boy's expression was calm and determined.

Taurellio studied her with his fire-opal eyes. "You will try this vintage from my home vineyards on Phrygio." He held out a glass of ruby liquid. It was too early for wine, but Serral toasted with the Syxarit, and drank a sip of what tasted like metallic fruit punch. Maybe he was testing her manners.

"How nice. I get to taste Hallenander's birthright."

"Ah, direct as the Imset always are. Understandable, for a people with so little time left."

"Exactly," she said tartly. "Something the Volterrans are familiar with, I understand?"

The large man opened his mouth and laughed again, "You are making me like you very much, dear. I am so sorry to say."

"I understand."

"Do you, though?" The lines below his cheekbones deepened and his thick lips flattened into a line. "You have taken my son flying. Taught him to murder. You think that makes you an expert in his future subjects?"

Serral tried to remain calm. "Sire, do you believe he will succeed? In becoming your heir?"

The older man picked up a small cake, sniffed it, and put it back on the plate. "I do. And the reason I am so sure of this, Tseeroolk, is because I worked very carefully for many years to make it so."

She nodded. "Yes. You even threatened to abdicate your throne if the powers that be do not fall in line, I understand."

"I think not," his eyes narrowed. "Our world is not as cynical as yours. Your culture is shallow, crass and silly. We enjoy brief bouts of it," he smiled condescendingly, "but yours is not a real civilization."

She flashed hot and cold, but a voice inside her told her he was trying to get a reaction. She tipped her head to one side. "I see your point. Why bother saving the Imset? We are not as refined as you. The universe is better off without us, am I right?"

"Ah, Lady." Taurellio made a sad expression with his thick, black brows and pursed lips. "Must we be frank with one another?"

"I have a proposal for you." Serral smelled something like roasted plums and newly cut reeds, a rare perfume. There was a door tucked into a nearby alcove, a perfect hiding place for Harb servants, or eavesdroppers. "Would you like to invite the Syxarim to discuss the matter with us? Or will she just tell the others later what she hears surreptitiously? Make fun of Hallenander for wanting to raise a scrap rat out of the dirt?"

Taurellio boomed theatrically, like a man hiding his rage.

"Oh, you are indeed something." He called out, "Come in, darling. The savage won't bite you."

A woman entered the room, straight and tall, carrying her long-crested head on slim shoulders like a precious object. Her skin was the color of young wood, her gown, a fine golden linen embroidered with shimmering white. Taking a hard-back chair behind her husband, Miranxis eyed Serral with contempt. Serral thought of the photograph of Taurellio with Elva and understood that the old Emperor had loved his Imset Companion, that the woman now standing behind him never warmed his heart the way Elva had. Miranxis must know this too, her pride stung beyond remedy.

The Volterran queen's gaze traveled insolently from Serral's feet to her head, but she voiced no opinions. She did whisper something low to Taurellio, who answered with a dismissive clicking sound.

Serral rose and moved behind her chair, as if to shield herself. "Okay, now that we're all here, I would like to propose a plan. This is not a negotiation. You can either accept it, or I tell your son everything I know about what you are really up to here."

Miranxis spoke harshly into her husband's ear. Taurellio held up a hand, "I am willing to hear you, little white mouse."

Serral told him her terms. As she spoke, he crossed his legs comfortably, Miranxis' large eyes darting between them as the Imset language flowed past.

Taurellio nodded. "My son is no fool. But I see you are wiser than even he is."

Serral looked at her toes, tears threatening behind her eyes.

Miranxis said, "Sad girl. Love the Minsyx. Stupid girl."

"I agree to your terms." Taurellio said. "It is a good enough plan."

"Hallenander must never know." Serral eyed the Empress. "It would only hurt him. He must believe your people to be good, and kind, and all the stuff you tell yourselves: you are so civilized, so much better than others. Hal must believe that what he is doing is for the greater good. Or he'll become angry and bitter, and the people who stand between him and his destiny will see that."

Now Miranxis spoke. "Why do you care, girl?"

Serral held her head high, "Because Hallenander is a good and noble person, and he deserves a chance."

"You love him," the older woman said with a sour expression. "Why? He is ordinary."

"Of course, to you he is ordinary, only a hybrid, a Rakki."

The woman's body stiffened as if hit by cold water. Taurellio raised his brows.

Serral held out her hands. "To me, of course, he is perfect."

"You sound a bit like the Harbingers, the gray people, Tseeroolk."

"What a funny coincidence."

Taurellio looked from his wife to Serral. "Then we are agreed."

He held his hand out for her to shake in the Imset style. Serral hesitated. "If you have your soldiers move too early, the whole scheme will backfire. If he sees how inhumane you are willing to be to get your way, he will walk into Volterra hating it and hating the people he is meant to serve. You and I both know that his enemies would use that against him. I know what has to happen. But I don't want him to know."

Taurellio spoke very quietly, "I believe you are correct, Tseeroolk. If our dear, young Minsyx witnesses how the world must be, he will lose heart. Though, only for a while. He cannot change what he is any more than you can, little mouse. He shall be a great man." His opal eyes sparked, "And great men must sometimes do terrible things."

"If you say so." Serral glanced at Miranxis, and then to the opal-eyed man. "May we speak privately, sire?"

Taurellio said something in Volterran about shame and honor.

Miranxis gave Serral a long look. "You are not a bad girl."

Serral nodded to the older woman, who disappeared. The door closed with a thud. "I'm not going to ask if you believe the other children will follow him to Volterra."

"But of course, I do."

"And I'm not going to ask if they are all your progeny, because they must breed together one day."

"Exactly. Most are. Some are not. The staff know."

"But I do want to ask one thing," she said. "Was Elva his mother?"

Taurellio scowled. "Do you think me an evil man? I have not killed. I have not taken life as you have done."

"Taurellio. I do not blame you for the war. Your grandfather, your father, they watched the Harbs lure Imseth into the Cataclysm."

"The Imset destroyed Imseth," Taurellio said. Then he fell silent.

"The Imset were foolish," she said. "They entered into a war they didn't understand, because they felt their very existence was threatened."

"We can argue this for weeks, my dear, and never agree. There is the matter of Alliance Law."

"Which the Imset didn't have any part in creating."

"You know nothing about it, child. And it matters not to you, now."

"I've seen people killed, lots of people, innocent kids who had no chance. You might not be guilty of directly killing Volterran children, but you bear responsibility for causing them never to be conceived. And, if you command the Xaff, you're a murderer a million times over."

"No one commands the Xaff," he said, not unkindly. "You auger with them, so you know that. You know they work for their own purpose. I am only trying to ensure stability for my people. As any ruler must. "He waved his large hands, as if to swat invisible insects.

Serral stifled a gasp. "You know I auger?"

"Of course, I know. And I know what they think you are. Your mind has traveled far and wide in this universe, Tseeroolk Brook. Your heart has no secrets. Our people are not simple like you are. They do not offer such pure will, such passionate loyalty. You are a real Imset warrior, and I am sad you have to die."

"Right." Serral reached out her hand, and they shook. "Good luck with your court case, with the Jalophians and the Eloxiture and all the rest."

Taurellio rang a bell. "She loved me, as you love him." His expression grew sad, "too much. Her heart was like yours, Tseeroolk, like the Imset. Too much feeling, too much sorrow."

Serral swallowed the rest of her awful wine and stood to leave.

He took her small hand in his large one. "I will not forget your sacrifice." His voice dropped to a whisper, "The Imset will live on in the same manner as the Volterran people as equals. Because of my efforts, because of my work. Try to remember that, yes?"

"I'll do my best," she said softly in his ear. "And you remember that the law applies to everyone. No matter who they were born to be. Powerful or helpless, Ysk judges all the same."

He looked confused.

She smiled. "The Thantons told me that."

"Ahem." Hallenander entered the chamber looking somber.

"Thank you for the talk, your Sevenni Highness." Serral curtsied. "I learned so much."

In the hallway, Hallenander gripped her left arm, and she winced.

"What was that?" he said softly.

"He loved me. He is letting us spend the rest of the day and the night together. Then you must go to Volterra, and I will follow, you know," she shrugged, "later. I'll fly in secretly."

"He actually agreed to that?"

She nodded, her heart grinding into bitter dust. He looked into her eyes for several long moments. Then he smiled, his eyes dancing. "Well, come on then. We have things to do."

# 46

—·—

C hapter Forty-Seven

He grasped her hand, and they slipped unseen to Hallenander's private chamber,  avoiding the Volterran guests who ate and chatted at the long banquet table below, head crests unmoving, eyes not traveling to the mesh opening above. Dozens of uniformed Harbs poured hot drinks and offered trays of food. From the walkway above, Serral saw a frail-looking Volterran girl in a wheelchair, sitting at one end of the table, Bellex.

Hal pulled her on, and they ran silently down the carpeted hallway, then over two arched bridges, and finally, into the towering turret of Hallenander's chambers.

"We are not to be disturbed for any reason, and no one is to know where I am or who I am with," Hallenander commanded a team of four Helpers.

They bowed; their head domes puffed with approval.

Hallenander's chambers were beautiful but simple, a private refuge more than a showplace. Its five rooms were full of wonders, and he repeated his delight that she be allowed to share it with him.

"My father must see you as I do," he said, "as the best of allies."

"He has your best interest at heart." If she lived, she would be haunted by these lies. But she did her best to look happy.

"Obviously," Hal replied with a look of relief on his face. "You can relax now, right?"

"Oh yes," she rubbed her stiff shoulder. "Everything is going according to plan."

He showed her his most precious books, his globes, and pictures. Helpers brought them food and wine, and he told her about his latest insights into Volterran politics. They talked throughout the day and into the twilight, then kissed. Serral pushed him down onto his bed.

He watched her with his large, glittering green eyes. "I've dreamed of having you here."

"An Imset woman in the palace? You dirty boy." She straddled him.

He wrapped his arms around her waist, kissing her shoulder. "Does it hurt?"

"No," she lied.

"Lie down. You look exhausted."

"I'm fine." She kissed him. "I'm stronger than I look."

He kissed her hard.

Below Hallenander's tower, on the balconies overlooking the gardens, Harbinger helpers led guests inside for late night delicacies and rare cordials, so they would not hear the sounds coming from above.

Later, Hallenander and Serral lay entwined under the skylight, looking up at the stars.

"Are you still afraid of the constellations you don't know?" he asked, running his fingers through her hair.

"Not at all," Serral replied. She thought back to her hex tattoo and the days of her younger self. "Feeling small and insignificant is sometimes right. Don't you think?"

"You? Small, perhaps. Insignificant, never."

Serral listened to his chest rise and fall as he fell asleep and traced one of his arm tattoos in the moonlight. He looked so unguarded it brought her to tears. She silently donned her dress and sweater, took up the pearls and ring, but left the wig. She had no reason to stall other than she wanted to find something of his, a photograph, a talisman. something to prove this wondrous night had been real, that she had once been his Companion then his friend. That he loved her. She picked up his pocket watch. She kissed his cheek.

She slipped the watch, along with an engraved lighter, and a couple wax tapers into her pocket. Then she walked silently to the Harb kitchen and its the secret passage. Its fresh smell told her the Harbs had not used it recently. She lit one of the candles and walked down the narrow staircase that led deep into the catacombs. Passageways back into the castle led in all directions, and they smelled well-used. She chose one at random, and it exited onto a carpeted hallway on the ground floor where sconces burned merrily and Volterran music played. She moved slowly down the hall. Low voices, male and female, spoke conversationally. She caught a few words about *loyalty,* and *gamble*, and something to do with *head crests*. People laughed. Helpers passed in and out of doorways carrying trays but did not notice her. Three open salon doors stood between her and escape. She flattened herself into a dark corner next to a large armoire. Her fingers felt the wall, hoping to find a Harb door. Sure enough, when she pressed gently, a panel sprang open. She had just turned to open it all the way, when a voice spoke from behind.

"Going so soon?" It was the girl in the wheelchair. She wore a fine white ball gown and a crown crafted of tremulous golden leaves. Serral hesitated. "Unfortunately, I have an appointment."

"You aren't supposed to leave. Peoplewill be annoyed. Everyone wanted to meet you. We've all heard so much about you."

"Come on. He trusts you."

Bellex's face took on an expression of fury. "As well he should since I am his kin and have his interest at heart."

"I spoke to the Emperor. He and I have an agreement."

"Oh, please. As if an agreement with an outlaw has any weight." Bellex rolled nearer. "You don't look like a mighty warrior. Does the plane make you feel important? Relevant? Legitimate?"

"Please." Serral inched toward the opening. "Why are you stalling me?"

Bellex laughed. "Because I am curious, obviously. We all are. Everyone wants to know what he sees in you. What an Imset woman even looks like."

"Now you've seen."

"Not really. I don't know what you look like, under that costume. They say your kind has tiny little parts. The men find them entrancing. Don't they? Your masters, I mean? The people who own you?"

"I heard Volterrans are noble. High. Moral."

Bellex's laugh was a shriek. "Who told you that? We're bored and sterile. And that is all we are. What did Hallenander say about us? He doesn't know. He is only just about to find out. How jealous and petty and depraved we really are. But at least we're not Imset. At least we don't have to do what you just did. In order to survive."

Heat spread through Serral's skin. She wanted to push Bellex to the ground, bring her heel down on the girl's neck. But even in the wheelchair, Bellex looked vigorous and strong, large like all Volterrans, and just as mean.

"You don't want him to find out that you've hurt me."

"Oh, please. Because he loves you?"

Serral's throat closed. "I have to go."

"I think I will call the guards."

"No. Hallenander must go to Volterra and win over his new subjects. You know this. If you don't care what happens to him do it for the emperor and your people, who need him. I trust you will help him. Because like you said, it's in your interest not to have your family's house fall to ruin."

"You, trust me?" Bellex's face darkened. "Wow. Thanks so much."

"You will help him. You will look out for him. Promise me."

Bellex touched the tip of her head crest absently. "I don't have to promise you anything."

"If you call the guards, he'll find out that you harassed me, and he won't like it"

"How will he find out?" The girl's blue eyes flashed.

Laughter sounded in the next room.

"The Harbingers will know. And they will tell him. And he will never forget your cruelty."

"I'm not cruel," Bellex wheeled closer, her perfume reaching Serral's nose. "Your people are the killers. They're ones who kill planets."

The same voice in Serral's head that counseled her not to let Taurellio rile her, helped control her now. This girl wanted Serral to leave. She loved Hallenander, Serral knew it like she knew his watch and chain rested on her hip inside her pocket.

"Help me leave. I'll tell the Harbingers to tell him you tried to save my life. Do it for his sake. He'll love you for it."

Bellex grew livid, her spine straining with rage. "You impudent vermin."

"Show him your loyalty. He needs an ally, Bellex."

"Fine, but I need to let the others have a look at you. Just let us ask you a few questions about your relationship. We need to know how experienced he is, what his skills are. Wait here." She rolled toward the nearest open door.

Serral smelled pipe smoke. Mimellio. Bellex's father, her enemy, was on the other side of the wall, most likely with his friend Zinnerit.

The moment she left the room, Bellex began shouting in Volterran, her voice full of outrage, rising to a horrified shriek.

Serral ran full bore down the hallway.

Yelling and footsteps followed behind. Mimellio, Zinnerit, and others calling out for her to stop. Serral pushed through a Harb door, then fell into cool air at the base of a set of stairs, and scrambled out into the night's darkness and a strong smell of lubricant.

The garages. A stroke of luck.

She augered without hesitation, *I need a Bisbee!*

*You are not authorized, Mistress. We are terribly distressed to deny you. We have missed you.*

*No, you don't understand.*

*We heard your need. But these machines belong to the Sevenni...*

*This is to help the Rakki!*

The river hesitated, debated.

She repeated, *The Rakki! I need a Bisbee to help the Rakki children.*

Immediately, a tiny, nimble, racing Bisbee hovered over the flagstones toward her.

*Thank you, friends!*

*The guests require you to wait, Mistress!*

*The guests can go...*

People tumbled out of the palace's large carved doors, indistinguishable Volterran shapes in the darkness, shouting and laughing as if an Imset girl running for her life were oh so amusing. A game. Serral gunned the little craft, up and over their heads, bumping someone she hoped was Zinnerit hard in his head crest. For a moment, Serral's eyes locked with Taurellio's. She was not sure, but she thought he gave her a small nod of his long head.

The Harbingers turned their attention to placating the Volterran courtiers, assuring them the Xaff were out in numbers, and they would no doubt hunt and kill the escaped prisoner soon. The thought river soon swelled with voices affirming that everyone was dutiful, all had worked for the best of their team, and the guests might be more comfortable inside, where there would soon be spiced drinks and small pies. The sounds of shouts and laughter disappeared as Serral breezed out the gates and onto the open road.

Serral gunned the craft southward, out over the perimeter and into Xaff territory. Her Bisbee's shadow followed swiftly below, racing her in the moonlight. Monkeys screeched in the warm, green-scented night. Serral tried to keep her mind off the thought river, but she felt Xaff coming at her from the airfield. She navigated the Bisbee into the trees, trying to stay hidden, but that only slowed her down. There was no use trying to hide. The Xaff knew where she was.

Once again in the open, she sped toward the southeast quadrant and felt them coming, though they had no urgency. They were waiting for her to arm herself for battle. She was afraid to open her mind to them. Because if she did, she risked the barrier between herself and the collective mind remaining permanently open, her consciousness no longer her own. How long until that boundaryless existence drove her insane?

The Bisbee slid into the side of Hallenander's hangar, throwing Serral painfully onto the Tarmac. She brushed dirt and blood off her knees, hardly feeling the scrape. The door flew open, and hands grabbed her.

"Get in here, now."

# 47

Chapter Forty-Eight

Serral let the hands help her to her feet.

"They won't come in here," Geddon said while checking her over. "Are you alright? Let me disinfect those scrapes."

"No time," she said. "Where's the entrance to the tunnel out of here?"

"Why are you concerned about that?" He stood back. "I have the Ecto ready for you."

He brought her to a worktable, opened a metal box, and took out a can. He sprayed it onto Serral's scraped knees and elbow. Adrenaline kept her from feeling much of the sting.

"Change of plan," she batted the can of first aid spray away. "We need to get to the Reykos."

"Do we?" His salt-and-pepper brows rose higher. "And who precisely do you mean by we?"

"Can you summon the ladies?" She riffled through cupboards and found plain underclothes and a pair of worn coveralls.

Geddon produced a small device from his coverall pocket. "Chi Chi, this is Papa Bear, over."

Serral told him what else to say. He looked skeptical but repeated her words.

"They'll meet us there in half an hour," he said, appearing calm.

Serral sketched out her plans. "We need you and your crew."

His face lit up. "You got it."

Serral laced on space shoes. She pocketed her trinkets and tossed the dress into the closet.

"Only one detail I don't yet understand, Crigsen Brook."

"You are going to ask me how we will get to the towers, right?"

"The tunnels are clear north of here. But to the south, the path to the towers, that's harder."

"Blocked by Xaff, I know. Let's take a quick look at Hal's collection."

Not fifteen minutes later, an Ecto blasted out of the southwest quadrant. It shook the piles of components so that parts and pieces fell, ruining the careful spirals. It opened a shallow crater inside a black star on the tarmac. The small ship, a minute pod, was dwarfed by its massive, fiery engine. It grew tiny against the blue-black sky and then winked out of sight. As it left the atmosphere, a sound wave rumbled across Evincio.

In the Palace, Hallenander opened his eyes.

A camera feed in the main Xaff control center was left unwatched. The entire force of warriors rallied into motion, moving with well-trained precision toward a set of armored vehicles. Had anyone been paying attention to the liquid portals, they would have seen a mismatched pair of Harbingers in space suits and helmets driving a Bisbee away from the commotion, toward the perimeter.

Whizzing by runways and landing pads, the odd pair hovered along in silence, their gloved hands gripping side arms, their helmeted heads turning from side to side nervously. In the distance, armored Bisbees raced across the airfield toward the southwest quadrant. Lights flashed. Alarms sounded.

The pair raced in the opposite direction, gaining speed.

Serral felt a tingle. She tapped Geddon's wrist in warning and showed him that she had her gun at the ready. They could not make eye contact within the Harbinger costumes, but he understood her meaning and did the same. A pair of armored Bisbees loomed ahead in their path, four helmeted Xaff waiting silently. She resisted their effort to break down the walls of her mind. She clutched the older man's arm for strength.

He tensed. "Keep it together, Child," he whispered through the Harb suit.

I'm trying," Serral said.

"Just another minute now."

They slowed to meet the Xaff. Serral's stomach lurched, the pressure of their thoughts hammering away at her in waves, eroding her will. Pulling up the mask of her Harb helmet, she retched over the side of the craft, her breath ragged, sweat breaking out all over her body. Her vision was beginning to fray, the black dots swam in her peripheral vision, and a terrible feeling of violation pressed in on her. The Xaff spoke in a scratching, confusing babble that threatened to drag her, kicking and screaming, onto the thought river. The level of violent intent was red-hot. If Serral surrendered to them, she knew she would never come back out. She put her gun to her own temple. Geddon turned. "What are you doing, Serral?"

Before he could grab her pistol, a huge explosion erupted to the south. The shock waves rocked Hallenander's hangar, sending a red fireball into the air, debris flying, alarms sounding.

Without hesitation, the Xaff turned their Bisbees and streaked toward the melee.

Serral pulled the mask up and retched again. Geddon gunned the Bisbee toward the northern fence, cursing. Behind them, Tekkus rose like a swarm of metal bees and spread out across the sky. They looked like saucer-shaped silver raindrops. There was no end to their numbers.

"Is that swarm of fighters part of your plan?" Geddon asked as they rose up over the fence line, skirting treetops.

"It's unavoidable," she said, breathing purposefully. "But I think I have an idea of how to deal with them."

"Does it involve blowing your brains out?"

She heard the anger in his tone. "I'm sorry. I'd rather not. But if it comes to that, you know what to do."

"No. Stop that. You are needed."

"I'm a liability."

"Because you're powerful. You have no right to stop now."

She took off the costume helmet and rubbed her eyes. The dots were receding; her breathing was steadying. "Who said anything about stopping?"

Throwing his helmet over the side, Geddon looked at her sideways. "No more Imset ghosts on Evincio. I command it."

"Yes sir," she said, steadying herself.

They dropped their altitude and hovered just below the treetops. To their left lay the charred remnants of jungle where the Xaff had attacked the Wilter. Serral smelled death. Carrion birds sat lazily in the sparse branches and watched them pass.

"How many Wilter are left, now? You think one or two?"

"Don't. You cannot do anything for them. They're true believers."

"So am I, and so would you be, if you could remember what you believed."

"Shhhh," he said. They passed over a creek traversed by a makeshift log bridge. "They've been here recently."

Suddenly, bullets sounded like rain on the thick-leaved vines around them. One shooter either stopped or ran out of ammunition.

"We don't have time," Geddon hissed.

"Stop now, old man. Please."

They glided to a standing hover.

"Soldier, this is Pilot Crigsen Serral Brook of the Imset Air Guard. Identify yourself."

Twigs snapped. A white Imset head appeared on the jungle floor below.

"Throw down your weapon." Geddon leveled his pistol at the Imset.

A bloodied young face turned upward.

"Hands in the air," Serral called out. "State your name and rank."

"Pilot Crigsen Liphal," The woman said. "Spooky, is that you?"

"Liphal?" Serral called out.

Geddon and Serral exchanged a look.

The Bisbee cruised through the still jungle, now holding three people.

"Stay low," Geddon commanded.

Liphal cried softly in the back, cradling her wrist, hunching over her bloody midsection.

"You're messed up," Serral said. "We'll get you some help."

"I got hit pretty bad. But everyone else is dead, so I guess I made out alright."

"You're sure?"

Liphal nodded. "We were shot down during that final offensive. After the Tuval took off, we knew we would never be rescued, so we formed our own squadron. Pointless, I guess, but what else were we supposed to do?"

"I get it. As long as you avoided contact with the Harbs, you were still enlisted. How many Imset are out there, would you say? I thought the Harbs killed everyone."

"There's more. We are hard to kill, as you know. Spook, what's happening? We saw you die."

Geddon looked surprised. "You died?"

"She's the bravest pilot the Imset ever had," Liphal said, smiling through her tears. "Crazy Col."

Serral turned toward the young, injured soldier. She spoke softly. "You wouldn't believe me if I told you. Rest now."

Liphal closed her eyes. Perfect round shadows of Tekkus passed rhythmically across the swath of terrain between the jungle wall and the road, their engines faintly whirring in the night air. Geddon steered the Bisbee just outside the line of trees.

"What are they doing?" Geddon said under his breath.

Serral watched as the Tekkus formed a grid, then rose to higher altitudes in an impressive show of force. "They're going to hunt the Ecto."

"You bought us some time."

"Down there." Serral pointed to the entrance tunnel. Before them, the Reykos stood resplendent in the sun, their angular blue-and-green surfaces reflecting the trees and sky.

"The boy trusts you. So, I suppose I can too."

"Well, I haven't told him the whole truth. But..." she said, willing herself not to feel the overwhelming grief swamping her heart. "I've got a job to do."

"Take it easy. You're not alone anymore."

Geddon guided them down into the tunnel.

Chapter Forty-Nine

Serral was gone. Hallenander ran to the hall and summoned Helpers.

"Where is she?" He looked imploringly into their black eyes. "Surely she augered with someone before she left."

"Your Sevenni Highness," the Harbingers answered, four voices together, "Your Companion has closed her mind to us."

"I don't believe you."

"Please, sire," they continued, "she is hardly an Imset anymore. When she ceases to be Imset, she can no longer belong to you."

"What is that supposed to mean?" He reached for the nearest Helper, its head dome puffing and then narrowing in fear. "How does a person stop being Imset?"

Then he dropped the Helper, who stood silently, ready for more punishment.

"Take me to your team leader."

"Our team leader?" The four little mouths said, heads accordioning.

"Where do you live? Where do you go when you are not here?"

They looked back at him but did not respond.

"Never mind. I don't have time for your..." His voice rose. "Nonsense."

The door to the Harb kitchen was open a crack. He pushed his body into the narrow space and followed the stairs down and down until he landed on a larger platform. The space was dark, but he felt his way, following the Harb stench to his right, and then into a wide, lantern-lit set of stairs.

Warm, musky air rose from below. In a few meters, the walls were covered by red membranes that grew thicker the deeper he went. They rippled with life. Disgust rose in his throat, but he ignored it. The ground became slippery, and he was forced to steady himself with the vicious, blood-colored wall. A deep throb surrounded him. He plodded until finally, Hallenander stepped out into a cavern that resembled the inside of a blood cell, moist and red, veined and pulsating. The smell was different here, less pungent, more mineral. It took him a few moments to understand what he was seeing.

In front of him lay a huge tub. It roiled as would worms under a lifted stone. Hallenander gagged. The room was carpeted across a hundred meters or more and seethed with naked, gray Harbingers, touching, locked together, writhing ecstatically. Head domes rose and fell in unison, their bodies forming a coil that moved in an endless circle around a fixed point, each body having its turn in the central position, then was subsumed into the wriggling mass, the next Harbinger taking its place. Hallenander fought for breath. He had never seen anything so alien.

And these were the creatures who were, at that very moment, pursuing Serral.

"Wake up, Worms!" his voice boomed. "It is time to do your duty!"

"Sire?" voices responded. A pair of helpers, dressed in thin fabric wraps, peered up at him, waiting at the edge of the vat. "We are afraid the team is unable to hear you at this time. But the two of us are available. What may we do to help?"

Hal bent close to speak to them. "What did Serral the Thanton say before she left the Palace?"

They went into the briefest of augering trances. "Nothing, sire."

"Don't lie," he said, pacing. "You must know something. Who did she auger with? Who among your kind helped her escape?"

A sound, like a massive wave hitting a beach, roared from the tub. The Harbingers had been interrupted. A thousand black eyes stared at him. Their head domes slowly drew in, and they broke apart to watch him. Hallenander felt their menace and noticed a dark, vinegary smell.

"Please, Helpers. I am begging you. Serral is in terrible danger. The Xaff will follow her, you know they will. They will find her and force her to fight them until she goes mad. They will auger her to death. Please. Is that what you want for your Thanton?"

A terrible cacophony rose up. Hallenander felt chaos building. It was like something heavy being dragged across pavement, the hysterical laughter of hundreds of naked Harbingers.

"Sire," said the two sarong-wearers, "respectfully, if your companion wanted you to know her movements, surely she would have told you herself?"

"I can't protect her out there, don't you understand?"

"Her destiny is to serve, as is ours. As is yours, Minsyx."

"She's supposed to serve me!" He grimaced in frustration.

"She did serve you, your Sevenni Highness." They bowed, unruffled. "But she has surrendered to her destiny."

"Meaning what?" He ran a hand over his head dome, through the sweat from the fetid heat. "She is supposed to let the Xaff do what they want with her? Let her try to return to the Imset? They will kill her on sight! They believe her to be a criminal. Surely you comprehend the direness of her situation."

The two Harbs blinked at him slowly. "Sire, did your slave fail to train you to fly a star ship? Our Medics healed her for you, as you asked, and she taught you."

"And now I'm asking for something else, something more! What right have you to question me?"

"Profuse apologies, Highness." They eyed him glassily, their faces reflecting red. "But you are Rakki."

His mouth dropped open. "How is that relevant?" He felt dizzy from the focused energy of so many gray people on him. They did not move or speak; they watched him grow more and more agitated.

"The Rakki are the best of people. The chosen ones. Those who shall inherit the green world," they said. "It is why we made you. It is the only reason why."

"What?" He spun around in a circle, feeling the floor slip under his feet. "What are you talking about?"

The sound of a thousand bodies changing position echoed across the cavern.

"We are despondent!" The two Helpers threw themselves on the floor, pressing their foreheads down. "We are but servants! Ysk knows how hard we try! Ysk has a plan for all, for us unworthy slaves, for you, the blessed Rakki! We act according to Ysk's plan!"

"What is Ysk's plan for Serral?" Hallenander hunched to speak to the pair. "Tell me!"

They hid their head domes under their hands, cringing. "We are only helpers, sire!"

"She will be murdered by your kind," Hal said through clenched teeth. "And it will be on your heads!"

A wave of shrieking poured over him. A thousand head domes moved like demented insects all around in the red half-light. Hallenander felt afraid. He turned, his feet slipping as he ran back the way he had come.

When he entered the palace, Hallenander went straight to his father's chambers. Taurellio acted surprised, but his son recognized comprehension in his opaline eyes.

"Oh, no," he tied his robe and followed Hal out to the antechamber. "What awful news."

With great effort, Hal made his face into the blank mask. "I want to go after her. I want the Xaff ordered not to touch or disturb her."

"I see," Taurellio said slowly. "Very well. I'll tell the Xaff not to interfere with your Companion's flight."

"I can tell them. As long as you will back me up."

"Fine." The Syxarit rang a bell, and two black-uniformed Helpers came through the door and bowed.

Hallenander had not seen them before. He ordered them to send out every Tekku on the planet and find the ship that had recently blasted out of Evincio.

"The Ecto," the two said. "It is out of our exosphere, sire. In un-governed space."

Hallenander felt sick. "An Ecto? Has she gone mad? She took off in an ECUnit?"

Taurellio signaled for the two Harbingers to leave. They made a salute Hal had never seen before and left the room.

"Son, forgive me for my ignorance, but what is an Ecto?"

He leaned over his knees. "It's nothing. It's not even a ship, it's more of an emergency escape pod."

Taurellio spoke gently. "And why would your friend choose a vehicle of that type?"

Hallenander walked to the window. The midday sky was a mockingly gentle blue. "I can only guess. I think either she intended to commit suicide, or she wants to risk stasis."

"I still don't quite understand," Taurellio said tightly. "Where could she go in such a tiny craft? Could such a ship be safe in asteroid belts or resist magnetic storms?"

"Yes. It would just bob along, like a cork in the sea." Hallenander looked at his father for a long moment. "Serral could put herself into stasis. Neither dead, nor fully alive. She might last a hundred years. If she were ever found, which is unlikely, history will have moved on."

"There will be no Imset left, then."

"Apparently." Hal felt despondent. "Helpers, bring tea. Immediately."

He watched the two gray Harbingers scurry away to comply with his wishes. He was not thirsty, but the sight of them turned his stomach, and he wanted them out of the room.

"So, she is gone forever then?" Taurellio put his arm around his son consolingly.

"Is she, Father? You do not think the Xaff will follow my orders?" Outside the window, Tekkus rose into the air, first a dozen, then more and more. But Hallenander realized how futile the situation was. He could see it in the old man's eyes; he had known. Serral had forewarned him. She had paid for their night together with something. Was it her life? "I'm sure the gray people will do what they think the law requires. You are learning how difficult they are to control."

"I am learning how helpless the Volterran race is."

"Ah," the older man said. "Never let them hear you say as much."

Hallenander estimated the number of Tekkus. A hundred, two hundred. They flew with precision, silver plates flung into the air in exact, even rows.

The Helpers placed a tray in front of him.

"Get gone, you two," he growled.

"Servants, you have done well," his father said, "and you will be rewarded."

The Harbingers bowed, heads puffing, and disappeared. Hallenander closed his eyes until they were gone.

Hallenander's voice grew weak. "It was a stupid idea, keeping her with me. She knew it would not work. She told you as much, didn't she?"

Taurellio watched the Tekku armada through the window. "They are remarkable, aren't they?" He looked tired, his cheeks deeply shaded.

"Who are?"

"The Imset." He turned to his son. "They simply never give up. It seems unfair that they are eternally punished. If it were up to me, I would let them live, and make an end of this war."

Hallenander sat down by his father's side. "Would you, now?"

"But if the people, your subjects, those lofty souls of Volterra, were ever to catch the faintest whiff of such sentimentality toward the Imset, your opportunity to be made heir would melt away to nothing."

"And after I am enthroned?"

"Ah, then you will need the people's goodwill, son. If you get to that day, and I pray you will, that will be only the beginning of your efforts."

"I'm not sure I'm up to it, father." Hallenander fought to keep his voice steady.

The older man's demeanor turned cold. "It is far too late for doubt. You have done an admirable job of resisting your uncle's undermining. Even the Syxarim has come around to your cause. Your cousin Bellex is half in love with you. You have told me a thousand times how my pleasure is your only concern. Has any of that changed?"

"No. But you've kept much from me."

"So?" Taurellio snarled, "Do you think any of my power has happened without effort? Without careful orchestration? Patience? Difficult choices?"

"Clearly not."

"No. Clearly not." He grabbed Hallenander's head in his arms, forcing it under one arm. He hissed, "You think that people would ever come to accept this head without my explicit patronage, boy? Knowing what you are? Where you come from? Are you mad?"

"This was your idea. Not mine." Hallenander wrenched away, "Perhaps it is you who are mad."

"Perhaps I am." Taurellio's eyes blazed angry, "But you have been my best option, and the best option for the Volterran people. For decades we have educated you, given you every privilege, allowed you to learn. To fly." He gritted his large teeth, "And you are now losing your nerve because suddenly you realize how difficult it all is?"

Hal moved to walk away, but his father gripped his wrist.

"It is a lovely planet, and I am glad you have enjoyed yourself," the emperor breathed heavily. "But you don't know what you're in for, boy. Unless you change your outlook, Volterra will eat you alive. You will wish you could fly away. You'll wish you hadn't been born so pretty, so lucky, the favored son of me."

"There were strategic reasons I wanted to bring Serral with me. She speaks the language of the servants and would have given me tremendous advantage."

Taurellio let go of Hallenander's wrist.

Hallenander continued, "I feel blind without her. But I never said I wouldn't do what you ask."

"Oh, you will. I know you will. But you need not have an augering whore in order to do as you're told." Taurellio's lowered his voice, "And what's more, you'll never bring up this absurd infatuation again."

The sky was empty. The Tekkus had passed off into space.

"Why would I?" Hal brushed his wrist as if to brush off lint. "The two of you have done an admirable job of solving my problem for me. I assume my only option is to continue to dance on your puppet strings, father."

The old man crossed his legs in a leisurely motion. "That is well."

"Am I allowed to leave the palace grounds?"

"To go and visit the rest of the women, in the jungle?"

"Believe it or not, I have no idea where they've run off to."

Taurellio waved a dismissive hand. "The Xaff know. They wait for my order to finally clear the planet of Imset contamination. That is all. Tell me, there was a dark-haired girl, whom everyone thought would become yours. What became of her?"

Hallenander paused in the doorway. "Was there? I don't know, father." He grinned. "All the Imset look alike to me."

He bowed and then walked out of his father's chambers.

— • —

C hapter Fifty

By early evening, the Tekkus had returned en masse. Serral watched them from the glass-skinned blue Reyko dome.

She spoke to Geddon through her walkie talkie: "Whoever isn't here in the tower with us, had best run now."

Geddon sent a crew member to explain to the few Imset left in the jungle that they needed to get as far as possible from the towers. The rest, two men from his former crew of twelve and six former Companions stayed behind. Over the past hours, Geddon and his crew had found seven remaining Imset soldiers living in a deep valley on the other side of the continent. And now, those white-haired pilots were working with Liphal and the rest of Geddon's former crew. Half stood at consoles in the high-ceilinged room, doing cross checks and calculating navigation protocols. The others worked in the green tower, across the narrow divide, doing similar tasks.

"They're headed back to the caves," Geddon's voice rasped into Serral's device. "We're ready for your signal."

Serral spoke quietly to Uniaah and Piettu, repeating instructions they had heard several times before.

"Child, you are very brave," Uniaah said, taking Serral's hand in her withered, gray one. The old woman had convinced the hundred odd

Harbs who staffed the Reykos to stay aboard, and those Harbingers had agreed to keep their minds unconnected for a period of hours, to go invisible to the thought river.

"You truly believe the risk is worth it?"

"You've met Taurellio. Do you trust him?"

Uniaah's black eyes blinked slowly, her bulbous gray head shifting softly. "I've been on this project since the very beginning, child. He has seen to it that we have succeeded. It has taken many years."

"Do you think the emperor cares what happens to the Rakki kids if they can't come to Volterra?"

"It is hard to say," Uniaah said. "He has many of his own problems to solve."

"Your people aren't going to fix the Emptiness. Ever. Are you?"

Uniaah's head pulled tight in a gesture of resignation.

"So, this plan will work."

Uniaah stroked Serral's small hand in her two long-fingered gray ones. "The law is the law, child. Unless the Volterrans accept Rakki as part of the Alliance, unless they give Hallenander citizenship, all of this will be for naught."

"I know." Serral teared up. She whispered to the old woman, "I wish you could know Hal as well as I do. I believe he will keep his promise."

"You have your own destiny. You know that."

Serral stared into the old woman's strange eyes. "Me? Besides being so connected to the Harbs that anywhere I go in the universe, unless I'm in stasis or protected by Air Guards, they can track me down and force me to kill them? Auger me until I lose my mind completely? What other use do the Harbingers have for me? Do you know?"

Uniaah took Serral's hands in hers. "It is true. You were made for this task. And you have served admirably."

Serral stared. "I what? I was made? For this?"

"Yes. We made a bargain with your mother. On the planet where you were born."

Serral stood. "My mother?"

"She was very fine scientist. She studied the carvings of the Ancients. Her idea was to upset the balance of power by giving an Imset child the gift of telepathy. So that my people could know you, the way I know Hallenander and the children here. As people. As similar to our own kind. Not enemies. Not worthy of endless suffering because of ancient laws. But friends."

"You made a bargain with my mother?" Serral burst into tears. "That's why I was given over to raiders when I was born? She sacrificed herself so I would be able to auger?"

Silence fell over the room. Several people quietly left.

"You and Hallenander have set something into motion that cannot now be undone. Look around. All the children here, all those in the cities, all those who remain hiding on planets in hopes of a miracle, depend on Hallenander caring enough about you to do what must be done. His path is hard. But I believe you touched him in the way only a real, unwiped, sincere planetary girl could."

"Who are you?" Serral stepped away from Uniaah. "Who do you think you are? A god? An agent of Ysk?"

Uniaah made a small smile with her line of a mouth. "I am a Harbinger. You know exactly how we think. You are in danger of coming to think like us, if you aren't more careful now about how you use your mind."

Serral sobbed into her hands. "You're a danton. Evil."

"No, no," Uniaah chuckled. "That is no way to speak of your godmother."

"I'm going back to the Imset. You can't stop me."

"Nor would I have any reason to. You are not safe here, and you put the children in danger with your presence."

"What? The Xaff can't track you?"

"Oh, no. The helpers here have all modified ourselves to be undectable to the warriors. We will be quite safe. Even our ships are almost invisible in space. All of this has been carefully planned. We are prepared to wait, until we are called to repopulate the Eight Worlds."

Serral put her hand on her stomach, trying to calm her breathing. "So this was always the plan? To replace the Volterrans with Rakki?"

"Not replace. The children are half Vol. Half Imset. You see? No one is exterminated. Everyone gets to live. A beautiful life as a perfect kind of person. A balanced person, with innocence and cynicism in equal measure. Neither too stuck in tradition, nor wild and impetuous. People worth being. Worth being born."

Serral choked. "You did this for the Harbingers. Because you believe you want to be reborn as something new. You're over the Imset and the Volterrans. You want better lives."

"Can you blame us?" Uniaah moved toward a console and began moving the levers. "The Imset doomed themselves. The Volterrans simply stopped growing. Nature doesn't like stagnation. It's not healthy. As a planetary, you should understand that."

Serral leaned onto the console. "And if you're wrong, and no one gets reborn, and all of this has been murder and genocide for no good reason?"

"You know it is not. You who could have become a Thanton. You have seen the other side. This is the wrong question."

"Oh?" Serral stood up and faced the window. Outside, the sunset was tinted blue. "What is the right question?"

"If you can convince your people to stay in the fight. To rejoin the larger world, when and if Hallenander topples the alliance."

"He doesn't even know who made the alliance."

"He will not be without help, child. Even without you by his side."

Serral rubbed her eyes. "The Imset will never listen to me. I'm a traitor."

"Are you?" Uniaah asked. "How will they know? If you slip quietly into the worlds, with all your knowledge, and find a way to spread hope? Convince your people to elect someone to parley? When Hallenander comes asking for renegotiation?"

"And you think I can do that?"

"Who else? Are you willing to risk not going, allowing the chance of a future on planet to slip away because no one knew to look for it?"

Serral dried her tears on her shirtsleeves. "I'm the chosen one, because you chose me."

"Yes. You are the chosen one because I and your mother chose you, one day when she used a relic she found in a cave to call to me, and I answered. As my training taught me to do. Because some of my kind have been trying to make peace for a very, very long time."

"Being with Hallenander wasn't the reason you made me."

"No. It is only how you came to be here."

"Does he know?"

"Not yet."

"It's more useful to take away his hope."

"His path is hard. He needs no distractions."

"You are a Harbinger. You think people are easily replaceable. Interchangeable. Just experiments to use in pursuit of an afterlife. But you're wrong."

"And so you see why we could never allow the Imset to be wiped out completely. You really are so deeply loveable."

Serral bit her lips to keep from cursing.

Later, a team of four Harb medics came near and helped Serral onto a gurney. The sun was setting over the islands to the east and turning the ceiling into a prism of rainbows. She settled back onto the pillow, and they inserted an IV.

"What's your count?" she said into the radio.

"Down to one landing per minute. I think they're almost all in," Geddon answered.

"Sounds about right. They'll be reporting to Taurellio about now."

"Telling him you're dead," Piettu said.

"That I'm lost in space, which is the same to him."

Uniaah sat at her bedside. "He'll see through your ruse. He's not a fool."

"I know. The ruse isn't for his benefit." Serral looked up at the ceiling. The silver rain of returning Tekkus had ended, and all that remained were pink-tinged clouds.

"Remember," she smiled at Piettu. "If things go wrong, even your father can't protect you from the Xaff."

"But you can. Don't you think they believed you when you led them on a wild chase after an empty escape pod?" Piettu walked over to a console where crew members focused on checking, double checking systems. They adjusted levers and discussed plans. "Thanton? Isn't that what they call you?"

"Hush. Serral is mortal now," Uniaah said softly.

Piettu looked puzzled. "Why would you want to be mortal?"

Serral did not answer. She nodded to the contrivers and crew members across the room. They called out to one another, hands now moving quickly over the controls. Power surged throughout the building.

Serral grabbed Uniaah's. "If you see him, please tell him the truth."

"May Ysk reward you in the Ouserium, child."

"Give it a rest, godmother."

Serral closed her eyes. The building around her burst to life. It vibrated like a living thing, the sound of engines stirring in levels far below.

**49**

— · —

Chapter Fifty-One

Together and at once, the two shining glass towers rose into the air. The land shook, and the people in the palace ran outside in confusion. A crowd of Volterrans gathered on a balcony and watched the twin flames crawl upward into the dusk. Taurellio and Hallenander emerged in the courtyard. They spoke heatedly to a group of Harbinger servants who threw themselves onto the cobblestones in supplication.

To the south, where minutes before hundreds of silver saucers had returned from space, their fuel tanks empty, their pilots exhausted, the airfield sat inert. Darkness fell on Evincio. No ships stirred. Not a single warrior was visible.

And then, a shock wave boomed through the atmosphere as the twin star ships pierced the atmosphere and continued onward and upward into space.

The two men in the palace courtyard stood talking for some time. Finally, Hallenander turned and walked back inside.

Taurellio stood alone then under the sky, rubbing his head in frustration. He yelled out in Volterran. No one heard him but the servants who lay unmoving, like supine statues on the ground.

Later, in the pitch-black night, flames erupted on the plateau across from where the Reykos had once stood. The tall, black-and-gold building capping the once-beautiful Xalavria, sparked up quickly with a roar of wind. The topmost floor was consumed first, followed by the remaining six levels. No one came to put out the conflagration. The palace saw its tongue of black smoke. By morning, the building was reduced to ash and blackened metal.

Hallenander watched from his Bisbee, smoking a tintorello. When the sun peeked over the eastern jungle, he turned his vehicle around and hovered out of the resort, leaving the silver gates ajar.

**50**

— · —

C hapter Fifty-Two

The *Sevenni Barge*, which struck Hallenander as a humorous name for a star ship, had been built in the style of the Capitol on Thrygia, all blue with golden stars, a motif celebrating the Eight Worlds. He strolled the ship's many hallways, often becoming disoriented and needing redirection by the Harbinger crew, as he went looking for windows to peer out into space.

He knew looking was futile. Serral was gone. But still, he looked. As often as he could during the fifteen-day flight, Hallenander gazed out at the stars. He knew also that searching for a damaged Ecto was pointless. He did not believe Serral had been aboard. The theft of his siblings' towers had her contrivance all over it. And while it helped him to think she had betrayed him for a good reason, he could not deny the mistrust her actions revealed. Not lack of faith in him, exactly. She was correct that his plan to keep her with him was impractical. But on top of her deduction that remaining with him was too risky, she evidently felt that the Rakki would not be safe on Evincio. She believed that he would not become legal Heir and provide the children with a civilization to inherit. Or perhaps she planned to keep them hidden until later. Either way, her willingness to risk Xaff wrath on the two Reykos rankled him. What right did she have to place the children in harm's way? He boiled. Serral obviously did not expect him to succeed. Pondering her meeting with his father a few hours before she fled did not help his mood. What had Taurellio said to her?

Hallenander could guess. But since he and his father were the only people in the civilized world aware of the existence of the Rakki children, he would never know. If no one knew the children existed, no one could feel threatened by them or insist they be eradicated. She had saved them. He was glad enough of that.

His father had easily concocted a story to explain the flight of the Reykos; simply that the Harbingers had business with the two colorful ships, and they would return when the business had concluded. The guests, used to accepting whatever the Harbingers did with perfect passivity, asked no questions. They had barely noticed the two glittering buildings in the first place.

There was a chance, Hal supposed, that someone else had contrived the theft of the Reykos, and Serral was at that moment in stasis, somewhere in the Obnney Void. He did not want to contemplate that future. He hoped she remained alive. The servants only said that Serral the Thanton was dark to them. When the liaison team had met with him and his father outside the palace during the Reykos hijacking, they claimed the Xaff had refused to bring the towers back, because the Thanton had ordered them not to.

He brushed lint from his jacket, smelling smoke. Never mind. There was plenty of conversation, wine, and amusement to keep his mind occupied and would be for as long as he remained among Volterrans. He would try to content himself with that.

Still, he was drawn to the windows, and could not keep himself from searching the starry, black sky.

**51**

— · —

C hapter Fifty-Three

The two glittering conjoined ships moved like a pair of glassy crustaceans through the Obbney Portworm. When they reached the point of no return, halfway down the starry passage, a tiny grain of silver popped from a tube near the stern. The twin hulls sped on. The metallic grain, a single-person Ecto without identifying marks, floated like a leaf on still water. A small orange beacon light blinked, faint against the worm's bright, curved wall.

Below a small port hole an Imset woman lay, already deep in stasis, her hibernation undisturbed by the void's solitude. Under her folded arms was tucked an envelope, a label bearing the words, *For Air Marsiant Slook, Imset Air Guard, Mollith.*

The double-hulled star ship reached the end of the tunnel and turned out of sight. The Ecto remained inert, alone and tiny in the vastness of the starry tunnel.

# 52

hora Wolf is a writer living in Los Angeles. When not writing about intergalactic empires and glamorous prisoners of war, she enjoys hiking with her Aussie shepherd mix.

Empire of Stars and Opals is her first novel.

For news about a sequel or to join our mailing list, go to: thorawolf.godaddysites.com

# About the Author

Thora Wolf is a writer who lives sometimes in the forests of the Pacific Northwest, and other times in the Santa Monica Mountains of Southern California.

thorawolf.com